MY NAME IS JUSTICE

Published by Red Kimba Press

Paperback ISBN-13: 978-1-7398510-2-6
eBook ISBN-13: 978-1-7398510-3-3

Printed in the United Kingdom

Cover design and layout by www.spiffingcovers.com

MY NAME IS JUSTICE

GABRIEL GALLETTI

Chapter 1

I step towards the figure bound to the table. His body quivers beneath the restraints and his eyes search for an escape. The moment is delicious in its intensity. I move slowly to stand beside him. His five colleagues, conspirators in his crime, sit staring into oblivion. My only regret is ending them with the precision of the bullet rather than inflicting the prolonged pain they deserved. The morally bankrupt should understand that their actions have consequences.

I bend down so he can see me.

"Hello, Dan," I whisper.

His eyes are questioning, pleading.

"Who am I? Is that what you're asking?"

He makes no sound, but a tear trickles out of the corner of his eye.

I lean into his face, eye to eye, then murmur, "My name is… Justice." I move back a little, but still hold his terrified stare. "I have a question for you."

I hold a photograph in front of his face, "Remember her?" His eyes roll as he rummages through his memory. Searching, probing, dredging through time.

At last, recognition.

And with recognition I see he comprehends. Excellent. It's his final thought. That's enough for me.

The blade glistens as it descends. One down, five to go.

Chapter 2

Chad Hilton sat in the cramped confines of a holding room somewhere in the bowels of the Customs Hall in Sydney International Airport. The two burly coppers who escorted him from the plane stood backs to the wall and took most of the remaining space. What was this about?

"Look," said Chad, "I've been on a plane for twenty-four hours and I just want my hotel and my bed. Can you tell me what the hell's going on?"

He stared at one then the other. They must teach that 'look straight ahead and say nothing' shit at Police Training School, he thought. Above them, a clock with a cracked plastic face was pinned to the wall. The room was small, ten feet by six, and had a table with a white Formica top and two metal chairs. Chad sat in one, but the other was vacant.

Chad turned as the door opened. A guy stood framed in the doorway. He looked about sixty, but was probably younger. His thick dark hair was unkempt and swept back above a broad forehead with deep chiselled frown lines. Dark bags spoke of little sleep, and a flushed complexion indicated blood pressure issues, which a bulbous nose reinforced. His eyes, however, were as sharp as needles. Blue grey, they looked like they'd pierce rock at fifty paces. He wore a Hawaiian shirt, jeans and a crumpled leather jacket, and Chad reckoned he'd seen smarter tramps. After dismissing the two coppers with a nod, the guy offered his hand. Chad decided it was better to shake it.

"Pleasure to meet you, Mr Hilton," he smiled. "And, ah, look, thanks very much for popping in and sorry for the clumsy methods we've employed. What with the press waiting for you at baggage reclaim I reckoned it was easier to grab a word now. My name is Ruben Murray. DI Ruben Murray of the homicide squad."

Chad said nothing and waited.

"So, mate," Murray continued, "I know about your profiling work in the UK and that you pieced everything together to nail that killer back in Leeds a couple of months ago." He shifted in his chair then rubbed his ear, his eyes darting from Chad's to the table. "Sorry about your wife, that must have been terrible."

Chad remained silent.

"Anyway," said Murray, "the press here have been doing exposés on you and your mate Freddie Jackson ever since." He paused.

Chad held his eye. He and Freddie were supposed to have flown together, but Freddie had cancelled and booked a later flight.

"And, incidentally, he needs to keep out of trouble when he gets here."

Freddie Jackson was a famous sporting icon in Australia, but it seemed the cops knew about his nefarious activities back in Leeds.

"Now, look," the copper tapped the table with his forefinger, "I don't give a toss whether you two were footballing gods with Leeds United and Sydney FC, but..."

"Well, if you've been reading that stuff," Chad interrupted, "you'll know I didn't play for Sydney, that was Freddie."

"Yeah, whatever, but what with your profiling work and coaching the Rest of the World team in the soccer match here next month, mate, you're big news and to prove my point there's a gaggle of hacks waiting for you in arrivals."

Chad rubbed his knee. It was an old habit. How long would it take for the copper to get to the point?

"Chad, mate," Murray looked across the table. "You don't mind me calling you, Chad, do you?"

Chad shrugged.

"I could do with your help, hence this little chat. You may have read that we've got a serious shit show going on in Sydney? It happened a few days ago, when some lunatic committed multiple homicides in the boardroom of a company in the Central Business District."

Chad nodded, recalling the newspaper headlines he'd seen on the flight.

"Horrific doesn't cut it. We've got as much manpower as I can muster working flat out on it, but we're getting nowhere fast. A psychologist working with us reckons the killer could strike again, so time isn't on my side. I'm hoping you could look at the files we've done so far and see if you can help point us in the right direction. What d'ya think?"

Chad felt fatigue sweep over him. He wasn't here for this. And, sure as hell, he wasn't ready for it. "You seem to know lots about me," he sighed, leaning in towards Murray to emphasise his point. "This trip is an extended break to help me recover from the carnage that went down at home. The last thing I need is to get embroiled in another mess. Sorry, but no, I can't help." Chad held the detective's eye.

"I appreciate that," said Murray.

Chad raised a sceptical eyebrow.

"No really, I do." The detective stretched his legs and eased back into the seat examining one of his fingernails, then idly scratched the top of his head, before turning slightly so that Chad caught his eye, "but the world isn't like that, mate."

Chad noticed the clock ticking on the wall. He leaned back in the seat and waited, as Murray tried to use the silence to his advantage. Pointless. Chad knew that game. The big cop leaned across the table and pointed a finger in his direction.

"Do you think the media give a flying fuck about some crappy soccer game? Eh, do you? They'll maybe do a couple of spreads on

Freddie Jackson, yeah, sure, but the authentic story they're after is you." He let out a laugh, then using both hands typed on an imaginary keyboard, "Can Chad Hilton, the ex-soccer pro turned celebrity profiler catch the Boardroom Beast?"

"Don't be ridiculous," groaned Chad, "and cut that 'celebrity profiler' crap. I'm a psychologist."

"I'm not being ridiculous. If you don't believe me, see how many newspaper and TV crews there are waiting for you to collect your luggage."

The room was hot. A trickle of sweat rolled down Chad's back.

"You can't win, mate," Murray went on, "and to be fair, neither can I. If I don't use your expertise, I'll get pilloried," he looked to the ceiling as if considering this eventuality. "If I do, they'll ask why I can't solve the case without using a Pom profiler," Murray rubbed his eyes and blinked. "Same for you. If you don't help us, the media will slag you off big time. I can see it now: '*Pom profiler ignores pleas for help*' or '*Hilton says no*'. And, if you help us, they'll expect instant results. After what you did back in Leeds, they're already trying to turn you into the next Sherlock Holmes. I agree you don't want either of those outcomes, but I'm sorry, mate, they're inevitable."

A fly landed on the clock face. Jesus Christ, thought Chad, this is blackmail. He interlocked his fingers and then rubbed his hands on his thighs. What the copper didn't understand was that it was taking all his time and effort to keep himself from sinking. Flashbacks, PTSD and grief were heavy burdens that had got little lighter in the three months since his world had exploded.

He could barely help himself let alone anyone else.

And he didn't need the media spotlight, because here he didn't even have the sanctuary of his home to hide in.

The fly circled the room before landing on the big cop's shoulder. Murray seemed to recognise Chad's conflict. "I know, mate, I know. It's shit. But look, I'll arrange transport to get you and your bags to your hotel, avoiding the press, then I'll send the case files to your email. Have a read when you've slept. If asked, I'll say that any help the police get from members of the public is welcome, but we understand you're here for the footy and nothing else, how's that?"

Chad looked across the table. Rock and hard place, he thought. "Are we done?"

"We're done," said DI Ruben Murray.

Chapter 3

Chad's chest tightened, his breath came in short, sharp irregular bursts, his heart rate frenzied. He was on his back, faces peering over him, then someone was putting a water bottle to his lips. But the water tasted bitter. The sky was receding. Dying. He was dying. Panic pushed open the doors in his psyche.

He heaved himself up from the pillow and fought for control. The images were like napalm, bright and intense; breathe in and count to four, hold for four, breathe out. Repeat. And again. His pulse slowed, the throbbing beat of his heart pounding in his ears faded, and calm returned. "I don't need this shit," he muttered. Since Angie's death, sleep was more an aspiration than a reality, but here, jet-lagged to hell, it was way out of reach.

He swung his legs out of the bed and walked the few steps to the window then pulled open the curtains. Street lights gave the scene outside an eerie neon glow. Elizabeth Street was a six-lane thoroughfare that spent most of the daylight hours gridlocked. Now it lay deserted. Chad stared at a movement across the road. Making its way, in no great hurry, across St James' Park towards the metro station, like some sort of animal kingdom commuter, plodded a possum. A possum, he thought. Wow, don't get many of those wandering the streets back home in Harrogate.

Chad stared into the neon. Murray was right, he thought, better to have the cops on his side and help keep the press away. And what to make of Murray? He'd been as good as his word, Chad supposed. He'd arranged for an unmarked police car, with his luggage already in the boot, to chauffeur him to the hotel and there hadn't been a journo in sight. But all that would change soon enough when he realised Chad's newly gained 'celebrity profiler' image was about as much use as a chocolate fireguard.

Right, come on, let's read this email.

Chad opened his MacBook and saw the name Ruben Murray in bold at the top of his in-box. In the body of the email Murray had written:

It happened two days ago, when some Joey accessed a business on the eleventh floor of a block on Castlereagh Street. Shoots five of the directors in the boardroom, then leaves with no one seeing or hearing a thing. No one reported the crime for five hours.

Five victims? The press reports said six?

Chad resumed reading.

Five killed with single shots to the head but the sixth was different. You can read it in the report, but we kept it away from the press. It's a shocker. No forensic clues and no ammo casings. It's a seventeen-floor building and there's nearly two thousand people work there. Hoped that as you go through the file, you could give us a pointer on what's driving the killer. Any ideas welcome.

Chad opened the attachment and skim read the police procedural stuff – time, officers attending, pathologist and forensic officers' names, then scrolled down to the crime scene photographs.

"Jesus Christ," he whispered. He assumed the first photo, a wide-angle shot of the boardroom, was taken from the doorway. The room was around twenty feet by fifteen. Floor to ceiling windows hinted at spectacular views over Sydney, but, in the photo, reflected the grisly spectacle in the room. The table was oval, mahogany and highly polished. There were six chairs, one at either end and two on each side. The gunshot victims occupied five. On one wall was a large screen showing a profit-and-loss table with graphs, the trajectory of which suggested a business doing very well. To the right, on a mahogany table, water and biscuits sat untouched.

His phone vibrated on the bedside table, so he walked across the room to retrieve it. The screen showed a text message from Jas Carter. DS Jas Carter.

Hey Hoppy, not sure whether you're behind or ahead of Leeds time, but thought I'd check you'd arrived okay, since you couldn't be arsed to let me know. How ya feeling? XX

He smiled. She'd christened him Hoppy when they worked together on the mayhem in Leeds. "Cheeky bugger, she knows I don't even limp anymore. Hoppy, for Christ's sake."

Lucky for you I'm an insomniac 'cos it's four in the morning! Yeah, got here fine. I'll call you in a few hours. You, okay?

The reply was instant. *Yep, I'm fine. Missing you though. Call me when you can xx.*

Chad took a deep breath and turned back towards the desk. He stopped halfway across the room. What had bothered him about Jas's text? Guilt? For what though? His attraction to another woman so soon after his wife's death? Maybe. Jas was stunningly beautiful, kind, funny and seemed to find him attractive. Psychoses and all. The downside was that she was a copper, and worked for his mate DI Lee Wallace in Leeds. Lee had been firm with Chad before he'd left for Australia. "Make your mind up, but don't mess her around," he'd said. "Understand where you want the relationship to go, pal, and don't bugger it up through your inability to decide. She's been good to you."

He'd put it on hold like all the other decisions he'd had to make. It was good to hear from her, though. Sitting down at the desk he pushed aside the newspapers. The Globe's headline screamed '*Carnage on Castlereagh*' while The Bugle declared '*Bloodbath in the Boardroom*'.

He clicked the mouse, and the boardroom returned to the screen. He scanned the main photo glancing from chair to chair. The images caused his heart to pound again, and he felt the onrush of panic. Standing, he reached for a water bottle on the table and drank, then regulated his breathing.

"Christ, I haven't got past page one and look at me."

He sighed and looked at the screen. He put the victims' ages between thirty and forty. Casually, but expensively dressed. A Mulberry handbag beside one female, a Rolex on her male colleague. He enlarged the close-ups one by one. Three men and two women faced the table. The killer had wound masking tape around their chests and the seat backs holding the bodies upright. He'd taped more around their wrists and the arms of the chair. Chad looked from one to the other.

"Why not fight, or shout? Christ, there's an office full of people twenty feet away."

He inspected the photos. The perp had shot four of the victims in the back of the head and pools of blood shimmered on the table in front of them. The fifth, a man he'd shot in the forehead. His head tilted backwards, eyes staring over the skyline A muddy puddle lay on the floor behind him.

Chad looked closer at the photo. "Why four from behind and one from the front?"

Chad forced himself to enlarge the last photograph. The sixth victim was the killer's pièce de résistance. A man lay lengthways on the boardroom table facing the screen. The man's legs and arms were bound tight with tape. More tape stretched over his torso and under the table. The victim was bound like some sort of grotesque pupae, or a mummy awaiting a sarcophagus and there were several strips of tape over his mouth. Chad's stomach lurched as he examined the close-up.

"Jesus Christ." A gaping hole lay garish and bloodied in the centre of the man's chest. "He cut his heart out."

Chapter 4

Sleep had eluded him for the remaining hours of the night, so after recovering from the jolt of reading Murray's email, Chad picked up his phone, clicked on Jas's name and dialled.

"Hey, how's things? How's sunny Leeds?"

"Ha, hilarious, it's been chucking it down all day. What's it like in Oz?"

Chad looked out of the windows. The sun had climbed above patchy, fast-moving clouds behind which an azure blue sky gave the promise of a beautiful autumn day in Sydney. "Well, the forecast is saying sunny and twenty-five degrees today so I'm not complaining. By the way, I'm nine hours ahead of you, try to remember that."

"Okay, but I have no concept of time. Anyway, how was the flight, are you alright?"

"Stop worrying, I'm fine. Well, I'm fine apart from getting my collar felt by your Aussie equivalents before I'd even got off the plane, and nothing to do with Freddie."

"What? You're kidding, right?"

"No, really. I got escorted off the plane which wasn't embarrassing at all, then met with a guy called Ruben Murray who's Lee's opposite number over here. Turns out they're hunting a killer who murdered a board of directors, and they want me to help. They're not taking no for an answer."

"Chad, it's too soon. Don't get involved."

"Easier said than done, but I'll try."

"Well, try hard. Anyway, look, I've got to go, will you call me same time tomorrow?"

"Yeah, will do and sleep well."

Chad put the phone on the desk. "Nothing in your life is straightforward, is it?" he muttered. DS Jas Carter, another complexity to add to the fucked-up life of Chad Hilton.

Back to business. Chad picked up his phone and typed a message to Ruben Murray.

Got the email. I understand why you've kept the gory bits from the press, but that may cause your perp to react badly. He wants to revel in his achievement not have it hidden.

His phone pinged, *Gotcha. Talk soon. P*

"P? Shouldn't it be R?" Chad mused, returning to the police report. Closing the MacBook, he rubbed his eyes. Knowing what he needed to do didn't make it easier. Would he cope, and what if he didn't? He tapped out a text, looked at it, sighed then pressed send. *Can I see the crime scene?*

The reply was instant, *Yep. I'll meet you there in an hour.*

*

Chad walked down the wide spiral staircase to the ground floor foyer then navigated the drop off point at the front of the hotel. The bell boys were under starters orders, luggage trolleys at the ready, as two limos pulled in, judging the amount of the tip by the size of the limo. Fair enough, he thought, everyone plays the angles.

"Hey, Chad, welcome to Sydney, mate." The shout came from Chad's right where a guy with a ponytail, high viz jacket, shorts and hiking boots was pointing a camera at him. Chad tensed, how the hell had he forgotten about the press?

"Thanks very much. Glad to be here."

"Any thoughts on our boardroom killings, Chad?" yelled a guy holding out his mobile phone to catch a reply.

"Chad, are you helping the police?" shouted a female hack.

"I'm just here for the game next month, guys. And a bit of R and R. The police don't need my help. Anyway, thanks for the welcome and I hope you make it to the game, I'll look forward to seeing you there." Chad patted his pockets, "Oops, forgotten my wallet." He ran back into the hotel. What a prat. He could do with Freddie being here to distract them. Chad stopped halfway across the reception area and pulled his phone out. That's a point, he thought, where the hell is he? Checking the screen, he saw two missed calls and a WhatsApp message all from Freddie.

Yo bro, have you arrived okay? I'm in room 524. Catching up with friends today. I've booked a table tonight for us at the Meat and Wine Company, 8 p.m. That work for you?

Chad typed a reply. *Two armed plods escorted me off the plane and the cops blackmailed me into helping them on a horrendous murder case. Oh, and hounded by the press. Other than that, all good. Cheers. See you tonight.* He added a crying emoji for good measure.

What murders?

For fuck's sake, Freddie.

*

Chad found the rear exit through a single door that led out onto Castlereagh Street. He checked both directions, then adjusting his Ray Bans, he stepped out and headed north.

He walked beneath the canopies that shaded the windows of exclusive jewellers and designer clothes shops. These soon gave way to the office blocks of the Central Business District. Walking past Martin Place he approached the junction of Castlereagh and Hunter Street. Chad stopped and looked up. This was it.

Nothing about the building distinguished it from its neighbours. Just another skyscraper of glass and concrete. Chad headed to the entrance. Visitors were able to look up to the roof thanks to a large atrium. Chad checked the digital directory of businesses and found Medics4U listed on the eleventh floor. He keyed in the floor number to a screen in front of the lifts and waited. Two other travellers joined him before the doors closed and they rose at speed. Both of his companions exited at floor nine leaving Chad alone. As the doors opened at the eleventh floor, he stepped out of the lift and straight into the bulky figure of a uniformed policeman.

"Sorry, mate, this floor's off limits at the moment." The copper held out an arm to emphasise the point.

Chad smiled. "Oh, I'm meeting DI Murray, is he here?"

"And who might you be, sir?"

"My name's Chad Hilton." Chad had learned from working with the police in Leeds that it was best to leave it at name, rank and number with the type of copper confronting him now.

"Well, Mr Chad Hilton, you won't be meeting anyone here today not even if Pop and you are best of buddies. I need to sign you in and get you police issued ID before you can enter."

"Pop?" asked Chad.

"Well, I guess you don't know him after all. Anyone who knows DI Murray knows him as Pop."

The guy's tone was annoying him. "Right," said Chad, understanding the 'P' from Murray's earlier message. "I'll drop him a text, see if he can sort it out."

Jobsworth at the lift won't let me through. Help required.

Chad waited and looked around. Two businesses occupied the corridor, one in front of him opposite the lift doors and the other, Medics4U, at the end of the corridor, protected from prying eyes by police tape. "Is there a fire escape or only the lifts?" he asked.

"Yeah, there's a fire escape right down the end, but I'd guess you'd have to be super fit to want to use it. There's close to one hundred and eighty stairs."

"Mr Hilton, thanks for coming across," Ruben Murray's voice

sounded strident in the confines of the passageway. "Cheers, Constable Swift, I'll take it from here. Follow me, Chad."

The detective, resplendent in a purple Hawaiian shirt, led the way to a large plate glass door on the left. Chad entered a bright, sparsely furnished reception area with a desk, a computer and a phone. Medics4U was emblazoned in blue lettering on the wall opposite the door. Above the motif were a series of clocks stating the time at various cities across the world. A corporate cliché, Chad reckoned. Ruben Murray let the door glide closed behind him and indicated for Chad to follow him.

"Yeah, sorry about the guy at the lift, but we can't stop people accessing the elevators at the ground floor so I need him there. His attitude might be iffy but no one's going to get past him."

"Good advert for the force then?" smiled Chad. "What's Medics4U's line of business?"

"Recruitment. They supply doctors, nurses and other healthcare staff to hospitals."

"Jesus," said Chad. "What is it with the recruitment industry? A recruitment company was at the centre of the chaos in Leeds."

"Really?" Pop turned mid-stride to look at Chad before continuing. "Down there is a sales office," he waved an arm towards it. "But this is where the action was."

Chad entered the boardroom where the sun gleamed through the windows. As Chad had expected, they gave a splendid view across Castlereagh and up towards Elizabeth Street. Cranes filled the skyline and enormous billboards advertised the new metro station at Martin Place. A plastic sheet, the only sign of the forensic team, covered the boardroom table, where dust motes swirled in the shafts of sunlight.

"How did he get in?" asked Chad.

Pop ran his hands through his hair, "Well, that's the million-dollar question, mate. Lisa James, the receptionist, swears blind that no one entered or left the room from the time the board meeting started at 9:30 a.m. until she went to check why they hadn't broken for lunch and found the shit show you've seen in the photos. She was at her desk out the front there the whole time."

"And no one heard anything?" Chad remembered something that had bothered him about the photos. "I mean, only one of the six had tape across his mouth, so why didn't the others at least shout for help when he started shooting?"

"No idea. We questioned everyone in the office but no one heard anything. It's crazy. Any thoughts from your reading of it?"

"By displaying the guy on the table and cutting out the heart, he wanted to create a place of theatre for you, a work of art, hence why it'll have pissed him off that you omitted it from the press coverage."

Pop looked out the window, "Yeah, that's pretty much what our own profiler said. It's a no win. Put it in the press and we'll have chaos, panic and every nut job on social media adding their ten cents. Don't put it in and this maniac will do something else to show off. Look, we are having a briefing meeting at 6 p.m. tonight if you can come along? You can meet my team and the other profiler, does that work for you?"

Chad sighed. "I'm here to get my head straight and relax with a bit of football. I'll come to the meeting, and I'll help if I can, but that's all. By the way, why do they call you Pop?"

D.I Ruben Murray turned and looked at Chad, "Yeah, well, I've got another bloody Pom to thank for that. Alan Jenkins, a Londoner who worked with us in Sydney years ago. Anyway, think cockney rhyming slang and Indian food mate and I'm sure you'll work it out."

Chapter 5

Chad opened his eyes. Shit, where the hell was he? His heart slowed as he recognised the corporate style furniture of his hotel room. Sitting upright, he blinked and checked his watch. 4:30 p.m. Wow, he'd slept for two and a half hours in the middle of the afternoon. That's bloody jet-lag for you. Fall asleep at the drop of a hat, hungry at the wrong times and a constant foggy brain. What had woken him? He checked his phone and found a missed call from Pop. He clicked on it and waited for the connection.

"Listen mate, can you get down to meet me now rather than leave it till this evening? I wouldn't ask, but it's urgent."

"Don't give me that," Chad moaned, "of course you'd ask. Anyway, what's the urgency?" He could hear voices in the background and then a loud sigh from Pop.

"Ah, mate, it's crazy. I can get everyone in the same room in half an hour. Can you make it?"

"Jesus Christ," Chad paused. This was turning into a busman's holiday. "Yeah, I suppose so. Where are you, what's the address?"

"We're at 192 Day St, back of Darling Harbour. Cheers, Chad, see you shortly."

*

As his taxi sped along the inner ring road, Chad scanned the skyline where cranes like storks rose high into the sky. More vanity projects and for what? To assuage the lust of the global accounting and technology businesses whose garish neon signs dominated the horizon. Progress? Yeah, right. In contrast, he noted, as the taxi pulled to a halt with a squeal of brakes, was the police station on Day Street. Sandwiched between the glitz of steel in Darling Harbour and the Victorian splendour of Sydney Town Hall, it sported a down at heel, seen better days vibe. It looked incongruous amongst its neighbours, like a guy in jeans and sneakers turning up at a black-tie dinner. The Asian taxi driver demanded his fare in a tone that told Chad that hanging around here wasn't good for business. He paid the guy and climbed out.

Straightening his jacket and running his hands through his hair, he checked his watch. 5:05 p.m. He inspected the building in front of him then took a deep breath and walked towards a set of double doors. On their left was a mosaic of blue and white chequered squares and a large sign declaring Day Street Police Station. To the right was an intercom. He pressed the 'Reception' button and informed a crackling voice why he was there. One of the automatic glass doors slid open and Chad entered.

His only previous exposure to a police station was in Leeds, where taxpayers' money had built a brand spanking new headquarters. The resulting glass and concrete structure continued to be a bone of contention in the city. Day Street was the opposite. If tired best described the exterior, then the interior was thoroughly exhausted. Chad looked around the entrance foyer. Cracks and scuff marks grazed the ancient lino on the floor, and in places around the walls the paint peeled lazily away, revealing brick work beneath. There were two chairs near a grubby table, on which leaflets reminded the public to keep socially distanced and to use hand sanitiser. Chad decided not to sit.

"Well, wherever else Sydney spends its money, it isn't here," Chad muttered. His words hung in the fetid air. If the building had air conditioning, someone had switched it off or overuse had broken it. His shirt clung to his back. The place held a sickly, cloying smell and the heat smothered what air there was. The smell, Chad decided, was a remnant of the fear induced sweat of previous visitors. Chad heard heavy shoes coming down the stairs at the end of the foyer.

Pop stood about halfway down the staircase and beckoned Chad over, "Come on, Chad, follow me. Thanks for coming in. What a nightmare. Unreal."

Chad followed Pop up the stairs and along a dingy corridor on either side of which were several wood framed doors each with a frosted glass panel. "I see they don't enjoy spending civic money on creature comforts for you boys," Chad commented. "This looks like one of those 1950s Hollywood movie sets, is Humphrey Bogart going to emerge from behind one of these?"

Pop laughed. "You're not wrong there, mate, but on the plus side working in this shithole means we never get visits from the top brass. They're in a state-of-the art, no expense spared new build in Paramatta."

A throb of noise emanated from behind a door, the sound amplifying as Pop leaned on it. Entering the dilapidated room, Chad decided it looked less like an office and more like a storage unit for unwanted furniture. Fighting for space in the cramped confines were several old wooden desks. Around the walls filing cabinets leaned like debauched drunks. Some tilted forwards with drawers open, while others with no drawers, seemed to accept that their functional prime was long gone. Two electric fans hummed and attempted to shift the warm air from one part of the room to another with little success. But despite the conditions, there was a buzz of vitality and urgency generated by the seven or eight detectives in situ. On the wall inside the door, someone had fixed a large wipe board which held photos of the Castlereagh victims. Their names, addresses, and ages underneath. Chad folded his arms and leaned against the wall as Pop called the room to order.

'Okay, everyone listen up," bellowed Pop.

Gradually the noise in the room died, and Chad appraised the team. First impressions were always important. Perched on a long wooden table were three men and one woman, while two or three other detectives and several uniformed coppers busied themselves at desks around the perimeter. The detectives clasped tablets or MacBooks and they all looked in their late twenties or early thirties. No lifers here. Except for Pop. The team shared a collective intensity, the physical manifestation of which was clear. Hands ran through hair, feet tapped incessant rhythms on the floor, and sweat rings stained the shirts and blouses that clung to their occupants. Chad had learned from the cases he'd worked on in Leeds to keep his mouth shut until spoken to. Opinions from outsiders like him needed to be asked for, not offered. "See all, hear all, say nowt," as they say in Yorkshire.

"Right, thanks, everyone. A couple of intros first. Bloke leaning against the wall there is Chad Hilton. He's a criminal psychologist from England. Okay, he's a Pom, but try not to let that cloud your judgement. And I don't want the press to know he's assisting, so keep his name out of it. Clear?"

A murmur of understanding greeted Pop's comments and Chad smiled as the team turned towards him. He noted the female detective appraise him from head to toe but the men barely glanced at him. Could be worse, he thought.

"Mel Keane's at the back, you've worked with her before. Welcome to both, I'll gladly accept any help you can give us."

Chad straightened and peered across the room. Seated under the window was a lithe, tanned, blonde woman around his own age. It's her, he thought. It must be fifteen years since he'd met her at a conference here in Sydney. Shit, small world, and she'd aged well. He wondered if she'd remember him. She was smiling at Pop but turned to Chad and winked. Yep, she did.

Pop began, "So, let me summarise current status then we can pick up on some specifics. First, who went where on the morning of the murders?"

Chad hid a smile. In his only previous exposure to a police team briefing, the cops all had Yorkshire accents so Pop's Tasmanian drawl sounded somehow out of place.

Pop continued, "We've checked with businesses on each floor of the building and they've identified their own employees from the CCTV footage we've got. That eliminates most people, but we've still got a further thirty-seven individuals that used the lifts that morning. Lucy, have you identified those?"

Lucy, the sole female detective was a willowy young woman of African heritage with a fabulous afro. She read from her notes. "We're working our way through them, Pop. We've identified sixteen so far and all are bona fide visitors to the building, we're still trying to tie down the other twenty-one so until we've confirmed who they are, and why they were there, they remain persons of interest."

"Okay," Pop said, "if one of these twenty-one turns out to be our perp that will be fantastic, but my instinct says that won't be the case. If I'm right, we can be pretty sure that our perp did not access the eleventh floor using the lifts, so he used the fire escape, which is accessed from the underground garage area. CCTV's in the garage but not the stairs. José, how are we doing checking that?"

A tall guy with dark wavy hair dressed in jeans and a New York Jets tee-shirt scrolled through his laptop. "I've checked all the vehicles in the garage and confirmed they belong to various personnel working in the building. Nothing to link them to the killings. The CCTV only covers the parking bays and the exit ramp, so we have no sight of the fire escape. But he'd have had to enter and exit via the ramp, I assume."

Chad shuffled his feet. Trickles of sweat rolled down his back and pooled in his waistband.

Pop was using a biro to point at the photos on the wipe board. "Alright, so our working assumption is that our perp and his victims have some connection. Unless, of course, these are totally random killings which Mel and Chad might shed some light on a little later." Pop paused for a moment, then continued, "Background checks on the victims, Dimi, how are you doing with those?"

Chad glanced at the young guy dressed in skinny jeans, and a black tee-shirt. He had tight black curls, trimmed, and John Lennon glasses which gave him a slightly academic look. Dapper, that's the word his mother would have used, thought Chad.

"Nothing to cause any immediate concern and their private lives don't provide any obvious motive for their murders. No dodgy mates, no drug habits or gambling addictions, nothing that brings them into contact with anything more unsavoury than the occasional bar brawl on a company night out. None have a criminal record; the odd jay walk caution but otherwise all six victims have led blameless lives. They're a bunch who've worked hard and made some money for themselves. They've all worked for Medics4U for years, Jonathon Hope and the CEO, Dan Hopkins, have been there since they founded the company."

"What about their employees, José, anyone leaping off the page at us?" asked Pop.

"Working our way through them, Pop. There's eighty staff currently employed by the company and they've had a twenty percent staff turnover for the last five years giving us another eighty we need to check on. We are updating the spreadsheet as we go and that's stored in the cloud so you can check on progress anytime anywhere. No obvious leads. We're doing the hard yards but it's time consuming."

"Josh, any forensic leads yet?"

The man was over six feet tall with a thick beard.

"Nothing at all," Josh pushed a recalcitrant strand of hair behind his ear. "No fingerprints, no extraneous clothing fibres, no shell casings. We'll know the calibre of ammo used when the pathologist's report comes in but looks like nine-millimetre parabellums. Clearly the weapon had a suppressor otherwise it would have alerted the rest of the office. Whoever did it was uber careful and cleared up after himself. Everybody working at Medics4U that day was very clear that no one entered the boardroom after 9:30 a.m. Seems that board meeting days were sacrosanct and there were often heated words coming from inside the boardroom so everyone was careful to keep clear. Lisa James the receptionist swears blind no one entered."

"Thanks, guys. Key area of focus, how did our killer get in? Anything on CCTV around the building?"

"Still going through it, boss," said Lucy.

Pop shuffled his feet and reaching over his left shoulder, massaged the muscles in the back of his neck. "Mel, Chad, you've both read the reports and heard from the guys here. Any initial thoughts or observations?"

"Ladies first," Chad smiled.

"Bugger that," Mel retorted, "but, yeah, okay, I'll kick off. I'll come to the front, so you don't all have to crane your necks." Chad returned her smile and made a conscious effort not to North and South her. Difficult, though.

Mel cleared her throat. "A couple of broad assumptions: Worldwide, ninety-eight percent of all multiple murders are carried out by men. In Australia that number rises to ninety-nine-point two percent, so it's odds-on the perp is a bloke."

Chad noticed the detectives were busy making notes.

"Second," she continued, "if the perp used the fire escape to get in and out, he'd have climbed one hundred and eighty steps and still been ready to do his work. That would show a reasonable level of fitness. That he knew to use the fire escape suggests someone with local knowledge. Add those together and I'd suggest you're looking for a local man, in an age range anywhere from late teens to, I dunno, I suppose a fit sixty-year-old could have done it."

She took a sip of water from a bottle she was holding. "The

manner of the killings is interesting. Why shoot five, but then torture the victim on the table? Torture is more personal therefore indicative that the killer has some type of connection to the mutilated man – Dan Hopkins, the CEO. If so, then the killer's not a random attacker." Mel caught Chad's eye, "Chad, anything to add?"

Chad rubbed his knee, an involuntary action that did not go unnoticed by the group. "I agree with Mel that the savagery singles this victim out from the others, and that it's worth focussing your attention on Dan Hopkins, the CEO. What is the link between him and the killer?" He paused. "We know that no staff member went into the boardroom after 9:30 a.m. so how did the killer enter and why didn't anyone raise the alarm?" Chad looked at the detectives, "The CEO had tape across his mouth, the other victims didn't, so why didn't they shout?" He shrugged, "That's it so far from me." Then he turned to Pop, "Oh yeah, one more thing. Crimes of this type usually have rehearsals, so I'd suggest that if you haven't already done it, that you check for ritual killings or those with a similar MO. If there are none, then you'll have to discover why this has happened now. What's the catalyst?"

"Thanks Mel, thanks Chad. Food for thought. I agree we dig deeper into Dan Hopkins' background. Guys, let's go further into his working life if his private life isn't giving us anything. Maybe he's upset someone in the past and they hold a grudge. Alright, let's keep going. Make sure you update the Google sheets before you finish tonight so we can all see what the hell we've been doing. That's it, folks. Mel, Chad can I have a quick word?"

*

Chad followed Mel down the tatty corridor to where Pop held open the door to another office. The scent of her perfume for a moment lifted the stench of sweat.

"Dingy doesn't do this place justice," muttered Chad on entering. "How the other one percent live, eh?"

"Funny bugger," said Pop.

"Don't sit down, Mel, God knows what those stains are," Chad pointed to the only seat, which was tinged with a brownish smudge.

"Don't worry, I won't. I've been here before, remember?"

Pop closed the door. "Yeah, yeah alright, that's enough. The good citizens of Sydney like to know their coppers aren't getting soft so they keep us here. Get bloody used to it. Look, joking aside, thanks for your insights in there. Mel, I have a budget that'll pay for your help on this one, but I'd appreciate it if you could collaborate with Chad and share any thoughts you may have." He turned to Chad. "I can't pay you, mate, but I'd appreciate it. Two heads being better than one. By the way, you two seem very chummy to say you've just met."

"Who says we've just met?" asked Mel. "We go way back, don't we, Chad?"

"We do indeed. That's flummoxed you, hasn't it?"

Pop frowned. "I daren't ask, but…You two weren't an item, were you?"

"No," Mel and Chad replied in unison.

"Okay, that's alright then," Pop chuckled, "I'll keep you both up to speed with developments and if you attend the team briefings that would be great. Oh, and Chad, make sure your mate Freddie doesn't get into trouble."

Chapter 6

Chad's shoes stuck to the lino as he walked across the dismal foyer of the police station. To the side of the sliding doors was a large green button underneath which a helpful sticker advised 'Push to exit.' Chad needed no second bidding. Once outside, the dry heat, unseasonal for May, immediately enveloped him and like an invisible bloodsucker drew moisture from him. He stepped to the side and Mel followed him out.

"Well, long time no see," he said. "How long is it? Fifteen years?"

"Yeah, it must be. Anyway, why don't we adjourn to a bar and get a cold beer?"

*

Chad bought two schooners of Toohey's New from the bar at Cyren and headed outside to where Mel had found a table. The bar sat on the north side of Darling Harbour next to the Sydney Exhibition centre outside which a huge, lascivious Rolling Stones tongue invited visitors to an exhibition of the band's memorabilia.

"Cheers," he chinked his frosted glass against Mel's. "Not sure I remember anything from that conference, except we were like a couple of kids knocking off school."

"No, nor me, except my liver needed several days to recover."

Chad took a long drink and relaxed. She looks great, he thought, sneaking a peek over his beer. Long blonde hair parted in the centre framed a small impish face. He remembered they were the same age, both late forties, but unlike his own, her skin was expensively smooth, tanned and wrinkle free. She wore no wedding ring, her only jewellery being a gold chain hung around her neck which glistened against her sleek white dress. Looked like a Zimmerman, one of Angie's favourites. "So, tell me," he asked, "what have you been up to over the years? Married? Kids?"

"My marriage ended a few years ago. We just ran out of stamina in the never-ending marathon of job, home, kid. Amicable enough, though. We've got one daughter, Jodie, she's fourteen and lives with her dad. I have her at the weekends. How about you, any kids?"

Chad smiled and shook his head.

"Chad, I've seen what the press has said about you, it was big news over here, so I asked Pop how much of it was true. Don't be cross with him, he felt it would less awkward if I knew. Anyway," she reached across the table and covered Chad's hand with her own, "I'm so sorry for your loss. How are you coping, are you okay?"

Chad sighed. What to say? Right now, he felt at ease although he recognised residual panic was never far away. He wasn't angry with Pop for telling her the facts; the guy was trying to make the relationship work so his investigation could be a success. He rubbed his knee, then stopped when he realised. "I'm fine," he said, then smiling added, "I think."

He let his eyes roam over Mel's kind, serene face and wanted to talk. "Grief seems to creep up on me and belt me when I least expect it, but I'm coping, thanks. Or, at least, I'm getting through the days. I've been having regular counselling sessions with my therapist, Veronica, and a couple of people I'm close to, Jas and Freddie, also look out for me. Being here makes what happened at home seem surreal."

"You don't have to go through it with me if that's difficult. Sorry, Chad, I don't mean to pry."

"You're not, and it's okay. The media circus at home has been tough. It's expected that you show the world a brave face, but

Christ, I've lost count of the number of times that I'd shut the front door and sit on the floor with my back leaning on it until I heard the photographers outside eventually disperse. I thought I'd put that behind me until Pop collared me at the airport and put me straight." He took a sip of beer, "What's Pop told you?"

"As much as he knew, I think. Kidnappings, murders, your wife killed and you working out who the killer was. It sounds the stuff of nightmares," said Mel.

Chad looked at Mel and took a deep breath. "We kept from the press that Angie and I had split up. I'd been on painkillers for years to cope with the football injuries, but in the final few months I'd become addicted to Fentanyl. I'm not sure whether that pushed Angie away, but it can't have helped. Couples split up all the time, right? But you don't expect your wife to die. Not because of that. The guy who did it was an evil bastard. He shot a couple of my mate Freddie's young guys en route to killing Ange, and Freddie won't forgive that."

Mel leaned across the table and whispered, "you don't have to do any of this. Don't get involved, I'll tell Pop. Just enjoy the soccer and rest up. No worries." Her hand touched his cheek, "I'll get us another beer."

She picked up the two empty glasses from the table.

"Thanks, Mel," Chad held her eye. "But say nothing to Pop, let's play it by ear. We need to catch whoever massacred those poor sods."

*

Chad's phone pinged. Freddie.

Bro, just checking you're still okay for dinner at 8 p.m.?

He looked up as Mel returned from the bar, "Hey, Mel, what are you doing tonight? Why don't you come to dinner? You'll get to meet Freddie, the guy I just mentioned. Freddie Jackson. I'm not taking no for an answer." Chad peered over his phone as he typed his reply.

Mel was smiling at him, eyes wide, "*The* Freddie Jackson? As in star of Sydney FC? That Freddie Jackson?"

"Yep, but he's got an ego the size of Australia at it is, so don't massage it."

He finished typing and pressed send.

Yep, all good. Add one more to the reservation. I'm bringing a friend of mine.

He saw Freddie was typing so waited for the ping.

Cool, that'll be four of us 'cos I'm bringing a guest too. It'll be a blast.

Chapter 7

"That's the Intercontinental Hotel," said Mel. They were standing on Macquarie Street and Chad followed Mel's outstretched arm. The Intercontinental was yet another unremarkable skyscraper, this time rising higher than its neighbours by dint of being at the top of Bridge Street, a steep incline that ran from George Street in the west and climbed to their current vantage point.

Chad saw a sign for the Meat and Wine Co. As they waited for the beeps at the lights to tell them when to cross, Chad nudged Mel. "What happened to brash, devil-may-care Aussies? Everyone's so law-abiding. No one just crosses, they all wait for the lights."

"That's because we have jay walking fines that the police can impose on the spot if they catch you."

"Jesus, when did you lot become such a nanny state?"

*

Freddie ushered them towards their table, treating Mel to the full Jackson charm offensive. "Anyway," he said, "let me introduce you to my other guest."

Chad was aware of Freddie's voice but the words didn't register. What the hell? He knew he was staring but couldn't stop himself. Behind the table sat a young man in his late teens or early twenties whose enormous physique was such that he looked like an adult sitting at a child's play table. His skin was a deep mahogany, lightened to give a milk chocolate tone, and his features were of

Northern European origin. He wore his thick black curly hair braided in ringlets. But none of that, Chad later reflected, would have made him stand there staring with his jaw hitting the floor. No need for a DNA test, because the paternity of the young colossus was not in question. Wow. Well, well, Freddie Jackson, you've kept this quiet. Secrets, Chad thought, no good ever comes of them.

"Hey, bro, aren't you going to say hello?" asked Freddie.

Chad realised Freddie was talking to him and that the young man opposite was holding out his hand. "Yes, of course, sorry, I'm Chad."

"Pleased to meet you, Chad, I've heard a lot about you. I'm Junior."

Chad caught Freddie glancing at him from behind his menu and decided that a raised eyebrow was a suitable response. As Mel engaged the young guy in conversation, Chad appraised him. There was nothing brash about him, none of the extroverted, in your face, alpha male that epitomised his father. Chad didn't know how the hell genetics worked, but he realised that while the boy may have inherited his father's looks and build, his personality hadn't come from Freddie. Junior was thoughtful in his response to Mel's questions, softly spoken, holding eye contact only occasionally. Chad perused the menu wondering how Freddie had kept his son secret. And why? Ostrich skewers leapt off the page at him. No, don't think so. Kangaroo steak. Nope. As the waiter hovered Freddie excused himself and went to the bathroom and Chad reached the conclusion that a ribeye and salad would do fine.

He was glad that Freddie held court on his return. It meant he could relax for the first time since he'd touched down in Australia. That Mel was in awe of Freddie was clear. But it was also clear that he reciprocated the feelings. Mel laughed at Freddie's jokes and Freddie, in return, was asking all the right questions about Mel's work, family and leisure pursuits. Chad could tell Freddie liked her because he was listening to her answers.

He's a dad, Chad thought, and if tonight is anything to go by, Freddie may have found a soulmate. He drained the last of his wine then looked across the table at Mel. Well, bugger me, he thought. Mel had her chin resting in her cupped hand and was gazing like an adoring teenager at Freddie.

"So, Chad, Dad says you're a psychologist, is that right?" asked Junior.

"I bet he called me a shrink," laughed Chad, "but you're right, I am a psychologist," Chad smiled. "Does that sort of stuff interest you?"

"The science of it does, I suppose, but I'm less into humans and more into AI and digital tech development. That's what I'm studying at college."

Chad stifled a laugh. "Really? Well, your dad is a complete Luddite in technology. Apart from posting endless photos of himself on Insta, he has no idea."

Junior looked at Chad from under hooded lids. "Yeah, I'm finding that out."

"Right, guys, if you'll excuse me my Uber has arrived," said Mel. "But I need that selfie first. You too, Chad, I need you in this."

Chad stood and placed his arm around Mel's waist while Freddie on her left did the same but with one long outstretched arm holding Mel's phone. Chad noticed another camera to his left and a bulb flashed bright.

"Hey Chad, Freddie, how's it goin' welcome to Australia," yelled a dark-haired woman pointing a phone at him.

Chad recognised her as the reporter from the hotel earlier. Shit, Pop won't want the press linking me and Mel together. "Thanks, yeah, great restaurant." He hurried towards the door but the journo stepped into his path and he felt a small hand press something into his. As Freddie and Junior pushed passed them to the exit, he glanced over his shoulder to see the diminutive reporter smiling and waving at him.

"Shit, I'd better let Pop know, just in case," Mel remarked, as they exited the restaurant.

"Yep, I think so,' replied Chad. "Jesus, that's my fault, I should have known that might happen. Anyway, it was great to see you again. No doubt I'll see you soon at that pig-sty they call a police station, but before then we should compare notes on what we think is going on."

"Let's do that, I'll call you tomorrow."

*

"So," Chad stared at Freddie, "spill. Why the hell haven't you told me about Junior? Why did you leave me to find out tonight? I thought we were best buddies." Chad knew the emotional blackmail stuff always worked on Freddie.

"Look, yeah, I know and I'm sorry bro, but it's complicated."

Chad rolled the Highland Park around the cut glass whisky tumbler. No rush, he thought.

"His mother made contact out of the blue a year ago. Sent me photos and videos but I swear that was the first I knew of him. I was gutted. She'd kept me in the dark, out of his life and said there'd been no point telling me. I'd just finished playing in Sydney and gone back to England and she didn't want an intermittent presence in his life. She's never married. Brought him up on her own. I could have helped, man. I could have helped."

Chad saw Freddie's eyes fill up and leaned across the bar stool and pulled his friend into him. The noise in the Sheraton bar seemed intrusive now, and Chad wished they'd gone somewhere quieter, more discreet.

Freddie sniffed, wiped his eyes and continued, "She eventually decided that as he was now twenty-one, she should tell him about his father. Said that whenever he'd asked in the past, she'd told him that his dad had left before he was born. When she told him, he got furious. Not with me but with his mother." Freddie paused, pulled on his drink then resumed, "Anyway, bro, long story short, I've spoken to him every week since then, but Covid meant I couldn't see him. With all the shit you've had in your life, I reckoned it was better to wait till we got here to tell you. I came a day later so that I could meet him on my own."

Chad let the news settle. Freddie was a dad, amazing. He couldn't blame him for not discussing it, Chad decided. Freddie needed his support, not brickbats.

"I'm delighted for you, buddy, and I'm looking forward to getting to know Junior better. Wow, mate, you're a dad. That's fantastic news."

"Thanks, bro. I might stay for a couple of months after the game to make up for lost time. I want to be a part of his life."

"What about his mum?" asked Chad. "Are you going to see her?"

"Yeah, I'm going to see them together tomorrow. They live in Bondi."

Chad smiled, "Well, here's to you, Junior and fatherhood."

Freddie raised his glass, and Chad clinked his against it.

"Oh, I forgot," said Freddie, "Odd Job and Tony are coming over for a few weeks. My thank you to them for everything they did when the shit hit the fan with Angie. It'll be an enjoyable break for them."

Chad stared at Freddie and laughed, a chuckle at first, but then he couldn't help himself and fell into a deep, uproarious, hysterical belly laugh. He saw Freddie smile at the other punters who were now staring and casting disapproving looks his way, but Chad didn't care. This was the funniest thing he'd heard in ages.

"You're joking, right?" said Chad, between gasps. "Those two, here, can you imagine?"

Freddie was staring at him then nodding and smiling again at the other customers. "No, bro. No joke, they'll be here tomorrow.

What's so funny?"

Odd Job. Chad had given him the epithet when he'd first met him a few months ago during the murderous maelstrom in Leeds. He'd reminded Chad of the eponymous bad guy in Goldfinger and the name had stuck. Odd Job was Freddie's chauffeur, chef and general factotum. He was also as scary as fuck. Six feet five tall, bald like Freddie, ebony black and built like a mountain range, he was Freddie's fixer-in-chief. Chad closed his eyes. And Tony, shit. Freddie's go to muscle of choice. Ex SAS of Pakistani origin and utterly ruthless.

Chad's stomach was doing cartwheels as he realised Freddie wasn't joking. "How will they get into Australia? The guys at immigration will just laugh at their application for a holiday visa. They're not exactly ideal tourists, are they?"

"Bro, they have more passports than you've got dollars. No problem. Odd Job can get us a car while he's here, drive us around, no more Ubers."

Chad stared out of the large plate glass window in the bar and considered his situation. Being blackmailed by Pop into work he wasn't fit to do. A lunatic on the loose. Press hounding him. Panic attacks daily. And now Freddie introducing two of his compadres that made the Kray twins look like winners of the Nobel Peace Prize.

"You couldn't make this up," he muttered.

*

Chad emptied his pockets onto the bedside table. Falling face up next to a couple of twenty dollar bills was a glossy business card stating The Globe, in a large gothic font. Printed below was the name Andrea Byrne. The reporter at the restaurant. He turned it over to see a message written in a neat script.

'Give me half an hour to buy you a coffee tomorrow and I promise

not to hassle you. It'll be worth your while. Starbucks on the corner of Elizabeth and Market, 9ish? A.'

"Shit."

Chapter 8

'Justice delayed is justice denied.'
William E. Gladstone.

The woman in the flowered print skirt tries to move her arms and then attempts to stand but she completes neither movement. Sweat is pouring from her, mixing with her perfume, making my nostrils twitch. Gross. Her eyes flicker around the room, widening in shock, tears welling, desperate for help, but no help will be forthcoming. Her chair shakes as she writhes to free herself. I savour her fear and wallow in her misery. Magnificent. Three others sit silent at their desks. All is well. But time is against me so I can't prolong my enjoyment.

The woman blinks rapidly, shaking her head from left to right. She stops with a jolt as her eyes alight on me. I wanted her to see her colleagues first, but it is what it is. Trying to make sense of what's happening gives way to terror. She'd scream if she could.

From the full 'In' trays to the bulging files piled on each desk the office exudes an air of casual incompetence. It's a story of negligence, of ineptitude, but worse it proclaims that those who work here don't give a shit about those outside. Those whose lives are on hold waiting for these lazy bureaucrats to be bothered with them. Or not. And money talks, of course. If there's a pecuniary gain to be had, these faceless custodians of the state will move the files in the pile. C'est la vie. I know that better than most. But today is different. Access has been simple and unhindered. My previous visits had confirmed that the right people were in the right place. It would have made things trickier if they'd worked in different offices but like everything in this place nothing ever changes. These four all worked together twenty years ago and they work together now. It was that sort of job.

A musty smell pervades the air. I'm sitting in an old-fashioned wooden chair with worn leather padding and cracks in the seat which is not built for comfort. But it gives an unobstructed view of the occupants in the room. Two men and two women. They seem of an age that they'd be retiring soon. They all have grey hair and wear what passes for a uniform in here. Stained baggy chinos and polo shirts for the men, shapeless flowery skirts and non-descript blouses for the women. The obligatory family photos on each desk. No one will miss them. Least of all me.

The office is small. Two steps are all it takes for me to reach the oversized industrial shredding machine which I pull over to stand in front of the woman whose previous shaking and twitching has given way to a catatonic stupor. She stares, eyes bulging, as if the appliance is going to eat her. I step behind the woman to the window. Above it is a large steel hook once used to winch things from the ground floor but now it's the lynchpin for my pulley. From the pulley, a rope falls to the floor. Lifting it, I give it a sharp tug and see with satisfaction how the woman jerks in her chair.

Moving in front of her and pulling a photograph from my pocket, I put it in front of her face. She stares and shakes her head, then stares again. The tape on her mouth prevents her from speaking but an answer isn't necessary. She can't distinguish this one face from those of the countless other people she's harmed. My time is up, so replacing the photograph and stepping behind her I lift the rope. She rises from her seat like a fish on the line. As she twists towards me her eyes are protruding and the veins in her neck appear close to bursting. Soon she's swinging free of her seat and I hoist her further till the top of her head is the same height as the pulley. I tie the rope around the cast iron radiator below. Positioning the shredder below her feet she sways gently like a sapling in a breeze. I open my jacket. The long knife seems to hiss as it's released from its sheath. Standing in front of my catch I place the tip of the blade against her chest. Nearly unconscious, her body still jerks as she feels the cut, then as the dagger sinks deep inside her head lolls forward and eventually the involuntary twitching of her legs abates. Her body says its last goodbye.

Two down.

Chapter 9

Chad opened his eyes and blinked. His phone was buzzing and doing a jig on the bedside table like an irate bluebottle on its back unable to right itself. The information on the screen answered the questions in his head. It was 7:07 a.m. and the caller was Pop. Neither of these two answers appealed to him.

Chad dispensed with any attempt at civility. "What?"

"Get your arse out of bed and meet me at the immigration office on Lee Street as soon as you can. I've called Mel, and she's on her way. We've got another shit show down here. The press are crawling all over the place. I don't need them recognising you, okay?"

Chad eased himself up onto his pillow, "What's happened?'

"Just get down here, I haven't time to give you chapter and verse. Four more bodies and at first sight looks like the same MO."

Chad stared at the phone as the black screen showed Pop had ended the call. Jesus, what was happening here? He clambered out of bed and sent a text to Martha Kennedy at Sydney F.C, telling her he'd have to cancel their 10 a.m. meeting then hurried into the bathroom.

He heard the knocking on his bedroom door as he was towelling himself dry. "Bloody hell, this is ridiculous," he muttered, "who the hell is this?"

He faced the door. "Yes, what? Who is it?" he asked hoping the tone of his voice conveyed what he really meant. Pissed off didn't cut it.

"It's Mel. I thought it would be easier to dump my car here, pick you up and grab a cab. There's nowhere to park in Haymarket."

"Okay, I'll just be a couple of minutes," said Chad, scrambling to get his jeans on.

"No probs, I'll wait downstairs."

"Okay. Oh, and Mel?"

"Yes, what?"

"Don't buy the coffee from the foyer, it's thirty-five bucks for two, but there's a Starbucks on the corner."

"I appreciate the heads up, but why am I buying?"

"'Cos you're getting bloody paid and I'm not."

*

Chad pulled the baseball cap a little lower on his forehead and adjusted his Ray Bans as he walked towards the police crime scene tape which was stretched across the road. Held back by another cordon of police were a couple of dozen news hacks. Pop was correct about the press getting here sharpish. Several TV crews were setting up just beyond the police perimeter. Chad checked his watch, 7:52 a.m. Christ, this would be on all the breakfast TV news channels. He followed close behind Mel as she showed her police pass to a copper who, having muttered something into his radio, lifted the tape for them to pass through. He heard questions being yelled by the journalists.

"When will we get a statement?"

"Who are you, lady? Who are you, sir? What are you here for?"

Chad glanced across the street then quickly turned his head away. A photographer was aiming a lens at him. Shit, he thought, that's all I need.

The building that housed the immigration department was a 1960s concrete block that looked like it had Stalag Thirteen to thank for its design. It stood in an L-Shape sandwiched between Sydney Central Station and the inner ring road. Chad entered a large soulless foyer and left the noise of trains and rush hour traffic outside. Mel was identifying herself to another policeman and beckoned Chad across.

"Fifth floor, take the lift," The copper pointed at a bank of lifts against one wall.

"I shouldn't be here," muttered Chad as the lift doors closed.

"Why not?"

"If the press find out about my involvement, it'll be an excuse for them to throw more shit at Pop's fan."

"Well, let's hope they didn't spot you then." She held Chad's eye, "I take your point though."

The lift reached the fifth floor and the old doors creaked open. Chad stepped into a maelstrom of activity. Crime scene techs in one-piece protective gear hustled along the narrow corridor, while outside each of the doors tooled up coppers stood sentry. Photographers, detectives and assorted medics jostled for space. Throbbing above the bustle were a hum of conversations, urgent in tone, but from which, Chad could only pick out random words and phrases.

"Ah, you've made it." Pop emerged from a room at the end of the corridor, "put these on." He passed them each a protective suit still in its polythene wrapper. "Last room on the left and, fyi, it ain't pretty."

Chad slipped into the one-piece suit and as he considered what he was walking into, his heart rate stepped up. His mouth filling with acid bile and the sweat breaking out all over his body confirmed what he already knew. Panic attack inbound. He took several deep breaths which calmed him, but his hands remained clammy and wet. He straightened to see Mel watching him.

"Chad, are you going to be okay?"

"Yeah, yeah, I'll be fine."

"I told you yesterday, you don't need to put yourself through this. I'll talk to Pop."

"I know, thanks Mel, it'll be fine. To be any use at all, I need to see what you see so we can get inside the perp's head. Come on, let's crack on, I'll be fine."

Mel stood in front of Chad as he tried to move. As she leaned towards him, he noted her perfume held subtle floral scents which he found weirdly soothing.

She spoke in a soft low undertone, "Chad, it's okay to be messed up by what you experienced back home. For God's sake, it was only a few months ago. No wonder the idea of going into a crime scene is freaking you out."

He held her gaze, "Thanks, Mel. I'm fine. Honestly. Now, coming? Or shall I go on my own?"

"Okay, but if you pass out, I won't catch you."

'Visa and Immigration Department' was stencilled on a brown varnished door. Once inside, Chad felt like he'd stumbled into an artwork created by someone having a bad hallucinogenic trip. He stood, mesmerised by the catastrophe in front of him.

The room was rectangular and perhaps four metres by three. There was nowhere to hide from the carnage, and dominating all else was the centrepiece. Chad stared across the room. Underneath the window was a large shredding machine, from which two blotchy legs protruded. A yellow flowered skirt covered the thighs but created a grotesque twisted pose hanging over the side like someone's dirty laundry. The killer had stretched a rope from the shredder to a pulley above the window.

"He's hanged her then stuffed her in here," shouted Pop, pointing at the lower part of the shredder. "But look at that."

Chad followed Pop's outstretched arm. There were four desks in the room. Three had chairs, each occupied. Seated, heads flopped backwards, mouths open and eyes staring were the other employees of the visa and immigration department. Each had a bullet hole in the centre of their forehead and on the walls behind them their brains and bone fragments created a macabre mosaic.

The fourth desk, to which Pop was pointing, was empty except for a two-tray filing system in blue plastic. The bottom tray bore a white sticker saying 'Out' and the upper another, 'In'. Sitting on top, like a disgusting paperweight, a large dripping piece of meat leaked gunge onto the desktop.

"What the hell is that?" said Chad.

"It's her heart," said Pop. "He's cut her frigging heart out."

The horror of the scene had paralysed his other senses, but they reactivated as Chad looked away and the stench assaulted him. The bitter metallic reek of blood mingled with the smell of faeces and urine creating an overpowering odour that seemed to have its own physical presence. Like an abattoir. Chad stepped into the corridor.

"Are you okay?' asked Mel following him out.

"Yeah, I'm fine, I just need to clear my head," Chad replied. "You?"

"Likewise. This is horrific."

*

Chad leaned against a wall. Sweat poured from him and nausea rippled through his abdomen. He closed his eyes. The noise in his head was like a storm at sea, roaring, raging, rising and falling. Crashing. Somewhere a tiny lucid fragment of his brain was saying '*breathe.*' Breathe, he thought, just breathe. Some calm returned, the noise beginning to abate. Chad heard Pop's voice, echoey and distant.

"Any first thoughts?"

He wasn't ready for this; it was too soon. He couldn't help Pop because he couldn't help himself.

"Are you okay, Chad, you look bloody awful, mate?"

Chad looked up to find Pop staring at him, "Yeah, yeah, I'm okay. Just wasn't ready for that on an empty stomach."

Mel cleared her throat, "This looks like the same MO as

Castlereagh Street, one victim mutilated, the others shot. As we saw at the Medics4U murders, our perp seems to have focussed his butchery on one victim, in this case the lady in the shredder. Who is she, what's her name?"

"Janice Short, she was the head of the department," Pop checked the notes on his pad. "The pathologist reckons they've been dead for between twelve and sixteen hours. We've been told that they always do overtime on a Tuesday, so it's likely our perp arrived after 17:00 last evening. Anyway, I'll have to get moving so call me when you've made an assessment. And avoid the press on your way out, Chad."

Chad looked up and nodded. Pull yourself together, he thought.

"Right," said Pop, "whatever the sicko is thinking we need to find what links Dan Hopkins to Janice Short, and try to join the dots. Talk later."

Chapter 10

Chad waited, holding the door for two giggling Chinese students each clutching a Frappuccino, then he stepped into the large, busy Starbucks. He saw Andrea Byrne seated in a corner at a table for two, with a mocha in a glass in front of her. "Can I get you another of those?" he asked, as he approached the table.

"No, thanks. It's my third of the day and I'm caffeined up. Anyway, I said I'd buy so what would you like?"

"Fair enough, I'll have a black americano, please. Large."

As she sauntered to the serving area, he sat and removed his baseball cap then ran his hand through his hair which felt damp to the touch. Sweat. No bloody wonder. The coffee shop was bustling, and he wiped some crumbs from the table. Why was he here? He couldn't answer that. The reporter returned and placed a large white mug in front of him and sat down opposite. He put her in her early thirties but knew she could be any age from mid-twenties upward. She had jet black hair with a fringe cut to the line of her eyebrows and the sides cut in a long bob, falling to her shoulders. Her eyes were dark, almost black, her skin tanned. She had a small diamond stud nose piercing and wore a yellow baggy tee-shirt with jogging bottoms.

"So, what can I do for you?" asked Chad.

"I think it's more what we can do for each other," she smiled. "An exclusive interview would be great, but, for now, I'll settle for a heads up on developments a few minutes ahead of the competition. I'm not asking for exclusives, nothing attributable, just sources close to the investigation."

"And what investigation is that? I'm here to coach a football team."

"Ah, Chad, look," she drummed a biro on her notepad, "I'd hoped we might skip the bullshit and cut to the chase. I know you've met with Ruben Murray and the lady you were with at the Meat and Wine was Mel Keane, one of our most illustrious psychologists. Now, I can control the narrative around that, and trust me it's far better to have my paper and our TV network on your side rather than making your stay miserable." She paused and sipped her drink, "Just a head start, that's all I want."

"Look, lady," began Chad.

"Call me Andrea."

"Okay, Andrea. If I could offer the police any help I would do it unpaid, and if Mel wants to get my thoughts, then fine, it's an exchange of ideas. But right now, I know only what's been in the press."

The reporter leaned back with an air of disappointment, like a parent finding out their teenager was dodging school. "Fair enough, Chad, have it your way. But be careful. If I hadn't intervened, you'd be on every news bulletin already."

"How so?" asked Chad.

"Because when one of my fellow hacks at the crime scene asked 'who's the bloke in the baseball cap, looks like that fella, Hilton?' I said 'Nah, it's not, he's a pathologist from Paramatta, I've seen him before.' Now, I think one favour deserves another, don't you?"

He could almost feel her claws biting into him.

"Anyway, think about it, Chad. You've got my number. And as a gesture of goodwill, how about this? I have a source and he said to say – to show you he's credible – that the murderer shot one victim at Castlereagh differently to the others. Now I don't know what that means because Murray has released little information, but I'm told it'll mean something to you. That source could be very useful to the police investigation, wouldn't you say? I'll keep tapping him for what he knows, and you can drop me a little heads up from time to time. How about it, Chad?"

"I've got to be going. Thanks for the coffee," Chad pushed his chair back from the table.

"Cool. No worries. Call me anytime, Chad. Phone's on twenty-four seven."

*

Chad's phone vibrated. He answered, "Hey Freddie, how are you? How did it go with Junior and his mum today?"

"Not bad, man. Not bad. For the first half hour, it was a bit awks, but after that she loosened up. Remember, I haven't seen her for over twenty years and then I only knew her on a sort of casual basis, if you know what I mean. We have little in common, but I thanked her for raising Junior to be the young guy he is. I think we've agreed on how we operate going forward and she knows I'm going to hang around for a month or two, so that should help build a relationship. So, yeah, bro, all cool."

"How was Junior?"

"He was cool, too. The whole sitch must be weird for him but he chatted along and helped keep the convo going. Yeah, he was fine, he's a good kid."

Freddie's voice seemed to fade away and Chad wondered whether his buddy understood that son and father were very different characters.

"What you been up to, bro?"

"Not much," said Chad. "Apart from the police calling at 7 a.m. telling me there's been more murders and to get my arse down to the crime scene."

"Shit, man, what the hell is going on? Mel said you'd met again through work. Nice lady, by the way. Very nice, even if she's a shrink like you."

"We're not shrinks, we're psychologists, there's a difference."

"Whatever, so what have you got dragged into?"

"Mel is working on the case and a copper called Ruben Murray who's leading it has asked if I'll help her. It's becoming a busman's holiday. Oh, and to top it off I got tapped up by a journo asking for tip offs."

"Jesus, Chad, you shouldn't be getting involved in that shit. It's too soon. The docs back home told you that. You need time away from getting into psychos' heads."

"Believe me, I'm trying not to, but, Freddie, let me tell you, these murders are horrendous and whoever is doing them needs catching – pronto. I may not be at full speed, but if I can help, I will."

"Well, I'm watching, bro, so tell Ruby or whatever his name is to back off, okay? I'll get Odd Job to look after you."

"Okay, okay. Let's grab a cab together to the ground and get some training done. You need to be ready to play a game in a few weeks."

"That's cool, bro. I was born ready."

Chapter 11

Chad sat at the desk in his hotel room and concentrated on the laptop screen. Pop's team meeting was in full flow, but he'd advised Chad to join by Zoom. The press had set up camp outside the station, so getting in or out without being seen would be impossible. Chad had been happy to oblige. He didn't want to push his luck, or get himself in hock to Andrea Byrne.

Pop was revving, "Okay, so we've got absolutely fuck all. Again. No forensics, ammo casings, nothing. The number of visitors to the office makes fingerprinting pointless." The detective's exasperation was flooding Chad's hotel room.

"We've located each of the remaining visitors seen on CCTV at Castlereagh Street, but as you thought, Boss, all legit," said Lucy, whose afro, Chad thought, seemed, if anything, more impressive on screen.

"Great, bloody marvellous. What else? Has anyone found links between the two poor sods that were butchered, Dan Hopkins and Janice Short? Well? Dimi, anything?"

Dimi's face filled the screen, "Nothing, Pop. Neither appear as a contact on the other's email or phone, unique backgrounds and acquaintances. They live at opposite ends of the city and their paths have never crossed. I'm cross checking whether any of the other victims in Lee Street had any dealings or contact with the victims at Castlereagh."

"Do we have anything?" yelled Pop.

Chad could make out the sweat rings on his Hawaiian shirt as he threw his arms in the air and paced the confined space of the squad room, staring from one team member to another. "Anything at all?"

Dimi reappeared on the screen, "We are getting lists of all service contractors and we'll check their schedules to see which were in the buildings at the times of the killings.

"Okay, good Dimi, let's have that done asap. José, what does the CCTV at the immigration place give us?"

José looked up from his laptop. "Yeah, well that's another issue, Boss," he began, "there's been an employee campaign against the use of CCTV as the staff believed it was an infringement of their privacy. As a compromise they agreed CCTV could operate from 10 a.m. until 3 p.m. which is the last entry time for visitors. But only in the foyer, until the employees' union and the management can agree otherwise. So, we've no idea how many people were in the building."

"Jesus H Christ. What is happening to the world?" bawled Pop. "Do we know yet how he gained entry at Castlereagh or Lee Street?"

"Nothing yet, Pop."

"Okay, background checks on all the victims. If you've done them once do them again. I want to know why some lunatic has topped them. Anything from anyone else before we wrap this up?"

Chad could see Mel's arm raised on the edge of the screen.

"Yes, Mel?"

"Thanks, Pop," her voice was calm, like a soothing balm. "That you didn't find any direct connection between Dan Hopkins and Janice Short, doesn't mean that there isn't a link so don't stop looking."

"What do you mean?" asked Pop.

"What matters is that the perpetrator has linked them. They mean something to him and he's singled them out by the way he killed them. They were paying a price, we don't know for what, but the perp does."

"So, what are we looking for?" asked Lucy.

"Well, that's the million-dollar question. And I don't have the answer. I'm sorry to be vague, but what I'm saying is you should treat the murders of Hopkins and Short as linked even though you cannot find a physical connection between the two. There'll be a connection somewhere, maybe in the past. It may be organisational, for example, somewhere they've worked. Or it may be some sort of social connection, perhaps schooling or sports."

"Thanks, Mel." Chad noted the lack of enthusiasm in Pop's response. "Anything from you, Chad?"

"No, Pop. Not much at this stage. Although Mel is right, there is a connection somewhere. By the way, could I have a word after this meeting?"

"Yeah sure, no worries."

*

"What's up, Chad?" asked Pop.

"I got accosted by a journalist called Andrea Byrne at a restaurant. She asked for a 'mutually beneficial' meeting so I grabbed a coffee with her yesterday."

"Yeah, I know her. She works for The Globe. Brash and ambitious. And? Anything interesting or was she just grubbing around?"

"She wants the heads up on lines of investigation you may follow and…"

More Pop invective cut Chad short mid-sentence.

"How the bloody hell does she know about you and me? Jesus, I thought we'd kept that quiet."

"No idea, but she knew alright, and she knew about me and Mel." Chad decided not to mention that the reporter had seen them together.

"Bloody reporters, the job's hard enough without them muddying the waters. Why the hell would we give her a heads up? Tell her to bugger off."

"She said she has a source."

"What sort of source?" Pop's frown was deepening by the second.

"She reckons her contact told her that the killer had shot one victim differently from the others."

Pop's eyes bored at Chad through the screen. "How's that got out, we didn't mention it in any of our press briefings? Probably a copper. We have leaks all over the place, but," Pop paused, "if it's not a copper then her source would be a person of interest to us."

Chad let the implications sink in.

Pop resumed, "Let me have a think. Part of me reckons it might be useful to have an 'in' with the press to get our message across without it coming directly from the police. And, as I say, we need to find whoever her source is. Don't give her anything without clearing it with me, okay?"

"Yep, no probs, will do."

"Right, catch you later." Pop's face disappeared from the screen.

Chad pushed his laptop away and stared out the window. Vague formless ideas that had been lurking in his mind were taking some shape. Not enough to run by Pop yet but worth trying to verify. The head shots were a conundrum but may mean nothing. Nagging in Chad's mind was another. What set of circumstances could be so bad that none of the victims try to raise the alarm? A thought lingered in his mind for a moment, then vanished.

Chapter 12

Chad sat at a table for two at Mordeo, a chic Mediterranean style restaurant on Philip Street and decided that he was getting over jet lag. Four days since he arrived, so he should bloody think so. A few punters sat around the bar area, but most diners occupied aluminium tables in a foyer that reminded Chad of a shopping mall or the entrance to a large office block. He'd arranged to meet Mel for their 'comparing notes' catch up and saw her before she saw him. Wonder whether she's been in contact with Freddie? Today, she wore jeans, Gucci trainers and a floaty lemon coloured blouse onto which her blonde hair tumbled.

Mel kissed him on both cheeks, "Hey, sorry I'm late, have you been here long?"

"No, five minutes that's all. Where did you park?"

"I didn't. I got the train, it only takes ten minutes. It means I can have a drink if I'm not driving. Fizz maybe?"

"Hell, yes," Chad beckoned to a waiter.

While they waited for their salads and a bottle of prosecco, Chad regaled her with the tales of his training session with some of the world's greatest prima donnas.

"Seriously, I kid you not, one of them who shall remain nameless was demanding a separate locker room for himself and his entourage. He wants his own physio and a guarantee from me he'd take any penalties awarded in the match. They make Freddie look modest and self-effacing by comparison. Anyway," he continued, "it's a bit of light relief from the other shit going on.

How's Pop, have things progressed?"

"Not much, no. I think forensics have confirmed the calibre of ammunition but whether that takes them any further I don't know. They're drawing blanks everywhere, pardon the pun, and I feel impotent. We've got nothing to go on and it's so difficult to understand what's driving the perp. I'm struggling to make an assessment," she paused.

Chad could see her ticking through the problems.

"When he uses the gun, he shows a callous, almost methodical approach, but then he displays an emotional barbarity and cruelty towards the victims he puts on display. In my experience it's one or the other. Cold, calculating and unemotional or passionately brutal and cruel, I've never come across both types at a single crime scene. It's contradictory. The theatre of it, the positioning of the bodies, removal of the heart, but it's also intrinsic to the perp's motivation. Jesus, Chad, it feels like I'm blind."

"In the kingdom of the blind, the one-eyed man is king."

"What do you mean?"

"Maybe the perp is laying a breadcrumb trail. We can't see where it's leading yet 'cos there aren't enough crumbs, but he knows that Pop will follow the trail. He knows where the path will lead and where it will end," Chad paused. Something about what he'd just said made him go cold. A feeling of dread creeping over him.

"And we've got the same conundrum at both crime scenes," said Mel. "How did he get in and why did no one raise the alarm?"

"Yeah, agreed, I'm still struggling with that." Chad took a sip of prosecco and gathered some salad leaves onto his fork. "I have an idea but not one I'm ready to volunteer till I've given it more thought. And then there are the locations."

Mel stared at him, "How d'ya mean?"

"The locations are important to our killer, he has a sense of place. It would have been so much easier to kill Dan Hopkins and Janice Short either at home or elsewhere and do the job with far less risk attached. Take Hopkins: he was in a boardroom less that twenty feet away from a busy sales office with upwards of forty people in it. So, for the perp to take the risk it must mean that the place he kills them is part of the story." Chad ate another mouthful and sipped his drink. "Why them, why now and why there?" The prosecco was sharp and ice-cold. "A boardroom and a pokey immigration office, why would they be important to the murderer?"

Mel ran her hand through her hair then said, "God knows, but if you're right about the breadcrumb trail, then we are treading water and it's a matter of time until the next one. Anyway, enough of talking shop, how are you? Coping any better?"

"I'm okay. I think," Chad smiled across the table. "I mentioned to Pop that a journo called Andrea Byrne doorstepped me. She was at the Meat and Wine place the other night, remember?"

"Oh, yeah. I think I've run into her once or twice."

"She knew you by repute if nothing else. Anyway, she is trying to get us to give her an early heads up on any developments. In return I avoid press intrusion and they keep shtum over my involvement with Pop. Nice, eh?"

"Just what you need. What did Pop say?"

"He didn't instantly dismiss the idea and thought she may give us pointers that we wouldn't hear otherwise. She reckons she has a source and knows stuff that wasn't in the press. I'll keep her warm without giving much away if I can. That's if we have anything to keep her warm with," he sighed, "which we don't," Chad paused and saw his own frustration reciprocated in Mel's face.

Chapter 13

Andrea Byrne leaned on the railings of the balcony that provided a boundary to her two-bedroom apartment overlooking Centennial Park. She sipped her wine, then took a long draw on a Marlboro and watched the smoke swirl away into the evening air. She checked her watch. Twenty minutes till the call. Looking out over the evening sky she reflected on events.

Had it only been two days ago? "Seems longer," she muttered. She'd been at her desk in the open plan third floor office of The Globe in Surry Hills, thinking about calling it a day and heading to the gym, when her phone had pinged. No name, just a number.

Consider yourself lucky that I've chosen you. Did you know there was a difference in how the victims died? Interested to know how I know? Then maybe we can help each other. Call this number tonight at 7 p.m.

She shivered recalling the adrenalin rush that hit her when she'd first read the text.

If fifteen years in journalism had taught her anything, it was to be cautious when assessing the viability of both source and material, but she had struggled to contain her excitement as she'd hurried home reading the message several times on the train to Bondi Junction. She'd poured over the police briefing notes on her tablet. Read them twice through. Her memory had been correct. Nowhere had the police mentioned that one victim's shooting differed from the others. Normally a ten-minute walk, she'd been climbing the stairs in her fashionable apartment block in less than seven. She'd thrown her bag onto the leather settee and poured herself a large glass of a crisp Pinot Grigio she'd opened the previous night, then re-read the message again.

At 6:59 p.m. that evening, with an unexpected hesitancy, Andrea had picked up her phone from the table, held it up for face recognition and then tapped on the number showing at the head of her 'Recent' list.

"Hello, Andrea, thanks for calling." The accent was New South Wales.

"Hi there, well, you have the advantage on me because you know my name. What's yours?"

"Call me Trevor."

"Okay, Trevor, thanks for the text and thanks for taking my call."

"Andrea, one quick ground rule, please. You do not record any of our conversations. Do you understand?"

"Okay," Andrea paused, how would he know if she did or didn't? Still, he hasn't said don't make notes, she thought. She switched the 'Record' button to off. "So, what can I do for you?"

"By now you will have checked your notes from the police briefings and realise that my source was correct. There will be more information forthcoming, which I will share with you. There is, naturally, a quid pro quo to the arrangement."

"Which is?" asked Andrea.

"The police will give you the 'heads up' on any developments in their investigation, and you pass that information on to me."

"What do I get from the arrangement?"

"Once we've established the information flow, both parties will agree what you can take to print. But being ahead of the rest will give you scoops galore."

Andrea needed to buy time to let her think. "So, Trevor, why me?"

The voice remained calm, measured, "Why you, doesn't matter.

But we both know how this will affect your career."

Andrea considered this. Absolutely she knew, but could she pull it off without knowing more about this guy? "How do I know you're not the guy doing the killings, 'cos that's a bargain neither myself nor my editor wouldn't countenance? No matter what."

"You don't. It's all about trust."

"Why don't you go to the police yourself, Trevor, and tell them everything you know? That might put a stop to these murders. That's the right thing to do."

"Andrea, let's just say it impossible for me to do what you suggest. Right and wrong doesn't come into it. I don't have a choice. For the duration of this call, you do. You either agree or not. If not you, my next call will be to Jason Austin at The Bugle, he doesn't have the scruples you do. So, are you in or out, Andrea?"

Shit, shit shit. Austin was an unethical bastard who'd jump at this. What could she tell her bosses? "*Oh yeah, guys, I got the opportunity first but decided against it, I let Austin at The Bugle have it.*" That would go down well. Career limiting didn't come close. The silence on the line felt like the defining moment of her life. She looked out of the window, the pulse throbbing in her ear felt like a clock ticking.

"Okay, I'll do it," she said. "But I need something more than you put in the text. You said the shootings differed. How?"

"I'll save that for later. The answer will give them confidence in us," said Trevor. "First, hook up with a guy called Chad Hilton. Do you know him?"

"Yeah, sure who doesn't? The Pommy soccer guy turned shrink?"

"That's him. He's just arrived in Australia and I know that he's been talking to Murray, the officer leading the case. Reach out to him, he'll be your way into the cops. I'll call you in a day or so. It'll be a different phone; this one is now obsolete. Glad you're onboard, Andrea. Talk soon."

And that was it, the line had gone dead. She'd held a moral and ethical debate with herself, but it hadn't lasted long. If the coppers agreed to play ball, then it was their lookout not hers. But if she could pull this deal off, her career possibilities were limitless.

Since that evening forty-eight hours ago, Andrea reflected, things had gone to plan. She'd got close to Chad Hilton without overplaying her hand and felt sure he was interested. He was a sharp cookie, so she'd have to be careful with him, but she knew he'd have told Murray about their conversation. The killings at the visa department had the city in a frenzy and desperate for information. The call in ten minutes should elicit more.

*

"No, Andrea, you listen to me. I gave you some information last time but have received nothing in return. That was not our agreement. I'm wondering if Austin at The Bugle may even yet be a better bet? You need to keep your side of the bargain, Andrea. I hope I'm making myself clear?"

"Yeah, okay, look these things take time. I've met with Chad Hilton as you suggested and things will move. So, what have you got for me?"

The silence seemed to go on forever. Angles being checked, chess pieces arranged and decisions made.

"Nothing more, yet," said Trevor. "Not till I get something back. Don't disappoint me Andrea, that wouldn't be good for you." The line went dead and the chill from her wine glass seemed to flow through her body.

Chapter 14

Chad thought it odd that the text said to meet Pop and Mel at The Juice Guru. It seemed an incongruous venue for the type of conversation Pop had said he wanted to have, but Chad wasn't complaining as it was only a couple of hundred metres from the hotel. Martin Place was a sea of commuters hurrying to work but the crowds thinned somewhat on Bridge Street. Chad walked into the brightly painted bar where in-your-face marketing teased that freedom, excitement and wellbeing were just a juice away. Yeah, right.

Chad saw them immediately, tucked in the far corner of the room sitting side by side with their backs to him. Pop's Hawaiian shirt of choice today was blue with green parrots sitting on branches. This, combined with his slumped shoulders, gave him the appearance of a weary tourist seeking refuge from the heat and the crowds. A weary tourist that appeared to have got lucky with his companion. Mel looked immaculate, even from behind.

Chad ordered himself a concoction including ginger and chilli that promised an invigorating, uplifting experience that would set him up for the day. He would let the judges decide. The drink arrived in a transparent plastic container with a domed lid through which a straw poked. Really? Couldn't they have gone for a coffee?

"Morning, all," said Chad, squeezing past Pop and edging behind the table into a bench that ran along the wall. He smiled at Mel. "Everything okay?"

"Everything okay? You've got to be bloody joking, mate," Pop replied, then took an angry suck on his straw.

"Pop's just been bringing me up to speed," said Mel, "it's fair to say progress is slow."

"Slow, it's non-existent. Hence this meeting. And I wanted it somewhere no one knows, so the Juice Guru it is. Apologies for that."

Chad contemplated his drink and finally took the plunge. At first a velvety fruity smoothness hit his tongue, sensuous and mellow, lulling his taste buds into a sense of security. False as it transpired, for no sooner had the liquid hit his throat than the spice of the ginger and the heat of the chilli entered. "Jesus Christ," he gasped. He looked up to see Mel smothering a giggle and Pop contemplating him in the manner of a French maitre'd observing a Brit trying snails for the first time.

"Bloody hell, there's a bit of a kick to that. I see what they mean about invigorating," spluttered Chad.

"Yeah, well," Pop offered Chad a napkin, "if we can get away from these bloody awful drinks for a minute, I want to hear your thoughts. We've got bugger all to go on, and every tinpot superintendent from here to Canberra is on my back. No forensics, nothing from the ammo and nothing to link the victims to each other. We've hit a dead end on Hodges and Short. They've never met, never contacted each other and never worked together. We've identified every person on CCTV at Castlereagh, and ruled them out so we are back to square one. Sometimes I like to get away from the office and get creative. Take a fresh perspective and see what comes of it. A bit of left field thinking, if you will. Which is where you two come in. Where have you got to in your assessment?"

Chad looked across the table at Mel and raised an eyebrow. "Go on, you fire away," he said.

"Look, Pop," Mel ran a hand through her hair pushing one side back over her ear, "it's the same for us. We have little to go on and what we have is contradictory."

"Contradictory how?" asked Pop.

"Our perp is displaying two contrasting personalities at each of the crime scenes. One is the cool, calculating, unemotional killer that goes from victim to victim putting a single shot from very close range into their heads. That personality seems at odds with the brutal, passionate, ritualistic venom exhibited in the killings of Hodges and Short. It's almost like there's two different perps."

"Jesus Christ, am I hearing this correctly?" Pop stared from Mel to Chad. "You think we may have a double act?"

"That's not what we're saying," said Chad, pushing the volcanic juice away.

Chad saw exhaustion, stress and frustration writ large on Pop's weathered face. He needed a shave and a damn good sleep. Chad continued, "We believe this is the work of one killer, but a killer capable of displaying two contrasting psychoses at each crime scene. The victims he shoots are incidental to the main event, therefore he doesn't waste time on them. He's clinical, dispassionate and ruthless. He displays a complete emotional detachment. But for Hodges and Short he takes his time, savouring the moment and the power before unleashing a passion and an anger. Now that may not sound much, but it's unusual. It also links Hodges to Short irrespective of the fact that your team haven't been able to find out how. There may have to be another victim before the jigsaw takes some shape."

Pop rubbed his eyes then leaned back and stroked the stubble on his chin. His right leg tapped out a steady rhythm. "Okay," he said, "so you know little apart from the perp exhibits conflicting behaviours which may or may not mean something. So, let's hypothesise instead. What thoughts are buzzing around your heads? Let's throw out some wild whacky ideas and see what happens. It can't do us any harm 'cos we're going nowhere fast. How the killer gets in and out? Educated guesses on why none of the victims scream blue murder? One view is that the receptionist at Castlereagh went to the toilet, left the door ajar and in came our boy. And in Lee Street, well, he could have been there all day given the situation with the CCTV."

Mel was clasping and unclasping her hands then looked at Pop under hooded lids.

"Pop, we can speculate all you like but it won't get us anywhere because we can't verify things. Chad, you said something about a breadcrumb trail. Want to share?"

Chad sat back and saw the expectancy on Pop's face. "Each crumb is a clue," he began, "but you can't see the end without following them all. So, we'll only understand what links the victims when we have more crumbs. More deaths." Pop's head sunk onto his chest. Chad continued, "How many more, only our perp knows. Therefore, Pop, I'm up for trying to short circuit our killer's plans, even by taking some guesses and see where they get us. There's also someone else we can use."

"Someone else? Who?"

"Andrea Byrne." Chad raised his hand to cut off Pop's imminent explosion. "Hear me out. You want supposition? Well, what about this? Suppose that whoever leaked the information to her wasn't a copper. Let's look at that. If it's not a copper, then who are they, and why are they approaching a journalist?"

"Not a copper?" Pop muttered as if he had never considered this before. "Go on."

"I don't think it was a copper," said Chad. "Otherwise, they'd have gone for the bigger news - the murder of Hodges. Heart cut out and all that. If it wasn't a copper, it's someone close to the killer or maybe even the killer. So, why don't we feed her something and see if we can leverage that to get more info from her?"

"Any suggestions?" asked Pop.

"Confirm that the killer shot one victim at Castlereagh in the forehead and the rest in the back of the head. If she uses 'sources close to the investigation' in her article then you can always fall back on not confirming or denying. Giving her that means we can ask for something in return. It links us to her contact."

Pop sat silent looking neither at Chad nor Mel, but his eyes were alert, searching, probing, working out the consequences, playing the politics. "Okay, let's do it," he said. "Give her that information, but quid pro quo. Tell her we need more to verify her contact is close to the killer. Ask if the contact's a copper? And tell us something that only we and the killer would know. That'll give this mystery caller some credibility."

"Cool, I'll do that. Just one other thing while you're here, Pop."

"Fire away."

"I'd like another look at Castlereagh. Can you get me access?"

"Yeah, of course. Why?"

"A blue-sky theory I want to test. I won't trouble you with it till I've checked it."

"Fair enough, I'll get you access for later this morning if that works?"

"Yep, great."

Chapter 15

Chad exited the lift on the eleventh floor and saw the same copper was on duty. At least this time the policeman expected him. "G'day Mr Hilton, how's your trip goin'?"

"Bit too much like work if I'm honest, but hey, the weather's great so I'm not complaining. I thought they would have closed this down as a crime scene?"

"They have, I'm here to make sure you get what you need. As soon as you're finished, I'm off." Constable Swift leaned towards him, "How are you going on training all those prima donna soccer players? They tell me that Messi might play is that true?"

"Well, if it is, I haven't seen him and you'd think I'd be the one to know given that I'm the bloody coach. No, Messi won't be there but there are some big names. Freddie Jackson, you may have heard of him? We've also got two Brazilians, two Argentines and a bunch of top Europeans. It should be great. Have you got a ticket?"

"Nah, I prefer Aussie Rules but if there's a freebie ticket available, I'll give it a go."

"Leave it with me, I'll get a couple of tickets and drop them off with Pop, how's that?"

The copper's face lit up like a beacon, "Wow, thanks, Mr Hilton, that's fantastic."

Chad could see that he needed to take advantage of his current god-like status to get clear access and no hindrance, "Can I go through to Medics4U, there's a couple of things I need to do?"

"You go right ahead, they're expecting you."

"Any press nosing around here?" asked Chad.

"No, sir, they couldn't get past me if they tried."

"And what do the staff in the office think I'm here for?"

"There's only Lisa James and one other, the rest are working from home. No one wants to be reminded, eh? They think you're from the forensics team. What exactly are you doing here?"

"Oh, just checking on a couple of theories. Anyway, thanks, I won't be long."

Chad smiled, relieved that they hadn't used his real name and hoping now that whoever was in the office didn't recognise him. He had a fallback story ready just in case. He walked the thirty yards to the glass door of Medics4U, which was held slightly ajar by a small rubber door jamb. Obviously expecting him. He pushed it open then held the glass, so it swung gently back onto the rubber.

"Hi, can I help you?"

Chad looked around to see a petite woman in her twenties with long auburn hair that swung over one shoulder, dressed in a one-piece orange dress with a small black cotton cardigan over it.

"Hi, Lisa, is it, I hope you're expecting me? I only need a couple of minutes then I'll get out of your hair."

"Yes, that's me. You're from the police, right? I've answered thousands of questions already."

"Don't worry, I don't want to cover old ground," said Chad. "The policeman at the end of the corridor will be happy to vouch for me."

"No, that's fine, they told me some forensics guy was coming, so it's okay. Where do you need to see?"

"Just the boardroom, if that's okay?"

"Yeah, fine, it's down here, follow me."

The girl led Chad back down the hallway. Reaching the boardroom door, Lisa produced a key and opened it, took two steps inside and then turned to face him with her arms folded and a look Chad couldn't quite place. Defiance maybe? Frustration? She was expecting him to say something, that was clear. He decided against it.

She shrugged and brushed past him, "Fine, just shout when you're ready. There's nothing to see, your lot have been over it with a fine-toothed comb." She pronounced tooth as 'tuth.' Welsh maybe?

The sun filtered in through the windows and, as on his previous visit, the dust motes swirled in playful patterns illuminated by the rays then invisible without them. They'd removed the profit-and-loss chart, leaving the coffee cups standing on the long trestle table as the only sign of occupancy. Chad pulled the seat nearest him away from the table, then sat down and closed his eyes. He wanted to feel the essence of the place, to let it wash over him, to inhale it, to sense its presence. He breathed deeply. Time meandered. He could feel the warmth of the sunlight on his eyelids.

"You were here before any of them arrived, weren't you?" he whispered.

The silence engulfed his words and, as if in some weird symbiosis, Chad saw himself sitting in his bedroom in Harrogate three months previously. He was typing his explanation for the killings and chaos in Leeds for his friend of twenty years and his erstwhile employer DI Lee Wallace. The words as clear as if he was writing them now. *Classic Sherlock Holmes. Remember? When you have eliminated the impossible whatever remains, however improbable, must be the truth.*

The killer wasn't a ghost, that was impossible. He didn't have the means to transport himself unseen through an office block. That was impossible. But he had got in somehow. Chad's eyes roamed across the walls, up to the ceiling then out of the enormous windows into the blue of the Sydney sky.

"There is only one sensible explanation of how he got in. And if that explanation is correct, it also explains how he might have silenced them. But I need to check." The dust motes seemed to quiver in anticipation. "Why do it like this? Why take the risk? What's so compelling that he puts himself in jeopardy?"

The table was a crimson colour and glowed in the sunlight. He rested his arms on the table, leaned back in the seat and closed his eyes again. He pictured the scene from the photos Pop had sent him. Dan Hodges head on the table where his hands were now. "What made you do it here? Why is this place so important? And why the theatre?" The walls kept a stoic silence.

Chad sat back and rested his chin on his cupped hands and let his thoughts swirl. No answers being forthcoming, he roused himself and stood, then took a couple of steps and inspected the air conditioning control panel on the wall opposite the windows. It registered twenty-one degrees and a minimum fan speed. He looked back into the room then opened the door. Lisa was standing in the hall outside.

"You wanted to ask me some questions?"

"Just one, if you don't mind?"

"Fire away."

"I know it's difficult but cast your mind back to the day of the, er," Chad paused, "attacks." Lisa folded her arms, her eyes not leaving his. "Did you notice anything odd when you entered the room?" Shit, he thought, she was looking at him as if he'd gone mad. "I'm sorry, I'm not making myself clear. I'm not talking about what happened to your colleagues or what you saw, I'm thinking about other things, extraneous things. The air conditioning, for example. Did anything strike you about that?"

Lisa frowned but held Chad's gaze. "It did, but how did you know, and what's it got to do with anything?"

Chad shrugged, but did not elaborate.

"The fan was on its highest setting and it was blowing a gale."

"And I take it that's not normal?"

"No, when I'd gone in before the meeting to put the coffee out, the air con was at its usual setting. I always check, 'cos Dan would get cross if it was too hot or too cold."

"So, when did you put it back to its normal setting?"

"I didn't. One of your guys must have done it 'cos it was at its usual setting when I next went in."

"Thanks, that's very helpful," Chad looked at the girl. "So, who is running the business with the directors gone?"

"It's difficult. We have a chairman that we can contact if we have problems but he's based in the UK. He said he's sending someone out this month."

"I see. What's the chairman's name?"

"Richard Ashcroft."

"Do you have a number for him?"

"Yes, just hold on, I'll get it for you."

Chad walked into the reception area where the four clocks on the wall beat out the inexhaustible rhythm of time passing in London, Sydney, Dubai and New York. He remembered a line from Macbeth, 'Tomorrow and tomorrow and tomorrow creeps in this petty pace from day to day to the last syllable of recorded time.' Where the hell had that sprung from?

"Here you go," said Lisa, handing Chad a business card bearing the Medics4U logo on one side and Richard Ashcroft's contact details on the other.

"Thanks very much, Lisa, and sorry to have troubled you."

Chad pulled open the glass entrance door.

"That's okay," said Lisa, "by the way, do I know you from somewhere? You seem familiar."

"Don't think so, and I'm sure I'd remember," Chad smiled. "Oh, one more thing, you never left your desk that morning, not even to go to the loo?"

Lisa's eyes flared, and anger turned her cheeks red. "No, I never."

"No, I didn't think so." Chad replied. She'd removed the rubber jamb so the door closed quietly behind him.

Standing outside Medics4U, Chad waved to the duty copper

who remained standing by the lifts at the end of the corridor then pointed to the fire escape door on his left and gave a thumbs up, which the copper acknowledged with one of his own. At the end of the hallway was a green door with a push bar running across it and white lettering denoting 'Fire Exit'. Chad pushed on the bar and walked through. Concrete steps on his right led upwards while to his left a flight disappeared to the floors below. Chad looked up. Above his head was what he'd expected, but that wasn't what he wanted to see. He scrutinised the floor area in which he was standing then edging towards the wall on his left, bent over, licked his finger and pushed it onto some tiny black rubber fragments on the floor.

"Rock and roll, Chad, boy. Rock and roll."

Chapter 16

Chad exited the building via the elevator accompanied by his new best mate who chattered on like they'd known each other for years.

"Anyway, it's been good to see you again, Mr Hilton, going anywhere nice?"

"Off to Bondi."

"Well, have a good day. You won't forget those tickets?"

"No, don't worry, I won't." Chad's outstretched arm drew the attention of a taxi which pulled to the kerb. The copper opened the rear passenger door.

"Hotel Ravesis, please," said Chad, settling himself into the seat.

Twenty minutes later as the cab swung left on Bondi Road, he saw the vista of sea and beach that adorned travel agents' posters across the world. The sight lifted his spirits and brought a smile to his face. Simple pleasures, he thought. He asked the driver to pull over, paid and climbing out of the taxi adjusted his sunglasses. A teeming mass of humanity waited at the traffic lights, many armed with multi-coloured surfboards or more manageable, but no less dangerous, skateboards and rollerblades. They jostled for position like there was a prize for getting to the other side first. As a stationary pedestrian he realised he would soon become collateral damage in the unceasing mid-afternoon stampede that was Bondi Beach.

The Hotel Ravesis stood on the corner of Campbell Parade, like an indulgent grandparent surveying the chaos with a world-weary acceptance. The building had three storeys and dated back to 1914, when its first use was selling groceries. It still maintained a colonial, turn of the century architectural charm. Since 1989 it had been a bar and hotel and didn't seem to have changed much since Chad had last visited fifteen years previously. Music blared from a first-floor balcony where there was an afternoon party in full swing. At ground level two burly security guards stood either side of the main doors checking the ID of everyone entering, but they nodded Chad through. Too bloody old. No ID required.

The bar ran the length of the far wall and the other two external walls were glass. These gave punters inside the bar a live stream to the mayhem on the street outside while enjoying a beer. Chad found Andrea Byrne sitting at a table for two, near what looked like a DJ's decks next to one of the open windows.

"Can I get you a drink?" asked Chad.

"I'm a journo, what do you think?"

Chad smiled, "Okay what would you like?"

"I'll get a Pinot Grigio, please, with ice."

Chad wandered to the bar and ordered the wine and a Tanqueray 10 with tonic and lime for himself. Just the one for you pal, he thought, she'll be able to drink you under the table and you need your wits about you.

"How's your stay going?" asked Andrea, as Chad deposited her drink on the table.

"Yeah, well, thanks. The coaching is fun, if you ever need exposés on the ludicrous foibles of some of the world's best football players come to me."

"I may do that." She sipped her wine." Now, to what do I owe the honour, you said you wanted a chat?"

"Straight to the point, eh? Time's money and all that," said Chad.

A gaggle of tourists outside caught his attention. They were following a small Chinese guy with a red umbrella which he held aloft. This had got itself attached to the pointed end of a surfboard. Said surfboard belonged to someone who looked straight outta

Baywatch and who, unaware of his new appendage, was heading off in a different direction to the one its previous owner had wanted, accompanied by a posse of bewildered tourists.

Chad lifted his glass, "Okay, cutting to the chase I have some information for you, but I need a quid pro quo in return."

"Go on, I'm listening."

"The police are concerned about the identity of your contact," Chad sipped his drink and looked at Andrea over the rim of the glass.

"Really?" queried Andrea. "Why?"

"They're concerned he may be a copper leaking information for his own gain. We need you to find out."

"And if he's not?"

"Then we'll to get our collective heads around what that means, but let's deal with one thing at a time."

Andrea drew patterns in the condensation on the side of her glass. Chad waited.

"And what do I get?" she asked, drying her finger on her jeans.

Chad leaned back on his stool. "Well," he said, "the killer shot four of the victims at Castlereagh in the back of the head, but one in the forehead. You can use that. The police haven't released it. By giving your contact that information you'll be verifying that you are close to the police." Chad took another sip of his gin and let the mellow icy chill of the drink flow over his throat leaving a slight citrus flavour behind.

"I can print that as well?"

"Yes, you can," Chad smiled. "That'll put you ahead of the rest of the pack."

"Anything else?"

"Don't push it, Andrea," Chad pushed his drink away and stood. "Oh, and one more thing. Any information must be stuff that only the police or the killer would know. That'll give us some confidence in him. Right, get us what we need and I'll expect a call tonight."

He walked towards the door, past the security guards and into the tumult. "You're getting quite good at this inscrutable hard man routine," he muttered.

Retrieving his phone from his pocket Chad typed a message to Pop.

Interesting session at Castlereagh need to meet up and fill you in. I think I've figured out how the perp got in, but I need to verify a few things. Are you free to meet tomorrow morning? Met with Andrea gave her the info we agreed and told her I need a call tonight re whether her contact is a copper.

The response took a matter of seconds. *She'll have to be bloody good to get that in return for info he already knows, but let's see. And yes 7:30 a.m. your hotel. You can buy breakfast.*

"7:30 a.m.? I'm on bloody holiday."

Chapter 17

After his meeting in Bondi with Andrea, and his subsequent text exchange with Pop, Chad had a sense of impending trouble. Like the killer had established a chain of events over which neither Pop nor he had control. Refreshed after a shower and change of clothes back at the hotel, he sauntered along Elizabeth Street before hanging a left and heading for the intersection of Hunter and Pitt. The apprehension from earlier remained, his heart beating too fast and a tremor in his hands.

"Breadcrumb trail, what a nightmare," he muttered, his thoughts and anxieties given voice. The words drifted away into the early evening air. The sun was dipping away leaving an orange glow in the sky and he breathed in the warmth. "Come on, shake yourself out of it."

Freddie had said to meet at Taylor's rooftop bar which was lodged on top of the Republic Hotel. The security guys on the door didn't want to see his ID. How the hell old did he look? He took the stairs realising too late that there were several flights and the lift would have been a better option. Rounding the corner at the top of the last set of stairs Chad walked into the rooftop bar breathless. After work punters packed the place. Inside the door and to his left a large group of boisterous twenty-somethings were singing Sweet Caroline for reasons that Chad couldn't fathom, while further into the space a gang of ten or more girls whooped as a champagne cork popped. That'll be on Insta before you can say cheers, he thought.

One area of the bar seemed less packed than the rest of the

place. Maybe because the punters had taken one look at Odd Job and Tony and erred on the side of caution. No one needed to get on the wrong side of a guy who looked like he bullied The Rock for funzies. Nor the guy nailed on to be 'Lead Mercenary' in the next Fast and Furious movie. Freddie, seemed positively benign compared to his two mates, as he stood glass in one hand and his other arm draped around an embarrassed looking Junior. The intimidating group, seeing Chad approach, let out a collective yell then hugged, embraced, fist-pumped and high-fived. Incongruous didn't cut it.

"Yo Chad, bro, I told you they'd get here. Breezed straight through immigration, didn't you, boys?" laughed Freddie.

"No problem," said the mountain range. Chad wondered whether he'd heard Odd Job speak before.

"Why, Mr Hilton, you didn't think we'd have a problem, did you?" Tony's broad Bradford accent was utterly out of place on a rooftop bar in downtown Sydney.

Chad laughed. It felt good to see these guys. "I may have mentioned to your boss that I thought the chances of you boys being welcomed into Australia were slim to none, but, hey, what do I know? Anyway, great to see you."

"Cheers," said Freddie, handing Chad a glass of champagne from a bottle in an ice cooler next to him.

"Cheers," Chad replied, clinking glasses with Freddie and noting that Odd Job and Tony had glasses with orange juice and still water, respectively. One or two of the champagne drinking girls had recognised Freddie and came over to ask for selfies with him, requests he took obvious pleasure in agreeing to. Chad turned to Junior, "How's things, are you and your dad getting on okay? It must have been quite tricky meeting him for the first time?"

Junior's massive hand twisted the braid in his hair. "Yeah, we're doing fine." He gave Chad a tentative smile and shrugged, "Like, yeah, you know, it's okay. We're different, I'm not like him, I prefer to be, you know, in the background." As if to emphasise Junior's point, Freddie was now surrounded by the group of girls and had joined in with their raucous shrieks and laughter.

Chad ushered Junior a few steps away to give him space and time to continue.

"I don't know whether he's disappointed that I'm not sporty or what," the words hung in the air as the young man seemed to appraise the statement. Chad waited. "But anyway, we're getting along. I don't think he gets what my life has been like."

Chad steered Junior to a vacant table away from the throng and sat down. "In what way?" he asked.

"Being this size, man, coming from a single parent family and mixed race," Junior paused, his eyes focussed on the tabletop. "At school I was a target for the dickheads who needed to prove how macho they were by taking on the biggest dude in the year. Me. So, I learned the hard way how to blend into the background." Junior wiped away some crumbs from the surface of the table. "And I've always been into techy stuff, okay, I'm geeky, my mum says, but I do like some sports, basketball, Aussie Rules, but hell, man, what can I say? I'm more into gaming." Junior looked across at Chad, "Do you get it, mate? I don't add up to my dad's view of what his son should be like, you know?"

Chad nodded.

Junior took a sip of his coke, "I've been fending for myself all my life and me and mum get along fine, so it's him that's going to have to adjust to me, not me to him."

Chad took his point, but Junior needed to know there was more to Freddie than the kid had seen. "Trust me, Junior, your dad will have your back no matter what. I don't know if he held expectations you'd be just like him, but he's not stupid, and he'll come to terms with the fact that you're not." Chad watched the bubbles in his champagne rise. "And that won't matter to him. You're his son and to him that will be all that matters. Anything he can do to help you he will. Anything at all. I know from experience that his loyalty is unconditional. You may not have wanted him in your life, Junior, but if he hadn't been in mine, I wouldn't be alive today. That's not bullshit, it's fact."

Chad saw Junior was staring at him with intensity, and hanging on his words. "But look," Chad continued. "if you need any help with the situation, call me anytime. Okay? I can say things to your dad that you may find hard."

Junior assessed the statement for a moment. "That's cool, thanks, mate," Junior smiled. "Are you on WhatsApp?"

"I'm on bloody everything, unfortunately," said Chad. "Follow me and you can DM me if you need anything."

"Anyway, enough about me," said Junior. "Dad's worried about you, ya know? Reckons you shouldn't be helping the cops, but I think it's cool. How's it going?"

Chad looked up at the young man. "It's difficult," he began. "Progress is slow. I've got a couple of ideas, but… We'll get there."

Junior leaned in towards him across the table, "What's your process? I mean how do you work out a profile for the dude when there's nothing to go on?"

Chad smiled, surprised by how much he liked Junior being interested in his work. "I start by applying logic to the situation."

"Like what? How d'ya mean?"

Freddie, Odd Job and Tony plonked their glasses on the table and sat down.

"You two seem as thick as thieves," said Freddie, then chuckled as something in the remark appealed to him.

"I'm explaining how I apply logic to my work."

"Shit," grunted Freddie. "Where's the logic in poking about in crazy dudes' heads?"

Chad smiled as Junior held his eye then raised a questioning eyebrow.

"I'm interested," said Junior with the hint of a challenge to

Freddie in his tone.

Freddie shrugged and sipped his champagne. Chad looked from father to son. More similar than they think, he decided. "Well, without going into details, here's an example. You've read in the press that the first killings were in a boardroom twenty feet from a busy sales office?"

"Yeah, I have. How did he do it without being heard?" asked Junior.

"That's my point. That's where I apply logic. When you rule out the impossible, whatever is left must be the answer."

Junior leaned in again prompting his father to do the same, "Come on, tell us what you're thinking. We won't spill."

Chad stared from father to son. "Look," he said, "I don't think any of the victims were conscious, but I haven't worked out how they became unconscious. Some sort of nerve agent I reckon, but I don't know which. As I say, it's work in progress."

Junior tapped the table with his forefinger, and a huge smile lit up his face. "Nitrogen, bro. He used nitrogen."

Chad let the remark drift around his mind. He saw Freddie staring at him for some sort of confirmation. "What makes you say that?" he asked.

"We did it once in Chemistry. Increase the ratio of nitrogen to oxygen in the air supply, and anyone in the room passes out."

"I told you he was smart," shouted Freddie. "Obvs gets his brains from my side of the family."

Chad raised an eyebrow then looked at Junior, "Are you sure?"

"Yeah, man, I'm sure. Yeah, yeah, don't you remember?"

"Remember what?"

"A couple of years ago the Russian special forces were dealing with a hostage situation in a theatre or somewhere and my teacher reckons that's what they did. Increased the level of nitrogen till everyone including the terrorists keeled over, arrested the bad guys then reset the air supply till the hostages woke up. Collateral damage to one or two of the hostages but not much."

Chad stared at the young man.

Freddie leaned back in a self-congratulatory manner, "Chad, bro, that's my boy right there. Sharp as a needle, man. Right, come on and drink up, it's Wings Wednesday at El Camino Cantina with as many Mojitos as you can manage, and I've got to be somewhere later. Odd Job, you can wear the Sombrero."

Chapter 18

Andrea sat on the leather settee in her apartment and waited. An omelette remained untouched on a plate on the coffee table in front of her, but the wine bottle that sat in a bucket of ice was three-quarters empty. Five large glasses already today and they hadn't hit the spot. That Hilton had been forthcoming with some information was a positive, but whether Trevor saw it the same way, she could only wait and see. So how could she find out whether Trevor was police?

"Fucked if I know. Cash maybe? Coppers always need cash," she exhaled, blowing her cigarette smoke in the general direction of the open doors leading to the balcony.

Her phone vibrated on the table in front of her. A number, no name.

"Hey, Andrea, how are you?" said Trevor.

"Yeah, I'm good thanks, and you?" Andrea had aimed for a cheery, positive tone but wasn't certain she'd hit it.

"Yes, I'm well, thank you," replied Trevor. "Now, do you have anything for me?"

"I do, yes. I told you these things take a little time, but I've been in discussions with Chad Hilton earlier today and got things moving." Stop rambling, she thought.

"And?" prompted Trevor.

"And, to recap, you told me in your original text that one shooting at Castlereagh was different to the others and when we spoke you asked me to get you some information to seal our deal, so to speak."

"Yeah, Andrea, I know all that, what have you got for me?"

"The killer shot one victim in the forehead, the rest in the back of the head. They've never released that."

She could hear him breathing down the line.

"Well, I suppose that's something, and it shows me that the police accept our proposed arrangement."

Andrea listened but could only hear Trevor's breathing. Time seemed to grind to a halt as she waited.

"Ask Chad Hilton," he resumed, "if they find it… what's the right word? Intriguing yes, intriguing, that only one victim at each crime scene could not speak. And what conundrum does that leave for the police to solve?"

"That's vague," said Andrea.

"It won't be vague to Hilton or Pop. In fact, I'm sure the implication is taxing their minds as we speak. Anyway, whether it's vague to you is irrelevant, you are a conduit of information back and forth. You don't need to understand."

"Do you know the answer?"

"Perhaps, yes."

"One thing that is concerning the cops is whether you, or your contact, is one of them, in which case I've been told there'll be no further information forthcoming. So can you reassure them on that point?"

"No. I can't," he snapped. "And I won't. Don't ask again. Who I am or what I am is not up for discussion. Likewise, my contact. Tell them that."

"Okay, okay, calm down. But it seems like they might end this before we've really got started. I'll go back to them with your latest teaser and see what they say, but don't blame me if they don't answer. They are adamant about needing to know if you're a cop."

"Then we'll have to see what they say," he said. "Although I'm sure the snippet I've given will whet their appetites enough for them to want to continue our dialogue. I'll call you tomorrow and I'll look out for your ground breaking revelations in The Globe. Oh, and by the way, why did you pick the Ravesis? Haven't been there in years. Goodnight." The line went dead.

Andrea stared at the phone. What the actual? Goosebumps covered her arms, and she shivered. Jesus, what had she got herself into? Picking up her phone she opened her WhatsApp and found Chad.

Spoken with our guy tonight. Couldn't elicit whether he's a copper. My guess is no, but hey, what do I know? Told me to ask you if you think it's intriguing that only one victim at each site couldn't speak? That may mean something to you. Let me know how you want to play it. BTW he knew we'd met at the Ravesis, ffs, think he was there.

Andrea downed the remaining wine in her glass, poured another then wrote her copy for her editor to review. She stopped typing and leaned back. Something Trevor had said was bothering her. What was it? Not the Ravesis bit, though that was freaky. No, he'd said something that had sounded wrong. What the hell was it? Have some more wine, it'll come to you.

*

Chad lay back on his pillows. As soon as he'd reached the hotel he'd googled as much as he could find on the Russian hostage situation. Although the Russians never confirmed the details, some commentators had speculated that nitrogen was involved. Well done, Junior, he thought. With his phone on the table in front of him, he hoped it wasn't too late for Mel to take his call. He wanted to talk her through his theory, in part as a dress rehearsal for his breakfast meeting with Pop, but also he valued Mel's opinions. She answered on the first ring.

"I haven't disturbed you, have I?" he asked.

"No."

She sounded flustered. Chad could hear music in the background.

"I know I'm getting old," her composure was returning, "but I still stay up past 10 p.m. Sometimes anyway. What's up, did you go to Castlereagh again today? Any joy?"

"Yeah, I did, and I wanted to run it by you and sanity check things so I don't make a fool of myself with Pop tomorrow."

"Fire away, I'm all ears."

*

"Yeah, that makes sense," said Mel, when Chad had finished. "Well done, you. It'll be interesting to see if it stacks up once you've made the checks, and to see what Pop makes of it. You'd think the police would have already considered that angle, wouldn't you? Any more on whoever is leaking stuff to that journalist?"

"No, she couldn't prize that out of him."

"Really?" Mel's tone was thoughtful rather than confrontational. "My inclination is that it is someone on the force. I can't understand the motivation otherwise."

"We'll have to agree to disagree on that then," said Chad. "I'm in a different camp. I think our perp has some leverage over Byrne's contact and is using it to find out where Pop's investigation is at. If the perp's a copper he wouldn't need to do that. Anyway, thanks for the chat, sleep well and I'll let you know what Pop says tomorrow."

Chad held the phone, staring at the screen. Every intuitive nerve ending told him that Mel was entertaining someone.

He'd lay big money that it was Mr F. Jackson.

Chapter 19

Chad hadn't realised till now that there were two 7:30s in the same day. He used his room card on the reader outside the dining room and as the door hissed open, entered to find that breakfast was in full swing on the twenty-sixth floor of the Sheraton.

"Must be bloody insomniacs," he muttered at several guests tucking into mounds of food. He wiped sleep from his eyes and contemplated the splendour of the views over Sydney afforded by the floor to ceiling glass that ran the length of one wall. He took a table in the corner furthest away from the buffet bar, not that this had been difficult at this hour. Settling himself with a large black coffee, he waited for Pop and mulled over what he was going to say. The police must have considered his theory, mustn't they? And discounted it because Pop would have said otherwise?

Chad heard a waiter say, "Just over here, sir." And looked up to see Pop approaching in a blaze of red silk, embellished with what looked like monkeys climbing a palm tree. The accompanying jeans and leather jacket looked more crumpled than usual, creating a compelling picture of a hobo that had found someone else's shirt.

Chad stood, "Do you have three hundred and sixty-five varieties of those shirts or, if I stick around long enough, will I see them all reprised?"

"Funny bugger," replied Pop, sitting down and ordering a coffee from a lurking waiter. The stress Chad had noted the day before on Pop's face remained in place. Black lines under his eyes spoke of lack of sleep and three days' stubble did nothing to help. You don't want to be in front of the press looking like that, Chad thought.

"Still no progress?" asked Chad.

"Nah. None. Well, I say none, at least none that is pointing us further forward. More things to check and more people to interview as we talk to the victims' relatives, but no chinks of light yet." He ran both hands through his hair then rubbed his face, as if the actions would somehow rectify the situation. "And, as you can imagine, my arse is being kicked from pillar to post by my superiors. Ever supportive. Not."

"I can imagine," Chad used as conciliatory a tone as he could muster.

The waiter arrived with coffee and Pop ignored Chad while savouring the drink like it was an elixir from the gods. Chad waited.

Pop replaced the cup in the saucer and continued, "We've held the press back for a day or so, but they'll be clamouring for information following Andrea Byrne's front page spread today. Have you seen it?" Pop stared across the table.

"No," said Chad, "what does she say?"

"Oh, nothing more than we gave her, but she speculates on whether the choice of shot – forehead or from behind – was a calculated move by the killer or just random shooting. Then she waffles on about being at the cutting edge of the investigation. Our media people have been fielding calls from the crack of dawn from the other hacks wanting to know how Byrne got that info. Fun and games. What do you make of the text she sent and the comment about only one victim being able to speak?"

"I think it confirms that her contact has accurate insights into the killings. He's showing us he's close and that he has access to the killer. It's information that only the killer and us would know."

"Still could be a cop," Pop mused. "One of my team."

"Maybe. That is a possibility, but I'm inclined to think not. I think he's playing a game with us, but what game and to what end, I don't know," Chad paused. "We'll have to think how we use Byrne to get close to whoever this is. I thought it was more interesting that her contact had seen us at the Ravesis. He must have been following her, which is worrying."

Pop seemed to give this some thought as he sipped more coffee before pushing his chair back and standing. "Mind if I get something to eat?" he nodded towards the buffet. "Can't remember my last meal."

"Be my guest."

Pop returned with a tray piled with food. Yoghurt, juice, toast and a plate of eggs and bacon. "Anyway," he began, settling a napkin onto his jeans, "your text said you reckon you know how he got in and out at Castlereagh. I'm all ears. I could do with some good news. You talk and I'll eat."

Chad took a sip of coffee. What if he was wrong? His hand shook as he set the cup back down on the table.

"Okay, it's just a theory and one I'm sure you've already considered, but I think it's worth checking out."

"Fine, I'll check it out when you tell me what it bloody is."

"Look, Pop, we are all agreed that the perp's entry point was the fire escape? He didn't come up in the lift. Your guys checked the CCTV, and that's clear. So, unless he got through sealed windows eleven floors up, then those stairs are the only plausible entry and exit point. Where I differ from your team is this…"

He took another sip of coffee and a deep breath. If Pop was listening, he gave no sign of doing so, concentrating as he was on his food.

"Your guys think he slipped past Lisa James on the desk, which he'd have had to have done twice, once on the way in then on the way out. She's adamant that she never left her desk," he looked at Pop, "and what reason would she have for lying? If she's telling the truth, then he didn't get in through the main office door."

Pop swallowed, took a slurp of juice then wiped his mouth. "Come on, then," he said leaning back in his seat. "He didn't come up in the lift, didn't get through the windows and didn't walk through the reception. But he got in somehow. So how did he bloody do it?"

In for a penny. "He was already there when everyone arrived for work. I reckon he was in the air conditioning shaft. He'd accessed it from the fire escape at some time prior and he was waiting for them."

"Yeah, yeah, yeah, my boys thought that had to be the way in but it doesn't add up," said Pop, waving a fork in Chad's direction. "Someone in the office would have noticed a noise above, and he'd have needed ladders. Now, say what you like, but I reckon some bugger climbing out of the ceiling might have caused those directors to raise the bloody alarm. And we know they didn't."

Chad rummaged in his pocket and pulled out a small cellophane bag.

Pop peered at it across the table. "What's in that?"

Chad opened it and emptied the small black rubber fragments he'd collected from the fire escape onto a clean white napkin. Pop leaned forward his face almost touching the cloth.

"And? Come on fella, don't leave me guessing just get on with it."

"Get these checked by forensics, but I think they are rubber fragments from the feet of a ladder that he used to get into the air vents."

"Well, bugger me. Where did you find them?"

"By the wall in the fire escape, directly below the air vent."

Pop's leg was twitching more than usual. "Well done, mate. Good work. You've put my guys to shame. Still, not sure how much further it gets us," Pop rubbed his eyes. "Doesn't it leave us with the same issue, like why didn't the directors yell when they see a ladder descending from the ceiling?"

Chad felt the adrenalin rush. "Because they couldn't," he said. "They were unconscious."

Pop looked up, mouth open and his loaded fork in no-man's-land. "Is that a guess or can you offer proof?"

"It's the only rational explanation remaining when you rule out all the impossible scenarios." Chad sipped his coffee. "I've got a theory of how he did it, but before I go into that get your pathologists to re-examine the bloods for higher than usual traces of nitrogen. It may be marginal but if there is more nitrogen than normal then that will give the guess a bit more substance."

They sat in silence for a minute, then Pop pushed back his chair and stood. "You can explain that nitrogen thing to me once the pathologists have checked. You reckon he used the same method at the immigration office?"

"Yes," said Chad. "I do. Don't ask me why he's done it that way, that's a far more complex and difficult issue and I've always said that the why is much harder to fathom than the how. Anyway, let's wait for the pathologists."

"Thanks for the breakfast, Chad," Pop wiped his mouth and threw the napkin onto the table. "First one for a couple of weeks that has tasted good." He turned half way across the floor and looked back at Chad. "And we need a chat about what we say to Byrne, I'll call you later."

Chad gave the thumbs up sign and decided he could now eat some breakfast.

Chapter 20

'Punishment is justice for the unjust.'
Saint Augustine.

This leech has come up in the world in the last twenty years. His crimes, like those of the others, have been no hindrance to his career progression. He carries the exalted title of Chief Executive Officer now, but whatever his status, the struggle he is putting up has become familiar to me from my previous forays. First the physical, trying to loosen the bindings that are holding him fast and then the mental, as he tries to comprehend what is going on. His struggles meet with the same lack of success as those of his co-conspirators. As he gives up the effort to release himself, his eyes dart from side to side. Excellent. Fear and panic cause him to emit a tight screech.

Amazing what the sight of an enormous axe has on the bodily functions.

His office occupies the whole of the top floor of the building. A complete floor for one man. No doubt guests to his office, or at least those not carrying an axe, would have been in awe of the achievements that allowed him to have such space.

They'd have used the main elevator and then taken a short flight of stairs, leading to magnificent double doors, through which his secretary would have given them entry. He has placed his desk and chair at the opposite end, so that his visitors, like courtiers, had to walk the entire floor before reaching him. During which they could understand the greatness of the man.

But not today. Today, his rise to the top of his chosen slimy pole is working against him.

And there won't be a tomorrow.

Fear commands his silence. He is now trussed up like my previous conquests and lies lengthways on the expensive teak desk, behind which I sit in his leather upholstered chair as the usurper. Time is not as pressing as it had been in my previous exploits, so I can relax and savour my quarry's distress. I stand. His eyes are following my movements. Walking past the desk I take several paces, his eyes still transfixed. I lift the axe above my head and begin the dance of death. I swirl it in great arcs up and over, around and around. It makes a *whooshing* noise as it slices through the air and I feel the cool of the breeze my movements create. The flaring of his nostrils and the wide-eyed stare tells me he's not enjoying the spectacle.

I lean the axe against the desk and take the photograph from my pocket. His neck and head dangle over the end of the table and I place the picture in front of his face.

"Do you remember her?" I ask.

Consternation? Perhaps. Indignation? Yes, I see indignation in his eyes as if he is wondering how such an insignificant person in his life could have led him here. Even I am amazed at the depth of his arrogance. He should suffer. I leave the axe where it is and revel in the sound of my knife unsheathing. Inside my head, the whispering begins.

'*Make him suffer.*'

His blood is reddening the carpet, and my anger is subsiding. It's time. I clean the knife and return it to its holder then lift the axe. No hubris now. His arrogance has evaporated. I stare into his eyes. Pain, fear, self-pity.

'*Go on, go on. Do it.*'

Placing the axe blade against his throat, I then lift it high above my head.

Three down.

Chapter 21

The sun was a glorious blaze of yellow as Chad followed the players off the pitch and towards the dressing room. If he was being honest, he was actually enjoying this coaching lark. Clearly most of these ex-players were self-obsessed, but being around people who have a total, if misguided, belief in their own ability was doing him good. They may once have been world beaters, but time had caught up with them. Not that you'd know it from their behaviour. No angst-ridden self-doubters here. He could learn a bit from them.

The clack of studs on the concrete floor and the smells of the dressing room generated a pleasant nostalgia.

"I can tell you still miss it, bro," said Freddie.

Chad stopped in the locker room doorway. "Do I?" He let the question hang. "Maybe, but I don't miss the injuries or the fact that I got myself addicted to Fentanyl to get over the pain. Or what that led to." He felt Freddie's massive hand on his shoulder and turned. "But do I miss the atmosphere and the adrenalin? Hell, yes."

Chad let the changing room door close behind him and would have joined in with the banter and noise had it not been for a large flat screen TV on the wall. Someone had turned the sound bar off, but mouthing animatedly into a camera was a woman with impossibly blonde hair, Gucci glasses and ten-thousand dollar teeth. Behind her, a scrum of photographers pointed microphones and handheld recorders toward a vivid red silk shirt, on which monkeys were climbing a palm tree. Pop. As Chad adjusted to what he was seeing, a Breaking News banner appeared at the bottom of the screen and a news feed scrolled in from right to left.

'We await official confirmation but sources say that Dr *Frank Cooper, CEO of Conway Private Hospital Group, is dead. His secretary found his body in his office in North Sydney. Chief Inspector Ruben Murray has arrived at the hospital and is leading the investigation but has so far refused to link this killing to the recent bloodbaths at Castlereagh St and the immigration office at Lee St.'*

"Jesus Christ," said Chad. He pushed through the naked and towel-clad players to his own locker. His phone lay where he'd left it and as he clicked on it, he saw he had several missed calls from Pop and Mel. His breathing quickened. Having failed to reach him by phone, Pop had then sent seven texts the first of which was; *Ring me.* Then each subsequent iteration developed more urgency until the final one five minutes ago which was brusque and typically forthright. *Where the fuck are you? Call me now.*

Chad could see on the TV the baying media mob still surrounded Pop, so called Mel first.

She answered on the first ring. "Hi, thanks for calling me back."

"What's happened? I can see Pop being grilled and something about a murder, what's gone on?"

"Yeah, I'm at the scene." She paused. "Oh, Chad, it's horrendous, and although he's not about to tell the press, he's linking it to the others. Wants you here pronto. Forensics are all over it. How long will it take for you to get there?"

"I don't know. I need to shower and change then I'll get a cab. Where is this place?"

"I'll text you the address. Be as quick as you can. More breadcrumbs, I'm afraid, Chad."

Chad hurried into the shower where Freddie was luxuriating in hot water and shower gel.

"Good session, bro. You should do more coaching, maybe have a think about taking it up as a career instead of that headfuck stuff you do. By the way, thanks for chatting with Junior the other night. He likes you, man. Thinks you're cool." Freddie turned his face towards the shower head to wash away the suds. Chad didn't answer but began hastily washing away the sweat and grass.

Freddie said, "Hey, what's up, bro? You look like someone died. Oh, sorry, man, I didn't mean to bring up… Yeah, well, sorry, man."

"It's okay," Chad, grabbed his towel, "I've got to run, there's somewhere I've got to be."

"Fine bro, no problem. Odd Job can take you; he's got the motor and I don't need it."

"Oh, that would be great, thanks, buddy. Catch you later for dinner?"

*

Chad's apprehension was twofold as Odd Job slowed the car a couple of hundred yards from a large hospital complex, set in its own grounds, around a mile north of the Harbour Bridge. The thought of walking into another brutal crime scene was making his hands damp with sweat and his heart rate was giving him a final warning. He needed to breathe. But compounding the ominous signs of an impending panic attack was Freddie's choice of vehicle. A black and silver Bentley. By the time he'd seen it there'd been no opportunity to protest, as Odd Job ushered him into the cool leather upholstered interior.

"Don't let the press see you," Pop had said. "Be unobtrusive, below the radar."

For God's sake, he thought, unobtrusive? The press will have a field day if they see me getting out of this bloody thing.

"Drop me here if you can," said Chad. The Bentley slowed to a halt. The media seemed to mill around inside the hospital grounds so ditching his ride a couple of hundred metres away might let him get away with it. Or so he hoped.

"G'day, Chad, isn't it? My name is Jason Austin and I'm with the Bugle. Do you have a comment for us? Nice motor by the way. Treating yourself while you're in Sydney?"

Shit. So much for hoping. Chad smiled and stepped onto the kerb. "No, the car's not mine, it belongs to a friend, and we thought we'd take it for a spin. Now we seem to have got lost. We're trying to find our way back to the CBD which way is it from here?"

"Really, mate?" Austin's tone held incredulity. "And what? You got lost and found yourself at the site of another murder? As coincidences go, buddy, that's right up there."

"Well, the truth is sometimes stranger than fiction," replied Chad, opening the car door and getting back inside. And as clichés go, he thought, that's right up there.

"Drive," he said.

"Where to, Boss?"

"I don't know, just drive."

*

It'd taken over an hour to get back to the hospital, but Mel had finally directed Odd Job to a private car park at the back of the main building. Chad had hurried across the tarmac, to where Mel stood holding open a rusty red door, on which someone had painted 'Private' in white gloss. Her face was flushed and Chad saw a small line of sweat beads on her forehead. He ran his hands through his hair and breathed deeply. It must be bad if she's flustered. He followed Mel inside. No stairs, no other offices, just an elevator with no button or other obvious means of calling it. Mel typed a message into her phone and seconds later the lift doors opened. "Can't be accessed externally, Pop's just let us in." She explained.

Ascending they both stared at the metal door of the elevator.

"It's horrendous. If anything, worse than the others. Are you going to be alright?"

"I hope so," said Chad. "How's Pop?"

"Going off his nut."

Chad inhaled a lungful of air, held it and slowly exhaled. He repeated the process several times as the lift ascended, reaching its destination with a tremor and a bump. The doors opened into a frenzy of activity. There was a tall white screen immediately in front of him, which Chad took to be shielding the corpse. Just as at the immigration office, uniformed police were there in numbers along with pathologists, forensics, assorted detectives, and Pop bawling at someone. Chad took a couple of paces to his right into the main part of the room and registered his surroundings.

The office was rectangular and some twenty metres long, he guessed. At the far end was a set of open double doors outside which two uniforms stood guard. From the rear, one of them looked like Chad's new best buddy from Castlereagh. Inside and on the left of the doors was a fully kitted out kitchen and a small, but expensive, dining table and chairs. Several large leather settees and coffee tables occupied the remaining open space. But it was the walls that attracted Chad's attention. Photographs adorned every available space, each of the same man. Chad assumed this was the deceased. They showed him at work; all expansive smiles giving out prizes or making speeches. At play; surfing, horse riding and cricketing. At home; family man with wife, kids and dogs. 'All-round good bloke', Chad reckoned, was the image the subject in the photos wanted to present. Look at me, the photos seemed to say, I'm just a regular guy like you. Just richer, more successful, more talented and more attractive.

Chad's eyes followed the lines of photos which stretched from the far end of the office back to another elevator exactly opposite the one he'd just exited. Separating the two lifts was an enormous teak desk. Prostrate on the desk was the body of a man, strapped to the table in the same way that Dan Hodges had been at Castlereagh. Chad blinked, his eyes watered, and he felt unsteady on his feet. His legs seemed to dissolve. He felt a small, strong hand close around his forearm and saw Mel at his side.

"It's okay," she said.

But it wasn't okay. It was about as far removed from okay as it was possible to imagine. Where the man's head should have been was a bloody mass of skin and tendon with pale spinal bone protruding. An enormous pool of blood lay on the floor underneath. But that horror was as nothing compared to the main spectacle. The man's severed head sat like some sort of big game trophy in the centre of his torso, eyes staring vacantly out into the office.

"What the hell is that?" stuttered Chad, pointing. "What's in his mouth?"

A booming voice reverberated in his ear as Pop strode up the office. "That's his cock, Chad, mate. That's his cock."

Chapter 22

Chad's limbs seemed disconnected, each undergoing involuntary spasms independent of each other. He opened his eyes and blinked. Where the hell am I? Images hurtled into his brain; blood and bone, grinning death heads. He was lying somewhere, but where? A voice boomed nearby.

"Is he okay? That's all I need, a shrink who can't stand the sight of blood. That's a massive help."

"He's got PTSD, as well you know, Pop. Give him some breathing space and I'll give him some water. He'll be fine."

Chad sat up to find he was on one of the leather sofas in the victim's opulent office. Mel offered him a glass of water which he had trouble keeping steady enough to drink. He could feel her body, tense but protective, leaning into him as she perched on the arm of the settee. "Don't worry, you passed out, that's all. I warned you about doing that."

Chad felt blood rush to his face. Passed out? Jesus.

Pop was in full flow. "Right, everyone stop what you're doing and stand still. No one leaves till I say so and that won't be till we've logged each of you as being present. That way if any leaks occur, then I know they must have come from someone in this room and I will find out who. Is that clear? No one talks to the press except me. Got it?"

Chad looked around the room. Pop had certainly got everyone's attention.

"Failure to comply with those instructions," Pop continued,

"will mean disciplinary action which, if I have my way, will mean getting fired. I don't care which department you work for, Forensics, Pathology, Homicide, I'll make sure of it. And you will communicate nothing you've seen in here to any external source. I will brief the press, but give them no details. Questions?"

"Yeah, Pop?" Dimi's arm was raised.

"Yes, Dimi, fire away."

"Wondered what makes you think that the leak in the press today, about the shootings in Castlereagh, came from someone on the force?"

"I'm not saying it was, but the report in The Globe today contained information that was not previously released so somebody did some talking. I want to make certain that the press gets nothing from anyone in this room, and boy, are they going to be digging. Let's all keep our mouths shut. I don't want the population of Sydney to panic any more than they already are, which is why the manner of Dr Cooper's death must not get out."

Chad felt Mel squeeze his shoulder. Forensics has placed screens around the table so he could no longer see the grotesque corpse and by regulating his breathing he was quelling the tremors. As Pop was finishing speaking, Chad could see the pathologists step forward, and he hoped to hell that this meant they were removing the body.

"Okay," Pop concluded, "carry on everyone. My homicide team, please, plus Mel and Chad."

Chad saw Pop staring at him.

"That's if you're okay to join us? Right, gather round in that kitchen area. Thanks, everyone. Constable Swift, can you make sure everyone has signed in, name and department, please."

"No problem, sir."

Chad made a mental note he recognised as ludicrously trivial in the circumstances, to remember to get Swift's tickets for the game.

"Are you okay?" asked Mel.

"I think so," said Chad. "Christ, I've dealt with some mad, murderous psychos in my time but I've seen nothing like this before."

"Don't worry, I don't think any of us have. Can you stand? Here take my arm, probs best not to keep Pop waiting, not when he's in this mood."

Chad stood, his legs steadying, but his clothes sticking to the ice-cold sweat that was covering every inch of his body. Or so it felt. He rubbed his face with both hands to get some colour into what he knew was a deathly pallor. '*I'm neither use nor ornament.*' He turned his back to the spectacle on the desk and walked towards the kitchen area. Those already there had the good grace to ignore him.

"Right, all here?" Pop looked around. "Good. We'll deal with the method of killing when Mel and Chad have gathered their thoughts and see what it tells us about our killer. For now, we need to focus on proper, old style police work. We check everything, we dot every 'i' and cross every 't'. No stone unturned. Find out everything there is to know about our victim and see if there's anything that links him to Short or Hodges."

Lucy raised her hand. Pop nodded. "One thing differs from the previous killings," she began. "We know how he got in and out. The lift over there on the right where the forensics boys are. Some blood stains in there."

As the team all turned to look, Pop added, "Yeah, well, I'm hoping to confirm the method of entry and exit from the other two sites later today when some fragments Chad found at Castlereagh come back from analysis at the lab."

Chad looked up to find the homicide team staring at him. Pop continued. "But you're right about the entry point here, Lucy. Which presents us with another tricky problem. According to Dr Cooper's PA, er," he checked his notebook, "Danielle Oban, that lift is for private access only. To use it, you need a key card which only she and Dr Cooper have. Or, he could have buzzed the killer in using the button on his desk. But either the killer somehow had a key card or the doctor let him in."

"What about the lift on the other side of the desk?" asked José. "You don't need a card to come up in that?"

"No, but you can only operate it from inside the office, so the victim would have had to let him in."

"Why the hell are there two lifts anyway?" said Dimi.

"Again, according to Danielle Oban, it's because before our victim took the entire floor for himself the layout was different and the lifts gave access to different areas."

Chad raised his hand.

Pop nodded. "Yes Chad, go ahead. Are you alright, by the way, that fall has made you look kinda pale?"

"Yeah, I'm fine. Look, entry and exit are just another riddle the killer's set to occupy our time. There's another question that's much more pressing and is the same for the other two murder sites."

"Go on, what's that then?" said Pop. "Explain."

Mel answered. "Why did he kill him here where's there's risk and difficulty involved? Why not get him somewhere else, like his home?"

"Exactly," said Chad.

Chapter 23

Andrea jockeyed for position with the rest of the press pack outside the Conway Hospital. Everywhere she turned her media competitors were staring at her or making barbed jibes. One journo's gain was everyone else's loss and no one liked to be behind the eight ball for breaking news. Andrea knew that her stock had gone through the roof since her first edition splash that morning, which meant that all the hacks on show here would have their editors kicking lumps out of them. "How come Andrea Byrne and not you? What am I paying you for?"

The comments she'd received since getting to the hospital had ranged from the jealous, "You lucky bitch, where did that scoop come from?" to the insulting, "Which copper are you shagging to get the inside track, Andrea? Or should I say how many coppers are you shagging?"

She didn't mind. Even her boss, Tom, had been grudgingly pleased with her work and she'd been name dropped on Fox and a host of other channels since first thing that morning. But once ahead she needed to stay ahead, and she was as in the dark as the rest of them regarding events at the hospital. She'd tried calling and texting Chad Hilton, but not received a reply and her mysterious contact hadn't called either.

A commotion near the main entrance set a stampede going. Andrea felt herself being carried along with the rest, but got her phone onto 'Record' just as she came to a juddering halt in front of the steps leading into the hospital reception. On tiptoes and peering round a malodorous photographer, she could make out Ruben Murray looking even more haggard than at the press briefing earlier outside police headquarters.

"I'm going to make a brief statement and will not be taking questions," she heard him shout. "At 1:07 p.m. Miss Danielle Oban, personal assistant to Dr Frank Cooper, CEO of Conway Hospital Group, found Dr Cooper's body in his office. His death is being treated as suspicious and until our investigations have progressed, I can make no further comment."

Hundreds of shouted questions pursued Murray as he disappeared through the glass doors to the obvious anger of the scrum outside. Andrea pushed her way out of the crush and headed for the main car park. She stopped and lit a cigarette.

"Shocking habit, not to mention bloody expensive."

She turned to find herself eyeball to eyeball with Jason Austin from The Bugle.

"I wasn't aware you were so protective of my health, Jason, but thank you."

"I'm not, but you seem to need some friends these days. I bumped into Tom yesterday at a lunch and he wasn't exactly complimentary about you. But twenty-four hours later and look at you now. I bet he thinks you're the best thing since sliced bread today. Anyway, well done on your leader this morning, that's set the cat amongst the proverbial."

"Why, thank you." Andrea made a small curtsy. Tom Greenwood, her boss. Bastard.

Austin carried on, "I realise that you have a PHD in unrelenting ambition, Andrea, and er, what was it?" Austin's eyes searched for a memory. "Oh yes, a poor second class in journalism."

She knew her anger showed in her face, the heat from the blood rushing there making her glow.

Austin's smile was unctuous and just the wrong side of lecherous. "So maybe it might pay you to heed my advice," he cooed. "If it seems to be too good to be true, it probably is. Anyway, got to go. Look after yourself." Andrea watched her rival take a couple of steps before turning back to smile at her. "By the way have you been keeping tabs on Chad Hilton?"

"Who?"

"Chad Hilton, you know, the ex-soccer player turned profiler. You must know him? He's been big news."

"No, can't say I know anything about him. Not much interested in soccer."

"Oh, okay. Just thought I'd check. Bye."

Andrea took a long pull on her cigarette. God, did she need a drink.

*

Andrea had felt grubby and tired when she finally got home from the hospital so had showered, put a few leaves in a bowl with some cold chicken she had in the fridge and poured herself a large glass of an ice-cold pinot. They say the first sip is the best. Bugger that, she thought, placing the bottle in the ice bucket, the first bottle maybe, she'd give them that.

She'd spent the journey home mulling over Jason Austin's comments about Chad. What did he know, and what was he getting at? Tom, her boss at The Globe, had been cramming her phone with texts and voicemails demanding the inside track on this latest murder, given she'd whetted his appetite with her scoop on Castlereagh earlier. But he could fuck right off. Chatting her business with Austin. Cheeky bastard.

The anger at her boss hadn't abated since he'd perched on the edge of her desk a few days ago and à propos of nothing had launched in with what passed for an appraisal.

"You're good, I'll give you that. Tenacious and not afraid of treading on toes, granted. Goes without saying that you're a valuable member of the team but you know, Andrea, I just think there's something missing. Instinct, maybe, or perhaps you've not got the nose for it." He'd walked away from the desk with the air of a disappointed teacher returning her homework.

She'd reminded him of those remarks when she'd sent her copy last night and again when callers jammed The Globe's phone lines this morning. "No nose for it, eh, Tom? Well, what do you call this?" For the umpteenth time she'd decided he was a wanker. He smoked cigars for fuck's sake. Irrespective of all that, it was her own career that was of most concern and she had no means of accessing inside information unless Trevor called.

As if someone was listening to her thoughts, the phone on the table vibrated. She picked it up, looked at the number and answered, "Hi, this is Andrea."

"Good evening, Andrea, how are you? I guess you've had a busy day?"

"Hi, Trevor, yes, you could say that. How are you?"

"I'm okay, thanks, but I've just put the phone down from my contact and he's eager to hear news from you regarding what the police are thinking about this latest incident at Conway Hospital."

"Well, I'm sorry, Trevor, but I can't help you with that." Andrea gulped some wine. "I've left messages for Chad Hilton but he hasn't come back to me and remember they still want to understand if your contact is a cop, so maybe that's why there's radio silence."

"I suggest, Andrea, that you do whatever it takes to get hold of Hilton. My contact knows he was at the Conway, so he must be able to tell you their initial thinking. However, as an olive branch here's something you can share with them."

"Go on," said Andrea.

"The victim's office has photographs lining the walls. On the right-hand wall there are ten. The fifth of these is interesting."

"Fair enough, but anyone who had been in that office may know that photograph. It's hardly unique information."

"True, Andrea, very true. But only one person, apart from the police, would know that this same photograph was not in its usual place, but elsewhere in the office. Now, that is unique. Goodnight, Andrea."

Chapter 24

Chad had drawn the curtains in his hotel room although the sun had not quite given off its last rays of the day. He lay cocooned in the darkness allowing the stillness to calm him and encourage his brain to emerge from the protective shroud that had enveloped it since he'd stared into the unseeing eyes of the severed head. Fainting at a crime scene, what the hell? Leaving the hospital without the press spotting him had been problematic until one copper gave him a police vest and cap. Then he'd jumped in the back of a squad car and kept his head down. He'd arrived at the hotel, minus vest and cap, some twenty minutes later.

He'd ignored text messages from Andrea Byrne and Freddie. The former rude and requesting an urgent call back, the latter concerned, *Yo, bro are you okay?* They'd have to wait, he needed time to think. Leaning over to the bedside table and turning on the lamp he retrieved his iPad and as thoughts darted in and out of his mind, he typed.

- *Risks too high, why take them?*
- *Why is place so important?*
- *Means of entry?*
- *Who is briefing Byrne and why?*
- *Why is this happening now? Catalyst?*

He lay his head back on the softness of the pillow and remembered the sense of dread that had come over him when he'd been discussing things with Mel at the Mordeo. He felt the same now. There was something he couldn't see, but could feel.

Something he was missing.

Risk, he thought. It comes back to risk.

He trawled through his memory banks of killers he'd come across. None, he reckoned, would have tried to carry out their murders within earshot of countless people. Likewise, none would have indulged in these 'locked door' mysteries. No, they'd have all chosen the easy option of a quiet secluded place with no chance of being disturbed.

So why was this guy different?

The rituals of the killings suggested vengeance, retribution. But for what? Pop's team could unearth nothing that linked Hodges to Short. Chad made a silent wager that they wouldn't find anything that linked Doctor Cooper to either of the other two. And yet three other people died at Lee Street and five others at Castlereagh. Why? Collateral damage? What sort of butcher were they dealing with?

Chad closed his eyes. So many questions, so few answers. As he lay still breathing deeply, two words kept floating across his consciousness.

Breadcrumb trail.

He felt his phone vibrate in his pocket and extricating it from his jeans saw a message from Jas back in Leeds.

Hey, Hoppy, out of sight out of mind, eh? Thanks, no really, thanks. 😟 How's things? I'm worried about you. Spoke to Lee and he agrees it's too soon for you to be working. So, stop it! Let me know how you are. Miss you. J xx

Christ, why hadn't he texted her? The two small xx at the end of the text held his eye. God, he wanted to feel her softness, her touch. He could almost feel the brush of her lips against his cheek, the scent of her perfume in his nostrils. Nothing had happened between them after Angie's death, but as he read the text, he wanted her now.

Hey, good to hear from you, and well done on remembering the time difference. Got to say it's batshit crazy out here. A serial killer racking up the body count and yours truly up to his eyes in it. But I'm okay... ish. Fainted at a crime scene today ffs. He paused in typing his reply, should he tell her that? Why not? He started again. *How's things with you? Missing you too.*

What??? Fainted??? Are you okay?

'Yeah, I'm okay. I'm told it's a consequence of the PTSD. I get panic attacks. In my defence the crime scene was horrendous.'

'STOP. NOW. If the Aussies can't solve these crimes without your help, that's their own fault. Chad, you need rest, not this shit. Promise you'll stop.'

'I can't just stop, I'm up to my eyes in it and you wouldn't be saying that if you knew how badly this perp needs to be caught. Look, don't worry, I'm okay.'

*

"No mate," said Chad. "You go, I'm tired so I'll just get something sent up on room service. I'll see you tomorrow."

"Hey bro, I saw that shit on the news tonight. The dude getting whacked at the hospital, is that where you were going earlier?" There was concern in Freddie's tone.

"Yeah, it was, and the Bentley did little for my low-key status. I've probably blown my cover as I got collared bang to rights by some journo. Just what I need - the press knowing I'm helping the cops with these murders."

"Maybe you should think about that, bro, and stop helping them. For your own good. How are you feeling?"

"I'm okay. I get shaky at the crime scenes and I'm getting the odd panic attack but I'm okay. Anyway, stop worrying about me, you're as bad as Jas."

"How d'ya mean, has she been in touch?"

"Yeah, we were texting a few minutes ago and you two are singing from the same hymn sheet. Anyway, go on, bugger off and have a wonderful dinner. Are you on your own?"

Why did I ask that, thought Chad?

"Yeah, who would I be with?"

Was that a slight delay in answering or was he imagining shit?

"Night bro. Get some rest."

Chad clicked the call off, but the phone vibrated immediately. Andrea Byrne. Shit.

"Hi, Andrea, sorry I haven't got back to you, been busy."

"Yeah, I know. Any news for me? Remember, if I'm going to help you and the investigation, I've got to keep ahead of the pack."

"No, nothing from today yet. "

"And what about the info I gave you yesterday? The stuff about only one victim being unable to speak. What can you give me on that?"

"Shit, yeah, sorry but events at the Conway have overtaken us so I haven't discussed that with Pop yet."

"Look, Chad, I need you to do that tonight and get back to me. I need to have something for tomorrow."

"It'll have to wait," said Chad. "It's too late to get hold of Pop."

"Chad, it has to be tonight." He picked up the irritation in her tone. "Oh, and my contact called me earlier with some info about the Conway which I can share with you in return."

"What's that then?"

"No, Chad, that's not how this works. Call me back when you've spoken to Pop. By the way, has a hack called Jason Austin hassled you?"

Chad felt a throbbing behind his eyes. "He saw me at the Conway today."

"Shit. He'll try to make some noise about that. Can you give me anything that I can run tomorrow as a plausible cover for why you were there?"

"Not off the top of my head. I told him I'd got lost. Thin, I know, but I couldn't think of anything else to say."

"Leave it with me, I'll have a think. You get onto Pop and call me back."

The line went silent. He scrolled through his recent calls and hovered over Pop. This was going to be a fun call. Not.

*

"Hi, Chad, did you speak to Pop?" Andrea's tone was peremptory.

Chad could hear her pouring something into a glass and decided he could use a drink. A large one.

"Yeah, I did," he replied.

"And?"

"And… I'm allowed to tell you that only one victim had tape over their mouth and that the investigation is pursuing various lines of enquiry regarding why none of the other victims raised the alarm. Now, what have you got for us from the Conway?"

Chad listened as Andrea explained that a photograph from the crime scene was not in its usual place and that there may be some significance to this. "Okay, thanks," he said. "Any thoughts on a cover story for why I was there?"

"I think we stick with what you told Austin. You were out for a spin in Freddie's car and the driver, who's a Brit, got lost. Keep it simple. I'll print that tomorrow as well. 'Night, Chad, talk tomorrow."

Chad threw the phone onto the bed and walked to the desk where his duty free bottle of Highland Park was calling to him. His phone pinged for the umpteenth time.

"Just piss off and leave me alone whoever you are," he shouted. He sipped his drink and retrieved the phone. A message from Jas.

Sleep well, Hoppy, and take these to bed with you.

Chad smiled at the big red heart and three kisses.

Chapter 25

There were several more people eating breakfast than the last time Chad had been in the dining room of the Sheraton. Business types, he reckoned. Opting for the same table that he'd sat at for his previous breakfast meeting, he ordered a coffee. If the telephone conversation they'd had last night was anything to go by, this meeting with Pop was likely to be less cordial than the last. He saw a waiter approaching being closely followed by Pop, sporting a worse than usual scowl. Probs best to leave the shirt banter for today.

Pop threw The Bugle and The Globe onto the table where the former's headline blared '*Hilton arrives in Style*'. Chad looked at the papers then at Pop, who sat down with a grunt.

"Look, Pop, I'm sorry but what could I do? Your messages said to get to the hospital as soon as I could and Mel said you were champing at the bit. Freddie offered me a lift and by the time I'd seen it was a friggin' Bentley it was too late to say no. And I parked away from the hospital, but that guy Austin was there. Anyway, nothing I can do now."

"Yeah, well, you probably owe Andrea Byrne a drink," said Pop, rummaging through The Globe's pages. "'Cos she's printed some bullshit about you getting lost and running into Jason Austin which sort of takes the wind out of his sails. Why the hell didn't you mention it yesterday?"

"To be fair, Pop, you had slightly more on your plate than my means of transport, and by the time I'd got into the Conway it wasn't the first thing on my mind either. What with a severed head with a cock in its gob staring at me."

"No, I suppose not," Pop scratched the top of his head and let out a long, heartfelt sigh. "Look, Chad…" Pop fidgeted with the napkin on the table then rubbed his eyes, a mannerism with which Chad was becoming familiar. He knew Pop was building up to something and his intuition was telling him that whatever it was, he wouldn't like it.

"What?"

Pop leaned back in his seat. "I think we should stop fannying around with the press and tell 'em that you're giving us a hand. Something like you've volunteered to give us any help you can, unpaid, blah blah blah."

"Why, though, why not leave things as they are?"

"Because, whatever Byrne may have written, the public will not buy that you just turned up at a crime scene out of the blue. So we may as well front it up and acknowledge that you're helping. At least it'll show we're leaving no stone unturned to try to catch this nutter."

"That may be fine for you," replied Chad. He could feel the blood rushing to his face. "But it'll mean I won't get a minute's peace. I'll have journos camped in the hotel's foyer and you know that as well as I do. They'll be all over me like a rash. It may deflect some of the heat from you, but I'm going to cop it. It's also not what we agreed at the airport. Remember what you said? I'm in a no win."

"Yeah, well, if you'd kept a low profile like I said we wouldn't be in this shit. If we say nothing it'll make us look bloody stupid. Better to acknowledge your help than not."

Chad stared at his coffee then at the big copper across the table who shrugged his shoulders and placed his hands palms down onto the table. "I'll think about it."

Pop pushed his seat away from the table and stood. "Right, I've got to go. I'll see you at the team debrief, yeah?"

"What time is that?"

"Midday, don't be late."

Chapter 26

Chad pulled his cap down as he pushed through a group of maybe fifteen reporters waiting outside Day Street Police Station. The latest batch in what had been a posse of journalists hounding him since Pop, without so much as a by-your-leave, had gone on TV after their breakfast meeting to announce that Chad was lending unpaid help to the investigation. Anger at Pop's opportunism and, as Chad saw it, betrayal, raged inside him.

"Hey, Chad, how long will it take you to crack the case?"

"Have you given the police any leads yet?"

He said a silent 'thank you' as a copper inside the foyer of the station opened the doors for him, while the reporters swarmed around him like piranhas. His shoes stuck to the battered lino as he made his way to the stairs, taking them two at a time before he hurried along the decrepit corridor. Chad opened the door and found the meeting in full flow. Clean air was at a premium and Pop was showing his frustration. Again.

"Come on, guys, we must have something. There's a reason the perp has picked these victims. Find it. And quickly. We know that they're not random attacks, but we can't see the motive. If we don't get somewhere soon, I'm reliably assured by my superiors that there'll be civil unrest, the blame for which will rest entirely at my door. So, have we found anything linking Dr Cooper to Hopkins or Short?"

"Nothing yet, Boss," said Dimi.

"Okay, but there's something that links them. What is it? Dig,

dig, dig. Come on, let's find out what it is. Before you all crack on though," Pop held up a restraining hand. "we have some good news. A bit of an upside. Chad's work shows how the perp got into Castlereagh and probably Lee Street. Chad, fill everyone in please."

Chad leaned against the wall and saw the expectant faces watching and waiting, but just looking at Pop was making his blood boil. He'd dropped him from a great height into a cesspit of hacks and now wanted his help. Chad looked around the ramshackle room. Why was it always him that drew the bloody short straw? Across a desk Pop raised an enquiring eyebrow. God, he could punch him.

Rock and frigging hard place.

Chad began. "I'm not sure whether you're all up to speed so stop me if I'm covering stuff you know. The other day, I found some fragments of rubber on the landing of the fire escape outside Medics 4U's office. I gave these to er… Your boss." Chad found it hard to say Pop's name. "Anyway, Forensics have now confirmed that manufacturers use this type of rubber as protection on ladders and other equipment. I also asked him," he pointed at Pop, "to check with the pathologists and see if they'd found slightly higher levels of nitrogen in the victims' blood. They have confirmed this to be the case, which supports my theory."

"Whoa, back up a minute, Chad," said Lucy. "I'm not sure I'm following you. Can you give us the context? I mean, why were you looking for something in the fire escape, and what has nitrogen got to do with anything?"

"Yeah, okay, sorry, I'll re-wind. Mel and I have been puzzling over the 'how' of these crimes, so I went back to Castlereagh and chatted to Lisa James the receptionist. She was adamant that she had not left the reception area that morning and I believe her."

"Why?" asked José. "Why believe her?"

"Because she had no reason to lie. If she had been, you guys would have found something in her background by now which would link her to the killer. But you haven't. Now, if she's telling the truth, then no way did our killer walk past her on the way in and on the way out. So, how did he get in? Once you rule out the impossible, sealed windows eleven floors up, lifts with CCTV, et cetera, the only route was up the fire escape and through the air conditioning shaft. To get in he'd have needed ladders and, hey presto, we get a bit of luck for a change, and we got some rubber off them."

"We've still got the problem of a bloke in an air vent dropping his ladders into the boardroom and no one in there saying a thing," remarked Lucy.

"Yeah, you're right." Despite being totally pissed off with Pop, Chad found he was enjoying this. "Which brings me onto the nitrogen. The only reason I could think why no one would raise the alarm is if they couldn't. What I mean is, they couldn't raise the alarm because they were unconscious. Nitrogen is odourless and altering the ratio of nitrogen to oxygen in air that people are breathing renders them unconscious. I think that's what he did, he introduced nitrogen to the air flow, probably by taking his own cylinder."

"Really? How do you know that stuff?" asked Dimi.

"To be fair, I didn't. Giving credit where it's due, a young friend of mine told me he'd learned it in a chemistry class. He also pointed me at an article on a terrorist attack in Russia, which speculated that Russian special forces used it to subdue the terrorists."

"Okay, so what does our perp do then?" said Lucy.

"Once he turns the nitrogen off, he re-adjusts the balance of oxygen to nitrogen by turning up the air con. I checked with the receptionist and she told me that when she went into the boardroom the air con was on the highest setting. The perp was blowing more clean air into the room to wake Dan Hopkins. My theory is that our guy wanted Hopkins and Short awake so he could watch them suffer. The other victims were collateral, so he shot them while they were still unconscious. As we know he used a suppressor on the weapon, hence why no one raised the alarm."

"Bloody hell," Dimi stared at Chad. "He went to a helluva lot of trouble. I mean why would anyone do that?"

"Yeah, good question, to which we don't yet have the answer. However, the place he kills them and the reason he kills them, carry as much weight in the killer's mind. They are both important to him."

"Okay," Pop intervened. "I get all that is plausible and the forensics and pathology would seem to support it, but why haven't we spotted the perp in the basement? There's CCTV in there if not in the stairwell. And do you believe he got in the same way at the immigration department?"

José was sitting on a desk swinging his legs and tapping a pencil. "Maybe we haven't looked far enough back on the CCTV. We've been looking at the comings and goings from around 7:30 a.m. Perhaps our guy was there way earlier."

"Maybe," said Pop. "Check it out. The immigration department at Lee Street is more problematic 'cos of these bloody rules for when and where they can use CCTV in the building. But let's go back over what we've got from start to finish. Also, let's check anywhere that sells cylinders of nitrogen and find out if they've got records of who's bought the bloody stuff. Right, now crack on, please. Back here at 6 p.m. Chad, Mel, can I have a quick word?"

The detectives bustled about gathering bags and equipment in the small confines of the room, but most had headed off after a minute or two. Chad hoped his expression told Pop how pissed off with him he was.

"Right," Pop snapped his laptop shut, "so, a couple of things for the guys to work on from that." The last member of the team left the room. "Let's see if the CCTV in Castlereagh gives us anything. A mugshot of a bloke with a set of ladders and a gas cylinder would be good, but I'm not holding my breath."

Either Pop was impervious to sullen looks and hostile body language, which Chad reckoned was possible, or he didn't give a shit, which was more likely.

"Anything from Byrne's contact?"

Chad said nothing.

"Hey, Chad, I'm talking to you. Have you heard from Byrne and, if so, any news?"

"Oh, I'm so sorry. Talking to me, were you?" Chad's anger spilled out like volcanic lava. "But you couldn't be arsed to talk to me before giving it large to the press, could you? Not even a heads up that you'd called a presser, you twat. So, muggins here is blissfully unaware of a mob of reporters waiting in the lobby of my hotel. You're one cheeky bastard." Chad knew his face was burning red but he couldn't stop now he'd started. "Since when, paps on bikes and in cars have followed me everywhere and bombarded me with calls and even DM'd on social media. So, I'm now checking out of the Sheraton and trying to find an Airbnb somewhere out of the city, where the press won't bloody find me. And, for the avoidance of doubt, I am extremely pissed off with you. Clear?"

"Abundantly." Pop leaned on the wall and inspected a fingernail.

"Right, boys, let's stop there, shall we. We have a maniac out there killing people and you two going at it like this will not make catching him any easier," observed Mel, stroking Chad's sleeve.

"Ah, that's good," said Pop. "There's another grown up in the room. Thank you, Mel. So, I repeat, is there any word from Byrne?"

Chad recognised defeat when he saw it. He'd been out-manoeuvred by a big Tasmanian with a penchant for dodgy Hawaiian shirts.

"Yes, there is," Chad responded. "According to her contact, there's a photograph which was not in its usual place and which might be of some interest. Do you know anything about that?"

Pop seemed to twitch. "Yeah, we found a photo underneath Doctor Cooper's body on the table. It was a group shot from 2002.

Normal place for it was on the wall. I've got a couple of the guys trying to trace everyone on the photo. That's a hell of a piece of information. Jesus, if it's not the killer it's someone very close, or," he paused mid-sentence, "it's a copper. Although I don't think many of the team even know about it."

"I hate to say it," Mel looked from one to the other, "but my view that a copper is involved is getting firmer."

"Nah, I'm still not with you on that," Chad scratched his head. "Could be, I grant you, but there are lots of other possibilities."

"Okay," said Pop. "I don't want Byrne printing anything about the photograph but confirm to her that the information is not without foundation."

"She'll want something in return, that lady does nothing for free. What can I give her?"

"Tell her she can print that we believe that the victims were unconscious when they were shot. That should also alert her contact that we might be slow, but we are getting closer to the killer. We are catching up."

"Okay, will do." Chad turned and headed towards the door.

Pop called after him. "There was no other way of handling the issue of you helping us, Chad. I'm sorry if you get hounded and I'll do what I can to keep them at a distance."

"Yeah, right. Nicely takes the heat off you and puts it on me though, doesn't it?"

Chapter 27

Chad's phone vibrated in his hand. Andrea Byrne. No point in putting this off. "Hey, Andrea, how's things?"

"I guess I'm a whole bunch better than you. Murray certainly stitched you up a treat."

"Yeah well, serves me right for rocking up at a crime scene in a Bentley. Asking for trouble, and trouble I got. Pop reckoned he had to come clean about me helping or it would have made it worse. So, I'm now experiencing the joys of the Australian press corps, of which you are a notable member."

"Indeed. Talking of which, we still have our arrangement right?"

"Correct, yes."

"Goodo. I'll do some nice background stuff on you and generally highlight what an all-round good guy you are," she paused. "Unless of course the information dries up in which case all bets are off. Did you talk to Pop about the photograph?"

"Yes, we discussed it. I can only confirm that your information may be useful and may have some basis in fact. But you can't print that. Sorry. Too sensitive. Your source is very good, maybe even too good, don't you think?"

"How can he be too good? If the stuff he gives us is accurate then that should help you guys, shouldn't it?"

"In theory, yes, unless he's using both you and us for his own ends. My colleagues think he's a copper, but you said the other day you didn't, why was that?"

"Gut feel, that's all. The information he's getting means there's three options: A, he's the killer; B, he's close to the killer or; C, he's a cop. I'm inclined to B but that's just a hunch. Anyway, if I can't go to print on the photograph what can I use?"

"You can print that police believe the gunshot victims at both Castlereagh and Lee Street were unconscious when they were shot. Hence why they didn't raise the alarm. Only Hopkins and Short had tape across their mouths which we believe means they were both conscious when he killed them. We'd be very interested to see if your source can confirm that."

"Okay, interesting. Does that get you any closer to catching this guy?"

"No, not yet, but we are beginning to make up ground on him."

"If you think they were unconscious that must mean you know how they became unconscious, right?"

"Maybe, maybe. See what your contact says."

"Okay, Chad, thanks for that, I'll call you tomorrow."

*

Freddie's voice boomed out of Chad's phone; he'd somehow got it on speaker. "Hey, Chad bro, do I look out for you or do I look out for you?"

Chad laughed. "Why, big man, what have you done now?"

"Only got you the best damn Airbnb in Bondi man, that's all. Halfway up Hall Street, penthouse, two bedrooms, two bathrooms and with stunning views. Am I your best friend or what?"

Chad had exaggerated to prove a point with Pop earlier, when he said he was looking for an Airbnb. He'd asked Freddie to do it for him. "How the hell have you got that?"

"Well, it being autumn sort of helps, but Junior's mum works at a medical practice and a doctor there owns it. When she asked, he said, too right, baby, all yours for as long as you want it."

"That's great, so when can I move in?"

"She's getting the keys first thing in the morning, bro, so I'll send Junior round to flat sit till you get there. Do you want Odd Job to take you?"

"Nah, it's okay, but thanks. Text me the address and I'll get an Uber over there. The Bentley's caused me enough shit."

"Cool, bro, see you tomorrow. I'm out tonight."

"Anywhere nice?"

"Just out, bro, just out."

Chad stared at the blank screen. Freddie and Mel. Why did he find that such a difficult concept?

Chapter 28

Chad lay staring into the darkness. Closing his eyes brought recurring images screeching across his brain. Like a TV recording on fast-forward. Faces staring down at him, the bitter taste of the water, the fleeting glimpses of his past receding. Dying. He was dying. Then Angie. Bright, beautiful, Angie, hair blown back, eyes wide in astonishment, laughing at something.

The clock on the bedside read 3:07 a.m. He sighed, Angie's smiling face disappeared, and he remembered the rows.

"Those pills are more important to you than I am. We can't go on like this. Get help or..."

"Or what? You'll leave me?"

She'd left him forever.

Here alone, he could feel her presence... Or, he thought he could. The sound of her voice was fading. He could picture her exactly as she was, but he was losing her resonance, her tone and inflexion. Why was that? Just time, maybe. He'd deleted her number from his phone and wished he hadn't. To hear her voice when he needed to.

"Hi, this is Ange. Leave a message and I'll get back to you."

Tears tumbled down his cheeks. "Oh God, Ange, my beautiful girl. I miss you so much."

Chad sat up and wiped his eyes. He couldn't blame jet lag, he was way past that. He climbed out of bed wandered to the window and looked across St James. "No possum tonight."

Restless, he turned to the desk and opened his Mac, then sat and stared at the screen. He was correct about ladders and nitrogen, but he was still missing something. The perp's job at Lee Street was easier. More people, no CCTV. "No, not Lee Street, I'm missing something at Castlereagh."

Chad tapped on the keyboard.

So, he rocks up gets into the air vent and turns on the nitrogen. He must have done that before? I mean you're about to slaughter six people and you can't afford a cock up otherwise it's over before it's begun. He must have practiced with the nitrogen. Where? On whom? Get Pop to check. And what about Cooper? Why would the doctor let the killer in?

Chad rubbed his eyes. A thought was nagging again. Something at Castlereagh, but what?

"Oh, shit."

Chad typed, hitting the keys hard. *How did he get out?*

*

Chad opened his eyes. "Bloody hell," he muttered, lifting his head from his folded arms. He was at the desk, his Mac open and his phone next to him. 6:45 a.m. He re-read his notes and unable to shed the sense of alarm from a few hours earlier, he opened his emails. Bugger Pop, he'd get hold of Lucy, she was a switched on cop. He hurriedly typed, requesting a meet at Castlereagh asap this morning. The reply was instant.

8 a.m. Okay? Is there a problem?

I'll explain when we meet. See you at 8.

Heading for the bathroom he texted Freddie.

Buddy, can you get one of your boys to pack my stuff and get it across to the Airbnb for me? Got an early morning meeting so I'll be at training afterwards. Hope that's okay, sorry to be a pain.

He put the phone on the ledge over the sink, then jumped into the shower. The hot water gushed over him, refreshing and cleansing. Jas, he needed to text Jas. Drying off he picked up the phone.

Morning, or should I say evening. Look don't worry about me I'll be okay. Freddie's looking after me.

His phone pinged. *That's what worries me. XX*

Chapter 29

Jas Carter sat in her blue BMW and swiped out of Chad's message. Freddie's looking after him, yeah, right. Reaching a decision, she clicked on her boss's number and held her phone to her ear, then waited. She'd parked at Sainsbury's on the Leeds outer ring road near Adel so that if he agreed to see her, she could get there sharpish. "Don't go to voicemail, come on, answer."

"Jas? What's up? I only saw you an hour ago, don't tell me we've had shit hit the fan in that time?" said DI Lee Wallace.

"Oh, hi, Boss, no, but I could do with a chat if that's okay?"

"Sure, fire away."

"If you don't mind, it'd be better to discuss it face to face."

"Sounds intriguing, can it wait till morning, I've got a parents' evening in a couple of hours at Hannah's school? Can't say I'm relishing it, but, hey."

"Not really, sir, it shouldn't take long it's just that, it's…"

"Come on, Jas, for Christ's sake, what's up?"

"It's, Chad, Boss." Jas listened to the silence at the other end of the line.

"You'd better come round," said Lee.

*

"Let me get this straight," Lee was perched on a stool in the kitchen. "Chad is helping the Australian Police with several cases in Sydney, but is doing so under duress, is that what you're telling me?"

Jas took a deep breath. "Not exactly duress, but he's got a DI out there leaning on him by saying the press are going to hound him if he doesn't help. He's got some journo tracking his every move and even Chad is admitting that he's struggling with his PTSD." She paused, then looked at Lee. "Boss, he fainted at a crime scene yesterday."

"Bloody hell, fainted? Shit. I'll ring him, or better still I'll call the DI and tell him to back off."

"Too late for that, Boss. I saw the New South Wales police on Twitter say that they're delighted that someone with Chad's experience is helping them with their investigations."

The kitchen door burst open and Lee's girls Hannah and Carrie hurtled in.

"We heard you talking about Uncle Chad, Dad, when's he coming home?"

"Not now, girls. Wait in the hall, I'll only be a minute."

Helen, Lee's wife, swept the children out of the kitchen then turned to Lee and Jas. "What's that about Chad?" she asked. "Is everything okay?"

"No, it's not." Lee stood and put his arm around Helen's waist. "He's got himself involved in some god-awful murders in Sydney and is struggling like hell with PTSD. If he's not careful, he'll end up having a complete breakdown."

"Yeah, I've read about those, they sound horrendous. I thought he was out there coaching Freddie for some charity game?" asked Helen.

"Yes, he is, but these cases seem to have hooked him in."

Jas saw Helen was watching her, a look of concern on her face. And something else.

"Only one thing for it," said Helen.

"And what's that?" asked Lee.

"You'll have to allow Jas some annual leave, I'm sure she has plenty owed, and she'll have to go out to Sydney and monitor Chad for us. He's our oldest friend and after everything he's been through nothing else will do. Freddie's hopeless and Chad's a liability. It'll be easier for Jas, a copper, to keep the Aussie police at arms' length."

Jas stared from Helen to Lee. Helen winked at her. What the actual? She'd never been further than Mallorca. Going over there wasn't part of the plan. I mean, shit, how do you even get there?

"Not as daft as it sounds," said Lee. "How about it, Jas, fancy a trip down under?"

"I dunno, Boss, I hadn't thought about it." As the words tumbled out of her mouth so the idea excited her. Why not? When would she get to visit Oz?

"What's your remaining annual leave entitlement?"

"Well, a few weeks, at least. I haven't had a break since… since Chad's wife died."

"Settled then," said Helen. "Leave it with me and I'll get Abi, my PA, to make the arrangements for you. I'd suggest we say nothing to Chad so he can't argue. Maybe give Freddie a call and let him know? Do you have his number, Jas?"

"Yeah, I have. I'll send him a text. Wow, I wasn't expecting this. When shall I leave?"

"Asap," said Lee. "Let's get your Visa sorted and get the first available flights."

Chapter 30

Lucy's afro was like a halo around her head and seemed to float in the breeze which made her instantly recognisable as Chad approached along Castlereagh Street.

"What's so urgent?" she asked.

"I've been thinking about those CCTV tapes and think we've missed something."

"Like what?"

"Like why our perp doesn't appear on those tapes on his way out. We know he could have gained access, perhaps hours before the killing, but he wouldn't hang around afterwards. It was around 9:30 a.m. so we should see him on the tapes after that. Unless you tell me different, no one on the team has spotted him?"

Lucy paused. "No, and you're right. He should appear minutes after 9:30 a.m. The tapes are back at Day Street. Anyway, we're here so we may as well see if they have copies. Let's go."

Chad followed as Lucy led him around the side of the building down a steep ramp and into the underground basement and car park. Chad paused as he entered. He breathed deeply and then exhaled, forcing aside the memory of another underground car park ten thousand miles away in Leeds where he'd come face to face with Angie's killer. A security office stood to the left as they entered, occupied by a guard who seemed to have modelled himself on Slash from Guns n' Roses. He wore an expression of bored cynicism like he was only doing this because his gigs had dried up. He examined Lucy's warrant card.

"We want to see the tapes from the day of the murders, please."

Slash considered the request. "You lot have been over these from thread to needle, but you're too late, anyway. Another copper took the original tapes for the whole twenty-four-hour period days ago. Sorry, mate, I can't help you."

"Oh, okay, sorry to have bothered you." Lucy turned to Chad. "Yeah, as I thought, they're back at the station."

Chad looked at Slash. "Excuse me?"

"Yeah?"

"How come this place isn't busier?"

"It's expensive, mate, and with the metro nearby who wants to drive to work? Why bother?"

"So, who uses it?" Chad looked towards the parking bays. "There are some cars here."

"Mainly people who work at the gym. Personal trainers who bring some of their own gear."

"What gym?"

Slash looked bemused, and pointed. "The door in the corner."

Chad followed Slash's outstretched arm. "Is it open to the public?"

"Yes, mate. There's a membership but early in the morning like now and after work it's heaving like a bar on Melbourne Cup Day."

"Does everyone have to go through the car park to get to the gym?"

"No, mate, there's stairs from the gym to the ground floor or they can use the elevator."

"Thanks, buddy. That's helpful."

"No worries."

Chad walked to the gym door that Slash had pointed out to them. No pass key or card was required, and the door opened onto a concrete corridor with a single glass door at the end, bearing the words Twenty-Four Seven Fitness Club in red lettering.

Chad asked Lucy, "Have you guys been here?"

"Yeah, we've interviewed all the trainers and eliminated them from the inquiry."

"Yeah, well, I wish you'd been clear about that at the briefings we've had," Chad couldn't keep the pissed off tone out of his voice. "No one mentioned a basement gym that doesn't show on CCTV." Chad looked around. "He goes from the fire escape to the gym, up the stairs and out into the foyer of the building."

"With a ladder and a nitrogen cylinder?"

"Maybe he's dumped those, or maybe they're still in the air vent. We should check that."

"Okay, I'll get someone to see what's there. Hang on, if he went into the foyer he'd show up on CCTV, wouldn't he?"

"Let's check."

Chad followed Lucy into the gym, which, as Slash had predicted, was heaving with sweaty bodies; running, lifting weights or cross-training. Chad felt tired just watching them.

"How do we get to the foyer?" Lucy asked a guy in a tee-shirt with Twenty-Four-Seven printed on and a set of weights as a motif.

"Door at the end, mate, then up the stairs."

Letting the gym door close behind him Chad climbed the concrete stairs where Lucy waited at the top. Opening the door, Chad saw they were outside the coffee bar some distance from the lifts.

"I'll bet you one hundred dollars there's no CCTV here," said Chad.

"I'll go check."

Chad waited as Lucy walked through the foyer and spoke to the security guard at the far end. From the way he was pointing and gesticulating, Chad knew he'd won his bet.

"You're right," said Lucy, shaking her head. "No CCTV here."

You've wasted a morning, thought Chad. It's obvious our guy wouldn't be obliging enough to appear on CCTV and you should have known about the gym. You're looking in the wrong place, Chad boy, looking in the wrong place. Wasting your own time and everyone else's. Sod it, focus on the why, focus on his motive.

Chapter 31

'Justice is the sum of all moral duty.'
William Godwin.

The anaesthetist is lying on the operating table. It'll be a novel experience for him being the patient. "Role reversal," I chuckle, although perhaps patient is the wrong choice of word. In more normal circumstances a patient on an operating table might expect to be in a pain-free zone created by the cocktail of chemicals calculated exactly by… the anaesthetist.

But he won't be getting an anaesthetic today.

'Kill the bastard, make him pay.' The whisper rattles through my brain.

Like my previous clients, the doctor lies prostrate, and begins the struggle that has become tediously familiar to me from my previous forays. First the physical, trying to loosen the bindings that are holding him fast and second the mental: comprehension. His struggles meet with the same lack of success as those of his co-conspirators. I've put his head on a pillow so he can watch the spectacle I'm going to provide. That he will have the lead role in my production is not yet clear to him. As he gives up the attempt to release himself, I note his eyes darting this way and that. It is a strange but inescapable truth that all my victims engage in this same exhibition. Searching. But for what? And why? Whatever it is, none of them have found it.

'Hurry up, don't waste time. Show him the photo.'

Ah, well. All good things, etcetera, etcetera.

I move from the head of the operating platform to the petrified medic. I place the photograph in front of his eyes. "Do you remember her?" He scans the image then screws his eyes tight shut, opens them again and stares at the picture. It's as if he feels that there may be redemption by giving me a correct answer. Into his eyes I see the recognition. He remembers and now he knows why he's here. Knowing, however, seems only to increase his distress. He wrenches and twists. Tries to raise his head, tries to scream. Fear and panic cause him to emit a tight screech. All to no avail.

'Slice him up.'

Next to the table is a metal tray on which are arranged the various tools of a surgeon's trade. Dissecting forceps, hinged forceps, tissue clamps, retractors – hand held and self-retaining, surgical scissors and, of course, scalpels. I pick them up and he watches me examine each and then replace it. I reach inside my jacket and add my instrument of choice to the tray. His eyes are bursting from their sockets.

There'll be no redemption today.

And no anaesthetic.

Four down.

Chapter 32

Chad smiled as Junior held open the door to the Airbnb. "Made yourself at home, I see," he said, looking past the young colossus.

"Yeah, mate, it's a flash place. Outdoor terrace with a barbie, fifty-two-inch TV and a games console, a couple of bedrooms and a kitchen. Man, I may move in here with you and give Mum some space, what d'ya reckon?"

"I reckon you couldn't afford half the rent, so you can bugger off."

"Worth a try," smiled Junior.

Chad followed Junior down the hallway and into the bright, airy lounge area. The sensations of space and light were fleeting as Chad felt his phone vibrating in his pocket, demanding his attention. Pulling it out he saw the screen was full. No sooner had one message landed than another fought for air space. Interspersed with the messages, he'd missed repeated calls from Pop, Andrea Byrne, Mel, Lucy.

"What the hell is it now? Jesus, I can't even get settled in." Chad noticed that Junior had put the TV on. "Put the news on for me, would you?"

The screen flickered as Junior found Channel Nine. There'd been another killing, but even that was competing for editorial space with shots of sizeable crowds gathering outside the Town Hall. Several were carrying home-made placards one of which he saw had the words 'Police where are you?' Another read 'Not safe in Sydney.' Guaranteed to create more tension, Chad reckoned, was a huge contingent of riot police.

In the TV studio, a reporter explained that the crowd had gathered in response to yet another murder. This time the police had found a doctor, dead in a mobile theatre unit.

"Uh, oh," muttered Junior. "This shit doesn't look good."

Chad took a deep breath as he felt a rising tide of panic welled in the pit of his stomach. He dialled Pop, but the call went straight to voicemail. No point in leaving a message. After trying Lucy with no luck, he finally got Mel.

"What's the story?"

"Yeah, looks like another one. Same M.O. Gory, ritualistic and utterly barbaric."

"I'm watching the news but I'm just getting shots of a mobile theatre unit somewhere. Where is it?"

"Randwick. Close to you."

"How do you know where I am?"

"Oh, I thought you were moving into an Airbnb in Bondi today, that's what Freddie…" her voice tailed off.

"Yeah, I have. I'll get an Uber and see you there, can you text me the address?" Chad took a couple of steps into the bedroom where Junior couldn't overhear. Stop being a dick about this, he thought. If they're happy, be happy for them. "Oh, and by the way," he said. "I have no problem with you and Freddie. Just saying, so you don't feel awkward."

"Thanks, Chad, it's something and nothing. Anyway, yeah, I'll text the address."

"Have you seen there's a protest at the Town Hall? There's a few there and the crowd's growing. To be fair, they have a point."

"Really? No, I haven't seen that. That's all we need. See you shortly."

Freddie had brought his luggage from the Sheraton, but unpacking would have to wait.

"Junior, I've got to go," said Chad, walking into the lounge. "I'll be back later. Where are the keys to this place?"

"On the table in the hall. Chad, can I stay here for a while?"

"Sure, yeah, no problem. In fact," Chad pulled out his wallet and extracted a few notes. "Would you put stuff in the fridge?"

"Yeah, sure, man, will do. Listen, Chad, you look a bit spooked. Are you gonna be okay?"

Chad looked at the earnest expression on Junior's face. Someone else watching out for him. Like father like son.

"I'll be fine, but thanks."

Chapter 33

Chad's Uber was grubby, in need of urgent repair and aesthetically the opposite of the Bentley. But it's presence was legitimate. The Prince of Wales Hospital stood modern, white and bathed in sunlight. The Uber got no closer than fifty metres to a pedestrian crossing at the glass covered entrance to the hospital such was the volume of reporters and TV crews, their numbers swelled by a significant police presence.

As Chad opened the car door a plethora of phones, mics and cameras immediately surrounded him. The noise generated by the melee made answering questions impossible, which suited him. What struck him, however, was the tone and attitude of the reporters. Maybe they'd sensed the mood of anxiety and terror that had surfaced at the Town Hall demonstration. Whatever, to Chad's eyes and ears there had been a substantive change. And not for the better.

He held up a hand and pushed his way through the jostling pack until a huge policeman unceremoniously thrust him forward. As he reached the hospital entrance, Chad saw Andrea amongst the throng. She caught his eye, and he saw her mouth the words "Call me" accompanied by the waving of her phone extended above her head. He nodded and added that to his mental to-do list.

Hospital administrators had attached the mobile theatre to the rear of the hospital, accessed through a set of double doors. A sign informed patients that the unit was a temporary measure for day surgery cases. This, it stated, would help deal with capacity in the aftermath of the pandemic and whilst one of the hospital's major theatres underwent a refurbishment. Chad stepped outside and inspected what looked like a series of shipping containers. A sign on the side said 'Day Surgery Unit.' The block was maybe twenty metres by twelve.

A ramp led to an open door where the forensics team were in full flow. Outside, leaning against the theatre wall, hair blowing in the breeze and his hands thrust in his jeans pockets stood Pop. Chad stopped when he saw him and said, "You look bloody awful, fella."

"Yeah, well, thanks for those helpful insights, Chad. Just what I need to speed the investigation along."

"How bad is it?"

"Well, if I thought you wouldn't pass out again, I'd say get yourself some protective kit, from the car there," Pop pointed to a squad car with its boot open. "Go inside and have a look. If you didn't enjoy the previous three, I can guarantee you won't like this one. The victim's name is Dr Tom Wise, an anaesthetist. I'm keeping my guys away, we'll just impede the forensic boys. We'll have the place to ourselves when Forensics leave."

Chad could feel the tension behind his eyes as he fought down the panic warnings, but looking at Pop made his own feelings pale by comparison. That the pressure was getting to him was to state the bleeding obvious. Hair a mess, big u-shaped black bags under his eyes and two days' stubble told their own story. Pop was struggling. "Have you seen the news coverage?" Chad asked. "The demo at the town hall is getting out of hand."

"Yep, seen it. The top brass summoned me and told me to wear a suit. After I've briefed the Deputy Commissioner, we're doing a presser at 6 p.m. tonight. It'd be helpful if we had some more firm leads other than just a ladder and a nitrogen cylinder. We've found those, by the way. In the ceiling over the fire escape. The rubber fragments are a match to the base of the ladders, so well done with that."

"Yeah, we need more. We need a break. I don't suppose your guys have found anything that links the victims yet, still drawing blanks?"

"No nothing, which is just plain weird. We can't find anything that connects the victims. All roads point in different directions. Either the perp is a random nut job or we are missing something."

Chad stared at Pop. Nothing to link them. Perhaps they were looking at the wrong things. But where should they be looking? Something was trying to push to the front of Chad's mind but he couldn't get it there. What was it? Anaesthetist, why was that important? Come on, think. Chad gave up. Whatever it was it, it needed time and space. Two commodities he didn't have. "Where's Mel, is she inside?"

"Yes, she is. Get your stuff on and join her. And stay bloody upright."

"Right," he said, "see you in a minute."

Once attired, Chad walked up the ramp to the door, put on his shoe coverings and stepped inside. He found himself at the rear of a reception area. Making his way towards a doorway, Mel emerged.

Her face mask muffled her voice, but he picked up her words. "Oh, hi Chad, follow me, are you okay?"

The theatre unit had connecting rooms. The reception led into a small anaesthetic bay which adjoined the operating theatre. Mel paused at the connecting door and asked again. "Are you sure you're going to be okay, it's another nightmare."

No, he wasn't bloody sure. "Yes," he said.

Technicians had ergonomically designed the operating theatre with every inch of room built for efficiency. They'd suspended circular light fittings from the ceiling on electronically controlled arms. Each fitting held a multitude of high intensity bulbs. With what Chad considered admirable attention to detail, they'd suspended a monitor over the operating table, next to which was a large computer that linked an assortment of other gadgets, wires and a blood pressure monitor. There were four forensic scientists blocking Chad's line of sight to whatever lay on the table.

"Excuse us, guys, could we look, please," said Mel.

Without a word the four crime scene investigators clad from head to toe in white, moved aside. Chad immediately wished they hadn't. Fighting for control, his legs wobbled, and he steadied himself against the wall. His mouth started watering and a need to retch was almost uncontrollable. He gulped some air, but it too tasted acidic.

The glare from the overhead lights enhanced a scene of total degradation. From nowhere, Edvard Munch's The Scream filled his head. But that was nothing compared to what lay on the operating table. A man, Chad presumed. Or at least the torso of one. It had undergone a series of amputations which were now symmetrically arranged on top of the body. The killer had removed both legs below the knee, and both arms at the elbow. These lay on the torso creating a kind of hashtag effect. The head, which rested precariously on the limbs, completed the scene. Scalpels and a large hacksaw lay discarded on blue sheets that the killer must have placed on the floor.

The SOCOs returned to their grim tasks. Chad followed Mel into the recovery room, then outside into the warmth of the afternoon. As the air hit him, Chad bent over and put his hands on his knees, like a late-night drunk leaving the pub, before emptying the contents of his stomach onto the ground.

"Told you that you wouldn't like it," said Pop. "Look, I'm getting the team together in an hour. I need you both there. I want to be crystal clear on all our current theories and lines of enquiry before my meeting with the Deputy Commissioner which might mean I keep my job for longer. We'll go through the whole thing from start to finish. I'll be very grateful for any ideas on the killer, the motive or his probable next steps. Oh, and Chad, clean yourself up."

Chapter 34

Chad asked Mel to drop him off in The Rocks. "I'm hoping the sea breeze will clear my head. Anyway, the walk will do me good."

There were plenty of tourists walking the quaint streets packed with bars and arty shops. The first foreign boats had docked here a couple of hundred years before. Chad sauntered along the pathway past the Park Hyatt hotel to Dawes Point, where the waves broke against the concrete and the breeze carried a salty taste of the sea. No cruise ships were in the harbour, so standing underneath the vast expanse of the Harbour Bridge, Chad had an uninterrupted view over the water to the Opera House.

He sucked in the air and closed his eyes, allowing the fog that had clouded his brain at the mobile theatre to lift. Anaesthetist. Why was that important? He allowed the question the space in his head to float unhindered. The wind rustled through his hair and the sun felt warm on his back. In his mind's eye he could see the boardroom at Castlereagh, then the dingy visa department. He pictured the ostentatious offices of the hospital where Dr Cooper died, and finally the mobile theatre. An answer shaped and formed itself in his mind. He probed and prodded looking for a flaw, and found none. That's it, he thought, that's what links them.

He looked out across the choppy, grey water. "Let's take the game to this bastard, my boy."

*

Chad dialled Andrea Byrne and waited.

"Hey, Chad, how's it goin'?"

Andrea had left the Prince Alfred hospital, thought Chad. The background noise had gone.

"Have you spoken to your contact?"

"Yeah, yesterday, he confirmed that when the killer shot the victims at Castlereagh, they were unconscious. That's what you wanted, right?"

"Yes, it was." That's something, thought Chad, but we've found the nitrogen cylinder and ladders which confirmed it, anyway. They were getting nowhere. "Andrea, we're going to change the rules of this game and start looking forward rather than backwards."

"What do you mean?"

"So far, this dude teases us with snippets of information about events that have already happened. I'm interested in what is going to happen. If he's the killer he'll know. If he's close to the killer he can find out," Chad paused. "And if he's a cop, he won't know 'cos the police are reacting to events that have happened. So whatever answer you get from Trevor will take us a couple of steps forward."

There was a silence on the line. A few seconds elapsed. "Yep, agreed," she concurred.

"Okay, when he calls you, tell him we won't part with any more information from our end, or confirm anything he tells you. That's over unless he can tell us if there's going to be any more victims. I need to know how many more the killer's planning."

"Why will he tell us that?"

"He's got nothing to lose by doing so. Just because we know there will be more doesn't mean who or when."

"So what use is that information?"

Chad weighed up the risks of trusting her. Too late not to, he decided.

"I have an idea about what links these victims. If I know how many more there'll be, that'll firm it up. Or at least suggest I'm on the right track."

"Right, I see," said Andrea. "And if he comes good, how do I know you'll keep giving me access to info ahead of the rest?"

"It's always me, me, me, isn't it, Andrea? For once try to see the bigger picture, and that this is far more important than you and your career," Chad paused, the wind picking up. "But yes, I'll give you more bits and pieces to keep you front and centre of the nation's consciousness."

"Okay, Chad, no need to get shitty. He'll call me later, I'm sure. It's his normal routine. Oh, while I've got you, you've left the Sheraton. I know you're hiding from my lot, but come on, Chad, where are you staying?"

"Ha, wouldn't you like to know? Anyway, let me know what Trevor says. Talk soon."

An incoming text prevented him from putting his phone in his pocket. Freddie.

Yo bro, how about dinner tonight? Booked the Chophouse. Btw I hear Junior's apartment sitting for you?

Yeah, he is, think I'll struggle to get him to leave. Thanks for sorting it for me. Oh, and thanks for delivering my luggage. What time have you booked dinner?

7:30 p.m.

Chapter 35

As Chad walked down the airless corridor, he could hear a swell of voices from the meeting room. Five minutes late, shit. He needed time alone with Pop before the press conference with the Deputy Commissioner.

"Ah, Chad, glad you could make it," Pop tapped his watch.

"Yeah, sorry I'm late, but look, Pop, I need ten minutes with you and Mel." Chad stood in the doorway and his foot drummed a nervous repetitive beat on the floor. He held Pop's stare, "Nice suit by the way."

"Thanks, cheeky bugger. Okay, Lucy, you take over. By the way, any luck on finding suppliers of the nitrogen cylinder, and anyone who's bought one?"

"No," replied Lucy. "Anyone can buy one online. It's a needle in a haystack."

"Christ," said Chad. "And the photo underneath Dr Cooper's body, have you identified everyone in it?"

"Yeah, we have. I've got the report here," José held up a brown folder.

"Okay, distribute copies and let's see if that takes us any further," said Pop, taking the folder and holding the door for Chad and Mel.

Chad headed down the corridor into an empty room on his left.

Pop took up a position against the wall, "What's up?"

"I didn't run it by you first but I've changed the rules of engagement with Andrea Byrne's contact."

"Oh yeah, why?"

"I've got an idea which might get us ahead of the game. We already know the info we're getting from whoever is talking to her. We need something we don't know."

"Go on. What's your idea?"

"As you know, I've been getting hung up over the risks the perp takes and reckon that he takes them because where he kills, the location, is critical. But why? Today, I looked at the crime scenes differently. What if it's not the place, but the activity that's important?"

Pop shuffled from foot to foot, Chad could see him assimilating the implications.

Chad wrote on the wipe board.

Recruitment – Visa - Health Administration – Anaesthetist -? -?

"What's that telling me?" asked Pop.

"Follow my logic here. I apply for a job but need a visa to get it. The job is in a hospital and the application handled by a hospital administrator. Then I work with an anaesthetist." Chad paused looking from Pop to Mel. "Who am I?"

Their thinking energised the silence. It was powerful and charged. Pop and Mel stared at the board and worked through what he'd told them. Then Mel slammed her hand on the desk.

"You're a surgeon, aren't you?" shouted Mel.

"Bang on," agreed Chad. "I'm a surgeon."

Pop stared at the words on the board. "But a visa suggests you're an overseas doctor, so, is a surgeon the killer?"

"No," said Chad. "More likely the next victim."

"Right. I like your thinking. But why is the killer giving us these pointers? Does he want to be caught?"

"No," said Chad. "It's the whole point of a breadcrumb trail, he lays it so we can follow it. He knows how this ends. We don't."

Pop stroked his chin. "What about that photo from the hospital?

Maybe our next victim is on there. Can you two go through José's report and I'll call you later? I've got to leg it and hope I survive the presser." Pop handed Chad the folder. "Feels like we might get somewhere at last."

*

"Two of these are surgeons," said Chad looking at the folder. "This is the overseas doctor." Chad passed Mel the one-page summary.

She read from the sheet. "Dr Theo Nefeli. A Greek national, came to Australia in 1999, worked from 2001 to 2003 at the Royal Prince Alfred. Retired in November 2003, returned to Greece where he died in March this year. Two months ago. No cause of death on here."

Chad shuffled the papers in the folder. "Right. So, the perp leaves a photo under Dr Cooper's body. To what end? We're assuming it's part of the breadcrumb trail in which case, the next victim is going to be the remaining doctor on the photo." Chad paused and lifted four sheets from the file. "Dr Jim Doyle, still alive and living in New South Wales. We'd better bring José and the team up to speed and get Doyle interviewed and some protection arranged." He looked at Mel. "Would you mind doing that? I'm meeting Freddie shortly for dinner. Maybe we could meet up with you later for a drink?"

"Yes, of course."

Chad wondered why Mel was staring at him. "What's up?" he asked.

"Oh, nothing," She smiled. "Let me know where and when. See you later."

Chapter 36

Chad checked the message from Freddie. The Chophouse on Bligh Street. Yep, this was it. He opened the double doors and saw the place was a reconditioned warehouse. It had a high ceiling, lots of steel and brick, visible air pipes and a wooden floor. Very much en vogue, he thought. The place was bustling with diners. Chad couldn't see Freddie which was unusual. Freddie's presence in any restaurant or bar meant that even if you couldn't see him, you'd hear him. Chad thought he'd get a drink and wait. Between him and the bar was a woman with her back to him sitting on a stool. Wearing a sleeveless red satin dress, her black hair tumbled over her shoulder and the shafts of light from overhead chandeliers glittered on it, creating a silk-like quality. The skin on the woman's arm was smooth, chocolate coloured, and glowed. Chad felt a small shiver as her lips in silhouette parted to sip her drink. Wow. Just wow. Then she turned to face him.

"Hello, Hoppy," said Jas.

Chad knew that his mouth was hanging open, but could do nothing about it. Questions competed for space. What's she doing here? How did she get here? Had he missed a text where she'd told him she was coming? An emotion he hadn't felt for so long pushed aside the jumble of noise in his brain. Pure joy. A tear rolled down his cheek as he stood, gormless and spellbound. He felt her soft fingers touch his face and brush the tear away.

"Bloody hell, Chad, give over with the crying, or you'll get me started and my mascara will run. I thought you'd be pleased to see me?"

At last, some words took shape. "You look amazing," he stuttered.

"Well, thank you. You're looking fab yourself. And you're tanned, I'm jealous."

A waiter approached, confirmed their booking, and led them to their table. Chad, recovering some composure, ushered Jas before him and took the opportunity of watching the gentle sway of her body as she made her way between the diners. An opportunity he noted, that a group of rugby players on an adjoining table also appreciated.

Chad leaned across the table and gazed into her eyes. "Come on, then," he said. "I'm dying to know it all, so leave nothing out. From start to finish please."

"Okay, okay. Can we get a drink first? Anyway, the answer is two words."

"Go on."

"Lee and Freddie." Jas smiled then added, "Well, no. Three: Helen, Lee and Freddie."

"That's four," said Chad.

"Pedant," she laughed.

Chad beckoned the waiter then looked at Jas, "Fizz?"

She raised an eyebrow, "What else?"

*

"And that was it," explained Jas. "Freddie did the rest. He refused to let me pay, then got me upgraded to First Class. I had imposter syndrome sitting there sipping champagne but loved every minute. Freddie sent Odd Job to pick me up from the airport in a Bentley and booked me a suite at the Sheraton. You've got a lot to live up to."

Chad smiled. "Yeah, looks like I have."

"Anyway, enough about me. The reason I'm here is to monitor

you. I want to know how you are. And don't bullshit, you know I can see through that from a mile away."

"I promise, I won't."

"Fainting at a crime scene, Chad?" she stared at him over the rim of her glass, one eyebrow raised. "And don't give me those doe eyes. Anyway, talk me through where you're up to solving these awful murders, and how you're coping with the press attention you're getting. Again, no bullshit."

"Yeah, I'll talk you through it. I'm interested in your take on things. What else?"

"The Freddie news, of course. He said he had something to share. I'm intrigued. Can I have a guess?"

"You can, but I bet you a grand you'll never get the answer. And is that it? That's a lot of talking from me, I'll bore you rigid."

"You won't, I'm all ears. Anyway, I'll be happy glugging away on the champagne, I've got a taste for it."

*

"And there you are," said Chad. "You're up to speed."

When the last of the plates had gone, Chad leaned back and sipped his Taittinger. "One bottle is never enough. Oh, Jesus, that sounds like something Andrea Byrne would say."

"She's the journo with the contact, right?"

"You have been paying attention."

Jas twirled her champagne flute between her fingers. "Freddie Jackson a father, who knew? You're right I'd have never guessed that."

"He's taking to it like a duck to water. Twenty years too late, but I suppose better late than never."

Jas laughed.

He loved her laugh. He loved making her laugh. How good was this?

"Let's hope you're right about what links these murders. Clever that you worked out that it's the jobs not just the places."

"Yeah, let's hope so. It doesn't move us that much further forward, but it's a start."

"That's why coppers like you."

"How do you mean? I'm a pain in the arse for them as you know."

"Yeah, but you have ideas that make us look good. I bet that guy, Pop, is telling his boss right now that it was all his idea."

Chad's phone pinged. Mel.

We're in Palmer and Co, a cool bar near Tank Stream Way. See you there?

"Fancy meeting Freddie and Mel, or are you tired?"

"Hell no, I'm not tired. I can't wait. Let's do it."

Chad paid and led Jas out into the cooling night air. She slipped her arm through his. It seemed a long time since anyone had done that and he pulled her closer to him. They walked in what he felt was companionable silence, taking a right on Hunter then crossing Pitt Street. Palmer and Co was down a tiny alley and guarded by an enormous security guard.

"Can I see your ID, miss?"

Jas pulled her passport from the clutch bag she was carrying.

"Thank you," he said, handing her back the ID. "No, it's okay, sir, I don't need to see yours."

"Ha," shrieked Jas. "You must be well old. Lol."

They entered down a stone staircase into a cavernous underground vault. It looked like a bar from the American prohibition days and seemed somehow familiar.

"This place is like Freddie's bar at home," said Jas.

Chad stopped. "That's it, of course," he said. "Typical Freddie, he's pinched the idea. I remember when I went to his bar in Leeds, he told me he'd copied the theme. This must be it."

They found Freddie and Mel wedged behind a small table next

to a well-stocked bar.

Freddie stood and enveloped Jas in a bear-like hug. "Hey, babe, how's the best-looking cop in the world doin'? Wow, if only they all looked as good as you, I might be nice to them."

"I doubt that, but good to see you, Freddie. You're looking great. And thanks for everything, I wouldn't have got here without you. You must be Mel? Chad's been telling me all about you."

"Oh no, has he?" laughed Mel.

"All good, I promise."

Chad ordered drinks while Jas grabbed two stools. He caught Mel's eye and noted a quizzical expression. She looked at Jas then back to Chad, then smiled and raised her glass. "Here's to you," she said.

*

Chad leaned on the balcony rail of his bedroom in the apartment. Away to his right he could see the beach bathed in moonlight and the gentle sound of the waves breaking from the ink black ocean reached his vantage point. Jas would be back in her hotel by now. He sipped his whisky. It was for the best. The breeze ruffled his hair and he caught the light touch of rain in the air. 'But boy, oh boy," he muttered, "I wish she was here right now."

Chad turned, walked into the apartment and closed the glass doors against the rain. Junior sprawled on the settee playing FIFA 22 on the games console.

"How'd it go today, Chad?"

"Not good, Junior, not good."

"I saw it on the news, man, I mean, why kill a doctor? I don't get it."

Chad sat down and sipped his whisky. "He was the next in a sequence."

"A sequence, like what?"

"The killer is picking off his victims in order, they're not random, but we can't see quite where it's leading at the moment."

"Yikes, Chad, so there'll be more, right?"

"I think you'd better bugger off home, Junior. I don't need a load of grief from your parents."

Junior heaved himself upright and reached for his phone.

"Have you got everything you came with?" asked Chad.

"I just need to find my keys." Junior began tapping on his phone.

"Well, you won't find them unless you look for them, rather than texting someone."

Junior looked at Chad and chuckled. "God, man, you're so old. I'm not texting. My phone is finding the tag on my keys. Jesus, how do you get by?"

A beeping noise identified their location. Junior walked out of the lounge then called back. "Can I come round tomorrow?"

"Sure, Junior, of course." Chad heard Junior collect his keys from the table in the hall.

Chapter 37

Andrea Byrne pulled on her cigarette and waited. She knew he'd call; it was just a question of when. On reflection, she reckoned Hilton was right. All Trevor did was give them titbits of info that the police already had. How he'd react to the new arrangement would be interesting. Her phone vibrated on the table in front of her. Well, here goes.

"Good evening, Andrea, how are you?"

"I'm good thanks. How are you?"

"I'm well, thanks for asking. Did Chad Hilton mention the photograph?"

"No, but the murder of the guy in the theatre unit has occupied everyone."

"Yes, to an extent it has."

Was that a laugh? Was Trevor laughing?

Andrea waited, she had to get the next bit right. "Look, Trevor, Hilton and the police don't think they're getting any value out of your contact. In fact, you need to tell them things they don't already know, or they'll stop the dialogue and close the comms line."

She listened hard but heard nothing. The silence felt ominous.

"What exactly would they want to know?"

Andrea plucked up courage. "How many more killings will there be?"

"And why would we tell you that?"

"Because you've nothing to lose by doing so."

The silence stretched into the night.

"I'll call you back." The line went dead.

Why, wondered Andrea, had Trevor said 'we' rather than 'he'?

She'd opted for a chilled bottle of a New Zealand Sauvignon Blanc. Change as good as a rest. The bottle was two-thirds empty when the phone vibrated again.

"Hello?"

"Andrea, we've agreed that we may be forthcoming with the material you requested, but… not yet. We believe that we've been more than generous with our information, but have received little or nothing in return. So, we'd like to know what Hilton thinks is linking these killings. It'll be Hilton joining the dots not the police. Oh, and what do they think of the photograph from the Conway? We hope that was of interest, but we'd like to know. Get that information, Andrea, and we'll answer your question. The ball is in their court."

"Okay, I'll ask."

Chapter 38

Chad checked his watch. He'd set off early and taken the bus to Bondi Junction then booked his Uber from there, because quick witted journos would be happy to flash some cash at the driver in return for Chad's pickup point. His stomach knotted, and he felt the familiar throbbing and pressure behind his eyes as he saw the TV crews and reporters camped outside the Day Street cop shop. A few hardy souls waving placards had joined them. It's a serious business this protesting lark, he thought. Up early, stay late, shift changes in between. Too much like hard work.

Climbing out of the cab he faced the reporters and tried to look calm. "Guys, I've nothing to add to what the Deputy Commissioner and Detective Inspector Murray told you last night. I've no comment to make. Now could you let me through, please?" They made room for him to walk into the foyer.

"You survived the presser then?" said Chad.

Pop stood on the staircase. "For the time being."

He had replaced the suit with a more familiar shirt. Coconut trees against a blue background.

"The Deputy Commissioner can't be associated with failure so he'll throw several of us under the bus to avoid that situation arising. Mind you, if we catch this bugger, he'll be front and centre for that press conference with yours truly nowhere to be seen. Any news?"

"Yeah, Andrea's contact said he'll tell us how many more killings there'll be but in return wants to know if we've joined the dots."

"Why would we tell him that?"

"We won't. But if we make him think we're further behind him than we are, then we've bought some time. He'll be calling Andrea again today so you need to decide what to tell her. Say nothing and my guess is that will be the end of the trail and we'll hear nothing more. Give him something and we keep the dialogue going and find out how many more victims he has in mind. Oh, and he wants to know what we made of the photograph."

"Let me think about that," said Pop. "Anything else?"

"No. Mel was briefing the team about the doctor in the photo who seems the obvious next target."

"Good, let's see what we've got." Pop opened the door to the briefing room. The team were already there and the mixed fragrance of various deodorants joined the bustle of activity and nervous energy. Chad saw that at least two still had wet hair from hurried showers.

Pop rapped a pen on a desk. "Right, guys, thank you. First, anything linking Dr Wise, the anaesthetist, to the other victims?" He looked around the group. "Don't tell me, let me guess. Nothing, nada?"

"No, Boss, nothing yet," said Dimi.

Pop stepped to his left and picked up a marker pen. "Chad has been saying that place is important to the perp. Yesterday evening he went a step further which provides us with something else to consider. Chad?"

"Oh, okay," Chad took the marker from Pop and turned to the expectant team. "You know about Dr Jim Doyle, right? But do you know why him?"

"No. Chad," said Lucy, "just that we need to get him interviewed pronto and subject to Pop's approval, some protection,"

"Okay." Chad turned to the board and wrote ACTIVITY in capitals and underlined it. "I want you to disregard the places our victims died for a moment and instead consider the activity that happens in them." Still facing the board Chad called out, "Medics4U, what do they do?"

"Recruitment," shouted Lucy. Chad wrote the word on the board.

"Lee Street Immigration Department?"

"Visas." They were getting the hang of this.

Chad wrote Hospital Administration and then turned to the group. "Which leaves us with an operating theatre. And apart from anaesthetics what other activity happens in an operating theatre?"

In unison the team shouted, "Surgery."

"Exactly."

José waved his hand in the air.

"Yes, José?"

"You think this guy Jim Doyle could be the next victim?"

"Yes, I do. He's the logical choice."

The group looked at the words on the board and Chad could tell they were checking to see if the theory held up.

José stood. "But Doyle's an Aussie. He doesn't need a visa."

"Agreed, but the overseas doctor in the photograph died a couple of months ago so we think Dr Doyle is the substitute."

"Okay, right, I get it."

Pop had perched on the end of a table and now stood. "It's the best we've got to go on. Lucy, can you organise for Doyle to be interviewed and a protection detail, please. Find out if he knew the other victims."

"What's up, Dimi, you look confused?" asked Chad.

Dimi scratched his head. "What's this about? I mean, what's he trying to say? Why is the perp doing this? It seems like he wants the story told."

"You're right, Dimi. The perp wants vindication, it's a narrative that he wants out there, in the news, on everyone's lips. He wants the headlines not about him, but about the story. The breadcrumb trail is his means of whetting his audience's appetite. We haven't found the principal plot line yet, but we will."

"Okay," said Pop. "Let's get to it."

*

Chad grabbed a coffee from Starbucks after the briefing before taking another Uber to training. With not long to go till the match the press coverage was ramping up and consequently his players were taking proceedings more seriously. No one wanted to look a dick on the night. The fitness of the guys had improved in the last few days. "Not for you though, Chad, boy. Not for you," he muttered. "That's a bridge too far."

His phone started buzzing. "Yeah, Pop, what is it?" Chad held his phone close to his ear so that he could hear over the squeal of the gulls.

"Been thinking about what we should tell Byrne's contact about the extent to which we've joined the dots."

"And?"

"I reckon we say that while the photograph is of interest, of equal interest is why he takes risks, which lead us to believe that the places are important to him. I don't think we should mention anything about the activities."

"Okay, Pop, I agree. If he thinks we are a little further back than we are, it'll make him believe he's got time. If we get a bit of luck, we may lift him as he tries to get at Dr Doyle."

"Righto, you give Byrne a ring and tell her that."

"She'll want something she can print, Pop, she does nothing for free."

"What d'ya reckon?"

"Let her lead with the photograph. Something like, the police are following leads from a photograph left at one of the crime scenes. That should keep her happy without it being too problematic for us."

"Yeah, okay, go with that. I'll manage the fallout from the rest of the media."

Chad clicked Pop's call off and dialled Byrne.

"Hi, Chad, what have you got for me?"

"I'm very well and thank you for asking."

"You said it yourself, Chad, time's money, so I thought I'd cut the pleasantries."

Chad smiled. "Okay, the locations of the murders are important to the killer. That's why he takes risks, because the places are a part of the story. That's as far as we've got."

"Places where he kills are important to him?"

"Yep, that's what we think."

"Doesn't sound much, but I'll tell him and let you know what he says. What can I print?"

"Me, me, me again, Andrea."

"Always. Come on, what can I print?"

"You can tell your public that we found a photograph at one of the crime scenes and are actively pursuing some leads that it has given us."

"That's it? Can't you tell me what these leads are?"

"No, sorry, that's confidential."

"Jesus, Chad, this is hard going."

"I'm sure you'll make it sound of earth-shattering importance by the time it's on the front page of The Globe. And it'll keep Andrea Byrne's name up in lights which is all that matters, right?"

"You're a quick learner, Chad, I'll give you that. I'll call you when I've spoken to Trevor."

"Remember, we want him to keep his end of the deal. How many more killings? Earn your corn, Andrea, get us the information."

*

Andrea pressed the phone to her ear to muffle the sound of the traffic. "That's what Hilton told me," she said. "The killer takes risks because place is important to him."

"That's it?" asked Trevor.

"Yeah, that's it."

The traffic noise seemed louder as Andrea listened to the silence down the line.

Trevor's voice then filled the vacuum. "Two."

"Pardon? What d'ya say?"

"I said two, Andrea. There'll be two more deaths."

Chapter 39

'The dead cannot cry out for justice.
It is a duty of the living to do so for them.'
Lois McMaster Bujold.

I end the call with Byrne, put my phone in my pocket then gaze out of the van window to the endless tumult of purple and white-tipped waves that roll and swell to the horizon. There's a tanker in the distance, the size of a matchstick, charting its course to who knows where. The clouds chase it towards the dying sun.

Today is my day off, and I have retreated to my safe space. I rented the house for this purpose. Down time, a place to re-charge my batteries and take stock. I open the door of the van and step out. From here the only other house is at the end of a deserted sandy track nearly one kilometre away. Nothing moving. It had taken time to find the property I needed, but the wait was worth it. I lock the van then walk along the side of the house and let myself into the kitchen. My footsteps echo as I walk through the empty rooms. My only furniture is a wicker rocking chair, placed in the front window of the property. Sitting in my eyrie, on the top of the cliff, overlooking the ocean. Wonderful.

"So far, so good." My voice echoes off the walls and reverberates around me.

Then the whisper. '*Yeah, but the hard part's yet to come. Don't fuck it up.*'

I sit rocking gently and remember that it was in exactly this spot three months ago that I had reached my decision. The anniversary of my mother's death. I can picture the day. Sunny, but the wind had risen and whipped dust and leaves onto the window. As I concluded my deliberations, I had wondered how far down my daisy chain of targets I'd get before the police cottoned on and I'd have to end the trail and disappear. I was prepared for that eventuality.

But that hasn't happened and my campaign for justice continues uninterrupted. I rock back in the chair and smile. Complete vindication. The system failed to deliver justice, so I have rectified that situation.

'Not finished yet, though. Don't fail me.'

Way below and far away from the shore a huge purple-hued wave is building, plunging then rising and gathering momentum. The waves usually calm me, but not today. Today, I feel a sense of unease. Hunter and hunted believe that the actions they take and the lies they tell are necessary to achieve their goals. The ends justify the means. I reflect on what Byrne has told me. They think the locations are important.

And that's why I'm uneasy.

Because I know they're lying. I know they understand the correlation between place and activity and think they know who the next victim will be. I smile. I know they are seeking to guard the doctor from the photograph. Ha, they've found the wrong tree and are barking up it. More fools them. If they'd done their job correctly in the first place all those years ago, then they wouldn't find themselves in their current predicament.

The wave has picked up pace and swallowed smaller swells to make an enormous roller heading towards the rocks.

So, why lie? I ruminate on that thought and explore its connotations in my mind.

'They're devious lying bastards. All of them.'

The answer is quick to arrive. They are trying to buy time. To make me believe they are further behind in the chase than they are. Lulling me.

The tumult crashes onto the rocks shooting white spray and spume high into the air, then the water settles into an effortless ebb and flow on the sand.

They're buying time, but that commodity, or lack of it, is also my biggest issue. There are two more criminals to whom I must deliver justice. The closer Hilton is getting to me the more hurried my planning becomes and therefore the greater the chance of error. I must rectify that.

I've told them there'll be two more deaths. Whilst accurate when I said it, now I know they've lied to me I feel within my rights to change the number as I see fit. As I contemplate my next move in this elaborate game, another idea leaps into my mind. I inspect it, examine it and test it. Oh yes, that is delicious and it'll slow them down alright. I'll keep that one back for a while. I chuckle. Being Chad Hilton isn't going to be a lot of fun.

In the distance a wave is building.

Chapter 40

Chad sat on the balcony of the Airbnb and checked his phone. 10:45 p.m. Jas had returned to the Sheraton struggling with jet lag. He hadn't wanted to suggest she stay in Bondi, but he'd felt equally uneasy about offering to take her back to the hotel. Christ, what did he want from this? Something, yes. But what? How did he know she wanted something too? Was it what he wanted?

"Bloody idiot, pull yourself together. You're not a kid. Talk to her, tell her how you feel. Have an adult conversation. What's wrong with you?"

He stared into the night sky. That was the million-dollar question, of course. How did he feel? He ran his hands through his hair. Until you can answer that to yourself, he thought, you can't talk to her. His neck muscles tensed. This is hopeless. You're allowed to be attracted to someone else, dickhead. Angie wouldn't mind.

"Oh, yes, she bloody would."

He opened his MacBook. "Come on, do something useful," he muttered. He skimmed his notes and looked for anything that seemed out of place. Hang on. Two more killings, Trevor had said. One's the doctor, but who's the second? We haven't given that any thought. Chad scrolled back and checked the photo of the wipe board in the briefing room. Visa, okay, that's Janice Short. Recruitment, Dan Hodges. Administration, Frank Cooper, Anaesthetics, Tom Wise, and yes, we think the next one's a surgeon. But what comes after that?

Chad scratched his head. "A doctor applies for a visa, gets a job in a hospital via a recruitment agency and then works in surgery. It must happen all the time, so why this mayhem?" Chad stood, went inside and poured a large Highland Park. He let a drop of water from a bottle on the table fall into the tumbler and watched the ripples it created in the amber malt. No finer sight.

What set of circumstances could have propelled our killer into seeking this… This what? Revenge? This felt different to revenge, Chad reflected. Different how? Chad sipped his drink and allowed the warmth of the liquid to trickle over the back of his throat.

He looked at his reflection in the glass doors leading to the balcony, the lights beyond emitting a flickering neon glow. The whisky seemed to unlock his mind. If someone wants revenge, he can carry it out anywhere, and its satisfaction is personal, it doesn't matter if anyone else knows. This is bigger than a personal vendetta. What then? Chad twirled the single malt around the glass, the amber and honey colours glowing in the dark. It's about justice, he thought. He's dispensing justice. And people need to see that justice is done.

The perp doesn't believe justice was done, and the wrongdoer got away with it. He's casting himself as judge and jury. But why? What could have happened that links the victims together? Who comes after a doctor?

Chad put down his drink on the table and picked up his wallet, as an idea formed. Pulling out the various dollar bills, he shoved them into his jeans pocket and shook the wallet upside down. A business card fell onto the table. Chad picked it up and held it to the light. Emblazoned in blue lettering was the Medics4U motif, underneath which was printed Richard Ashcroft, Chairman. Chad clicked on his phone and keyed in the UK phone number from the card as he made a mental calculation to determine the time back home. Yeah, just after lunch, should be fine.

"Hello, this is Richard Ashcroft." Clipped Surrey accent.

"Hi, Mr Ashcroft, my name is Chad Hilton and I'm a psychologist helping the police in Sydney, Australia, with their investigations into a series of murders here. Including the murder of Dan Hodges, your CEO, and his board of directors at Medics 4U."

"Yes, yes. I've seen your name in the press reports. Terrible business. Shocking. I don't mind telling you we're working flat out to hold things together."

Chad wondered why people internalised something like this. This guy sounded more upset about his increased workload than about the deaths of his colleagues. How bloody inconsiderate of the killer not to think of Richard bloody Ashcroft.

Ashcroft was still talking. "Thankfully, I have persuaded our UK Managing Director to spend six months there and recruit a new Australian CEO. He leaves tomorrow. Now, how can I help?"

Chad cleared his throat and tried to keep his irritation out of his voice, "How well did you know Dan Hodges?"

"Very well. I've known him for many years. He worked as a recruitment consultant in London when I was CEO and then opened our Sydney office. That was," he paused, "twenty years ago, now."

"Mr Ashcroft, we've linked the killings here to something that happened in the past, specifically the placing of a doctor into a hospital. Would you know anything about that?"

"Well, as you'll know, that is our line of business. We place many healthcare professionals into hospitals."

Slippery as a fish.

Chad tried to tie him down. "Did anything ever go wrong?"

The silence down the line seemed to stretch over the vast space between them. Chad waited.

"I assume you'll be referring to Dr Nefeli? But none of that was our fault."

Nefeli, thought Chad. The Greek doctor who'd died two months ago.

"That's right," Chad agreed. "What can you tell me about Dr Nefeli?"

"This was, I don't know, perhaps eighteen or more years ago," said Ashcroft. "There were some complaints made regarding Nefeli's competence, and a hospital administrator informed our office that an inquiry was being undertaken. He wanted us to confirm that we had carried out all the requisite background checks on Nefeli, including ensuring his qualifications were bona fide and his references exemplary. Anyway, cutting a long story short, after a rather tense few months, the investigation into Dr Nefeli was closed. We heard nothing further."

"Had you carried out all the requisite checks?"

Chad detected a slight hesitation.

"Without going into the technical machinations of the recruitment process, it is sometimes difficult when recruiting from one country into another to ensure we've dotted every 'i' and crossed every 't'. A qualification valid in one country, for example, may have less merit in another. The ultimate responsibility lies with the Immigration Department and the employer. They must be satisfied the doctor is legally entitled to work in Australia and is qualified for the role."

"So," said Chad, "did Medics4U make the checks?"

"As far as I'm aware, they did." A politician's answer. "The administrators found no wrongdoing."

"I see," said Chad. "But just because the inquiry was closed, doesn't mean errors didn't occur, does it?"

"Yes, it means just that. They brought no charges of any sort before the inquiry was closed," said Ashcroft. "You seriously believe the Dr Nefeli enquiry is linked to these awful murders?"

"We don't know. We are just following up any leads we have. Anyway, thanks for your time. I won't keep you any longer."

"No trouble at all, Mr Hilton. I hope you catch this monster soon."

"Oh, one last thing," said Chad.

"Yes?"

"Who carried out the enquiry?"

"I don't know. As I told you, an administrator at the hospital contacted us at the start, but we heard nothing further."

"Okay, thanks."

Chad watched the screen on his phone change to black as Ashcroft hung up.

Motive, he thought. We've got a bloody motive.

Chapter 41

"About bloody time too," Pop shouted with a broad smile on his face. "We've got something to go on. Well done, Chad, mate." He turned to the wipe board and wrote MOTIVE in capitals. "It looks like our resident nut job," Pop paused, looked over his shoulder and winked at the group, "no, not you, Chad… the killer."

Chad shrugged, raised his eyebrow at Mel, then chuckled with the rest of the team. Pop cracking funnies seemed light years away from where they'd been only yesterday.

Pop continued, "Our resident nut job has a grudge against a bunch of people who were all part of an investigation into claims of potential negligence against Dr Nefeli during his time as a surgeon at the Royal Prince Alfred. They proved nothing, but someone thinks there was wrongdoing. Maybe he's harboured a grudge and has decided now is the time to exact his revenge."

Chad raised his hand.

"Yes, Chad, something to add?"

"This isn't about revenge," said Chad. "Revenge is too petty. Granted, murders often have retribution as their motive, but not these. He wouldn't have taken the risks if it was simply revenge. Our killer wants everyone talking about this, sitting up and taking notice. That's because this is about justice, rectifying a wrong. And he must see justice done, hence the elaborate staging."

"Right, thanks, Chad." Pop addressed his officers. "I want that inquiry reviewed pronto, the names of the complainants against Nefeli, and where they are now. Lucy, can I leave that with you?"

"Yes, Boss."

"Dimi, get in touch with the Greek authorities and find out everything you can about Nefeli. What happened when he left Australia in 2003 and how did he die? Okay?"

"No probs."

"Have we got a team with Dr Doyle? I don't want anyone to get within one hundred metres of him without us knowing. Clear?"

"All done, Boss. Security detail attached and a strong police presence at his home," said José.

"Chad, two more killings, right? Doyle's one. Who's the second?"

"I don't know. Have you guys have identified everyone in the photograph?"

"Yeah, we have, but we don't have the resources to protect them all," said José.

"I understand that, but have you interviewed them and carried out risk assessments?"

"Not yet. We've only had the photo for twenty-four hours."

"Fair enough," said Pop. "The doctor looks like the first target, so we'll stick with him, but let's identify and interview everyone else on the photo within the next twenty-four hours. Right, anything else? Mel, thoughts?"

"I think Chad's assessment of this being about justice is correct. However, and this won't be popular, but you need to hear it. Worldwide, in eighty-five per cent of cases with 'justice' as the motive, the perp turned out to be a cop or someone involved in law enforcement."

Feet shuffled and hooded eyes cast wary glances. "Well, that's a cheery thought," observed Pop. "Back here 6 p.m., please"

Chad considered the stats Mel had put forward. Eighty-five per cent. That's massive. He'd resisted the idea that the killer was a cop but maybe he needed to revisit it.

Mel interrupted his reverie. "Hey," she said. "I like Jas, she's lovely. You two seem to get along great. Where's your head with that situation?"

"There isn't a situation. Although I kind of wish there was," Chad smiled. "My head's a mess already, but," he paused, "yeah, I like her."

"That's great. I think she'll be good for you. Anyway, maybe see you later?"

"Of course, yes. Catch you later."

Chapter 42

Chad turned the key in the lock and pushed the door open. Voices from the lounge said Junior was still in situ and had Jas for company. He'd spoken to her earlier, and they'd agreed that they'd get a microwave meal – a 'Poppety-Ping' as Jas had put it, rather than yet another restaurant meal. "I'll play FIFA with Junior, it'll be nice to get to know him," she'd said.

Chad walked through into the lounge. "Good day?" he asked.

"We've had a fab day, haven't we?" Jas replied.

"Yeah, mate, I've been showing Jas around Bondi, the bits the tourists don't see." Junior was in his familiar recumbent position on the long settee. "We got a selection of stuff for dinner, mate, some Thai, some Chinese and some Indian. Take your pick."

"And do I take it you'll be joining Jas and I for dinner?"

Junior looked sheepish. "If that's okay with you guys? Yeah, thanks, that would be cool."

Chad put his sunglasses on the coffee table and emptied his pockets of phone, wallet and keys. "Won't your mum be wondering where you are?" asked Chad. "And are we expecting your dad, Junior, is he coming round?"

"Nah. Mum says she's glad of the apartment to herself, and Dad reckons he's got something on tonight."

Right, thought Chad. I need a more direct approach to get Junior to go home.

Junior hauled himself upright. "How's the case going, Chad? Did my nitrogen stuff check out?"

"It did, Junior, thanks. Yeah, and I gave you a name check with the coppers."

"Ha, that's cool. Are you any closer to catching this bloke?"

Chad walked to the fridge and grabbed a beer. "Anyone else want one?"

Jas shook her head.

"Yeah, I'll have one, if that's okay?" said Junior.

Thank God, I didn't have kids, Chad thought. "I think we're getting closer but not near enough," he handed a beer to Junior. "Have you got any other little gold nuggets you can give me Junior? What with that nitrogen stuff you've got a lot to live up to."

"Not really, mate. But me and Jas have been chatting about it today and I'm trying to apply what you said about logic to the sitch."

Chad smiled, "And did you get anywhere?" He caught Jas's eye. She winked.

"Well," said Junior sitting upright and running a hand over his hair to straighten the braids. "I've been trying to fathom how the bloke carries out the attacks without getting caught. Logically, he should have been by now. How he gets away with it tells me what sort of bloke he is."

"Really?" Chad took a pull on his beer. "Let's hear it, Junior."

"Let's think about it this way. Who can get into places other people can't?"

Chad decided that Junior's question was rhetorical, so said nothing.

"How could he get people to let him in?"

Chad looked at Jas but got no clue. "Come on then, Einstein, you tell me."

"It's obvious, Chad," Junior was staring at him as if he was the dumbest kid in the class. "He's a cop. Chad, mate, he's a cop."

Chad paused, beer halfway to his mouth. Junior and Mel on the same page, he thought. "Go on," he said. "Explain how that's logical."

"The victims let him in. They think they're safe, that's why."

"If that's the case, why did he use nitrogen to knock 'em out?"

"There were more than one of them, so he had to neutralise them. When he did the solo victims like that last bloke, then I reckon he calls 'em up says he wants a confidential chat and they let him in."

"I don't want to burst your bubble, Junior, but that's not logic, it's speculation."

"Chad's right," said Jas. "You're guessing and the minute the police or psychologists do that, the whole thing goes pear-shaped. You're trying to make events fit your theory."

Junior reclined back on the settee and smiled. "Yeah, maybe, but it's fun trying to work it out, and I still reckon I'm right." He took a long drink from the beer bottle, then wiped his mouth. "Can I get first dibs on the Thai?" he said.

*

Chad stood on the balcony and sought the stars in the sky's darkness. He had an overnight guest, but it wasn't the one he'd hoped for. Junior sprawled in the lounge playing Call of Duty. His intended guest, meanwhile, was in an Uber back to the Sheraton. How the bloody hell has that happened?

Chapter 43

Life, Andrea decided, was on the up. Mind you, not before time. Success, she now understood, was getting the risk and reward ratio right. If she hadn't taken a gigantic leap of faith and accepted working with Trevor, she'd have never got the headlines that she could now write. It was about maximising the benefit from her good fortune. Telling her boss, Tom, he was a wanker remained high on her to-do list, but while gratifying, it wouldn't move her career forward. She needed to be seen in the public eye and that meant prime time TV.

One or two had made overtures. Channel Ten had called her but the daytime news show producer had pissed her off.

"Jeez, Andrea, you're not one of the Lara Vella's, but ya might make the back-up team."

Back-up team? Cheeky bastard.

She sipped her wine, took a deep draw on her Marlboro and blew the smoke out over her balcony. "Make the most of this opportunity, it won't come around often."

But how? That was the issue she faced. How to get Andrea Byrne as popular as the articles themselves? The latest exposé, '*Killer taunts cops with photograph*' had generated lots of likes and retweets, but the name Andrea Byrne was in the background not up front and centre.

An idea that had been forming nudged itself further into her consciousness. It was like an earworm, nagging and persistent.

"No," she murmured, "you can't do that."

She took a drag of her Marlboro. "Why not?"

The agreement with Trevor, she thought, is confidential. You can only print what Hilton tells you. Yeah, but eventually Trevor will dry up or they'll catch the killer then my usefulness is over. I'm back to playing second fiddle to arseholes like Jason Austin at The Bugle. But not if I make a move first. Leave them behind. I go direct to Channel Nine, Fox News and some others and sell a real scoop to the highest bidder. The bidding opens at offering me an investigative reporter role on prime time or my own show.

She took a long drink of wine.

And the scoop? That sources close to the police says there'll be two more killings.

She stared into the near empty glass.

It was risk versus reward. What could the police do? Nothing. Deny it, yes, but if there were two more killings, I'm prime time news. And if not, then I'm the hero that had prevented them.

She leaned forward, picked up her glass and drained it, the condensation on the glass damp on her hand. After that, who gives a shit? I'll be working in TV, having left those dickhead print journos behind.

Her phone lay on the settee and drying her palm she picked it up, clicked on a number, took a deep breath and dialled.

Chapter 44

'... There can be no justice without truth.'
Louis Farrakhan.

The brass name plate is around eighteen inches and has a gilt edging which glimmers in the sunlight. I read the inscription. Howard Trippier, Human Resources Director. Given that he has his name and title stencilled onto the office door, it's clear the occupant doesn't want visitors to be in any doubt about who they are meeting. The name plate is a display for his own gratification. Hubris and vanity. The same characteristics his fellow conspirators exhibited.

The owner of the soubriquet, however, shows no sign of vanity now. His eyes are doing the familiar searching, flitting left and right. Like the others he doesn't find whatever he's looking for. There is no one to disturb me so I can take my time with him. I won't rush justice. I have questions to ask.

"Your crime is worse."

He stares at me, terror writ large in his eyes. His toes tap the table. I have taped his legs together and suspended him from a pulley contraption I made in my garage and brought with me. The noose is tight around his neck.

"The others were incompetent and I don't forgive that, but it is at least understandable. Incompetence has its consequences, a price to be paid, and I have exacted the reckoning. But you," I pause and wave the machete in front of his face. "Yours was a deliberate act. You knew what you were doing."

'Too fucking right, he did. Come on, stop messing about. Get on with it.'

I walk around him and his head twists to see where I am. "Human Resources Director. Why did anyone think that a criminal like you should be an upholder of values? Who? Perhaps I will find out who appointed you and have a quiet word with them," I laugh, the thought amusing me.

'Come on, come on.'

I sit in his chair and check the papers on his desk. I read a letter he has written to an employee, communicating his decision following a disciplinary hearing. This employee has been in breach of company policy concerning the dishonest reporting of customer complaints. For this heinous crime, the Director of Human Resources has deemed that the punishment is dismissal. Dismissal, wow. The employee's life changed irreparably.

I look at the swaying monster. "You'll sack this poor bugger for telling a few lies," I wave the letter at him. "But you'll instigate and ratify a cover-up to protect your reputation, you miserable bastard. And protect the reputations of the other criminals involved in the deaths of innocent people. What sort of morality is that, Mr Howard Trippier?" I take out the photograph then reach up and hold it in front of his face. "Remember her?"

Stepping away I see a stain spreading slowly down his trousers.

Time's up. Time to make reparation.

Five down.

One more left, and I've saved the worst till last.

Chapter 45

"Are you watching the news?" Pop's voice boomed out of Chad's phone.

"Eh? No, you've just woken me up. What time is it?"

"Turn your TV on. Christ's sake, as if things weren't bad enough already."

Chad checked his watch. 7:30 a.m. Jesus. He reached for the remote and switched on the television. "What channel?"

"Channel Nine news. Call me back when you've watched it."

Chad clicked the call off and groaned as a smiling presenter announced that Channel Nine were delighted to announce that Andrea Byrne, Australia's top crime reporter, had agreed to join the Channel Nine team as their lead investigative reporter, and "strewth, does she have a scoop."

"More like self-appointed 'top crime reporter,'" Chad muttered.

Andrea appeared on the screen wearing a serious expression and trying slightly too hard to convey a gravitas in keeping with her new position. Gone were the baseball hat and nose piercing and in had come a dark navy suit and an expensive haircut and makeover. Before she opened her mouth Chad knew this would not be good.

"Andrea, welcome to the team and what have you got for us?"

"Thanks a lot, Jim, happy to be here. But I have some devastating news for our viewers and the people of New South Wales regarding the serial killer the press have dubbed The Boardroom Butcher."

Dubbed by you, Chad thought.

"Sources close to the Sydney Homicide Department have told me they believe there'll be two more killings."

"Wow. How are the police so certain of that number?"

Andrea tried, but failed to keep a smugness out of her expression.

"An unknown source, but one they believe to be close to the killer."

"So, do they know who these victims are?"

"No, they don't know the identities of the victims or..." Andrea stared into the camera, "who the killer is."

*

"What the hell is she playing at?" yelled Pop.

"How the hell should I know?"

"I'll have to deny it and then no more communication with Andrea bloody Byrne. And we'd better hope we catch the perp before he does another two. Bloody journos, they're all the same. Make out they're doing everything in the public interest when they're only in it for their own miserable careers."

"I'll try to speak to her," offered Chad, "and find out what's going on. I can't imagine her contact is going to be any too pleased with her either."

"Yeah, okay, let me know if you get hold of her."

*

Chad stared at his phone. He'd called Andrea seven times but gone to voicemail each time. He lay back on his pillows and turned off the TV.

"Andrea you're a bloody idiot." He closed his eyes. She hadn't thought it through. Cause, effect and consequence.

Cause: You decided that you need to make hay while the sun is shining. It's the biggest story you've had and you need to milk it.

You've used Trevor's insights as leverage with the TV companies. An excellent plan if you were in control of events. But you're not.

Effect: It's working to plan so far. A big new job which puts you out there front and centre, a supposed scoop that your new employers will love and the subsequent increase in viewers that justifies your appointment. Everyone's a winner. In your head, there won't be a downside. Either we catch the perp before he kills again, in which case that's fine. If he kills another two, you're proved right. And if he doesn't well, hey, that's because Andrea Byrne got close to him, so he stopped. Yep, in your head it's win, win.

Consequence: Trevor is going to be none too pleased with you, you've betrayed his confidence. You've also betrayed Pop, so longer term Channel Nine's lead investigative reporter is going to be behind the media curve with breaking news. Your employer won't like that.

Chad opened his eyes. "Holy shit," he muttered. "What the hell have you done, Andrea?"

He felt the muscles in his neck tense, tried massaging them, then got up from the bed and walked to the glass veranda doors leading to the balcony. The breeze was fresh. The waves crashed on the beach half a mile away. He pictured her at Starbucks and at the Ravesis, all aggressive pose and 'in your face' bravado. She'd employed a female variation of machismo to get her way. But it had blinded her. If Trevor is the killer, and she had pissed him off, she might be his next visit.

Chapter 46

Chad towelled himself dry, his mind still considering how to keep Andrea Byrne out of harm's way. He pulled on a tee shirt, then wandered to the kitchen where he poured a coffee from the pot he'd brewed before taking his shower. 9 a.m., and his day was already looking like a train wreck. He'd have to get to Andrea, but first he'd better get Junior up and on his way. He liked the guy, but they lived in different time zones. Junior spent the daylight hours asleep and the night time designing computer programmes or gaming. "Well not today, Junior." Chad muttered.

His phone lit up. Pop calling.

"Whatever you're doing, stop doing it and get your arse over to Darlinghurst. I'm texting you the address. We've got another."

Chad picked up traces of panic in Pop's voice. He knew the answer but asked, anyway. "Another what?"

"Another fucking murder!" Pop shouted. "Only murder doesn't come close to describing what he's done to this poor schmuck. And is the victim Dr Doyle? No, that would be too easy. He's tucked up safe at home with half of Sydney's finest camped outside his front door. How the hell did we get this so wrong?"

Chad felt logic and reason sliding through his hands. Not the doctor, then who?

"Who is it?" Chad asked.

"It's a guy called Trippier. He was the HR Director at the hospital in 2003 and he was in the bloody photograph. Oh, and one more thing, it ain't pretty, so get your act together. If you faint or spew when you get here, I'm going to have you locked up."

Chad picked up his keys and paused outside the second bedroom door where Junior was sleeping. He raised his hand to knock. "Oh, bugger it," he groaned and opened the front door, deciding to let the sleeping giant lie.

*

"You shouldn't be doing this, Chad, you're not well enough," said Jas.

"I don't have a choice. I'll be fine."

"Well, let me know when you're finished and I'll get Tony or Odd Job to pick you up."

Chad clicked the call off and opened the window in the airless Uber. He closed his eyes and went back over the last briefings at Day Street. Could he have done more? The police hadn't had time to assess the risks against anyone besides the doctor. And the next victim had to be a doctor? Immigration, recruitment, administration, anaesthetist – doctor, surely?

The suburbs raced by and as the car sped past houses and offices in a blur, so a thought, sharp, clear and cold filled his head. He ran his hands through his hair. Sweat formed on his upper lip and forehead. He shook his head, but the thought remained. He could see it and it had a name.

Doctor Nefeli.

He's already killed the doctor, that's where he started. Nefeli was the beginning of the chain. Your job to join the dots, and you didn't. You missed the most obvious. And now another victim has been butchered.

*

Chad stood in the car park of Australian Pharma, the pharmaceutical company for whom Howard Trippier had been the Human Resources Director. Police tape stretched some fifty metres in each direction and he could see Pop leaning against the plate glass doors of the two-storey building. Chad walked towards the detective and thought that even the parrots on Pop's shirt looked pissed off, and stressed.

"I need a word."

"Fire away," said Pop.

"I know it looks like we guarded the wrong person."

"We did," Pop interrupted.

"Okay, we did, but our logic was spot on. The natural target was a doctor."

"I wish it had been obvious to the killer, but it seems he didn't get the bloody memo."

"Pop, if Byrne's contact is telling the truth, there'll be one more victim so we've still got time to stop this guy before he kills again. I know who the next victim will be. Not by name but by occupation."

Something akin to hope flashed into Pop's eyes. "I'm all ears."

"Yeah, well, hold that thought till I've had a look inside here. Where's the victim?"

"Last office at the back of the building, follow the forensic boys round the side there and get some kit on," Pop paused then held Chad's eye. "Ah, look, mate, this is the worst of the lot, don't go in, Mel, can brief you. I've seen plenty of sick shit in my time but this about takes the biscuit."

Chad stopped mid-stride. Here we go again. His stomach was turning cartwheels, and he was trying to slow his heart rate. There was a pounding in his ears. Attractive as Pop's offer was, the crime scene was a glimpse into the killer's mind. Chad knew nothing could replace that.

"I need to go in. I may faint or be sick, no guarantees, but I need to see it."

Pop scrunched some gravel under his foot. "Okay, mate, but don't say I didn't warn you."

*

Someone was trying to force a water bottle into his mouth.

No, no. His brain screeched.

The water's poisoned, someone's trying to kill me. Sunlight flickered on his eyelids but something was different. Same words, different accents.

"He's fainted."

"Give him some water."

He opened his eyes. Where am I? What's happened? He blinked. His vision returned, and he saw Mel's face leaning over him. He could smell the floral tones of her perfume. Okay, he wasn't on a street in Harrogate having just drunk from a bottle laced with Fentanyl.

"You're okay, Chad. You were fine till you came outside then the fresh air seemed to poleaxe you. I could see you wobble and go, but luckily got my arm under you as you dropped so you haven't banged your head. Breathe, you'll be fine."

Chad sat up, leaned back on the wall, and did as she said. As he filled his lungs with air, his brain cleared. Images of the crime scene, like still shots from the most gruesome of horror movies, returned.

Hanged, drawn and quartered. Jesus.

Two guys in protective gear were sniggering, but Mel gave them a look and they shuffled off.

"Told you it was nasty," Pop emerged around the corner of the building.

"And I told you no guarantees I wouldn't faint."

"True. Thoughts?"

"You tell him, Mel."

"This is justice being delivered in its harshest sense. The killer believes the victim is more responsible than the rest, so he's escalated the violence to match the perceived crime of the victim."

"What crime does he think this guy Trippier committed? I mean, shit what could someone working in HR do that's worse than a doctor who killed people?"

Chad looked up, the morning sun flickering over Pop's shoulder. It skidded in and out of clouds which were blown fast by the breeze. "He covered it up."

"Eh? Explain."

"The report was a whitewash; they covered up the negligence of Doctor Nefeli."

"How do you know that?"

"I don't for sure but it's the only rational explanation. And I know who the last victim will be."

"And who is that?"

"Not here," said Chad. "I'll go through it with you back at the station."

Pop looked at Chad then Mel. Chad could see a renewed purpose in his eyes. A scrunch of footsteps made them turn to see Dimi coming round the corner.

"Dimi," Pop's voice held menace. "Total news blackout. And I mean total. I want everyone back at Day Street in half an hour. Let's get our collective act together before we give it to the press."

Chapter 47

Andrea Byrne checked her phone. She'd received congratulatory texts and WhatsApp messages from dozens of friends and ex-colleagues, but nestling amongst the celebratory were names and numbers she didn't want to hear from. Seven missed calls from Chad Hilton, and two from No Caller ID. She clicked onto her voicemails.

"Yeah, yeah, yeah," she muttered as she listened to Chad's urgent request for a callback. "That won't be happening, buddy."

She clicked onto the second voicemail.

"Andrea, what have you done?" Trevor's voice seemed to have garnered a more threatening tone. "I understand your need for career advancement, but we have a deal. Breaking your side of our contract before the project is over is not acceptable. Relaying information that I haven't authorised is likewise not acceptable. Nor is avoiding my calls. I will ring at 9:45 a.m. prompt, you will answer. Don't test my patience further. Be warned."

She checked the time. 9:43 a.m. "Shit." She lit a cigarette and took several deep draws, inhaling the smoke into her lungs then exhaling with a 'whoosh.' What shall I say? She wondered. Tell him to bugger off, game's over and I'm not playing anymore. I mean what can he do? Her phone vibrating interrupted her chain of thought.

"Hello, Andrea, it's been a busy morning for you. Name in lights and all over the TV. Well done you. However, I suspect that you only have this role because of information you shared, that was not yours to share. Am I right?"

She opted to ignore the question. "Hello, Trevor, how's things with you?"

"I'm fine, thank you. Now, to business. I need you to re-establish contact with Chad Hilton, who'll be as upset as I am about your misconduct." He paused. "Following today's murder, does he know who the last victim will be? Find that out."

Andrea stared at the screen, the appalling consequences of what she'd heard dawning on her. "Hang on a minute. Which murder, has there been another?"

"Andrea, while you've been smiling into the camera things have moved on. It won't please Channel Nine if their new celebrity reporter is last to the scene of the latest death, will it?"

Nausea consumed her. Her alternative universe had shattered. Trevor was still speaking, but she was barely listening as she watched the career she'd cultivated and the endless possibilities she'd created, drift away like the smoke from her cigarette.

"To avoid that, you must re-establish your side of our contract. The news hasn't broken yet."

Had she heard that correctly? "Say that again, Trevor, you broke up. Did you say the news hasn't broken yet?"

"Yes. Pop wants to keep it that way for as long as possible. Andrea, you can still be first to break it, but only if you call Chad Hilton immediately. I guess you'll need to do some grovelling, but you're good at that."

Andrea felt light-headed, nausea turning to euphoria. "Right, tell me again," she said, trying to give her voice a composure she didn't feel. "What information do you want?"

"Does he know who the last victim will be?"

"Okay. I'll call him now. He won't give me that information for nothing, what can I tell him?"

"Wait, Andrea," he said. "My contact is approaching the end of his mission and needs a little time to accomplish it. So, you will need to be at your devious best with Mr Hilton."

"Why?"

"With your help we are going to indulge in a little misdirection. You are going to plant a small red herring and send them on a wild goose chase."

"Am I? Really?" Andrea, bristled. "Why would I want to help you mislead the police?"

"Because, if you don't carry out this task, or if you break your contract again, then my contact will add you to his list. He's asked me to pass that information to you." She could hear his breath down the line. "Trust me when I say that's not a threat." A second's silence. "It's a promise."

Andrea felt her knees buckle and she grabbed the edge of a chair. Oh, Christ he's going to kill me, she thought. What the hell have I done?

"Now, Andrea, no one wants that, so follow my instructions."

"Er… okay, what do I do?"

"Find out if he knows the next victim's identity, then tell him the Greek doctor holds the key. Investigate him."

"What Greek doctor?"

"Andrea, we've been here before. You are the conduit, that's all. You don't need to know which Greek doctor and you may not use what I've just mentioned in your next broadcast, is that clear?"

"Crystal."

"Good. Now stop interrupting. You must convince Hilton of the importance of following up everything about this doctor. I'll leave you to get that across to him, without him sensing anything is amiss. I'm sure your natural creativity will come to the fore. Are you clear?"

"Yes."

"Good, and remember, Andrea, I'll know very quickly if you've carried out my instructions. I'll call you in an hour. Goodbye."

Chapter 48

Chad leaned against the wall in the squad room at Day Street, waiting for Pop. The place smelled worse than usual, so he moved a little closer to Mel and breathed in her perfume just as his phone pinged with a message from Jas.

What happened at the crime scene?

Chad paused. Should he tell her? If he couldn't be honest with her now, then what chance would a relationship have?

Horrendous… And I fainted again. Before you start, I'm okay.

Chad watched for a new message, but seconds elapsed and none came. How pissed off was she with him?

His phone pinged. Freddie this time. *Bro, what the fuck are you doing, man??? Mel says you passed out? How many times have I told you that you shouldn't be doing this? I'm on my way. If you can't look after yourself, then I'll do it for you.*

Jesus Christ.

Chad nudged Mel. "You grassed me up," he held his phone towards her so she could read Freddie's message.

"It's for your own good," her voice was so low he had to lean in to hear her. "Anyway," she continued, "who will you listen to if not the people who care about you? You're ill, for God's sake. Not physically, but mentally. You are in trauma and by continuing as you are, you're making the PTSD worse."

Chad hadn't heard Mel in this vein before. Say nothing, he thought.

"You've helped Pop," she continued, "and look where that's got you. He just blames you when things don't work out 'cos he knows he'll never have to work with you again. He doesn't give a shit if you faint or vomit. Or if your mental health is getting worse by the day. He doesn't treat me like that because I wouldn't stand for it. And he thought nothing of getting the press to direct their focus on you, remember? But you won't let anyone help you. I can't seem to get through to you, so I've made sure that the people you're closest to know which way this is going." Mel was holding direct eye contact Chad couldn't avoid. "And," she whispered. "I've just texted Jas, who says to tell you she's on her way here with Freddie and the boys."

What could he say? He knew she was right. He remembered his first thought when Pop had asked for help at the airport.

He could barely help himself, let alone anyone else.

Why had he ignored that? Chad shuffled against the wall. Mind you, he thought, what good the seventh cavalry in the shape of Freddie, Odd Job and Tony were going to achieve was anyone's guess.

Pop shouldered his way into the cramped confines of the room as Chad's phone vibrated. He checked the screen, then headed towards the door as Pop let it swing shut.

"Where the hell are you going?" asked Pop.

He held his phone out so Pop could see the name of the caller.

"Right, deal with that."

Chad clicked on the call, then made his way down the corridor.

"Andrea, better late than never, I suppose," he said.

"Yeah, sorry about that. I've been busy," she replied.

Chad found an empty room.

Then let rip.

"What do you think you're doing?" Mel's sharp critique had stung him so he let his anger and shame explode. "You don't give a flying fuck about the harm you've done. You'd do anything, anything at all, if you thought it would advance your poxy career, wouldn't you?" He didn't wait for a response. "People are dying and you've scared the average Sydneysider shitless, so then what do you do? Fan the flames. You really are a piece of work."

"It's not like that. It's complicated. But anyway, Trevor's called."

"I bet he was as pissed off as I am."

"Maybe, but look, you need to re-engage."

"You're even crazier than I think you are if you think Pop's going to be in the mood to play ball with you, Andrea. He's more pissed off with you than either me or Trevor. Talk about burning your bridges."

"You'll have to get him onside, Chad, you must."

"I can't work miracles. You told a couple of million viewers there would be two more victims. Reckless doesn't cut it. You knew that the public mood was borderline panic and then you pour petrol on it."

"Okay, okay, I hear you, but Chad, listen, Trevor said there's been another murder, is that right?"

Chad looked at the screen. He couldn't confirm that, he thought. "Did he say who, or where?"

"Chad, don't hold out on me."

What was that? Sounded like panic.

"It's not about getting the story first," she said. "Trevor's told me that unless we resume the dialogue between you guys and him, the killer is going to come for me."

"Look, Andrea, don't bullshit me."

"I'm not, I promise. That's what he said. Re-establish my side of the contract, get dialogue going with you and Pop. Or," there was a pause, "I'm next on the list."

Chad stared at the phone. Was this just more journo bollocks? He remembered his thoughts from earlier. Andrea hadn't realised she was playing with fire, but if she was telling the truth, Trevor had spelled out the consequences.

"Please, Chad."

"I'll have a word with Pop and see what he says. No guarantees."

"Thanks, I mean it."

"What information is Trevor after?"

"He wonders if you know the identity of the last victim?"

Chad felt his stomach lurch. "Interesting," he said. "And in return?"

"Well, he offered nothing up, but…"

"But what? I can't see Pop wanting to resume dialogue without getting something in return."

"Chad, you've got to help me." There was hysteria in her tone. She's terrified, he thought.

"You've got to convince Pop to resume talks."

Chad couldn't see how, but he sensed Andrea had something more.

"Look," she said. "There's something else. At the end of the call, Trevor sort of paused, like he was thinking. After a couple of seconds he said, 'tell Hilton he must dig up everything he can find on the Greek doctor, if he wants to find the truth.' That was it."

Chad let that sink in. What the hell was he missing about Nefeli, and why was it so important? "Okay, I've got to go. I'll do my best with Pop. Call me in an hour."

*

Chad opened the briefing room door to a crowd of coppers and saw Mel and Pop in conversation.

"I need a word, Pop. You too, Mel."

"Okay." Pop gave the thumbs up to the other officers. "Right, guys, I'll catch you before the presser."

Chad walked along the corridor, then held open the door. Pop and Mel filed in.

Pop positioned himself by the far wall, hands on hips and brow furrowed. Chad could see he was ready for a fight. Mel's face held the same angry expression as a few minutes previously.

"Okay, what did that silly bitch say?" growled Pop.

Not a verbal chess game then. "She didn't know the details, but knows there's been another killing. Trevor told her."

"Was she fishing for info so she can break the story first? Fuck that and fuck her. I've had it up to here with all journos, but Andrea bloody Byrne in particular."

Pop stalked around the room muttering while Chad, allowing him to calm down, ran a hand through his hair and counted the number of monkeys he could see climbing palm trees on Pop's shirt. Mel leaned on the wall.

"Come on, what did she want?" demanded Pop.

"Information."

"Information!" Pop slammed the wall with his hand. "I should be locking her up for obstructing a police investigation not sharing information with her."

Like a referee separating the pugilists, Mel jumped in. "Can you both please keep the conversation this side of confrontational? And keep your voices down."

"Yeah, okay, Mel, okay," said Pop.

Mel looked at Chad. "The call you took was from Andrea Byrne, I take it?"

"Yes, it was, which shows…"

"Which shows what?" Pop barked, clearly not looking for a peace settlement yet.

"That she's still got a line into Trevor,' said Chad, "which keeps us closer to the killer. Okay, she's a conniving, ambitious so and so and defo wants to be the first to break the news of the latest murder, but Trevor threatened her today. Told her if we don't resume dialogue, the killer would add her to the list."

"Mmm, I'm beginning to like Trevor," Pop grunted.

"Pop, be pragmatic. Trevor's after info and dialogue with him keeps us close."

"What does he want to know?"

"Have we sussed who the last victim will be?"

Neither Pop nor Mel reacted. Silence sat heavy, like another presence in the room.

"Which you said you knew, right?" said Pop. "So, come on then, who is it?"

Chad hoped to hell he was right. "It's whoever wrote the report into the negligence claims against Nefeli."

The words buzzed like a fly looking for somewhere to land. No one spoke.

Pop rubbed his face with his hands. "Go on, explain your reasoning for me."

Chad looked from one to the other. "We knew a doctor was next in line, right? We assumed Doyle, but we didn't know he'd already killed one. The Greek doctor. Nefeli. I reckon Nefeli was the first victim, at the beginning of the chain. He's no need to kill another doctor, so HR was next. Trippier. And Trevor confirmed to Andrea that we should dig up everything we can find on Nefeli."

"Really?" said Pop. "What did he say?"

"Just that. If we want to find the truth, investigate Nefeli."

"Okay, I'll allocate some resource to Nefeli, but I still don't get why he killed Trippier. Why HR, for Christ's sake?"

"Because the report's a whitewash, a cover-up. And he blames HR and the report writer."

"So, who's the report writer?"

"I don't know. Your guys investigated that."

*

"Redacted? What the hell do you mean redacted?" Pop's face was a livid purple.

"What I said, boss, someone's redacted the whole thing. From the title at the beginning to the paragraph at the end headed

'Conclusion', it's just a load of black lines. Looks like something from the JFK files," Dimi was trying, Chad reckoned, to say nothing to antagonise Pop further.

Chad thought Pop was going to punch someone as he banged from one wall to the next. "But our perp knows who the writer is," he yelled. "'Cos he's discovered everyone from recruitment through to the HR Director. Why can't we find out?"

Chad said nothing. This was the breadcrumb trail reaching the end of its road. He'd known they'd have to catch the killer before this moment, but they hadn't. So, here they were. Shit. They'd no means of preventing another death. Maybe investigating Nefeli might unearth the answer? Maybe, but something nagged at Chad. They'd reached the end of the trail so why was Trevor pointing them at Nefeli? Another crumb?

Chad stood. "Pop, I've got to go. I hope the press conference goes well. Will you call me afterwards?"

"If I'm still in a job, I will."

"We need to decide what we say to Trevor," said Chad. "In the meantime, do we let Byrne stew or do we give her the heads up on Trippier?"

Pop scratched his head. "Give it to her five minutes before the presser and tell her we want something concrete from Trevor in return." Pop turned to his team. "Right, guys, find everything you can on Nefeli. We need to discover what Trevor doesn't want us to know."

Chapter 49

Not even police cars used the station forecourt as a car park, Chad reckoned, let alone a silver and black Bentley. Until today. As Chad exited through the sliding doors with Mel in close order behind him, he could hear Freddie subjecting a city ranger to a charm offensive and explaining why he'd had to park right outside the door. "Ah, here he is now, officer," Freddie was pointing towards Chad. "I told you we are here on urgent police business, so thank you for your understanding." Freddie patted the Ranger on his shoulder. "Let's go everyone, come on, Chad."

Chad climbed in followed by Mel. Freddie joined them, and Odd Job closed the door. Jas was already inside, tucked in the corner. The smell of the leather upholstery and the frostiness of the reception reminded Chad of sitting in the back of his parents' car one cold Saturday morning. They'd come to collect him from the local cop shop where he and three of his mates had spent the evening sobering up after a brawl outside a nightclub. He'd been seventeen then. Thirty years later, the atmosphere in the car was reminiscent.

"Before you all start," he said, "I have to make a call." He dialled Andrea's number as the Bentley headed out of town towards Bondi. Driving into the suburbs, the sky was grey and threatened rain. He noticed a couple of Red Gums and remembered that the bark changes colour with age. Smooth and pinky orange fading to grey as they got older. These were grey.

Andrea answered. "Hey, Chad, what have you got for me?"

"First things first. Here are the ground rules. If you televise or print anything that you don't have permission to do, Pop will arrest you on a variety of charges, including aiding a murderer... If you're still alive."

"Yeah, charming, thanks, Chad. So, what can you give me?"

"You don't learn, do you, Andrea? I've got a bad feeling that's going to cost you in the end. Take Pop seriously or your career is in the gutter. Okay?"

"Yeah, okay," she sounded sincere. "Point taken."

"Tell Trevor we don't know the next victim's name, but we know what he did. And we know Trevor knows that. In return," Chad paused.

"Yes, in return what?"

"Ask him why we should look closer at the Greek doctor?"

"Fine, okay, he'll call me shortly so I'll let him know. Now what about this latest killing? Give me the heads up."

Chad checked his watch. Three minutes till Pop started the presser. We'll see how good you are now, Andrea, three minutes' start ain't much, he thought.

"The latest victim is a guy called Trippier. He was the Human Resources Director for a pharmaceutical company called Australia Pharma based in Darlinghurst. I reckon you have only a couple of minutes' head start, Andrea, so you'd better crack on. Call me when you've heard from Trevor."

The line went dead.

"Nice talking to you, too," Chad muttered.

*

Freddie had been lecturing Chad since the call to Andrea had finished. He was still in full flow as Chad turned the key in the lock. "Nothing seems to get through to you, bro. I know I'm going on about it, but I'm telling you, man, I'm this close," he snapped his fingers in the air, "to getting Tony to have a quiet word in that copper dude's ear. What's his name? Ruby?"

"That'll be a big help, Freddie. Just what the situation requires," said Mel, raising her eyebrows. "I think I should tell Pop that you're not fit enough to continue. End of."

"Even if that makes sense," replied Chad, filling the kettle, "I can't back away now. I'm the contact point from Trevor to Pop. Throwing a sickie doesn't work with serial killers. They operate under a different code of working practices." He smiled but got no response except a 'tut' and a sigh from Jas. "But I hear what you're all saying," he continued, "and I'm not ignoring you or my welfare."

Freddie plonked his vast frame onto the settee and accepted the offer of a coffee as Junior shuffled into the lounge in a tee shirt and boxers.

"Hey guys, g'day. What time is it?"

"Morning, son," said Freddie. "Coming up to midday. Did you have a late night, bro? Out chasing the girls, were you?"

"No," Junior rubbed his eyes. "I was gaming."

Freddie looked at Chad. "What's gaming, bro?"

"Hey, Chad, is that coffee?" asked Junior.

Chad poured another cup and handed it to Junior, who sat down next to his father, making the large three-seater settee look like an under-sized armchair.

"What's up?" asked Freddie, noticing that Mel and Jas were chuckling. "What's so funny?"

Junior grinned.

"Are they're laughing at us?" he nudged Junior. "Son, why is that?" said Freddie, his self-awareness plumbing new depths.

"I think it's 'cos we look funny sitting together on here."

"Funny? What's funny, bro? I don't get it."

"Never mind,"

Chad caught Junior's eye and smiled.

"Anyway," Junior looked from one to the other. "What brings all you guys here today?"

"There's been another murder," said Jas.

"Oh, shit," Junior looked at Chad. "Did you go to the scene?"

"We did," replied Mel, "and Chad fainted. Again. We're trying to convince him to back away before he has a breakdown."

There was a pause before Junior spoke. "He can't do that, Chad, mate, tell 'em."

"Tell them what?" said Chad, nonplussed.

Junior looked at Chad, then at his father. "That being involved is giving you purpose. It's helping you. Okay, so it's bringing back the memories of the trauma back home and that's not good, but the rest of it… It's stopping you from sinking."

Out of the mouths of babes, thought Chad. He turned to Jas, who reached out her hand and stroked his cheek.

"I don't know where he gets it from," said Jas, "but he's smarter than all of us."

A huge smile creased Freddie's face.

Chapter 50

The ceiling fan rotated above him. Given that there was air conditioning, it didn't need to be switched on but its motion helped Chad think. He stretched on the bed, wishing Jas was next to him. She'd left with Freddie and Mel and promised to return later. Everything seemed to conspire against them, getting time together on their own. Leaving, she'd turned in the doorway, reached her arms around his neck, then standing on tiptoes had given him a delicate kiss.

"It would be nice to spend some time together," she said. "How about dinner tonight, just the two of us?"

"Sounds great, but I reckon it's Pop and the killer dependant. I could try to get rid of my lodger and you could come here."

"Fab. Now get some rest. I don't care whether that boy's right about you needing to be doing this or not. You need rest."

And then there was Junior. Chad reflected on the boy's words. That he'd been correct was interesting, and said much for the guy's emotional intelligence, but also shocking that until he'd said it, Chad hadn't recognised the truth. Bloody hell, he thought, I'm like a drug addict with Stockholm syndrome. Addicted to and obsessed with the thing that'll kill me.

He leaned across the bed and picked up his iPad. Come on, do something useful.

Nefeli, he typed.

What did they gain by following the trail of the dead Greek doctor? If Chad was right, then they'd find the killer had murdered

Nefeli. And would the Greek authorities want a bunch of Aussies trawling through their investigation? "Not a chance," he muttered.

He tried to order his thoughts into a coherent sequence and addressed the black face of his iPad. "Trevor tells Andrea we must investigate Nefeli." Chad pushed himself up on his pillows. "Really?" he muttered. "Not, 'it might be worth our while,' or 'we should consider'. No, he tells her we must investigate Nefeli. Has Trevor been that overt before, so explicit? No, so what's happened here?" He gave that some thought. Why was Trevor pushing the police to investigate Nefeli? What would that accomplish for him? Chad considered the question. They'd go haring off, using all their resources investigating Nefeli, only to run into a brick wall called the Greek police.

A light shone in Chad's brain. Trevor knows Nefeli won't lead anywhere, but it'll buy him time. By sending us on a wild goose chase, he gets the space and opportunity to kill the last victim and end the breadcrumb trail, leaving us nowhere.

This is all about time. Trevor's playing for time. The fan above him whirred. Is it just about Trevor buying time to complete the murders? Or is it... distraction? We'll be looking in the wrong place. So, where's the right place?

He needed air, so opened the veranda doors to the balcony, inhaling the sea breeze and smelling the saltiness in the air.

The perp is exacting justice, he thought. We said it from the start. But justice for who?

The answer came sharp and clear.

For one of Nefeli's victims. Because someone close to Trevor was one of Nefeli's victims.

"Yes, that's it."

And their identity is in the report. But there must be a record of deaths at the hospital, regardless of the report being redacted. Narrow down the timelines to 2002 and maybe 2003 and filter again by deaths caused by surgery. There'll be autopsies, death certificates. And in the list of victims' families, will be the killer.

He pulled his phone from his pocket, tapped on it and scrolled down to find the name he wanted. He didn't have far to look.

Pop.

Chapter 51

There was a crowd of press and protesters outside Day Street yelling questions and abuse. So much for an afternoon off, thought Chad as he waited for the doors to open.

"You're bull dust, ya Pommie bastard," shouted a bearded protester. "Fuck off home."

The doors slid open and Chad went inside, shoes sticking to the tiles as usual. The place was getting him down. Couldn't they have a cleaning company come in and hose it down? He rushed to join the team in the squad room. The quicker they got on this, the quicker he could meet Jas.

"Great, we're all here," said Pop, as Chad entered. "Right, Chad, explain where we've got to. Fire away."

"I'll cut to the chase. The killer wants two things. One is to buy time, and the other is to create distraction. That's why he's trying to get us to divert our resources and energies into digging into Nefeli. But that won't lead us anywhere. It's a red herring. The next victim is the author of the report, but we can't protect him because we don't know his identity. Our only option is to catch the killer before he strikes again."

"Chad, mate, it's not like we haven't been trying to do that," said José, with a touch of irritation in his tone.

"I know, I know. I'm not saying we haven't, but we've been following the breadcrumb trail he's been laying," Chad paused. "Now, we must find a different way because there are no more crumbs."

"Which is?" asked Lucy.

Pop answered, "That we search the archived hospital files from 2001 when Nefeli started work at the Royal Prince Alfred, up to November 2003 when he left. We examine the deaths of any patient that died on his operating table. There can't be bloody hundreds, otherwise this would have been a massive scandal. We identify every living relative of the victims and we trace them."

"Bugger me, Boss," said Dimi, "not many victims, granted, but there'll be thousands of relatives. By the time we've traced them, I'll be up for retirement."

Pop scratched his head. "Yeah, I'll give you that. It'll take too long. Anyone got any other ideas?"

"Er, Pop?"

"Yeah, José?"

"Why don't we get some value out of Andrea Byrne?"

"Well, that would be a first. What do you mean?"

"We identify the victims, then she asks for relatives to come forward in a TV appeal. We set up a hotline to control the response."

Pop scratched his head. "José, mate, I hate to think you're losing the plot here, but I don't think the perp is going to dial that number and give us his name. Anyone else got any ideas?"

Chad ran his hands through his hair. Pop was right. How then?

"Narrow the search area down," said Lucy.

Pop rubbed his eyes. "How?"

"We'd have to make some operational judgement calls, but we categorise the victims." She walked to the wipe board and began making headings as she spoke, "First group, any victims who were children. Their parents are next of kin so they can easily be traced. But it's the siblings' names we want. Why would a parent leave it twenty years to start killing? Much more likely to be a child that's now grown up. The killer's a sibling, not a parent."

Good point, thought Chad.

Lucy continued, "Next group; adolescents, same criteria apply as for the kids' group. Third group are the adult victims. And here we'd be wanting to talk to their offspring, not the spouse. Do you follow me?"

"Yep. Sounds sensible," said Pop. "Let's get to it. We work as long as it takes to get the victims' names."

"Excellent stuff, Lucy. Nice work," said Chad.

Chapter 52

'Terror is only justice: prompt, severe and inflexible.'
Maximilien Robespierre.

I sit in my wicker chair. Outside the clouds and the sea share a similar hue: grey, interspersed with flecks of white and both swirl and change in a never-ending shape shifting. It's impossible to keep focussed on either such is the deftness of their movement, but watching gives my mind space and time to think.

Hilton and Pop have followed my little trail of clues and now understand what lies at the end.

The Findings of an Enquiry into claims of Death by Negligence against Doctor T S Nefeli. And that this report tells them… Nothing.

Redacted. The ultimate insult. The conspirators probably thought they were so clever. They basked in the belief that no-one would uncover the truth. No one would be concerned enough to look for it.

'Bastards, bastards, bastards. I hate them. Stop idling your time away looking out the window and finish the job.'

But I was looking for it. And found it.

Truth will always find a way to the surface. Okay, I may have had to cajole, negotiate and barter to get the information I needed but I used whatever means were necessary to achieve my ends.

The clouds skid overhead and a gull, shrieking, heads out over the cliff, its shape soon lost in the swirl. I make a mental note of the loose ends. How many are there? Two for certain, but there may yet be more. I'll deal with them soon enough.

My mind returns to the current issues at hand. Pop and his

homicide squad don't have the requisite skills to find the author's name, of that I'm certain. But what about Hilton? He's got them this far. He's found the chain, one or two mistakes along the way, but he's seen the links and pointed them in the right direction. What will he do? The question lingers. What indeed?

'Kill him as well. That ends the problem.'

I close my eyes and rub my temples trying to lose the voice. "Shut up, for Christ's sake and let me think. Killing him won't help, it'll make the situation harder."

Given time, Hilton will work out how I found the author. Before he does, that's a loose end I'll tie off. Even if the Nefeli bait that Andrea Byrne planted has worked, which I don't yet know, it won't be long till Hilton sees that for what it is: a red herring.

I need some other leverage to slow him down. The waves crash below, and the clouds tumble. Something more personal.

What about Pop and his merry men? If I sideline Hilton, what will they do? Not much. They're unaware of who the next victim will be and therefore of the eminent position that he now holds. But the criminal is aware I'm coming and has increased his security. He knows he's the last piece of the jigsaw and is taking steps to protect himself. Pointless, but the timing of his death and its manner require greater levels of planning than I have hitherto undertaken.

So where will Pop look now? They have hit a dead end and think time is against them. I haven't been a party to their recent deliberations but I know them and how they think.

I gasp as clarity arrives like a sharp shaft of sunlight. Of course, if they can't discover the identity of the next victim, they're going to try to find me instead. But how?

The swirling eddies of the tumult below and the churning clouds above merge into one grey shapeless mass, from which as always, I find the answer I seek. It sits in front of me stark, unequivocal.

From the hospital records. Ha, that's what they'll do.

Good luck with that.

That onion has multiple layers which, unpeeled, will get them… nowhere.

I'm gone like the clouds.

*

"Andrea, good evening, how are you?" I hear a glass clink. Drinking again. I check the time and wonder how many she's had, then interrupt her mindless chatter. "Andrea, my contact needs you to do something for him, no quiet please, just listen. We need you to find out if Chad has friends in Australia. We know all about Freddie Jackson, but is there anyone else?" She's slurring her words but I think she's understood my requirements.

"Good, Andrea, that's good. I'll call you soon, make sure you have some names for me."

Chapter 53

To be fair, Chad conceded, Andrea Byrne had made the couple of minutes head start work. Her face was on every news bulletin. Leaving Junior to Call of Duty he called her from the bedroom.

"Oh, hi, Chad, sorry I haven't got back to you, I've been busy."

Chad detected an exultant pitch to her voice. No wonder. She was on cloud nine. She'd be thinking the world was her oyster.

"Hey, Andrea, how's things?" He didn't wait for a reply. "I've got to hand it to you, you nailed the competition. I particularly liked the shot of you standing outside Australian Pharma with not another journo in sight, just you and the crime scene tape. Like you'd discovered the body. Well done with that. And you whipped up the local populace into a frenzy giving you a spin off story line. Clever stuff, Andrea, but careful it doesn't bite you on the arse."

"Well, thank you, but I'm not getting the crowds all juiced up. They're worried and angry 'cos this bugger's still on the loose. Are the police any closer to nailing him?"

"They're making steps in the right direction, but they need time. Having demonstrations on the streets doesn't help."

"Yeah, but, Chad, this killer isn't giving them time. They need to get ahead of him and soon. God knows what'll happen if there's another 'cos the mood on the streets is ugly. It might help if Pop would give me an interview, help to get the public onside, what do you think?"

Chad grimaced. "I think if you were the last person on earth, he wouldn't give you an interview."

He heard her exhale smoke.

"Worth considering, Chad. Maybe have a word with him. Give him the chance to let people know the police are doing their job."

"Let's move on, Andrea. Have you heard from Trevor?"

Chad listened, was that hesitation?

"No, I haven't," she replied. "Which is weird. He always calls within a few hours of the news breaking. Do you think something has happened?"

"No," said Chad. "I'd made a small bet with myself that you wouldn't hear from him. I'm not surprised."

"Why did you think that?"

"When this is done, I'll tell you. But in the meantime," Chad paused, "in the meantime, Andrea, be watchful and be careful."

"Why are you saying that, Chad?"

Chad removed the phone from his ear and stared at the screen. "You must be dumber than you look."

"Why? And none taken."

He smiled, "None intended." Chad paused. "Andrea, did it never occur to you that Trevor's the killer?"

The silence down the line told Chad all he needed to know.

"Yeah, maybe a while ago, but I sort of gave up on that idea. Do you think it's him?"

"Not for certain, but he's obviously a strong possibility. So, as I say, be careful. I don't think you'll hear from him again, but will you do me a favour?"

"Depends what it is."

"Reflect on your conversations with Trevor. Did anything he said strike you as strange or unusual? Something perhaps that didn't seem important."

"Yeah, okay, I will, why?"

"Because everyone makes mistakes. A word here, an unintended phrase there. Give it some thought, you never know."

"Fair enough, I'll buzz you if I think of anything. Now, you do me a favour and ask Pop if he'll do that interview with me. It would get the public behind him. Oh, and Chad?"

"Yeah, what?"

"Remember when I saw you at the Meat and Wine place?"

"Yeah, what of it?"

"Was that Freddie Jackson's son?"

Chad stared at his phone.

"Ah, come off it, Chad. They're like peas in a pod. Is there a story there?"

"Andrea, bugger off and do your job."

*

Chad lay on the bed, his hands behind his head. Andrea may be right, getting the public on Pop's side might just save his job. Pop had a bloody great target on his chest and 'scapegoat' written all over his face. He didn't deserve that. Would Pop countenance an interview with Andrea? Chad doubted it. And why ask about Junior? Bloody journos, he thought, they never let up.

He reached over and grabbed his iPad then created a heading in the centre of the screen.

Justice killings for Nefeli Negligence.

He started typing and dumped his thoughts onto the page.

- *How did Trevor know I'd met Andrea at the Ravesis?*
- *How did the killer get access to Cooper, Wise and Trippier?*
- *Why did they let him in? Is Junior right, it's a cop?*
- *Why did he take the risks?*

Calm, don't rush, just breathe. He closed his eyes and sucked in the air through his nose, letting it slowly leave his lungs before repeating the process over and over. A shape that he hadn't been able to grasp stabilised in his head. Out of the ether words formed, a question that had been hidden, finally emerged.

How did he find the report author's name?

Chad looked at the words he'd typed. Good point, Chad. With the report redacted, how the hell did he find the author? The killer couldn't have seen another copy, unredacted? No, it was a public document. One redacted, all redacted.

He stood and walked to the open veranda doors looking out towards the choppy seas. So, he's worked out the author's identity somehow. But how? Come on, Chad, think. As rain clouds gathered overhead, the answer zoomed into view. "When you rule out the impossible whatever remains, however improbable must be the answer."

He typed the answer onto his notes.

Chapter 54

To have one meeting at The Juice Guru was unusual, but a second seemed downright eccentric.

"We did some blue-sky thinking last time we were there," Pop had said when Chad had called him to request the meeting. "And we won't get hassled by irate citizens 'cos the only people who go there are tourists. I'll meet you there at 4 p.m."

"G'day, mate, what can I get ya?" asked the guy behind the counter.

The menu was on the wall. Nothing with chilli and bloody ginger, that's for sure.

"I'll get a bottle of still water, thanks."

"Oh, right," said the waiter. Chad admired the way the guy managed in just two words to convey his utter disdain for the choice. "Anything with the water, mate?"

"Yes," Pop's voice boomed over Chad's shoulder. "A double espresso and I'll get a Sex Me Up as well. I bloody need it."

The shirt was a teal green today, Chad noted, with several varieties of multi-coloured birds. Parakeets, parrots and at least one kookaburra. Same jacket, same jeans. Pop looked like the subject of a TV appeal to help the homeless.

"What's so urgent?" said Pop, when they'd got their drinks and sat down.

Chad had wondered in the cab up to town whether he'd been premature in asking for this meeting. He hoped he could articulate his thoughts because time was against them.

"Right, bear with me as I try to explain where I've got to. And try not to interrupt, just listen. We can debate it when I've finished."

"Okay. I'll give it a burl."

Chad stared at Pop. "Give it a what?"

"A burl. Yeah, I'll give it a burl. What do you Poms say?"

"I don't know what you're talking about, so let's crack on."

Divided by a table and their common language, Chad ordered his thoughts. "I spent a couple of hours earlier this afternoon mulling over some questions about the case. Didn't get very far with the majority, but one question stopped me in my tracks."

"Chad, I haven't got a few hours to chew the fat, so can you save the contextual background info and just cut to the chase? What was the question?"

Chad smiled. For all Pop was a big Tasmanian arse, Chad couldn't help but like him.

"Okay. The killer found the author of the Nefeli's report," he said. "How?"

Pop stopped sucking on his straw. "Yeah, how did he? 'Cos we bloody can't."

"It's a public document, so when someone orders a redaction, that's it. No copies remain un-redacted. So, he couldn't have read it. Which leaves only one answer."

Pop raised a quizzical eyebrow.

"Someone told him who wrote it."

Pop downed his espresso, his eyes darting around the café. "But who? Who would have known about it?"

"I've come up with one answer, no guarantees it's right, but it fits."

"I said cut to the bloody chase."

"Grumpy bastard," retorted Chad. "Who and why. You'll get who if you can understand why. Come on, Pop, you're the cop, work it out."

The seconds ticked by. Pop sucked hard on his drink, the thick orange liquid surging up the straw. Two minutes went by as Chad watched Pop put the pieces together. Just as Chad was about to answer his own question, Pop said. "The killer put the squeeze on someone from the hospital back in 2002. He's threatened them."

"Eureka. For a minute there, I was thinking you should seriously consider a career change."

"Funny bugger. But who has he got at? Which one?"

"The doctor he didn't kill," replied Chad. "The guy we were certain was the next victim, the bloke you had your officers guarding. I think the perp has got to Dr Jim Doyle."

Pop pushed his plastic cup away to the side of the table. "Yes, that fits. Right, let's get him interviewed." He stood to leave.

"Wait a second, Pop," said Chad. "Time isn't on our side and," he paused, "it isn't on your side personally."

"How do you mean?"

"By your own admission, the top brass have got you in their sights as someone to blame."

"Christ, don't I know it?"

"Pop, buy time for yourself and the investigation."

"How? What's your plan?"

"I think you should do a live TV interview with Andrea Byrne. You control the narrative and the questions. It'll help to get the public and your superiors off your back. If you want to finish this job, you should consider it."

Pop turned on his heel and stared at Chad. "Mate, good work on the Doyle theory, but an interview with Andrea Byrne… You can stick that where the sun don't shine."

Worth a try, thought Chad.

Chapter 55

Chad waited for Jas on the steps of the Sheraton. The bell boys were still under starters orders, but the press pack had disappeared. Chad chuckled remembering the guy outside Day Street who'd shouted abuse at him. He'd asked Pop what 'bull dust' meant.

"Bull dust means rubbish. He's saying you're rubbish, mate. But, Chad buddy, if you heard what they shout at me, you'd take bull dust as a term of endearment."

Jas emerged looking sexy as hell. Her hair was curled up onto the side of her head above her ear and held in place with a white rose. She wore a figure hugging sleeveless pink Chanel dress with a jewel neck. Her skin seemed to shimmer and Chad struggled to stop his eyes drifting onto her body.

"Hey, Hoppy, the face is here not there," Jas laughed pointing at her chin then her chest.

"Oops, sorry, but if you wander out looking that good you can't expect me not to stare."

"No," she said linking Chad's arm. "It's not that you're staring, that's nice. It's which bit of me you're staring at, you naughty boy."

"Guilty as charged."

"Where are we going for dinner?"

"I've got us a table at Café Sydney, it's in the Customs House on Circular Quay. I've asked if they'll seat us out on the balcony. There's a stunning view of the bridge."

"I seem to get a magnificent view everywhere we go, but I'll be the size of a house side if I keep eating like this."

Chad started laughing for the first time in ages. Then as a remembered phrase came into his head, he stopped walking and a fit of the giggles bent him double.

"What?" said Jas, his laughing making her chuckle as well. "Is being the size of a house side funny?"

Chad stood and leaned on the wall. "It's not that," he said gasping for air.

"What then?"

"Once, at a barbecue, Freddie told Odd Job that if continued eating, he'd look like a gable end."

Chad started howling again. "Anyway, a girl with us scowled at Freddie, so he says 'What's up?' and she says, 'Freddie, you can't call him a gay bell end.' Chad slumped against the wall, shoulders shaking.

"The tensions getting to you, Chad. Come on, let's go eat."

*

The lights of the Harbour Bridge twinkled so bright and so close that Chad felt he could reach out and touch them. Amidst the chaos and the carnage, he felt almost guilty for enjoying the simple pleasures. Mind you, he thought, simple pleasures didn't accurately describe the restaurant he was in, the views from the balcony or the company he was keeping. Jas sipped a Courvoisier, and he rolled his Highland Park around the glass. "I'll nip to the loo," he said.

Chad stood in the bathroom and washed his hands the water splashing on the stainless-steel bowl. What to do now? He'd walk Jas back to the hotel but what then?

He looked in the mirror. Angie's face looked back at him. She was blond and beautiful and smiling. Angie who had left him, but who wouldn't leave him. He closed his eyes then opened them again. His own face peered back at him. Not yet, he thought, it's not time yet, she's still with me.

He emerged from the bathroom and wondered what he could say to Jas. He couldn't be intimate with her when every time he closed his eyes Angie's face appeared.

Christ. Pull yourself together, he thought, arriving back at the table and sitting down. He smiled at Jas who held his eye and raised an enquiring eyebrow.

A voice behind him said, "Hello, Chad, fancy seeing you here."

Chad looked over his shoulder to find Andrea Byrne smiling, glass in hand.

"Hello, Andrea," said Chad. "They let you in here? Blimey, standards slipping, eh?"

Andrea looked at Jas then back to Chad. "Punching above your weight mate." She winked at Jas. "Aren't you going to introduce us?"

"Now, now," said Jas. "I'm Jas Carter and I reckon you must be Andrea Byrne, Chad's told me a lot about you, and of course, I've seen you on TV. Pleased to meet you."

"A pleasure," smiled Andrea. "From the UK by your accent?"

"Yorkshire, if you don't mind."

"Ah, apologies," laughed Andrea. "Anyway, I won't intrude, nice to meet you, Jas. Talk soon, Chad."

Chad watched her turn away then look back over her shoulder and give an exaggerated wink.

Chapter 56

Andrea leaned back on her settee and exhaled. The smoke swirled and swayed before dispersing. Not bad, she thought. Three weeks. From being a hack at The Globe to being on mainstream TV. Not bad at all. Twitter followers into the hundreds of thousands and in demand from every news network. Shit, she'd even done an interview with the BBC. Long may it continue.

The only downside was having to keep her drinking in check. Studio make up could cover a multitude of sins, but she'd discovered that if she'd hit the bottle hard the night before, then reading the autocue the next morning was problematic. Note to self: don't get hammered on school nights.

But, tonight was different. Tonight, she'd let her hair down. It was a mark of how far she'd come in such a short time she was considered high profile by her producers and worked Monday to Friday only. None of this weekend stuff that was for the reserve team. She sipped her wine. So, Hilton had a girlfriend. How did she feel about that? Part of her had wondered what he'd be like in bed, but she'd decided he was too old for her. Not to mention the fact that he'd shown no interest in her. Anyway, thanks to a colleague who owed her a favour and had tipped her off about Café Sydney, she had two names to give to Trevor when he rang, or indeed, if he rang. Hilton had wobbled her when he'd suggested that Trevor might be the killer. It made sense, of course, but she'd buried that suspicion. It had been better not to think about that. But Hilton had made her re-consider the prospect. She shivered. Give Trevor the names, she thought, and hope he'd bugger off.

She wondered if Pop would accept her proposal for a face-to-face interview. What a coup that would be. Pop. Something about saying his name aloud made her sit up mid-exhale. "Come on," she muttered, "what is it? What's bothering you about Pop?"

Before she could find the answer, her phone rang.

"Good evening, Andrea, I hope you're well?" Before Andrea could reply, Trevor continued. "Now à propos of our conversation yesterday, I wonder if you have some names for me? Friends of our mutual acquaintance, Chad Hilton?"

She took a pull on the ice-cold Pinot. "I've got a couple, yes," she said. "Look, nothing's going to happen to them, is it?"

"Don't discover a conscience now, Andrea, it's too late for that. And I've told you before, what'll happen is no concern of yours. To put your mind at ease, my contact wants a little leverage on Mr Hilton. An insurance policy. Now, names, Andrea."

Andrea jostled with the ethics but decided she didn't want the killer's spotlight back on her. She didn't need that shit. "Okay," she said. "There's a woman that he's seeing. I assume they were an item back in the UK. Her name is Jas Carter."

"Interesting, well done. And the other?"

"Freddie Jackson has a son, Junior, who lives over here. He's late teens, maybe early twenties. Hilton seems close to him."

Andrea waited. She could hear Trevor's breathing, but nothing else. Say thank you and piss off, she thought.

"That's good work, thank you. Now I have one last job for you, after which we can consider our deal concluded."

Andrea sat bolt upright, spilling her wine. "Oh, come on, Trevor," she shouted. "I've more than upheld my side of the bargain."

More silence, then "One last job, Andrea. Don't forget you broke the contract, and it's only because of our leniency that you're now a TV celebrity. That can all change, Andrea."

"What do you want me to do?" Jesus effing Christ, she thought, this is beyond a joke.

"I want you to talk to Chad Hilton... "

"What about?"

"Andrea, don't interrupt me again. Is that clear?" Trevor's voice was acidic.

Andrea took a sip of wine but said nothing.

"Good. I want you to tell Chad that he needs to stop looking for answers to puzzles. Stop helping the police. If he stops, Jas Carter and Jackson's son will be safe, but if not, then both would be in terminal danger."

Andrea saw an immediate flaw in the plan. "How will you know if he stops?"

"Once more, Andrea, that's no concern of yours, but trust me I will know the minute he ceases. Or indeed if he doesn't. You'd better make sure he gets the warning loud and clear, Andrea. I'll leave that with you, but expect that you'll relay our message to Hilton by no later than midday tomorrow. Okay?"

She recognised a rock and a hard place when she saw it. "Yeah, okay."

"Good night, Andrea. And let's hope it's also goodbye."

Andrea sat unmoving for several minutes after the call had finished. What to do? Her brain juggled a pros and cons balance sheet. Over the last few weeks, the risk and reward ratio was the deciding factor. This was no different.

Not risks or rewards to Jas Carter or Junior, or even Chad Hilton.

It was all about the risks to her career and what course of action would give her the greatest reward. The answer was obvious. Relaying Trevor's message to Chad just would not be a runner. She couldn't afford him to down tools on this, 'cos that would end her advantage over her competitors. And anyway, she reasoned, if Chad kept working on the case Trevor, or whoever was the killer, was more likely to be caught sharpish. Hell, she thought, there's only one remaining victim.

She was sorry that the world was shitty, but that wasn't her fault. She had to look out for herself, she decided, 'cos no other bugger would. If Chad hadn't got involved with Pop, this wouldn't have happened. So, it was Chad's fault, not hers if anything happened to Carter and the kid.

She poured more wine and mused that not unlike cocaine, she found her brain was sharp and clear with a couple of glasses inside her. As she put her glass on the table top, a memory surfaced. She replayed a conversation over in her head, verbatim, then remembered Hilton's comments about the killer making a mistake. "A word here. An unintended phrase there."

She lifted her phone and typed. When she'd finished, she read the message back and then pressed send. Not sure if that's what Chad meant, but hey, he couldn't accuse her of being unhelpful, even if she didn't pass on Trevor's message.

Chapter 57

Dr Jim Doyle bellowed the lyrics of Tom Petty's American Girl, reflecting that singing in the shower without the police as an audience was a luxury. Before he'd buggered off, the last copper had told him to attend an interview with Inspector Ruben Murray at 9 a.m. sharp at Day Street Police Station. "Nothing to worry about, sir, just tying off loose ends," he'd said. The police believed the threat to him was over.

He turned off the tap, grabbed a towel from the rail, Then checked his face in the mirror. "Say nothing tomorrow," he told his reflection. "You know nothing, not why these murders are happening or who's doing them. Say nothing and you'll be okay." In reality, of course, he understood why the murders were being committed, but he didn't know who was doing them. Telling the police would only put himself and his family in jeopardy. Therefore, he'd do as he'd been told and say nothing. No choice.

Drying himself, he stepped across the hallway to his bedroom. Mirrored glass wardrobes ran the length of one wall. Sliding one panel open, he pulled out a red tee-shirt and a pair of navy shorts. In the mirror, he glimpsed a photograph on his bedside table. He was smiling at the camera, one arm around his wife and the other around his daughter. He shivered and screwed his eyes tight shut. His wife had been dead three years, but her presence was everywhere. And his daughter… A tear fell down his cheek. His daughter, the reason he had found himself in this god-awful predicament.

'She's safe. If I say nothing to anyone, she'll stay that way.'

He fastened the button on the shorts, slipped the tee-shirt over his head, then sat on the bed and stared at the bedside table with distaste. Constructed in a solid looking pine, it had three drawers but it wasn't the material or the object causing him to grimace. It was what it contained in the bottom drawer. Clasping the brass handle, he slid the drawer open, then felt to the back. The plastic touched his fingers, and he retrieved the clear folder from the recess.

His hand shook as he pulled the sheet of A4 from its wallet.

I'm the justice that was never served. I have passed a sentence of death on you and your fellow conspirators. There is nowhere for you to hide. You will all die.

You, Dr Jim Doyle, have one small window of opportunity to save your own life.

- *The year is 2003 and you are working with Dr Nefeli at the Royal Prince Alfred.*
- *He has killed those he should have saved.*
- *You knew.*
- *They hold an enquiry.*
- *A cover up is instigated.*
- *Here is your opportunity.*

The report's author has to be named. By you. The name, no more. You will send it by text to a number you will receive at 4:30 p.m. If you don't, your opportunity is gone and you will die with the others. As an added incentive, failure to comply will mean the death of your daughter.

He'd received the letter four weeks ago and clipped to the back was a photo of Claire, his only child, standing at her front door with the key in the lock, looking over her shoulder as if disturbed. He'd complied. Who wouldn't in the same position? But now, having had the police camped in his house for days, he'd decided that keeping the note was dangerous. What if the police had found it? He'd burn it. Now.

Shoving the sheet of paper in his pocket, he made his way downstairs and was crossing the hallway when the doorbell rang. Stopping mid-stride, he looked over his shoulder.

"Who the hell is that?" he muttered.

He walked to the door and peered through the security spy hole. Shit, another bloody copper. Christ, they've only just left.

He opened the door and stood facing the policeman. "Forget something?" he asked.

"I'm sorry sir, just a couple of things, if I may?"

"What things? I'm meeting Inspector Murray tomorrow, so what the hell can you want?"

"That's why I'm here, sir. Inspector Murray has asked me to cover off any ongoing security arrangements, including making your property as secure as possible. It'll only take a minute. May I come in, please?"

"Jesus bloody Christ. Yes, I suppose so, come in." The copper crossed the threshold. "Lounge is up ahead on the right."

"Thanks."

Doyle shut the front door. They must think I'm still in danger after all, he thought. Anyway, it can't harm to have the house checked over and made secure. He walked up the hallway, home to various family photos and his qualification certificates, then entered the lounge.

Standing in the doorway, two thoughts flitted into his head. First, why was he staring at a handgun? Second, this was a mistake.

"You thought I'd let you live?" asked the man with the gun.

He opened and closed his mouth to reply, but no words were forthcoming.

"Wow, you did," said the man, smiling. "That's a tough break."

Doyle's head exploded, depositing the contents onto the door and wall. As his body crumpled and fell, the A4 sheet slipped from the pocket of his shorts.

The man picked it up. "Good on ya, sport. Saves me searching for it."

Chapter 58

'Justice will overtake fabricators of lies and false witness.'
Heraclitus.

I listen to the ring tone, come on, answer the bloody phone. I need to know how Hilton took my threat.

"Hi, this is Andrea." Her voice sounded anxious.

"Andrea, how are you today? Well, I hope?"

"Oh hi, Trevor," she says. "What can I do for you?"

"I'm checking that you've had a chat with Chad Hilton as instructed?"

A pause. "Yeah, yeah I spoke to him a while ago." That's all she says.

"And? Andrea don't play games with me, what did he say?"

"Well obvs it shocked him and he ranted, but after a couple of minutes he got a grip. He said he couldn't let harm come to Jas and Jackson Junior, so I reckon he'll back off."

I let the information sink in. It'll be clear soon enough whether he acts on my message. Or not.

"Well, thank you, Andrea. I've enjoyed our conversations and hope you agree that they've been mutually beneficial, but as they say, all good things must end."

"Er, right," she says. "Is that it?"

"That's it, Andrea. Goodbye."

I put the phone in my pocket and replay the conversation again. It feels like I'm approaching the endgame, the denouement. My planning is complete for the execution of the final criminal, and I'll expedite that as soon as I can. There is now only one other loose end to tie off.

Subject to how Hilton reacts to what Andrea has told him, I may have to implement a plan for the removal of Ms Carter and Mr Jackson Junior. I'll know soon enough. There's no point in making a threat if you're not prepared to carry it out.

*

The veins in Pop's forehead were close to bursting. "What do you mean there's no answer?" he shouted. "When I say 9 a.m. sharp that's exactly what I mean."

"He's not answering his phone," said José.

"Well, don't just stand there." Pop pointed at the two uniformed officers standing in the squad room's doorway. "You two, Swift, Dawson, get over to Doyle's house and pick him up. Cheeky bastard thinks he can piss me around. I want him back here in half an hour flat, sitting in an interview room shitting himself, is that clear?"

"Sir," the two uniforms bellowed in unison.

*

Chad was brewing more coffee when he heard his phone ring. He noticed he had a message from Andrea but reckoned that could wait. "Morning, Pop, what's up?" he asked, not looking forward to the answer.

"Dr Doyle was due to have his little chat with me at 9 a.m. this morning but didn't show. I sent a couple of uniforms to pick him up and when they arrived, they found the front door unlocked so went inside. The doctor was lying in the living room with blood and brain everywhere. Shot at point blank range with a nine-millimetre Parabellum by the look of it."

"Shit," sighed Chad. He poured coffee into a mug and headed for the lounge.

"So, we've obviously ballsed up again. I think the perp changed the order and did Trippier first. Then as soon as we stand down the security on Doyle... Bang."

"Maybe, but..."

"But nothing, Chad." Pop shouted. "Maybe the author of the report was Doyle. Who knows?"

Chad grimaced. "No, Pop it doesn't fit," he said. "The killer's only shot those he considered collateral damage," Chad paused. "Doyle was a loose end. He'd served his purpose by giving the perp the author's name but he couldn't take the chance that Doyle wouldn't talk. The killer may have known you were going to interview him."

"How the hell could he have known that, I only set it up yesterday?"

Moot point, thought Chad.

"Anyway," continued Pop, "it doesn't matter if it fits or not. He's dead and we are none the wiser. I will have to explain why I stood the security down. One minute we think he's a potential target, the next we don't. Then he gets shot. Doesn't look good, Chad. Maybe I'm at the end of the road."

Chad sat up. "Pop, take control. Do an interview with Andrea, explain that we think the author of the report is a target and ask that he or she makes themselves known to you so we can offer protection. Appeal to the author. It'll get you on the front foot and you never know the author may be so shit scared by now that he'll call. I mean, wouldn't you? It'll also make life a little tougher for the perp 'cos he won't know if the author calls you or not and therefore whether we are guarding him."

Silence. Chad didn't feel the need to break it. He knew this was tough for Pop, but he had to let him get there under his own steam. In the time it took for Pop to consider the proposal, thoughts swirled in Chad's head. There was one way the killer might know if the police received a call from the author. The same way he might have known that Pop was going to interview, Doyle.

Pop cleared his throat. “Get hold of Andrea Byrne,” he said. “Get her to set up the interview. Today.”

The line went dead, and as Chad clicked through to the home screen, he saw Andrea’s message and opened it.

You said to text if I remembered anything that Trevor said that seemed strange. One thing struck me as weird. Probs means nothing but… One of the first times he called, he was talking about the police and he used Pop’s name. I don’t mean his real name, Ruben Murray, I mean he called him Pop. Like he knew him.

Chad read it twice. “Shit, shit, shit.”

Chapter 59

Chad stood in the bar at the Sheraton and watched the big screen. Next to him, Jas and Mel, shuffled and fidgeted. They knew how these interviews went. Channel Nine had given the interview a big a build-up. Or at least as big as the short notice they'd had to arrange it, had permitted. Andrea was all over the bulletins, promoting her exclusive upcoming interview with a *'Breaking News'* banner running across the screen.

An announcer, with what Chad reckoned was an inappropriate amount of delight given the subject, intoned, "So, after this quick break we'll cross to Australia's leading crime reporter, Channel Nine's very own, Andrea Byrne. She'll be talking with Detective Inspector Ruben Murray who is leading the investigation into the horrific murders that have shocked Sydney over the last three weeks. She'll be putting to him the questions we know you're asking. Don't miss this, folks. We'll be right back."

As the adverts finished, the cameras zoomed in to Andrea Byrne and Pop in chairs facing each other. Chad felt disappointed that the habitual hobo look had gone. Not a Hawaiian shirt in sight. Instead, there was a suit and tie and the appearance of someone akin to a modern professional law enforcer. Pop had shaved, washed and combed his hair and was looking the part with, Chad guessed, a significant input from Channel Nine's makeup team.

Andrea couldn't keep the look of triumph off her face.

"G'day, Inspector Murray, and thanks for joining us in the studio today. I know you're busy so let's cut to the chase. Are you any nearer to catching the perpetrator of these outrageous murders?"

Chad shuffled from foot to foot. Don't fuck this up.

Pop cleared his throat. "Thanks Andrea," he began. "Murders like these are extremely rare and Sydney is one of the safest major cities on the planet. Fourth worldwide. I know, however, that the current situation is worrying for everyone," he paused. "But the killer does not commit the murders at random, there are specific targets and the public is not at risk."

"Well," she replied, with a sigh of relief to camera, "that's good news." Andrea, reprised faux concern as her expression of choice as she asked the camera, "Is an arrest imminent?"

Pop leaned towards Andrea. Not the only one who could play for the camera, Chad thought, he's not bad at this. Pop's face was serious but conveying a sense of reassurance. He was like everyone's dad: strong, safe and you knew everything would be okay. No irascible Tasmanian stress-head on display here.

"Andrea, for reasons that I'm sure your viewers and the people of Sydney will understand, I can't go into details of our investigation. But I can reassure them we have made significant progress." Pop looked into the camera. "Today, I want to use your show to make an appeal."

Andrea faced the camera wide eyed, like this was news to her.

"Go right ahead," she said.

Chad looked into Pop's eyes down the camera lens.

"I'm appealing for the author of a report commissioned twenty years ago to contact the police. This person knows they are in danger. He or she should make themselves known to me so that we can offer protection. There's a direct line which they can access."

Pop took a deep breath and pushed his shoulders back then, in a tone Chad recognised, said, "I don't need hoaxers and other idiots calling this number." That was more like it. Tasmanian arse back in town.

The number scrolled along the bottom of the screen.

"How does this person calling you move the investigation forward?" asked Andrea. "Does he or she hold information you need?"

"Andrea, we believe this person is in danger and should make themselves known to me as soon as possible. I have nothing else to say right now."

Chad turned to Jas, "He did well there."

"Yeah, he did. He was reassuring and calm which should keep people off the streets."

Chad nudged Mel and took Jas's arm, "Come on, let's go. Is Freddie on his way?"

"Yes, he is," said Mel. She looked at Chad. "With your protection detail of Odd Job and Tony in tow."

Chapter 59

'Justice is truth in action.'
Benjamin Disraeli

Sometimes it's necessary to give credit to one's adversary. And this is one of those times. Pop appearing on Andrea Byrne's TV show is a smart move. Gets the public off the backs of the police, makes out they're closer to catching me than they are and every right-minded citizen will think that the report writer is bound to call. I mean, why wouldn't he?

But if the public knew what I do about him, they'd realise there's no way he's going to call. He can't, he's too much to lose. But his arrogance – a common trait amongst all those involved twenty years ago – makes him think he can keep me at bay by increasing the security he has at his beck and call.

Oh dear, how little he knows of me.

I can see Chad Hilton's fingerprints all over the idea to use Andrea Byrne. What does that mean? Is he ignoring my threats? The wind outside is picking up and the white spume on the waves below, rising and falling, gives the ocean a restless energy that matches my own. I need more evidence before I decide on Hilton and his friends, but let's check first that Hilton is indeed ignoring me. I'll know if he is still involved in the case after my last execution. If he is, that's all I need.

Anyway, one thing at a time. Let's end the Nefeli nightmare then concentrate on the rest. I take a deep breath and turn back into the house. I need to prepare my apparatus.

Chapter 60

One of the two fans in the briefing room had shuffled off its mortal coil, the other was having no noticeable effect.

"Okay, guys, let's get started," Pop began. "Lucy, how far have you got in tracing the relatives of Nefeli's victims?"

Lucy was leaning against the wall, her afro like a black halo framing her head.

"We identified six patients that died because of Nefeli's surgery. It's a disgrace, really. It's clear that everyone knew Nefeli was a wrong 'un, but allowed him to carry on and it was even suggested he wasn't a qualified doctor," she paused, then looked at Pop. "Sorry, Boss, rant over. Anyway, we applied the criteria we'd agreed to these six victims and could eliminate four of the families."

"How?" asked Chad. "How did you reach the decision, are you certain that none of those four families could hold the key?"

"Yeah, we're certain, Chad. The spouse of the victim was the only living relative. Three have subsequently died and the one remaining is in a dementia care home."

Pop said, "Fair enough, what about the other two?"

"We have two families. The first is the Davis family. The mother died at the hospital leaving dad, John, and two daughters, Emily and Jo, now aged twenty-five and twenty-eight respectively. Emily, lives in Melbourne and, Jo, on a farm in Queensland."

"Doesn't sound very promising. Have you spoken to them?"

"Yes. Each of the women have alibis for the times of the

murders and John, the father, suffers from a degenerative bone disease rendering him wheelchair bound. Before you ask, yes, we've checked with his doctor."

"That's great," said Pop, with less enthusiasm than the words implied. "Our perp must be from the remaining family?"

"Yes, but it's never that easy, is it?"

"Jesus, I bloody knew it. Come on, what's the problem?"

"The Rasch family included two brothers aged ten and thirteen at the time. Nefeli killed their mother in 2002. They're now thirty and thirty-three. The father, Klaus, was of German descent, and had a history of alcohol abuse and domestic violence. The authorities deemed he wasn't fit to look after them, so the two boys David and Jonathon entered the care system."

Lucy scrolled through the notes on her tablet. "The younger, David, went to various foster homes, but we lose sight of him aged sixteen when he leaves the care system. We pick him up again aged eighteen when he's fined for being drunk and disorderly. No known whereabouts since then." Lucy looked up, "And to make matters worse, there are no records relating to the elder brother. He absconded from the children's care home two months after being placed there in January 2003. No trace since."

"Well, that's fucking bonzer," Pop yelled. "We finally get a lead and it turns to dust before you can say g'day."

Chad wiped the sweat from his face and forehead. The perp's laughing at us, he thought. He's known when we discovered the Rasch family, there'd be nothing there, just a spectre, a ghost. A big fat dead end. Trail over.

"Good work, Lucy," said Pop. "What about the appeal?"

"Nothing, Pop. A few idiots but no one of interest."

The silence sat heavy and oppressive. No one spoke, the ideas jar was empty.

Chad closed his eyes. He'd arrived at the last corner of a long, treacherous road. A trail he'd followed with the promise of closure.

But there was no closure, because the road went on away into the distance. What now?

Chapter 62

Jas sat on the stretch of grass that ran from Campbell Parade down to Bondi Beach. She'd arranged lunch with Junior and had some time to kill. Her idea was simple: watch the waves, enjoy the surfers, and chill. Straightforward as it was, gaggles of tourists throwing food from their assorted lunches to the gulls thwarted her plan. The birds swooped and hollered, fighting for each scrap, then loitered with intent and menace. Jas strolled down to the beach, away from the mayhem, sat on the sand and gazed out to sea. The sun was warm enough for tee-shirt and shorts. She wriggled her toes in the sand and her mind drifted to Chad. What are you going to do about him? Even the question was difficult, she thought, let alone the answer. Which Chad? The Chad with something akin to Stockholm Syndrome: needing his work to keep him sane, but going bonkers doing it? The man so wrapped up in Pop's case that he was mentally self-harming to the point of no return? That Chad?

She felt the breeze blow back her hair and pictured Chad a few months ago. A barely functioning drug addict, life in turmoil, needing work to keep alive. We're there again, she thought. Just without the drugs.

Or the other Chad? The man that was tearing himself apart with feelings of guilt about his wife's death. A guilt, Jas recognised, that his undoubted feelings for her compounded and increased. That he could not deal with those feelings, let alone articulate them, had been amply demonstrated when he'd walked her back to the Sheraton after their meal at Café Sydney. An onlooker,

Jas reckoned, would not have guessed that the man was a highly qualified psychologist such was his gauche, tongue tied and distressed attempts at expressing himself. But what could she do about that?

She looked out over the ocean. The colours; mixed purples and greens tinged with the odd shaft of bright yellow, jostled and mingled on the waves. You can't help him get over Angie, just be there when he does.

Two gulls, one with food and one without, fought an aerial duel over the water. Jas kicked the sand.

'Be there when he does.'

Really? Is that what you want? To wait? And for how long? Sitting on your hands and kicking your heels… For a bloke? Not really your style is it, girl?

Snap out of it, she thought. She pushed Chad aside and concentrated her thoughts on the case. After all you're here to help him, so if you can't get him to pull himself together maybe you can help solve these bloody crimes? The copper in her itched to be released, to do some good solid detective work. What about that idea you had?

Out at sea, a surfer, tiny in the distance, rose with balletic grace onto his board, crouched and skidded across the swell being chased by the crest. Then, his stature growing as he got closer, he somehow doubled back before finally rising, arms aloft, ride complete.

She pulled her phone from her back pocket and typed a message to Junior. *I'll grab us a sandwich and meet you at the flat, we've got work to do.*

*

Chad closed the door to the apartment and leaned back against it. His mood hadn't lightened since he'd left Day Street. If anything, it had worsened as the cab driver had insisted on participating, albeit virtually, in a radio phone-in dedicated to Rugby League, about which Chad knew bugger all.

The driver offered the same succinct summary to each of the callers' opinions.

"Talking shit, mate, you're talking shit."

Chad had found only partial relief that the driver didn't expect him to comment. He'd had several missed calls from Jas and a text saying *Call urgent.* on his way back to Bondi, but hadn't reached her. What could be urgent? Whatever it was, he'd decided, he couldn't take more shit.

"Chad, is that you?" shouted Jas from the lounge.

"Yep," Chad straightened, plonked his keys on the table with his cap and sunglasses and wandered down the hallway. "What's so urgent?"

A male voice said, "Hey, Chad, how's things with you today?" Only Junior's feet were visible, dangling over the end of the settee.

"I've been better, Junior." Chad saw from the TV screen Junior was playing FIFA 22. "But seeing that you've got to the semi-final of the Copa America has cheered me right up."

Junior's head appeared. "I love this game, man," he beamed.

"Well, can you pause it for a minute, please?" said Jas. She looked at Chad, "I need to run something past you."

"Right, okay. What is it?"

Jas joined him at the window and they looked down onto the afternoon mayhem that was Hall Street. She put her arm around his waist and then leaned in to him. "I've had an idea," she whispered.

Chad turned and faced her. "Really, an idea about what?"

"About the identity of the report writer."

Chad stared at her. Her eyes sparkled with life and excitement.

"Brilliant, go for it," he said. "I'm all ears, though I thought you were dead set against me being involved?"

"If I can't stop you, the least I can do is try to help."

From the settee Junior's yelp of "get in, you, beaut," suggested

Lionel Messi had just scored an injury time winner.

Chad took Jas to the bedroom and sat on the bed. "Right fire away, now we're not competing with the racket in there."

"Okay, and don't interrupt," said Jas. He felt the shape of her thigh as she settled next to him. "Every public body," she began, "has a complaints procedure that's documented and available on request. There are process maps detailing who handles each complaint, plus who hears any appeal."

"With you so far."

"Junior discovered that if a complaint was sufficiently serious, it got escalated to the relevant minister. In Nefeli's case there were several of these that went to the Minister for Health and Aged Care. He commissioned an enquiry and appointed its head. We looked back to 2003 to see who the minister was."

"And?" asked Chad. "Who was it?"

"It was a bloke called James Dignon, but that doesn't really tell us much because he didn't write the report. He sanctioned it and would have decided on the publication, or redaction. Anyway, he's dead now, so he's out of the running," Jas smiled, conspiratorial and excited, like a young girl about to confide a secret.

"But the Government deem their employees work in the public domain which is ideal from an investigator's viewpoint, because if you have the time, patience and Junior's hacking skills, you can find their names. And, bless him, he found the list of Dignon's aides and secretaries from 2003."

Chad stared at Jas' animated, beautiful face. Bloody hell, he thought, how smart is she? The air in the room appeared to be lighter and clearer than before.

"We couldn't discover who Dignon had appointed to run the enquiry, but found senior aides conducted investigations in other ministerial jurisdictions like Home Affairs and Treasury. It seemed logical that our report would be conducted in the same way. Dignon had four senior aides, any of whom could have investigated. And the good news is that we've tracked them down."

Chad said nothing, he didn't want to spoil her moment. She nudged him and he held her eye. "I think I might have found him. The report writer."

"Do you have a name?"

"Yep, I do."

Chad looked up. He'd been so intent on listening that he hadn't noticed that Junior was now standing in the doorway.

"You owe Jas and me big time. Tell him Jas, he'll love this."

"It's a bloke called Michael Wilcox, which probs doesn't mean much to you?"

"No," said Chad. "I can't say it does."

"Well, he's done well for himself," she paused. "Get your phone and google him."

Chad typed the name into the browser and pressed enter. The result was immediate, and alarming. "Shit," he stared at the screen. "He's the current Minister for Health and Aged Care in the Australian Government." As questions and actions competed for space, time seemed to stand still. He tapped his phone and dialled.

"Pop, get your arse over here now," he said when the copper had answered with a gruff, "what?"

Chad spent thirty seconds explaining Jas's findings, but when he finished, he could tell from the wheezing and occasional grunts that Pop was on his way. And he was running.

*

Chad felt euphoric as he pushed past Junior, clapping him on the shoulder as he went.

"Great work, you two. Brilliant."

That's a tremendous breakthrough, he thought. Whether the means employed to elicit the information had been legal, was a technical detail and not his concern.

"Any joy in identifying the families of Nefeli's victims?" asked Jas.

"Yeah, they've narrowed it down to one. The Rasch family. Mother died on the operating table and they did not deem father fit to look after their two children, boys, aged ten and thirteen. They went into the care system and disappeared without trace thereafter. They could be anywhere."

"Can we trace them?"

"We don't know, it's been twenty years. Pop's not sure where to start and time's against us."

Jas sighed. "Because there'll be another attack?"

"Yes," said Chad." But thanks to you we know who that will be and can stop it. Protecting Wilcox gives us more time to find the killer."

Chad ran a hand through his hair, then looked at Jas, "Anyway, it pains me to say it, but I think Junior's hunch about the perp being a cop may have some merit."

Junior sat up, smiling, "I told you, man, it was obvious."

"Yeah, well, we've got something more substantial than your intuition."

"Go on," said Jas. "What have you got?"

"Two things. First, the perp took the quick route to finding the report writer. He put the frighteners onto the only person left that knew the writer. A guy called Doyle, Dr Jim Doyle. Maybe the killer told him he'd let him live, I don't know. You remember we'd found a photo?"

"Yeah," said Jas. "At one of the crime scenes?"

"That's right. It was a group shot from the hospital where Nefeli worked back in 2002. The only one still alive was Doyle. Pop planned to interview him, but the killer got to him before that could happen," Chad paused. "Only a copper based at Day Street would have known of that arrangement."

"Shit. Yeah," said Jas. "What's the second thing?" she walked into the kitchen and opened the fridge. "I'm listening."

"Is there a beer in there?" asked Chad. "The second is tenuous but still adds up. I'd asked Andrea Byrne…"

"Andrea Byrne from the TV?" interrupted Junior.

"Yeah, that Andrea Byrne. Anyway, I'd asked her if anything had struck her as strange, when she spoke to Trevor."

Jas returned and handed Chad a beer. "Don't I get one?" asked Junior.

"Get your own, you big lazy lump. Go on, Chad, what did she say."

Chad pulled his phone from his pocket, scrolled though his messages and having found the relevant one, passed the phone to Jas.

She read it, handed Chad, his phone, then said. "Yeah, weird if…"

"If what?" said Chad.

"If the name Pop isn't common knowledge."

"I'm told it's an internal nickname and not known outside the force. Added to everything else it hangs together that he could be a cop."

"Or an ex-cop, I suppose," muttered Jas.

"True," said Chad. "Although an ex-cop wouldn't have known about Doyle." He took a pull on his beer. "I'm going to run the theory past Pop, when he arrives."

Chapter 63

Chad was expecting the knock on the door but it still made him jump. "Christ, Pop, knock any harder and the residents will think it's a raid."

"Was it loud? I didn't think so," said Pop, stepping past Chad and walking into the living room. "So, you must be Jas?" Pop held out his hand which Jas shook.

"Hi," she replied. "I've heard a lot about you."

"All bad, I guess?" Pop laughed.

"Yeah, most of it."

Chad knew Pop couldn't decide whether to take the comment at face value.

"Yorkshire girls always tell it as it is, Pop. Warts and all. You'd better get used to it."

Pop scratched his head then looked at Jas. "I should give you and the…" Chad saw Pop's jaw drop as he watched Junior uncoil himself from the settee and stand, "the er, young giant here, a bollocking for meddling. But under the circs, I'm going to give you both a bloody medal."

"I see we have resumed normal service on the shirt choice," said Chad, admiring what looked like blue and yellow Macaws swaying in the trees. "Did you rent the suit for the TV interview with Andrea? Seems pointless you owning one."

Pop plonked himself in the armchair near the dining table.

"You're about as funny as a fart in a spacesuit, Chad, but I'll give you ten out of ten for effort. You don't let up, do you?"

Chad grinned. "Can I get you a drink?"

"What'ya got?"

"I can do you a gin and tonic, a single malt or a cold beer?"

"Bloody hell, if I'd known you were that well-stocked, I'd have come more often," said Pop. "But, no, thanks, and you shouldn't be drinking either. We are going to meet the Right Honourable Michael Wilcox, Minister for Health and Aged Care, in an hour. Which brings me to why I've legged it here. Jas, would you mind showing me the work you did to find Wilcox? Are you sure it was him that wrote the report?"

Jas opened the laptop and scrolled through various sites talking and pointing as she went. "Wilcox was one of four permanent secretaries to the Minister back in 2003," she began. "Since then, one has died and two have moved to New Zealand and California. Wilcox is based in Canberra but lives here in Sydney. So, if there's going to be one more victim, then the guy living here looks favourite."

"Okay, so why the hell has he not answered our appeal?"

"Too much to lose," said Chad. "If he came forward now, we'd accuse him of covering up Nefeli's negligence and allowing the murders to happen. He'd have some impossible questions to answer."

"If I have my way," said Pop, "he'll still have to answer for his actions. Could make for an interesting interview later. Well, thanks again, you two." He turned and Chad held his eye. "Chad, you said on the phone there was something else, for my ears only?"

"Yeah, there is," Chad turned towards the settee. "Junior, bugger off home, please, I need a private chat with Inspector Murray."

"Nah, mate, I can't. I need to stick around, Dad's coming here shortly."

Pop raised an eyebrow. "Dad?"

"Freddie Jackson," explained Chad.

"Oh, er, right, I see."

"Talk on the balcony," said Junior. "It's private. I'll chill here out of your way."

"He think he owns the place," muttered Chad. "Come on, Pop, this way. And Jas should join us."

*

"A cop?" said Pop. "When Mel suggested that, you were dead set against it. What's changed?"

"It's the only logical explanation that fits the facts," replied Chad. "Remember what Mel said? Where justice is the motive, eighty-five percent of killers come from law enforcement. That's powerful. Add how the killer got four victims alone, and it's compelling. Also, only cops from Day Street knew Doyle was due to be interrogated by you. Circumstantial I know, but it adds up. And finally, Andrea, texting that Trevor refers to you as Pop. Now how would he know that?"

Pop wandered along the balcony, tapped the lid of the barbecue and looked out to sea. "Okay, suppose he's a cop," he paused. "How do we find out which one it is? That's another needle in a haystack. Christ, in your theory Chad, it could even be me."

"That's the tough part of this. Jas, any ideas?"

"A couple."

"Come on, let's hear them," said Pop.

"I think the murder of Doyle is the key, because the only people who knew about the interview were cops. No one else."

Pop ran his hand through his hair. Chad could see the cogs turning.

"I ran a briefing meeting at lunchtime the day before. I told the team that I wanted to interview Doyle."

"Who specifically did you tell to let Doyle know?" asked Jas.

"No one specific, the squad would divide tasks between themselves or give it to a uniform. My guys were all there. José, Dimi, Lucy, Jess, Josh and Ken plus myself."

"Anyone else?"

Pop raised his arms in outstretched appeal. "Christ, Chad, you know what Day Street's like, there are always loads of uniforms coming in and out."

Chad wiped some dust from the balustrade with his finger while Pop fidgeted.

"I won't believe that the killer is one of my squad," murmured Pop. Then louder said, "I've worked with them for years. I'd have seen something; I know I would."

"Okay," said Jas, "how about this?"

"Go on."

"Give me discreet access to your systems. I'll check both your homicide squad detectives and the uniforms based at Day Street to see who was on duty at the time of your briefing and who was on duty at the time of the murders. And if you can get me the permissions, I'll dig a bit into their backgrounds. If one of the Rasch brothers is a copper at Day Street, he must have told a lie on his resumé that might give him away."

Pop looked at Chad. "Why don't you have fantastic ideas like that?"

Chad smiled, "'Cos you don't pay me," he said. "On a serious note, Pop, if the perp is a copper from Day Street, we can't alert him. We need radio silence concerning our Michael Wilcox suspicions until we're ready to make a move."

Pop stood. "Yeah, I know." He stared at Chad. "I'm going to call my Super in a minute and update him but other than that not a word. Now leave it with me, Jas, and I'll get you access within the hour. Do you need a laptop?"

"No, I can use his," she said pointing at Chad's Mac. "Will I need some training on your systems?"

"Nah we're simple coppers, it's easy. If he can use it," Pop nodded towards Chad, "a clever girl like you will find it a breeze."

"Okay, get me some login details and I'll crack on."

Chapter 64

Pop parked up on Beach Avenue in the affluent suburb of Vaucluse. "How the other one percent live, eh?" he said.

Each property, Chad noticed, stood in its own grounds and large, often ornate, security-controlled gates protected them from the outside world. But the house outside which they'd parked was different. Chad could only see the red-tiled roof of the property. The rest hidden from sight by ancient trees and shrubs. Further setting it apart from its neighbours were two burly security men standing inside the gates. Both had bulges in places males normally wouldn't and they both wore black suits.

"Right," muttered Pop, opening the car door and stepping out, "I'll have a word."

Chad watched as he approached the gates and engaged in a conversation the result of which led to Pop producing his police ID for inspection. Thereafter a few words into a one-piece headset and the gates opened. Pop headed back to the car.

"Two recent additions to the minister's security, they work for Control Inc, which I know well," said Pop. "According to dumb and dumber," he inclined his head towards the two guards, "it's a private arrangement between the minister and the company, not paid for by the government. Interesting that our esteemed minister feels the need to beef up his protection with some private muscle. I know I'm not the sharpest tool in the box, but I reckon our boy must be expecting trouble."

Pop drove in through the gates and along a driveway shaded by overhanging branches. The drive curved to the right and Chad saw a man in a blue shirt and chinos beckoning for them to follow him, then pointed at a row of parking spaces behind the property giving them the thumbs up.

"Not too shabby, eh?" said Pop. "Even for a stinking rich ex-soccer player this is special?"

Chad ignored him and climbed out of the passenger seat then stood taking in his surroundings. Not too shabby indeed, he thought. From where they'd parked there was a clear and uninterrupted vista of the beach and the sparkling blue water beyond. Chad saw a pathway that he assumed led to the clifftop, along which more security guards patrolled.

"Detective Inspector Murray?" asked the bloke in the chinos.

"Yeah, that's right, and this is Chad Hilton, who's assisting the investigation."

"My name is Joe. The minister's expecting you, follow me, please."

Gravel scrunched under foot as they approached a black painted door, which the flunkey opened and held to let them inside. Chad walked a pace or so behind Pop until they reached the end of the parquet corridor, which opened out into a large, dome-ceilinged, circular vestibule with several polished doors around its perimeter.

"Follow me, please," said Joe, striding across the space and knocking on a door.

"Enter."

Joe looked over his shoulder, smiled at Pop and opened the door. "Just in here, please."

Pop advanced into the spacious interior, and Chad followed. He smiled and nodded as Pop made the introductions and dealt with the pleasantries. Enormous bay windows looked out over the front lawns and to the trees beyond, making the room bright and airy. It was old-fashioned in a shabby-genteel style. Books lined the walls and around the room photographs adorned a series of tables, the carpet was Persian. A large three-seater red leather Chesterfield sat at right angles to a vast fireplace. The minister's desk sat in the bay and was clearly antique. Wilcox was of British colonial stock, Chad reckoned.

"So, Inspector, what is so urgent that I had to amend my diary to accommodate you?" He waved an arm at two chairs in front of his desk.

As Pop explained the reason for the meeting, Chad appraised the Minister for Health and Aged Care. Late fifties, maybe early sixties, he had a full head of greying hair in a side parting and bushy sideburns. His eyes were blue, face tanned, and his skin showed little signs of wear and tear. He wore a white short-sleeved shirt and his forearms rested on the desk. They too were tanned, and silver hair bristled around a large, expensive looking watch. Tall and well built, Chad reckoned he stood around six feet two.

Although outwardly attentive to what Pop was saying, the polished arrogance of the successful politician was also on display. A tapping of the pen here, a shuffle of papers there, glancing at his watch, checking his computer screen. His time way more important than theirs.

"Can you confirm, Minister, that back in 2003 you worked as a senior private secretary to the then minister, James Dignon?"

"Yes, I can't remember the exact dates but what you say is broadly correct."

"Okay. In 2003 were you appointed by the minister to conduct an enquiry into a series of complaints made against a Dr Nefeli, working at the Prince Alfred during 2002 and 2003?"

The Minister looked at Pop. "No," he said. "I wasn't."

"Who conducted the enquiry?" asked Pop.

"I don't know, in fact, are you sure there even was an enquiry? I don't recall it being the subject of any discussions I had with the minister."

Chad had to hand it to him, he was an accomplished liar. No

obvious physical signs like looking up to the right, or squeezing fingers, but Chad was intuitive. He'd done hundreds of interviews with desperate people, their freedom dependent on the outcome. They were invariably, liars. And so was the minister.

"Oh, we know there was a report, we've got it," said Pop. "Tell me, Minister, why have you increased both your personal protection and your home security in recent weeks?"

"I'd have thought that was obvious," replied Wilcox. "I can tell you I'm not the only high-profile public figure to do it. There's some madman roaming the streets of Sydney, murdering people at will and the police," he leant across the table and pointed his finger at Pop. "specifically, you, Inspector Murray, have not apprehended him. Why the hell wouldn't I increase my security?"

Pop sighed. Chad thought he was doing well to keep his temper.

"Minister, we believe that the killer's next victim will be the author of the report commissioned into the activities of Doctor Nefeli."

"Hold on a minute," said the Minister. "If you've got the report, you must know the name of the author?"

"No," Pop leaned forward across the desk. "The report's redacted and despite a public appeal the author hasn't come forward. We've narrowed our search to four people. Two have emigrated, one's died, which leaves you, Minister. If you wrote that report you should tell me now. We can the offer appropriate police protection and deal with the matters arising from the report and cover up in due course."

Nicely done, thought Chad.

Wilcox stared across the table. If he was angry or frightened, Chad saw no sign of it.

"I have told you, Inspector, I did not write the report. I hope I don't have to repeat myself. The police would better spend their time and the public money catching the killer, than chasing the author of some ancient report. An observation I intend to make to my colleague the Minister for Home Affairs and to the Chief Superintendent of Police. Now, I have a busy schedule."

Wilcox pressed a buzzer on his desk, and Joe entered. "Ah good, thanks, Joe. Can you see these gentlemen out, please?"

*

"What d'ya make of that cocky bastard?" said Pop.

Chad fastened his seat belt as Pop reversed out of the parking bay onto the drive where Joe stood sentry making sure they left.

"I expected nothing else, did you?" said Chad. "He would never come clean, that's for sure. I reckon he's banking on us catching the killer at some point and feels safe enough with his own protection and security. Once caught, it's his word against that of a murderous psychopath."

"Yeah, I agree. Except he now knows that we know he wrote that report. I expect he'll put some pressure on my boss to make me back off him."

"You're probably right," sighed Chad admiring the stunning view of the sea as they approached the road. "And his current security arrangements won't be good enough to stop the perp getting to him."

"Yeah, I agree. I need a plan for that."

Chad continued, "There are lots of potential entry points into the house, and I spotted the air con vent on the roof. Wilcox will also have to travel to Canberra every week and our killer is resourceful."

Chad allowed silence to settle around them. Glancing across he noticed that Pop's habitual frown seemed more pronounced. Deep in thought, he looked exhausted.

They stopped at a red light, and Pop turned to Chad. "Here's how I see it," he said. "The killer won't give up, he'll get to Wilcox. I can't place a police security detail on him because, a, Wilcox won't have it and b, it will alert the killer that we know who the report writer is, which could send him underground. Time is on his side. Seems like we're caught between a rock and a hard place, what d'ya reckon?"

Chad mulled over Pop's depressing assessment. A car horn blared as the lights changed to green. "Ah, do one," said Pop giving the driver of the car behind the finger in the rearview.

"You're right," replied Chad. "Rock and hard place about sums it up. We can't protect Wilcox and we can't find what happened to the Rasch brothers. Maybe Jas will get us a break."

Chapter 65

I watch the car leave the driveway and rub my eyes in disbelief, gripping the steering wheel so tight that my knuckles are white. Opening the window, the breeze cools me and the cacophony in my head dissipates and fades into the distance.

I take several deep breaths, place my hands on my thighs and sit upright. Breathe, breathe. I remain in my trance for what seems like seconds but the clock on the dashboard tells me minutes have elapsed. Minutes since I'd watched Pop and Hilton drive away taking my plans with them. I sit still. Calm returns. But no answers. Okay, let's think straight.

What's changed? They've discovered Wilcox and I don't know how they did that, but…

Does Pop knowing about Wilcox change anything?

No. Wilcox won't admit to being the author. He can't. Which means the police can't protect him. In fact, their position is worse now than before they knew. Failing to protect a minister of state that they knew was in danger? That's career ending for Pop and reputation trashing for Hilton.

I relax. Getting at Wilcox was always going to be a tough challenge, but even after today's setback my plan to accomplish it still holds. And what about Hilton? Why hasn't he backed off? Does he underestimate me and think I won't carry out my threat? That's a serious mistake if so.

Best to double check. I pick up a phone from the passenger seat, another burner, and dial a number etched in my memory.

"Hi, this is Andrea, is that Jack?" her voice is light and excited.

Who's Jack, I wonder? "No, Andrea," I reply, "it's me, Trevor."

"Oh hi, Trevor," her voice becomes tentative, wary. "I wasn't expecting to hear from you again."

"Nor I expecting to call you, Andrea. However, I'd like to check something with you."

"Er, okay. What?"

"Can you confirm you informed Chad Hilton of my insurance policy in the shape of his girlfriend, who's name escapes me, and the Jackson boy?"

There's a slight pause, but not enough to cause me concern.

"Yeah, I told him. He ranted a bit but got the drift. Why?"

"Oh nothing, I just wanted to double check." I allow a small sliver of silence to amplify the threat in my next question. "You wouldn't be lying to me would you, Andrea?"

Another pause.

"Of course not. Why would I do that? Telling him was no skin off my nose, but I can't control what Hilton does with the information."

"That's true, Andrea. Okay. Thank you, bye now."

I throw the phone onto the seat, and look out through the windscreen. What was it that the soccer commentators say?

"Game on."

Chapter 66

Chad could hear voices and laughter as he held open the apartment door so that Pop could enter.

"Sounds like a house full," said Pop. "Anyway, I can't stay long, but let's see if Jas has made a start."

Chad deposited his paraphernalia onto the table in the hall alongside Junior's keys and Jas's sunglasses, and walked into the lounge. Freddie stood by the window pointing at something outside which Odd Job and Tony craned to see. Junior meanwhile had resumed his position on the settee. Chad felt like a Lilliputian in the land of giants.

"Hey, Chad bro, how's it going?" said Freddie, turning. Then, noticing Pop, "You must be the police dude. Ru…" Chad caught Freddie's eye and scowled in time to prevent the 'Ruby' that he was certain Freddie was about to say. "Pop, is it?"

"Yeah, that's right," replied Pop, offering his hand. "And it doesn't take Hercule Poirot to work out who you are."

"Hercule who?" asked Freddie. "Don't think I know the dude. Is he French?"

"Jesus, Freddie," said Chad, "he's Belgian." Chad noted the blank expression on Freddie's face. "Agatha Christie's detective? You must know her?" appealed Chad.

"These guys are talking riddles," said Freddie, turning for confirmation to Odd Job. "Agatha who? What sort of name is that?"

"Forget it," said Chad. He'd known Freddie for over twenty years, but looking at his best friend leaning against the wall, he wasn't certain whether he was taking the piss. "Where's Jas?"

"She's in the bedroom doing something for the feds on the computer." Freddie was smiling, but the smile didn't reach his eyes. "Hey, Pop, looks like you've got Chad and Jas and even my boy Junior all working for you for free. You need to tell me your secret, bro, because these dudes," he pointed to Odd Job and Tony, "expect paying."

"Call it philanthropy," said Pop, smiling back at Freddie. "A sense of civic duty. But yeah, you're right, I owe them a beer or two."

"Damn right you do."

Chad led Pop out of the lounge before the back and forth between his mate and the Tasmanian degenerated into something less friendly. He opened the door. Jas was lying on the bed, MacBook on her thighs, her back resting against the headboard.

"Hey," said Chad, wishing he could close the door, lose the MacBook and lie down next to her.

"How did you get along with the minister?" asked Jas.

"To say the guy's a tosser," growled Pop, following Chad into the bedroom, "is a bloody understatement. Denied everything, and smarmy with it. How are you going on, found anything?"

"Well, it took me longer than I thought to work out your catchily named Standard Operating Procedures for Rostering systems, but Junior helped me so I got there in the end."

"He won't hack us, will he?" asked Pop.

Jas laughed. "Nah, he promised he wouldn't," she winked. "I've made a start, but there are more coppers than I hoped there'd be on duty at Day Street on the relevant days." She looked at Pop. "I know major crimes like these attract additional personnel resource, but it doesn't make the job easy."

"Start with the uniformed coppers. I know my team of detectives inside out and I can't believe it's one of them. I know the coppers, but not as well."

"Okey doke," said Jas, "leave it with me."

Pop headed back to the lounge; Chad followed. "Looking like a long job," he said.

"Yeah," agreed Pop. "But your mate Freddie has just given me an idea about Wilcox."

"Really?" asked Chad. Apprehension clawed at him. Whatever the hell Pop's idea was, if it involved Freddie, it wouldn't be good.

"Er, Freddie, mate," said Pop. All heads in the lounge turned as if in sync towards Pop.

"Yeah, bro, what is it?"

"I'm wondering whether your friends here," he nodded towards Odd Job and Tony, "might fancy a bit of extra security work. Paid, of course."

Chad chuckled. Pop's request was staggering, but so was the reaction of the group.

Each looked from one to the other, before all stared at Pop. Junior's head appeared over the cushions and peered like a Meerkat.

Freddie coughed, "Let me understand what you said, dude. You want to hire Odd Job and Tony, right?"

"Right," Pop confirmed.

"But you're a fed, bro!" Freddie's face had incredulity written all over it. "You don't hire my boys, damn, you spend most of your time trying to lock 'em up. Anyway, you've got hundreds of your own, why do you need mine?"

"Look, exceptional difficulties require exceptional solutions, and I think these guys would be great."

Freddie appeared to give this due consideration. "What are you hoping we do?"

"I want you to monitor the Right Honourable Michael Wilcox, Minister for Health and Aged Care," said Pop. "Without him knowing who you are, of course." Pop looked at Odd Job. "Someone plans to kill him at his home in Vaucluse, and I need to stop that happening."

"He'll have his own protection, right? So why can't you use them?" asked Tony.

"The killer is resourceful and has already shown he can get past run-of-the-mill security, and he also takes risks. I need some, er, higher calibre help."

Nicely done, play to their vanity, thought Chad. Although in fairness, it was also true. Odd Job and Tony would be the last people you want on your tail. Chad knew that only too well.

"How will that work?" asked Freddie. "They can't very well turn up and just start watching the dude."

"No," said Pop. "I agree. But I'm going to get them employed by the private security firm currently guarding the minister. It's called Control Inc, and I know the owner. He owes me some favours. Now if you're okay about it, I'll make the call and then we can talk details… And money."

Freddie looked at his two fixers and raised an eyebrow. Both gave a barely perceptible nod.

"Okay," said Freddie. "Let's talk."

Chapter 67

Following her interview with Pop, Andrea had basked in the afterglow. Social media had gone berserk, her followers through the roof, and Channel Nine had already said they'd be happy to discuss a new contract. They were falling over themselves to pay her more after three weeks in the job. Indeed, she'd been expecting a call from a reporter at Time Magazine, Jack Ryman, who'd contacted her producer to request and receive agreement for an exclusive interview with her.

It was the only reason she'd answered a call from 'No Caller ID.'

She inhaled the smoke from her cigarette and stared at the phone screen.

Hearing Trevor's voice had freaked her. She'd almost forgotten about him in the euphoria of her success, but now as she reflected on the conversation, his "Hello Andrea" had wobbled her. She'd recovered well, she reckoned, aided by a deep pull on a cold spritzer, but she'd felt an icy hand grip her throat. It had been too late to change her story. She'd had to stick with it. But when he'd asked her to confirm that she'd discussed his 'insurance policy' with Hilton, doing so had left her feeling frightened. Scared shitless if she was honest. Being asked had confirmed to her that Trevor suspected her of lying, he'd said as much. Why though? She checked her watch. What to do?

Maybe she suggests to Chad he wants to keep a close eye on his girlfriend. Nah, she thought. Couldn't do that without setting the hare running. She lifted her glass and took another mouthful.

Trevor had seemed to believe her, by the end, or at least given her the benefit of the doubt. Did that mean she was safe? Maybe, 'cos he could never prove she hadn't discussed the insurance with Hilton. Not unless he was to have a cosy little chat with Chad.

"Oh hi, Chad, did Andrea mention to you that if you don't back off this case something nasty could happen to your girlfriend and Jackson's son? No? Oh, well, that was an oversight."

That wouldn't be happening.

She exhaled and blew a smoke ring which drifted in a perfect circle towards the window. Do nothing, she decided. Nothing. That was the best policy. And don't answer calls from 'No Caller ID'.

She felt better now she'd reached the decision.

Right, onwards and upwards. The patriarchy won't fuck itself.

Chapter 68

The Right Honourable Michael Wilkins paced the gardens surrounding his home and considered his position. That the copper and the other guy hadn't believed him had been clear. But they couldn't prove anything and if everything went okay in the next hour, then the entire episode would be closed. Two new security guards he hadn't seen before patrolled close by. Jesus, he thought, he didn't care who you were, you'd think twice before confronting those two. One was the size of the Empire State Building and the other looked like a guy a Columbian drug baron might entrust with guarding his kids. Good to see that Control Inc. were on the programme. These guys went some way to calming his nerves, but the butterflies in his stomach still fluttered.

From his jacket he pulled the folded sheet of A4 paper. He stared at the familiar transcript.

Dear Minister,

Trust me when I say that carrying out your execution and administering justice for your role in Nefeli's crimes would give me enormous pleasure. If you wish to avoid such a fate, then you will follow my instructions. Be present at your home in Vaucluse at 6 p.m. on 15th May. Leave the front door unlocked, be alone and waiting for me in your office at the rear of the house. You will have $4m dollars in an Escrow account and available to transfer. There won't be security guards on the property.

He checked his watch. 5:45 p.m. Fifteen minutes. He replayed his plan. Everything was in place.

"I've no choice at all," he muttered, "no fucking choice. I don't want to do it, but what else can I do?" He walked around the manicured border, head down. Stop it, he thought. Get your head on. You didn't ask to be blackmailed but you can't let it succeed. He raised his eyes to the sky. Okay, let's do this.

He headed past the swimming pool, up a flight of five stone steps and along a shrub lined pathway. The two additional security guards followed him.

"Right, you two remain outside, out of sight and call me on this when you see my visitor approaching." He raised his hand which held a walkie talkie. "Get the others to come to my office and do a full check inside. Okay?"

"No problem, sir."

A Brit security guard. Bloody hell.

His polished black brogues click-clacked on the parquet floor of the rear hallway, the sound audible throughout the vast empty house. He'd given Joe and the staff the evening off and wanted any prying eyes to see them leave. He'd also made sure any watchers saw a Control Inc van exit. Reaching the end of the hallway he stopped, nerves jangling, and shivered. Up ahead the door to his office stood slightly ajar. He was certain he'd closed it, so how come it was open? He looked over his shoulder. Nothing just the fading sun casting shadows on the walls.

"Hello," he shouted. "Is anyone there?"

He stepped towards the door and pushed it open with his foot. The door swung back on its hinges revealing his sanctuary and the holder of all his secrets. He exhaled realising he'd been holding his breath. "Come on, get a grip."

His desk occupied the far end of the spacious lounge he'd converted to an office and he covered the space between him and it in four long strides. Pulling the leather chair away from the desk he sat down, opened the top drawer on the right and reached inside. His hand felt the cold hard metal of the pistol. He took it from the drawer and felt his confidence returning as he weighed the gun in his hand. He checked the magazine. Full. The words of his golf coach came to him.

"Visualise the shot, play it in your head before you address the ball. How will the contact be? What's the ball flight, a fade? A draw? Where does it land? See it in your mind, Mike."

His nerves were shredding, but he played the coming minutes in his head. Footsteps should signal his approach, but the door handle turning definitely would. Guards behind the door. Grab and hold. No discussion, no words. Four paces, gun to the temple, fire once. Over. Guards remove body and dispose.

He'd decided against telling the security guys anything other than they needed to apprehend a known criminal. They didn't know he would shoot. Okay, he'd compromised them but he'd bung them enough to keep them quiet. Job done.

He checked his watch. 5:58 p.m.

Several sets of footsteps approached his office, and the security detail stepped inside.

"All done?"

"Yes sir, as instructed all doors and windows are closed except the front door which we've left open."

"Good. Okay, stand behind the door at the far wall. He may be armed so do what you need to apprehend him."

The four burly guards lined up against the wall. He could see bulges at various places on each. They're armed, fair enough. Okay, bring it on.

His walkie talkie crackled into life.

"Visitor in the grounds."

*

I watch as a Range Rover swings out of the gates onto the road. Two more cars follow and a van with the name of the security company on it. So far so good. I sit in the back of my van, parked three hundred metres away, and open my laptop. I've been watching the house for several weeks. Comings and goings, who does what and when. He's given the staff the night off, I think. Good. Obeying instructions. Very good. But I have left nothing to chance, because chance increases risk.

Planning is everything, so a couple of weeks ago when I'd seen the minister had hired extra security, I'd posed as a police consultant hired by Control Inc to check the place out. I love paranoia: it overcomes all obstacles and logic. The flunkey had said "make sure a bloody fly can't get in here without us knowing about it, mate." I had access to all areas and know the place like the back of my hand. Including how to enter the air con vents.

I tap an icon on my computer and the cameras I'd placed at various vantage points around the minister's home and grounds spring into life. Better safe than sorry. To become Minister of Health and Aged Care you're a slippery, devious sod, so I won't take chances. As I glance from screen to screen my stomach lurches…

Something is wrong.

I close my eyes and shake my head. What the hell? A path leads to the back door of the property. Half hidden by a tree I see two shapes.

"Who the bloody hell are you?"

Both step onto the path, looking around. Both are in black suits. One clearly has an intimate relationship with steroids, and it doesn't take a genius to see the other is ex-forces. Not regular security guards, I haven't seen these two before.

I feel the anger rise, burning my cheeks and filling my head. "Cheeky bastard," I mutter. On screen, Wilcox is fussing with something in a drawer at his desk. I see a gun in his hand. He looks up and I see his mouth move. Talking to someone.

"I set the traps, you wanker. Not you. Who the fuck do you think you're dealing with?"

A third camera shows me the roof. I zoom in, what is that? The pipework of the air con vents through which I've planned my entry, looks different. Someone has fixed a metal panel over the vent and welded it in place. I've seen enough. They know I'm coming and they know I'm going to use nitrogen. How?

Hilton and Murray. They are the only ones that know about it. Bastards.

I'll abort and re-think. But first… I'll discover what they had planned for me. My next move takes shape. I climb into the driver's seat then fire up the engine and drive the van past the gates, jump out and run fifty metres around the perimeter. I know they'll be waiting for my arrival, so I climb up onto the wall and shake two tree branches. That should do it. Mr Steroid spots the movement and talks into a handheld. Excellent, let's see what happens now. I jump sprint back to the van, and open the computer. There's only one camera I'm interested in.

"Gotcha, big boy."

Hiding behind the door that leads into the house from the roof are the two goons. That explains things. They were going to jump me as I entered the air vent.

"Okay, let's get out of here," I growl, "But Mr Fucking Minister this isn't over. What I was planning to do to you tonight, is nothing compared to what's gonna happen to you now."

*

Tony and Odd Job stood in the doorway to the minister's office. Michael Wilcox stared at them from behind his desk, then yelled, "So, where the hell is he?" He slammed his hand down hard onto the polished surface. "Why's he a no-show?"

Tony looked at Odd Job whose expression suggested that any more verbals from the jumped-up wanker screaming at them might cause the minister to have an urgent need for an ambulance.

Tony didn't think Freddie would appreciate that. Nor the copper. He decided that he'd better answer the question.

Tony held the Minister's eye, "He's been watching you."

"Watching me?"

Wilcox shook his head and rubbed his eyes. Apoplectic didn't cut it, Tony decided.

"How?" shouted the Minister

Tony shrugged. "The guy you were meeting had visuals on the house and grounds. You need to get a sweep done for cameras and bugs." He pulled a disc-shaped object two or three centimetres in diameter, and a few millimetres in depth from his trouser pocket. Two wires each around six inches, protruded from the back of it. "We found this near the air con vent. It's a micro-camera," Tony walked towards the minister and dropped the object on his desk. "It's a delicate piece of kit and he can access the recording from anywhere." Tony put both hands on the desk and leaned towards Wilcox. "He knew we were here," he inclined his head towards the other security guards. "And I reckon he knew you had these guys, as well. 'Cos there'll be a camera in here," he said, glancing around the office.

Wilcox stared at Tony then frantically around his office. "But how? How did he get them in here?" His voice tailed off. "So, he knows..."

Tony turned away from the desk. "We'd better be going," he said.

Wilcox sat alone and stared at the gun on his desk. His head throbbed and his leg wouldn't stop shaking. He ran his hands through his hair, damp with sweat and wondered what the hell to do now. '*The guy knows I was going to try to kill him.*' Jesus. Panic rose steadily from his feet to his head. He couldn't think and he could barely breathe. The phone in front of him jumped on the desk, vibrated and scared the shit out of him. He leaned towards it. A message from a number he didn't recognise.

Last chance to live. I'll tell you where to meet. Bring the money or die, your choice.

Fuck, fuck, fuck.

The screen lit again with a second message.

You look a little flustered, Minister. Put the gun back in your drawer, it won't do you any good.

Wilcox read the message several times then warily scanned the room. The killer had invaded his sanctuary. He pushed the phone away and stood gingerly, his beige chinos darkening around the crotch.

Chapter 69

Tony gave a succinct update on events at the minister's home in Vaucluse. His words came out fast and without superfluous detail. He talks like he acts, thought Chad. Freddie turned to Chad.

"Does Ruby know what he's up against? Ordinary schmucks don't get access to a politician's gaff and plant multiple cameras around the place. This guy is smart, bro."

"Yeah, thanks for that, Freddie, I think we know what we're up against," said Chad, ignoring Freddie's deliberate misnomer. "I'd better call Pop."

Chad picked up his phone from the table and walked through to the bedroom dialling Pop's number as he went. Pop remained unusually silent as Chad explained the events at the house, then said, "Yeah, my guys got there a couple of minutes too late. We had to keep our distance and wait for your guys inside to contact us. Wilcox was shouting the odds and asking why the hell we were there."

"By going for Wilcox, the perp's confirmed him as the report writer," said Chad. "That's something."

"Yeah, but the killer's wary now, more evasive. We need to think about our next move."

"Are the guys at Day Street aware that we think the killer's a cop?"

"Nah. I've told the Chief Super, which did little for his blood pressure, but no one else." Pop sighed. "Has Jas narrowed the search from the rosters? How about looking into their backgrounds, any joy?"

"I don't know," said Chad. "She's gone back to the Sheraton but I'll call her."

Silence filled the distance between them.

Chad felt an idea sharpen as he looked out the window. He'd have liked time to consider it but knew that time and certainty were luxuries he didn't have. Just say it, he thought.

"Pop, I've got an idea about next steps."

"Fire away."

"We burned our bridges as far as protecting the minister is concerned. The perp will have worked out that Tony and Odd Job were our boys, so he'll be changing his plans."

"For the umpteenth time, Chad, cut to the frigging chase."

"Okay. How do we protect him when he won't let us?"

"I don't know, we've tried Jackson's fellas which nearly worked, but as far as I can see he's tied our hands. What's your idea?"

Chad paused. "Provide Andrea Byrne with an unattributable leak that Wilcox is the report writer."

"What good will that do?" spat Pop.

Chad could hear that the mention of Andrea's name changed Pop's tone. "She'll run hard with it, she knows a gift horse when she sees one, so there'll be a press furore around Wilcox. Everywhere he goes the journos will be on his tail making it impossible for the killer to get to him. The killer will have to put his plans on hold. Meanwhile, Jas may come up with a name for us and we'll nick him before he can do anything else."

Chad waited. Seconds seemed like hours.

Pop's voice broke the silence. "Not bad, Chad. Not bad at all. Leave that with me, I'll make a couple of calls. You get onto Jas and see where she's up to. Call me if she's got something."

Chad dialled Jas's number. Voicemail.

He looked out to the ocean. Using Andrea Byrne was not without risk, he thought. A plan like this brought them into direct contact with the law of unintended consequences. What they couldn't know was what the killer would do if he saw his plans thwarted. What then? A shiver rolled up Chad's spine. What indeed?

Chapter 70

Jas leaned back and rubbed her eyes. She'd headed back to the Sheraton several hours previously so that she could work uninterrupted and without a constant background noise of one computer game or another. Junior had been a massive help, but she needed some peace and quiet. Staring at the computer screen had given her a headache. She stood and walked to the bedside table where a glass of water from the previous night remained untouched. She took a long drink then went back to her desk.

She'd created a spreadsheet into which she'd put the data she'd garnered from the SPOR system. What had begun as a straightforward one page excel spreadsheet had morphed into several inter-connected sheets. Officers' names ran down the first column. Across the horizontal, she'd placed several operations related headings: roster dates and hours worked, annual leave, crime scene attendance, overtime worked, on which dates. The headings went from column 'B' to 'M' – twelve headings in all. On another page she'd copied and pasted the officers' names but changed the horizontal headings to include personal details: date of birth, place of birth, ethnicity and several others. She'd applied various filters but had still ended up with a last sheet on which nine officer's names appeared. The killer could be any of them.

She ran her hands through her hair and stared again at the screen. This isn't much help, she thought. Nine names. That's too many. But what else could she do? She examined each page on the spreadsheet. Had she missed something?

Hang on a minute. The killer would need time to carry out his executions.

'So what?'

He couldn't afford to be called to another crime scene or interrupted by orders from his superior.

'And?'

So he'd have to be off duty when the killings happened.

'Forget who attended the crime scenes and check who was off duty at the time of the murders.'

She typed fast on the keyboard, filtering here, and deleting there. The spreadsheet updated automatically as she tapped the keys. Cross-referencing off-duty times and adding annual leave reduced the nine names to four. Four officers were off duty or on annual leave at the dates and times of killings. She reviewed the names. Three were female police constables and the remaining male was in his late fifties and up for retirement.

Could the killer be a woman?

Not according to Mel. Jas remembered Chad telling her that, Mel had shared a stat at the beginning of the enquiry. What was it? Yeah, ninety-eight -point two percent of all multiple homicides were carried out by men. It was still possible but not good odds. She stared at the screen. If it isn't a woman or the old boy, what am I missing?

She looked outside. Elizabeth Street was heaving. Cars and buses jammed the road in the early evening rush hour and wary pedestrians waited for the harsh *beep, beep, beep,* of the traffic signal to tell them when it was safe to cross.

The answer came to her as a car horn blared. "You bloody idiot, Jas," she said.

She sat and applied one more filter to the spreadsheet. Sick leave. How many officers had called in sick on the relevant days? The computer programme did its job. Black and white, no argument, no discussion.

Jas stared at the screen. From the hundreds of data entries she'd made, one name highlighted in yellow, sprang from the page.

"Bugger me," she said. "I think I've got him."

Jas saved the file and applied a password to make it harder for the likes of Junior to hack in. Then she rang Chad. Voicemail. She didn't leave a message, clicked the call off and dialled Pop's number. Voicemail. "Shit," she said. She rang Junior.

"Hey Jas, how's it goin'?"

"Hi Junior, I haven't got time to talk, is Chad with you?"

"Nah, he left a few minutes ago with my dad."

"Where's he gone, do you know?"

"I dunno, something to do with the soccer match they've got coming up, but I wasn't paying attention."

"Okay. I'll jump a cab and get over to the apartment. Wait there for me, there's something I want you to check for me. If Chad turns up get him to ring me, will you, it's urgent?"

"Cool, sure, no worries. See you shortly."

Jas tried Chad's and Pop's mobiles, then stamped her foot as they both went to voicemail again. She grabbed the MacBook and ran for the door.

Chapter 71

I've headed to Bondi after the debacle in Vaucluse and parked on O'Brien Street, a quiet suburban backwater which runs parallel to Hall Street. From my vantage point, I get an unobstructed view of Hilton's apartment. It's quiet. The occasional mum pushing a pram walks by and assorted surfer types head back home from the beach. Reflecting on the last twenty-four hours I can feel my anger rising again.

Wilcox. Oh, he is going to suffer. The hours I'd spent building the crucifix on which that slug would meet his end, wasted. But every plan has a setback, and that was all this was. A setback. I'd recover from it and make him pay in spades. Like I'm going to make Hilton pay.

My head is throbbing, and I rub my eyes. I can hear a murmuring in my ear, growing, getting closer, getting louder.

'Total failure, fuck knows why we thought you could ever be successful. One job, that's all we gave you, and you fucked it up. What are you going to do now?'

'You'd better complete the mission. Failure is not an option. You know the consequences. You fail, you pay.'

'Hilton's taking the piss out of you.'

The voices fade into a dull murmur, retreating, leaving me drained. Finally, silence returns. I open my eyes, push my hands across my head, then take a drink from my water bottle.

Movement.

From the rear door of the apartment block, Hilton and Jackson emerge. They're standing only twenty metres from me but don't even glance in my direction. A car emerges from the underground car park. A silver and black limo, a Bentley by the look of it.

The man mountain is driving and his mate is in the passenger seat. Hilton and Jackson climb in the back. Okay, have I got lucky? Junior isn't with them. Five minutes then I'll check the apartment.

I check my watch, 6:40 p.m. I look up to see Jackson's boy, if you can call anyone as huge as him a boy, is exiting the apartment block. He heads down a flight of steps next to the building. I wait minutes, then he returns with a box of groceries. He's been to the farm shop. Good, that means he's staying put. I want him and the woman together but I'll do one at a time if needs be. I'll give it half an hour more. She's been there every day so she'll come tonight, I'm sure of it.

Minutes pass, then a Thirteen Cabs taxi glides by and indicates, before pulling into the kerb. The rear passenger door opens and an attractive mixed-race woman steps onto the pavement. She turns, smiles and says something to the driver before closing the door. She looks around, clutching a shoulder bag. Heavy by the look of it. She's observant. I watch her assess the street. Like a copper would. She sees my car and seems surprised by its presence. I take a deep breath. Show time.

I open the car door and climb out.

"Er, excuse me, ma'am," I say raising my arm. She sees me and stops. "Are you Miss Carter?"

She looks at me. I hold out one of the many police identification badges I've acquired over the years. This one's from Bondi, more appropriate, I thought.

"Yes, is there a problem?"

"No, no problem at all, ma'am. I'm Sergeant Langer from the Eastern Suburbs PAC, based at Roscoe Street here in Bondi."

"What's PAC?" she asks.

"Oh, sorry, Police Area Command."

"Yes, Sergeant, how can I help?"

I detect a slight wariness, a reserve. She's on her metal, observant, suspicious.

"Detective Inspector Murray has asked me at the request of a…" I check my notepad. "a Mr Chad Hilton," I raise an eyebrow as I look at her, like I'm checking the name is correct, "to collect yourself and a Mr Jackson from this address and drop you off at Day Street Police station in the city."

"Really, why?"

"I don't know, ma'am."

She'll want reassurance and will call them. I need my luck to hold, but if it doesn't, I've got my taser ready.

"Please ma'am, call them. I'll wait in the car."

"Okay," she says. "I'll check what's going on and see you in a minute."

"No worries."

*

Jas hurried up the stairs to the apartment, dialling Chad's number as she went. No answer. Jesus. She rapped on the door.

"It's open," Junior's voice boomed from inside.

Jas ran in, "Any word from Chad or your dad?"

"No, none," replied Junior. "What's up, has something happened?"

"Yeah, I think I know who the killer is. But there's a copper downstairs who's here to take me and you to Day Street cop shop. Apparently, Chad's arranged it with Pop."

"Eh? Why me?"

"I don't bloody know, Junior."

"Are you sure about this?" asked Junior.

"No, I'm not but maybe they think we will be safe if something goes down."

"What if this cop downstairs is the bad guy?"

"He's not. I've checked his ID. He's a sergeant from Bondi called Langer. Our guy is a constable from the city, and ain't called Langer. I'll try Pop and Chad again."

She dialled both, cursing at the familiar voicemail messages, then made her decision. "Okay, I don't see we've much option, come on let's get to Day Street."

*

My heart races as I see Carter and Jackson emerge from the building. I climb out of the car walk around to the rear passenger door and open it.

"Ma'am, Sir."

She gets in first then the giant somehow climbs in beside her. Getting him out might pose a problem, I think. I've made sure it's hot in the back seat, and of course the windows don't open. Walking to the driver's side I get into the car and gain eye contact with the woman.

"It'll be hot back there," I say. "I'll put the fans on."

"Thanks," she says. The speaker implanted into the bullet-proof glass divider distorts her voice. I turn the ignition, then reach to my left and turn the nozzle on the cylinder in the passenger footwell. The pipe I've fixed runs into the car's AC system and straight into the back of the car. I indicate then pull away from the kerb.

Glancing in the rear I watch and wait. Seconds pass before I see her eyes roll in her head and she slumps forward held by the seatbelt. Jackson has fallen sideways and his head is resting on her shoulder. Excellent. I pull back into the kerb and park with the engine still running. I don't want them to die here but if it happens it happens. Jumping out I pull the rear door open, grab her bag and open it. Laptop and phone. Great. The Jackson boy is holding his phone which I take from him. I run to the other passenger door and having opened it, feel in his pocket. He has a lot of keys and coins in his right pocket, but only one in his left. I take it, close the car door with the engine still running and check the street. No-one.

I take the stairs two at a time, reach the penthouse and push the key in the lock.

"Please be the right one."

The key turns and the door opens. Thank you, God. I throw the bag on the settee and put both phones on the table, then turn and run.

Exiting onto the street all is quiet. I get in the car, close the nozzle on the bottle, open my window and drive.

Chapter 72

Chad wiped the sweat from his brow. Training in the evening meant the weather was cooler, and the guys were close to peak. He opened his locker and retrieved his phone. Seven missed calls from Jas. Shit. Maybe she found something, he thought. He dialled her number. It rang out to voicemail. He scrolled down and tapped on Pop's number.

"Hey, Chad, how's it goin'?"

"Have you heard from Jas?" asked Chad. "I've had a load of missed calls, but now I can't get hold of her."

"She must have found something 'cos I've got a load of missed calls as well. I've been with a bunch of jumped-up bureaucrats that think they're coppers. I'm leaving now."

"Okay, I'll try to get her at the Sheraton, but if she's not there, she'll be heading to the flat. I'll let you know and meet you at whichever. How did you get on with Andrea Byrne?"

"The top brass weren't keen, but they got there in the end. They don't need to have a minister murdered when they know he's at risk."

"I bet Andrea bit your hand off?"

"Yeah, she damn near wet herself. Got to go. Call me, let me know where Jas is."

"Yeah, will do." Chad clicked the call off, retrieved an email with the number for the Sheraton and dialled. The receptionist asked him to hold while she tried the room.

"No answer, sir, I'm afraid."

"Okay, thanks," said Chad. A gnawing alarm was pushing behind his eyes.

He dialled Junior's number. Voicemail.

Freddie, emerged from the shower. "Freddie," said Chad, "is Junior going out this evening?"

"Nah, bro, I think he was looking forward to having your apartment to himself. Why?"

"I can't get hold of either Junior or Jas. You try, will you?"

Chad showered, wrapped a towel around his waist then looked for Freddie in the locker room. "Any joy?"

"Nope, the dude ain't answering." Freddie looked at Chad. "What's up, bro, you look worried?"

"I just don't like not being able to contact them. Where are Odd Job and Tony?"

"Waiting for us in the car, bro."

"Okay, let's get back to the flat." Dressing in a hurry he texted Pop.

Meet us at the flat.

Chad turned the key in the lock, pushed open the door and called out, "Jas? Junior? What's going on, why haven't you answered your phones?"

The silence seemed to hold a threat.

He walked down the hall with Freddie and the boys in tow, his unease growing by the minute. It was clear no one was there. A box of groceries sat on the kitchen worktop and on the table, Chad saw two phones. One had a Leeds United phone cover and belonged to Jas. The second he gave to Freddie.

"Yep, that's Junior's," said Freddie. "They must have popped out."

It looked that way, thought Chad, but why leave their phones?

Freddie articulated Chad's thoughts. "No one leaves their phones, man, so they can't have gone far."

Chad noticed Tony checking the other rooms in the apartment.

He heard the doors to the balcony being opened, then a couple of seconds later, closed.

Tony walked into the lounge. "No one here," he said.

Turning, Chad saw Jas's bag on the settee. He picked it up and opened it. His rose- gold MacBook stared up at him. She wouldn't leave this, no way. Too much sensitive information on it to leave lying around, maybe even the killer's identity.

Panic welled like a rip tide and dragged him to the bedroom. He sat on the bed and tried to breathe but his head was pounding. Flashing images of Angie's broken corpse juxtaposed with a smiling Jas. He couldn't move. He was gulping air but his lungs couldn't hold it, the room spun into a darkening void.

He could hear voices but they sounded removed from reality. He could make out the odd word or phrase.

"Their phones are here."

"Leave him, he'll be okay."

"Give him air."

"Jesus, man what's happened?"

Chad, opened his eyes, blinked and closed them again. He could smell Mel's perfume and guessed she was leaning over him. "You'll be okay," she whispered. "Just lie still and I'll get rid of this lot."

"Everyone out, give him some space. He'll be fine. Make yourselves useful."

Chad gathered his senses. He opened his eyes, saw Mel and sat up. He let stability return after taking a couple of deep breaths.

"What happened?" asked Mel.

Dread gripped him tight. "Something's happened to Jas," he paused, "and to Junior."

"What makes you say that?"

"She's been doing stuff for Pop on my laptop and wouldn't leave it lying around, nor would she disappear without taking her phone. She'd rung me seven times for Christ's sake, and would have taken it with her waiting for me to call her back. And as for Junior, you'd need a surgical procedure to remove that phone from him."

"Mm, I take your point."

"Look," said Chad, sitting upright. "Just give me a minute to get my act together and I'll meet you in the lounge. Don't let Freddie and Pop get started."

Mel sighed, "I won't."

Chad stood and opened the doors to the balcony. Fresh sea air swept over him. Something had happened, he knew it, he could feel it. But what?

A discarded leather jacket lay on the floor near the bed. He bent and picked it up, feeling something rustle as he did so. He pulled out an envelope from the inside pocket. Inside were two tickets to the game next Sunday. The tickets he'd promised to get for the copper who'd befriended him at Castlereagh.

"Nah, I prefer Aussie Rules but if there's a freebie ticket available, I'll give it a go."

Chad looked out to sea. A series of unconnected recollections leapt into his brain, like someone moving apparently unrelated jigsaw pieces around a board. Through the chaos, a picture was forming. He closed his eyes, his nerve ends tingled. He was back at Castlereagh standing outside the lifts, the jobsworth copper blocking his access to Medics 4U. Constable Swift.

"Well, I guess you don't know him after all. Anyone who knows DI Murray knows him as Pop."

Now he was outside Castlereagh hailing a cab to go to Bondi and meet Andrea Byrne. *'A taxi pulling to the kerb. The policeman from the eleventh floor holding open the door. "Hotel Ravesis, please."'*

'Andrea's question: '"How did anyone know we were meeting at the Ravesis?"'

Chad knew the answer now. *'Because Swift had overheard him. That was how.'*

He kept his eyes tight closed and recalled Andrea's text from yesterday.

When he talked about the police, he used Pop's name. I don't mean his real name, Ruben Murray, I mean he called him Pop. Like he knew him.

Then, like a sharp slap, another thought hit him. "Oh no, why didn't you spot that earlier?" Chad leaned against the wall. "How have you missed that?"

The bedroom door flew open. "Who are you shouting at?" said Mel.

"What? Was I shouting? Right. Anyway, we've no time. It's staring us in the face."

"What is?"

"The answer. The perp. I know who it is and I've been so stupid."

"Calm down and tell me what is happening."

"Okay, but I need to tell Pop."

Chad raced down the hallway, Pop and Freddie stood either side of a seated Tony who had the MacBook open.

"Wait," yelled Chad, "I think I know who it is," he paused, expectant faces staring at him.

"Well, go on," said Pop, "who is it?"

"It's Constable Swift."

"What? Right, let's see if Jas's work corroborates that. Then you can explain your thinking." said Pop. "We've found an Excel document, but its password protected. Five letters, any ideas?"

Chad sighed. What would she use?

"Try Hoppy," he said.

Tony typed the letters in lowercase. Nothing. He tried capitals. Nothing. Then capital H with the other letters in lowercase. "Bingo!" he shouted, his Bradford accent lengthening and deepening the 'O.' He clicked into the spreadsheet then looked up at the faces peering at him. "Yep, she's got a name," he said.

All eyes turned to Tony.

"And?" asked Pop.

Tony leaned back in the seat, "Same name, Boss. Constable

Jonathon Swift."

Chad looked into the big Tasmanian's eyes. "Pop, it came to me in the bedroom, I can't believe we missed it. The word Rasch is a German word," he said.

Pop, turned towards the window and scratched his head. He let out a long sigh.

"Yeah," he said, "it means swift."

Chapter 73

Chad leaned against the wall as voices competed for space. Everyone seemed to talk at once. Pop was demanding to see the spreadsheets Jas had completed and how they'd led to Swift. In the next breath yelling at Chad to explain how he'd arrived at the same answer.

Freddie was pacing the room issuing Odd Job and Tony with instructions to speak to the neighbours and see if anyone had seen Jas or Junior entering or leaving. All done in a tone and manner that left no one in any doubt that he held Pop personally and the police generally, responsible for the disappearance of his son.

"We're dealing with the keystone cops, man," he yelled. "So, we won't get any help to find Junior from this lot. Christ, I thought the coppers back in Leeds were useless, but this dude…" Freddie jabbed a finger in Pop's direction, "and his crew of fucking morons take incompetence to a whole new level. They can't find their arses with both hands, let alone find Junior."

Chad raised an eyebrow in Mel's direction and said a silent thanks that Pop was too preoccupied to hear Freddie's jibes. He was barking instructions down the phone on a series of calls to his team, issuing commands, demanding information and co-ordinating Swift's capture. Chad ushered Pop into the bedroom. "Make your calls from here," he said. "You'll be able to hear yourself think. What's the plan?"

"I've put out an arrest warrant on Swift. We've got a team heading to his apartment in Randwick and another checking the

ANPR to see if we can spot his car."

Chad remembered from his work in Leeds, that ANPR was an automated car number plate recognition system. "I'll leave you to it. Have you told your boss yet?"

"No, so tell that lunatic mate of yours to keep the noise down, I'm ringing him now."

"He's worried about Jas and Junior, that's all. And so am I."

Pop looked up from his phone. "What are you worried about? They can't have gone far."

"I don't like it, Pop. Jas wouldn't leave a computer with confidential and sensitive information. She's a good copper. And kids like Junior would feel like someone had removed a limb without their phone."

Pop looked distracted. "True," he said. "Let me make this call to the Chief Super then we'll get our heads together. Check if Andrea Byrne has gone live with the Wilcox stuff."

Chad walked down the hallway into the lounge. Freddie's ire had abated now that Tony and Odd Job had left to talk to neighbours. Anxiety replaced the anger on Freddie's face. Chad picked up the remote and found Channel Nine news. Andrea was in full flow and banks of cameras were already showing Wilcox' home in Vaucluse. Another set were outside his office in Canberra. A banner headline scrolling along the bottom of the screen declared that the author of the report that had triggered the series of recent gruesome murders in Sydney was Michael Wilcox, Minister for Health and Aged Care. Andrea meanwhile was informing her audience that Mr Wilcox was currently unavailable for comment, but that she expected a statement from the Minister's office in due course.

"The police," she said, "are not confirming or denying the veracity of the information we've received."

Mel looked from the TV to Chad. "Swift won't be able to get to Wilcox now. He's untouchable. No one could get within a hundred metres of him."

"Yep," said Chad. "You're right, which makes me wonder what Swift will do next."

"Well, let's hope he's arrested before he can do anything else."

Chad recognised the feeling in his stomach. Terror. He's got Jas, he thought. Swift's got Jas.

Chapter 74

'Injustice is relatively easy to bear; what stings is justice.'
H. L. Mencken.

I'd thought it was going to be harder. It's no wonder they haven't caught me given the level of disrespect they have shown me. It's clear that Hilton believes I'm an idiot otherwise why disregard my threat? My passengers remain slumped on the back seat. Have I overdone it? Maybe they're dead? Well, that's not my fault, it's Hilton's.

Anyway, that will be the result eventually.

But it poses a problem. The woman's not an issue, I can easily lift her, but the giant is another matter. What the hell did they feed him on, for Christ's sake?

I indicate and pull into the deserted industrial estate I'd chosen earlier, parking behind a nondescript transit van. No one around. There never is after 6 p.m. I've checked. I climb out open both rear passenger doors to let some airflow through. Reaching inside the car I touch the woman's neck and feel for a pulse. Okay, that's good. Before I walk around the car to open the other door, I unclip my Glock. Just in case. He's way too big to fight. I check for a pulse and find one. Okay, they'll wake soon. I undo their seat belts then bind their wrists with double strength police zip ties. I feel in my pocket for the masking take tape and tearing two strips place them over the prone figures' mouths. Nothing to do now but wait.

The autumn sun has died an hour ago, so I stand in the darkness of the desolate industrial estate and reflect. A brief respite in a hectic schedule. I feel my anger rise again as Wilcox's smug face leaps into my mind. And then there's Hilton. He'll soon know I've got these two, but he's in no place to negotiate with me and there's nothing he can offer me. No, I'll just let him know he should have taken me seriously and that I've won. I'll leave the bodies somewhere for him to find. And then there's the final loose end, what shall I do about that?

I take a deep breath. Deal with it tonight then dispose of the two in the car. After that I'll be free to plan for Wilcox. I hear a rustling from the back of the car and step to the side. I see both my passengers are sitting upright and staring wildly around them.

"Okay," I say, standing a metre or so from the open door. "Get out of the car and into the back of the van. Any funny business and I'll blow your heads off. Am I clear?"

They nod.

I leave them and walk the couple of paces to the transit parked in front of the squad car. I unlock the double doors at the back, pulling them open.

"Come on, the pair of you. In there." I train the Glock on the giant's chest as he tries to get himself out of the back seat. They clamber out and stumble to the rear of the van. "In you get." They both sit on the rim then shuffle themselves along the floor of the interior. When all that's visible is their feet, I close and lock the doors. I return to the squad car and drive it to the southern corner of the estate and park it. No more need of that.

I stroll back to the van, checking there's no one watching. The evening remains silent and still. I unlock the driver's door, climb in and start the ignition. As the engine splutters into life the radio squawks at me and I reach to turn it off but stop, my arm poised in front of the knob.

A reporter is in mid-sentence, "... but we've still heard nothing from the Minister of Health and Aged Care, Michael Wilcox. Andrea Byrne of Channel Nine is sticking to her guns that the Minister is the author of the report. We'll keep you up to speed with developments as they happen, so stay with us."

I turn the radio off and try to comprehend what I have heard. Andrea Byrne? How the hell could she know? Think, come on, think. I stare, unseeing, through the windscreen. No way could she have uncovered Wilcox on her own. No way. So, how?

Minutes pass and I feel the pressure growing behind my eyes. Hilton and Murray must have told her. But why, what purpose is served? I drive slowly to the exit, then indicate and pull out into the traffic. Opening the window, the wind helps to clear my mind, and I see the logic behind their move. They are trying to stop me from getting close to Wilcox by having packs of journos following the bastard's every move.

Smart.

My anger and hatred are like a storm brewing inside me. I can feel the rage engulfing me and scream out through the open window into the night air. A howl of pain and fury. But they won't stop me. Not now. The two in the back will suffer. I had planned to shoot them, quick and easy, but not now. The whispering in my head is becoming louder and more persistent.

I yell. "Dad, leave me alone, I've got this."

The murmuring recedes but I hear the last two words clear and loud.

'Useless bastard.'

*

Jas and Junior had inched themselves backwards so that they could now sit with their backs against the panel separating them from the driver's cabin. Jas had a pounding headache and the movement of the van threw her against the side then back towards the middle where Junior's bulky frame prevented her from falling further. She breathed in through her nose and nudged Junior. Raising her eyebrows, she hoped he'd understand. '*Are you okay?*' He nodded an affirmative.

How could she have been so stupid? Why didn't she say no and wait for Chad to get back? Her head banged on the metal partition as the van bumped over a pothole. Recriminations were pointless, she thought. But if they hadn't complied, he'd have shot us back there. Or marched us out of the flat at gunpoint. She sat still, the common-sense analysis making her feel a little better about the situation. She felt Junior's arm nudge her and turned towards him. He winked at her then using his eyes showed she should look down his towards his feet.

What the hell's he doing?

Junior's hands were in his lap but he moved them to his right-hand jeans pocket and pushed a couple of his fingers inside the denim, then dragged them out revealing a set of keys. Jas looked from the keys to Junior's face, her frown and eyebrows asking, *'So what?'*

He frowned back at her and rolled his eyes which Jas took to mean *'Doh, stupid.'* She was missing something. He pulled the keys further out of the pocket. Attached to the key ring was a circular disc, half white and half black with the instantly recognisable Apple logo in the middle.

They stared at each other. If she could have kissed him, she would have. Apple tags. Euphoria swept over her. Then disappeared with the realisation they'd need somebody nearby to have an iPhone.

Would Chad or the boys be able to access Junior's phone tracker? Would they even think to look?

God help us, she thought. Her fate and that of Junior to be decided by the IT capabilities of a middle-aged techno-Luddite with PTSD.

Great. Just bloody great.

Chad Hilton, she thought, if ever you needed to get your shit together… It's now.

Chapter 75

Chad sat on the settee listening to Freddie rant. Pop had made his calls, commandeered a lift in a Bondi squad car, and rushed back to Day Street to co-ordinate the search for Swift.

"Freddie, just sit down and keep quiet, I need time to think."

"Time to think? It's a shame you and that idiot fed didn't think harder before this nut job kidnapped my son. Christ."

Chad heard footsteps and looked round to see Odd Job's enormous frame fill the hallway.

"Any joy?" asked Freddie.

"Yes, Boss," said Tony. "A guy across the road saw a woman and a young guy, both mixed race, getting into a Sydney City police car."

"Under arrest?" asked Chad.

"No, they got into the car voluntarily."

Shit, Chad thought, he's taken them. But why? What's he trying to do, what does he want with them?

I've no time to work that out, he thought. I must find them.

Tears welled into his eyes. Christ, he couldn't lose Jas. Not now. And if they lost Junior, he'd lose Freddie as well. Because Freddie would blame him. What a shitshow. He ran his hand across his eyes then wiped the teardrops on his jeans. Pull yourself together, this is no time for self-indulgence.

Chad dialled Pop.

"It's not a good time, mate. What is it?"

"Did you find Swift? Was he at his apartment?"

"Nah. The place has been empty for a while, judging by the mailbox. His car is in the car park so we don't know where he is or what he's driving. We're all over it though, we'll get him."

"Have you released his ID to the press?" asked Chad.

"Nah, can't do that yet. We've no actual evidence against him, not a shred. So we just need to bring him in pronto."

"He's taken Jas and Junior. A neighbour saw him."

"Shit. What was he driving?"

"A squad car."

"Okay, leave it with me and I'll get their descriptions out to all forces across New South Wales. Send me any photos you've got."

Chad clicked the call off and standing, scrolled through his photos till he found one of Jas and Junior together on the rooftop of the Glenmore pub in The Rocks. He forwarded it to Pop then put his phone in his pocket. He checked his watch. 7 p.m. Where to start?

"Where are you going?" demanded Freddie.

"I've told you," said Chad, "I need a bit of space to think without watching you pace around like a caged bear." Chad walked towards the hall, then turned. "And, Odd Job, sit the fuck down, you're blocking the light."

Odd Job looked startled, as if he'd suddenly seen himself for the first time. He nodded and eased his frame slowly onto the settee.

Chad looked at Freddie. "Mate, give me a couple of minutes to get my head straight. We must come up with a plan. Pop and the whole of the New South Wales police are searching for Swift but haven't got him yet, and I can't understand why he's taken Jas and Junior. We need a plan of our own."

"Too right," said Freddie. "The feds are useless."

Chad closed the bedroom door behind him and then lay on the bed watching as the ceiling fan rotated, cutting circles into the air.

"Why take Jas and Junior?" he muttered. "What the hell did he hope to gain?"

Chad closed his eyes. He allowed his thoughts to flow, unrestrained, meandering like a stream, seeing where they took him.

Revenge, maybe? But for what?"

It's personal, he thought. He's taken them to get at me, no one else, just me.

If the kidnappings were to get revenge on me, I must have done something. Or, maybe not done something. But there'd been no warning, no message, nothing. '*Come on, think.*' If he'd sent a warning, how would he have done it?

The room felt chilly and the blinds on the windows were rattling.

"The same way he communicated everything else. Through his conduit." Chad sat upright.

"Through Andrea Byrne."

He pulled his phone from his pocket, scrolled and dialled. The ringtone sounded shrill and harsh.

"Well, good evening, Chad, to what do I owe the pleasure?"

Chad tried to keep a hold on his emotions. "Andrea, did Trevor ever give you a message or a warning to pass on to me? I'm not talking about the information he gave about the crimes; I'm talking about something specific. A message for me. Not Pop or the police, just me?"

He tried to decipher the silence at the other end of the line.

"I can't think of anything, Chad." He could hear her exhaling smoke. "Why has something happened?"

"It's important, Andrea, think back. Any message at all?"

"No, Chad, I've no idea."

"Okay, thanks," said Chad. "Look after yourself." He clicked the call off. Was she lying? Probably.

He swung his legs off the bed and stood. Regardless of whether there was a message, or whether Andrea had given it to him, it didn't alter the facts. Jas and Junior were gone.

He opened the bedroom door and stood in the hallway. In

the lounge Freddie still paced, Odd Job still sat and Tony still watched from the window. Chad glanced to his right. The table in the hallway was bare. The clutter of keys and sunglasses that usually adorned the surface weren't there. Chad looked again then smacked the wall in front of him.

"Keys," he shouted, as all three figures in the lounge jumped. "Where's Junior's keys?"

They pulled cushions from the settee, checked the lounge and the kitchen but found nothing. Chad stood in the middle of the room and smiled.

"What the fuck, man?" said Freddie. "Why are we looking for Junior's keys, and why are you grinning?"

Chad didn't answer but ran to the second bedroom where Junior's rucksack lay on the floor. He emptied the contents onto the bed, but there was no sign of the keys amongst the assorted underwear and shorts.

"Okay," he said walking back into the lounge. "We may have a break. Junior has an Apple tag on his keys so he can find them if he loses them. If we can get into his phone, then we can track the tags which should give us his location."

"He's smart, bro, like his dad," said Freddie enveloping Chad in a massive Jackson hug complete with back slapping and a few kisses on the top of his head.

"Right," said Freddie. "But how do we get into his phone?"

Chad stared at his best friend. "Bloody hell, Freddie," he shouted. "You're a criminal mastermind and you don't know how to get into someone's phone?"

Tony turned from his vantage point at the window. "That'll be my job, Boss. And we're going to need a lot of luck."

Chad felt the euphoria being sucked out of him.

"How come luck, bro, you can do that shit, man, right?"

"I'm from Bradford," said Tony, the first 'd,' pronounced as a 't.' "You'd never survive if you couldn't do that stuff." He looked at them like he was teaching a class of kids. "Junior's phone can only find the Apple Tag if it's within a range of a few hundred yards."

Chad watched despair spread across Freddie's face, and felt his own hopes sink.

"Well, we're buggered then," said Freddie. "Wherever this Swift dude has taken them, he ain't gonna be around the corner, is he?"

"No boss, I don't think so. But there's still a chance, which is what I mean about getting lucky."

"Explain," said Chad.

"When we get into Junior's phone and start the search, any iPhone that's near the Apple Tags will connect with Junior's phone, and we'll be able to pick up the location."

"So, what you're saying, Tony," said Chad, assessing the implications. "Is that we are hoping Swift uses an iPhone?"

"Yep, that's about the size of it, Chad. Do you have a laptop I can use?"

"Yeah, sure."

Tony sat down at the table, opened the MacBook, and connected Junior's phone to the computer. "I'm gonna download some software called Tenorshare, it's an iPhone un-locker, is that okay?"

"Yes, fine." Chad hoped that the powers that be wouldn't have cause to examine his Mac.

Tony tapped away on the keyboard. Chad could tell from the tension in Freddie's enormous frame that he was struggling to contain himself as they waited for Tony to un-lock the phone.

Chad checked his watch. 7:56 p.m. Jas and Junior had been gone for at least an hour.

"Okay, Boss, good news we're in to Junior's phone."

"If you weren't so ugly," said Freddie, "I'd be kissing your face off."

Tony smiled and moved away from the table.

"Okay," said Freddie. "Come on, Swift, be an Apple user." Freddie sat at the table looking at the computer, then smiled sheepishly. "Does anyone know how this tracker works?" he said.

"Jesus," said Tony. "How do you lot get through life? I'll do it."

Chad peered over Tony's shoulder as he tapped on the Find My app, then found the Air Tag in the items list that appeared. He clicked on it and waited. The seconds drifted. Chad had his fingers crossed and Freddie was rubbing both hands over his bald pate that gleamed with sweat.

Tony looked at Chad with triumph on his pock-marked face… And a map on the screen.

"He's in Tamarama," said Tony.

Freddie jumped in the air then high-fived Chad and Odd Job before slapping Tony on the head. He looked from one to the other.

"Where the fuck is Tamarama?"

Chapter 76

Jas felt the van slow to a halt, and then reverse. Wherever they were going, she thought, they'd arrived. Keep your wits about you, you've got sight, smell and hearing, use them. She heard the driver's door open and footsteps walking away. Seconds later she heard them returning, heavy steps crunching alongside the van. A key turned in the lock and Swift pulled the double doors wide. The smell of the sea on the strong breeze filled the cabin, but the night sky was black and darkness enveloped them.

"Out ya get, the pair of you. Nothing funny from you, big boy, or I'll plug ya. Understand?"

Jas looked at Junior, and her eyes conveyed a warning. She shuffled forward towards the doors and let her legs drop over the edge. Junior followed suit. Standing maybe ten feet in front of her was the policeman, arms outstretched with a black pistol extending towards them from his hands.

"Good," he said. "Now, walk down the side of the house. Go in the door at the end."

Jas felt her feet touch the ground and stood, turning as directed, with Junior behind her. There was a garage on her left with double doors. He'd parked the van in front of it. On her right was the house. She counted the steps it took her to reach the door that stood open in front of her. Eleven steps. Thirty feet. She looked over her shoulder as she approached the door.

"In you go," shouted Constable Swift.

Jas stepped into a small kitchen. There were some functional units on the wall and another couple either side of a free-standing cooker. On the rear wall, underneath a rectangular window was a sink unit.

"Go out into the hallway, turn left and wait."

Jas did as directed, Junior followed. She entered the first of the three doors on the left in the hallway. A single unlit bulb hung from a wire in the ceiling and the moon cast spectral shadows on the walls. Against the wall opposite the door, a workman's bench ran along the entire length. It gleamed in the moonlight and Jas could make out the shapes of assorted metallic implements that lay on the surface. The bench looked solid and menacing.

"Okay, lady, sit yourself down on the floor at the far end of the table."

Jas sat, pushing her back against the wall and trying to see out of the window.

"Now you, big boy, go to the wall opposite and lie down on the floor. Try anything and I will put a big fucking hole in your head."

Jas locked her eyes with Junior's and nodded. He shuffled his way to the wall and lay face down. Jas saw Swift unclip a set of handcuffs, then walk towards her. "Hold your arms out in front of you." Jas obliged. Swift held the gun close to her face as he took something from the bench. A blade glistened in front of her. As terror swept over her, she felt the zip tie on her wrist being cut and springing free.

Swift dropped a set of handcuffs on the floor. "Clip your wrist to the table leg," he said, then screamed, "now, do it now."

Jas fastened one bracelet to the table, the other around her wrist. As she clipped it into place, she could see he'd bolted the table to the floor. Swift took a couple of paces towards Junior and unfastened something from his belt, but in the darkness, Jas couldn't see what. Seconds later she knew. There was a sharp *twang*, deafening in the enclosed space, and Junior's body twitched violently on the floor.

"Call it insurance," said Swift, holding the Taser.

He dragged Junior's huge, prostrate frame across the floor and cut the zip tie then attached another set of handcuffs to the table leg and Junior's wrist. He pulled the Taser wires from Junior's back and placed them on the workbench.

"Good," he said. "I'm going out, I've an errand to run. Sit still and keep quiet."

Jas watched as the dark shape, briefly illuminated by the moon, walked out of the room. His footsteps retreated into the kitchen and then stopped. What was that? Sounded like a push alert on a phone, she thought. Silence. She heard him heading back towards them. A silhouette framed in the doorway, then a screen lit up the room. His phone.

Two quick strides and the man was leaning over her, she saw his arm rise then as he brought it down, her face exploded in pain. Her head slammed into the wall and the room swam in front of her. She felt him pulling her legs and patting her front pockets before roughly turning her to check the back pockets of her jeans. His hand ran over her blouse, feeling her breasts and under her arms. He pushed her back against the wall where her head slapped into it again. His legs moved away, and she saw him step towards Junior and launch a boot into Junior's ribs. A long, low moan filled the room. Jas could see Swift repeating the rough search of pockets and body then standing upright holding a set of keys in his hands. The room became bathed in light as he clicked the torch icon to examine them. Jas saw him turning a disc-shaped object.

"Cheeky fucking bastard," Swift yelled. Jas made herself small not allowing the pain in her face and the throbbing in her head to find a voice. She didn't need his anger turned on her.

Seconds passed then Swift said, "This has just made it worse for you." He strode out of the room, stopped in the doorway, then swung a vicious kick onto Junior's head. Jas winced as she heard the thud of his boot connecting.

Chapter 77

Andrea leaned forward and made room for the phone on the table. Space was at a premium; there was an ashtray, a pack of Marlboro, a zippo lighter, an ice-bucket dripping condensation onto the glass surface and a half-eaten pizza in a box. She kept her wine glass where it had been for the last hour. In her hand. She let out a long sigh. Chad's call had put a bit of a downer on her evening, she thought. A bit of a buzzkill.

She hadn't thought twice about answering his call after the previous few hours. She'd thought he was calling to congratulate her.

Fat chance.

But what a day it had been. She smiled at the recollection. If the call she'd taken from Pop giving her Wilcox' name had been unexpected, then the response to her broadcast had exceeded all expectations. Channel Nine ratings were the highest ever, her followers were now into the millions and everyone and their brother wanted to interview her. Her producer had put the blockers on any external interviews, but had scheduled her to appear on everything from kids' TV to the late-night show, and pretty much everything in between.

She lit a Marlboro and sucked in the smoke. Wow. It hadn't been her place to wonder why Pop had given her Wilcox, but she'd defo made the most of it. Okay, the top brass at the TV station were getting pulled from pillar to post by government officials wanting to know where she'd got the information, and trying to kibosh it, but fair play to her bosses, they'd let her run with it. Now she wanted Wilcox. In the studio, one to one. Fuck, how good would that be?

She looked at her glass. The wine had a greenish tint and as she drank it, the sharpness of the Sauvignon Blanc made her shiver. Her mind returned reluctantly to Chad. Should she have told him the truth? Hell, no. What good would that have done? At this stage, for everyone concerned, she reckoned, ignorance was bliss. But something had made him call. The journo in her, wondered if there was a story, while another part wondered whether Trevor had cashed in his insurance policy.

Chad's tone, as much as the questions he'd asked, had worried her. No jaunty banter or even expletive ridden explosion as had happened before. Instead, she'd heard a deep anxiety. Ah well, she couldn't do much about it now. She refilled her glass and took a deep draw on her cigarette, then watched as the smoke ring she blew spiralled its way towards the veranda doors.

Then the doorbell rang.

*

The rain whips my face as I lock the back door and walk to the van. My house is on the clifftop which is just as well. I slam my hand against the side of the van and scream. My voice travels upwards towards the scudding clouds and twinkling stars that seem to laugh at my rage.

"I'm gonna kill you all!"

Walking further down the sandy driveway I head out onto the grassy headland towards the cliff edge. My mind is racing and I need calm, I need to think. To breathe and to think. The wind whistles around me and the waves crash and splinter on the rocks in the darkness below. The push alert means they've found the location of the keys. They've found my hideout. But who? The police? Hilton? How long have I got?

Not long, but I may shake them off. The Air Tag will alert them if the keys move location, so long as they remain close to my phone. If the gods are on my side then Hilton, or whoever, will follow the tracker wherever I take it. I turn and run back to the van, climb in and turn the ignition, then speed down the dirt track to the main road.

*

"He's moving," said Tony from the back of the car.

"What?" said Freddie. "Where?"

"I don't know, Boss, but I've just gone back into the tracker and the location's changed."

"Shit."

"Could he know we've found the Air Tags?"

"Yeah, man," said Tony. "The Air Tags beep if they've been away from Junior's phone for some time. He might have heard that. But he'd defo have received a push alert when we activated the tracker. If he had his phone on him, he'd have seen that."

"Jesus," moaned Chad. "I hate technology, it gives you something then snatches it straight back. Do we follow the tracker or stick with Tamarama?"

Odd Job drove in silence hands gripping the wheel, glancing at his boss alongside for instruction. Tony shrugged.

"What do you reckon, Chad, bro?" asked Freddie.

Chad looked out of the window as raindrops splattered against the glass. "I think we follow the tracker. It's the only sensible thing to do. Junior and Jas are safe if Swift is moving." His stomach knotted as another thought occurred to him. Unless they're already dead. "I'll call Pop," he said.

Chad dialled and held the phone to his ear.

"Yeah, Chad, where are you?"

"Looks like he's on the move."

"How do you know?"

"'Cos the location is changing on the tracker."

"Okay, call me when you know where the bastard's going. I'll keep my teams ready till we know the location."

"Yeah, will do," said Chad.

*

I drive two full circuits of the industrial estate. It's a risk, but one I must take. The place remains as I'd left it, deserted apart from the squad car I'd abandoned at the extreme edge of the estate. Two minutes, no more. I'll listen for two minutes, that should tell me all I need. I park the van behind the car, leaving the engine running and leg it to the blue and white police vehicle. I unlock the doors, climb in and turn on the police radio. Static hisses over the airwaves.

Silence ensues, just the hissing, I check my watch. One minute forty-five seconds. I hear a crackle and then...

"All units stand down, remain in position and await further instructions."

Is that good or bad?

'Swift is on the move, further instructions upcoming.'

The words hit me like a sledgehammer. They've got my name. They know who they're looking for. There's a buzzing in my ears and my head begins to spin, lights flash bright and garish. Then the whispering starts.

'End of the road for you, son. And as I predicted, you've failed. One job, that's all your mum and me gave you. One job. And you failed. Useless bastard. Well, fuck off now, we're washing our hands of you. We'll chat with your brother, David, to see if he can do better. He always was the smart one. We should have gone to him first. You're on your own now. Loser.'

The whispering stops, and the sudden silence startles me. I feel cold and the hairs on my arms are standing on small goosebumps. And then from nowhere, comes clarity. Of mind and of purpose. I feel a calmness descend on me and the stress and anxiety of the last few weeks lift. I know what to do. How many come with me I'll leave to the Fates, that trio of spinners who control our destiny.

Time to go.

Back in the van I head out onto the quiet highway. The rain is falling harder, and the sky is jet-black. A storm in more ways than one. Traffic is light as I drive past the Sydney Cricket ground and hang a left towards Centennial Park. There's no-one around and the lights in the buildings tell me everyone's indoors. Driving past the plush apartment block I'm looking for I find a space to park under a tree at the entrance to the park. I cut the engine, open the small holdall on the passenger seat and slide out the pistol, then screw on the suppressor, eject the magazine and check the stack. All good. It's full, I like it that way. I check I've got the keys and my phone. Okay, let's do this.

*

Andrea waited in case it was someone at the wrong flat. The doorbell rang a second time. She checked her watch, 8:35 p.m. I'm not expecting visitors, she thought. She moved to put her drink on the table, but seeing the mess, took it with her. "Just a minute," she called. She stood, somewhat uncertainly, and walked to the door of the apartment. Steadying herself with one hand against the door, she peered through the spyhole.

"Who is it?' she said.

"It's the police, Miss Byrne. Detective Inspector Murray asked me to pop round, if you'll pardon the pun, and check you're okay. Here's my ID. May I come in for a second?"

Andrea peered through the glass hole and saw the police badge of Sergeant Langer of Eastern NSW PAC. She smiled. First class treatment.

A fraction after she'd turned the lock and pulled the door ajar the alarm bell in her head went off like a claxon. She knew that voice. In the moment it took for the thought to register, a foot pushed the door wide.

She'd hit the floor before the trickle of smoke from the muzzle had disappeared.

Chapter 78

Chad phoned Pop, "Yeah, we'll meet you there, how far are you away?"

"Ten minutes," said Pop. "And keep Jackson and his bruisers on a tight rein. I don't need more bodies, okay?"

Odd Job had parked the Bentley on the roadside in a fashionable neighbourhood at the edge of Centennial Park. "Pop says to wait for him, he'll be ten minutes," said Chad. If Freddie heard him, the instruction hadn't registered.

"Right, dudes, let's go."

Chad sat in the back, dumbfounded, as Freddie, Odd Job and Tony, exited the car and ran across the road.

"Shit," said Chad.

Tony was talking into an intercom at the front of the building. Seconds later the main door of the apartment block buzzed open. Chad leapt from the car and ran to the door. In the entrance hall the three Leeds gangsters stood in a huddle. Chad closed the door against the rain.

"How do we know which apartment he's gone to?" said Freddie.

"We don't," replied Chad.

Chad checked the mailboxes that extended in four rows along the wall, each with a nameplate on the front. He read the names, recognising none, until the fourth row. His stomach lurched, and he felt bile fill his mouth, then the familiar light-headedness. He stretched out an arm to steady himself.

"Easy, bro, what's wrong?"

Chad tapped on a mailbox. "Andrea Byrne," he spluttered, "that's where he'll be."

Freddie noted the flat number then began striding up the stairway, two at a time, with Odd Job behind him. Tony grabbed Chad's arm and helped him to the lifts, then pressed the button for the fourth floor. As the lift clunked to a halt and the doors opened, Freddie and Odd Job appeared through a fire door.

Automatic hall lights came on as they walked down the corridor. The door to Andrea's apartment stood ajar.

"We wait for Pop," said Chad.

"Bollocks," said Freddie, pushing the door further open until they could see inside the apartment. Andrea lay on her back, arms flung wide, eyes open and a small round hole in her forehead. A broken wine glass had leaked its contents onto the wooden floor where the wine mingled with a red pool of blood spreading steadily towards the windows. On her stomach were a set of keys, an Apple Tag and an iPhone.

Chad pushed Freddie away from the door. "Don't go in, this is for the police. It's clear he's gone. We've missed him." He looked once more at Andrea's crumpled form. She hadn't deserved this, he thought. Abrasive, arrogant, ambitious. Yes, all of those. But tenacious, brave, funny and full of life. Those too.

"But what now?" asked Freddie, interrupting Chad's thoughts. He pointed inside the apartment. "I know you knew her, man, but we need to find Junior and Jas."

Chad turned away and dialled Pop's number.

"Christ almighty," said Pop, when Chad had explained where they were and who they'd found. "He's a complete bastard, he didn't need to kill her."

"She was a loose end," said Chad. "Bloody hell, I've made so many mistakes. I told you after Doyle's killing that he doesn't leave loose ends. I didn't do enough to protect her."

"Oh, shut up, Chad. Cut the self-pitying and whingeing. Pull yourself together."

Chad, stung by the tone as much as the words, straightened. "What now?"

"The forensics guys are on the way, then we resume the search."

Chapter 79

Chad sat next to Freddie in the back of the Bentley. Tony and Odd Job were in the front.

"Bro, we've no time to wait around for the feds," Freddie held Chad's eye. "The killer's got Junior and Jas and he'll top them too unless we find him and stop him."

"Finding him is the problem, though. He could be anywhere, Boss," said Tony.

A heavy, anxious silence descended on the occupants of the car. Chad rubbed his face to get the blood flowing and help him think. He wound the window down to let some air in. Raindrops found the opening and splashed on Chad's face.

"Hang on, if the tracker picked up Tamarama, that's where he took them," said Chad.

"Not necessarily," said Tony. "They'd been gone an hour when we picked up the trace. They could have been anywhere and Swift could have taken the keys to misdirect us."

Chad gave this some thought. "True," he said. "But he was in Tamarama, and that's worth a follow up. What was the address?"

Each looked at the other. "Shit, it was on the tracking map, which disappeared when Swift moved location," said Chad.

"Fuck," shouted Freddie. "Are you telling me we haven't got the address?"

"No, Boss," said Tony, "I'm just wondering where the hell you lot would be without this little lad from Bradford? I took a screen grab of the map. Let's hit the gas. Odd Job, put Fletcher Street,

Tamarama, into the Satnav."

Chad dialled Pop's number. "We're going to Fletcher Street in Tamarama, it's possible Swift is there."

"Don't let your mates take unilateral action, Chad, you hear me? You wait for us. Okay?"

"Okay," Chad put his phone in his pocket.

"Let me guess," said Freddie. "He wants me to wait for them to get there."

"That's about the size of it."

Chad looked into Freddie's eyes.

"And you know, bro, I can't do that. They had their chance. Now it's my turn."

*

Odd Job parked the Bentley at the bottom of a steep incline on either side of which houses stood in sleepy silence, silhouetted black against the sky. Chad hurried up the hill, Freddie and Odd Job were a few strides ahead of him and Tony brought up the rear. Chad noticed how Tony would run a few paces, then turn, face back down the hill, and check the street. Habits of a lifetime.

The street they'd climbed ran out of tarmac maybe thirty yards further on from where they stood, after which a sandy track led for several hundred metres to the summit of the cliff. Freddie ducked into a bus shelter at the side of the road. Two houses were visible. The first was twenty metres away, but the other was at the end of the track, perched on the cliff top. Chad reckoned to approach unseen would be difficult.

He checked his watch. Another five to ten minutes before Pop and his team arrived.

"Okay, big man, what's the plan?"

Chad's question was ignored.

Freddie, Odd Job and Tony stood in a conspiratorial huddle,

whispering and pointing. Tony taking the lead. He then ran towards the first house and disappeared around the back. Freddie and Odd Job had size and muscle, Chad thought, but when it came to operational tactics, Tony, ex-special forces, was the man.

"Right, the house closest isn't occupied," said Tony, sliding to a stop in front of the bus shelter. "So, Swift is in the one at the far end, but there's no cover between here and there. This one here," he pointed across the road, "has a garage on the side, just there." Chad followed the direction of Tony's outstretched arm. "It's got one window, side facing. From what I could see, the house up the road is the same. Keep low and head in a straight line from the side of the house here, to the side of Swift's garage."

"What will happen when we get to Swift's house?" said Chad.

"Leave that with us, bro. We've got into more houses than you've had hot dinners."

"Ready?" said Tony.

Everyone nodded.

"Follow me."

*

Pop checked his watch. "How much longer?" he barked.

"Sat nav's saying eight minutes, boss," José was driving.

Pop looked out of the back window and saw the four teams he'd deployed in close order behind them.

"Get your bloody foot down."

*

Chad's knee was complaining as he ran, bent almost double, following the others in single file. How the hell Odd Job and Freddie managed to run so fast and keep so low was beyond him. Tony was last in the line, doing the turning and checking routine.

The house was now about one hundred yards away and they were closing fast. Freddie's muscular figure seemed to glide over the ground, head forward, never taking his eyes off the target.

The garage was on the side of the house with a window facing them.

Tony squatted under the glass, indicating with hand movements for Odd Job and Freddie to go to his right and Chad to the left. Chad gulped air, trying hard not to make a noise. Tony peered over the window sill and checked inside the garage, then sat back down.

"One door leading into the house, probably into the kitchen," he whispered, then turned to Freddie. "There's a van out the front. Swift's here." Tony looked hard at each of them. "Keep your eyes and ears open," he said. "Odd Job, hide by the van, he'll need it to escape. Keep out of sight and be ready."

Odd Job nodded.

Chad reckoned that he'd never seen anyone more ready.

"Boss, we'll make entry round the back. Chad stay here, he may come out through the garage, so again be ready."

A noise in the distance made them all turn their heads like a row of pointer dogs sniffing the wind.

"What the fuck is that?" whispered Freddie.

"Police sirens." Chad replied.

"Christ almighty, do they want him to get away? If we can hear them, so can he. Shit. Tony, get moving."

*

I stand and look out of the bay window. The wind is strong whipping up the surf onto the rocks, which is good. I'll be returning to nature. My thoughts turn to Wilcox. He is a source of irritation for me. That my intricate plans were scuppered by Hilton and Jackson's goons rankles even more. So, in return, something they value will go. An eye for an eye.

I should have thought about trackers, but I've cut myself some slack. You can't foresee everything. Who knew the boy was a geek?

They are in the other room, hoping to be rescued. That won't be happening. How they die will depend on what happens from here on. But die they will. I look around the door, they're where I left them. The young giant has regained consciousness and is leaning on the table leg. The woman, alert and watchful. I return to my vantage point in the front room and empty the contents of my backpack onto the wicker chair. Passport, cash, drivers' licence and credit cards. The paraphernalia attached to the new life I was going to lead. The life of Constable Swift would have been joining that of Jonathon Raschs in the bucket marked 'history'. But not now. I came close, but not close enough. The thought of Wilcox roaming free is my only regret. I check the pistol. One shot fired so nearly a full stack. I've two more magazines which I put in my pockets. I'll take as many with me as I can. Time to go.

Faint and some way off, I hear the distinctive wail of police sirens. More than one. So, where are Hilton and Jackson? Maybe they're already here. Let's see. I look around my lair one last time. Okay, showtime.

*

Pop turned to José, his face a livid red. "Tell them to turn those fucking sirens off. Jesus Christ, let's give the bastard some advance notice so he can complete the job. Sometimes I can't believe how stupid my colleagues are."

"Boss, we're travelling at high speed through a residential area and we're required to have them on."

"Not today, we're not."

Chapter 80

Chad pressed his back into the garage wall as he sat on his haunches. The wind had picked up, and the sky was black, the rain more persistent. Chad listened, but either the wind had drowned the noise of the sirens, or they'd been switched off. He wondered how the hell Tony and Freddie planned to get into the house. They knew what they were doing, he supposed. And what if they got in? Fear gnawed at his innards. Was Jas still alive?

Chad thought he heard something as the wind dropped for a second. What the hell was that? Front of the house? He'd been told to wait at the garage, but if Swift was taking them out the front, he needed to get there. Chad made his decision, then stood and ran to the van where Odd Job was crouched. Odd Job put a warning finger to his lips.

The sight in front of Chad made his legs turn to dust. Swift stood fifteen to twenty metres ahead, near a small fence at the front of the property. Junior and Jas, hands bound, stood alongside him. Both looked injured, Junior more than Jas. Chad glanced to the left and saw Freddie come into view from the opposite corner of the house. Swift waved a gun at him.

"That's far enough, ya fuckin' goon," he shouted. Freddie stopped mid stride. "One more step and I'll blow your son's head right off his fucking shoulders, ya get my drift? And where's your mates, eh? Call them over and we'll get this party started."

Freddie glared.

"Better call 'em, mate. I'll count to three and then start shooting.

One..."

"Guys, here to me, now," yelled Freddie.

Odd Job rose from behind the van and stepped forward. Chad saw Tony walk to stand next to Freddie.

Swift smiled and said, "Looks like we're missing someone. Where's Hilton?"

Chad stood and edged in front of the van.

"Ah, Mr Hilton, I'm glad you could join us. Now, all of you walk along the path you can see on your right. We're going to take in the view from the cliff edge. Nearly the witching hour. Appropriate don't you think, mate?

"You hurt that boy, bro, and I'll..."

"You'll what?" Swift interrupted Freddie. "You and your steroid buddies will do fuck all."

Chad stepped out across a small patch of scuffed grass onto the path. Freddie and Odd Job, framed in the light of the moon, edged forward and joined him. Tony followed suit, his eyes never leaving Swift's face. Chad looked across the ground and caught Jas's eye. There was something wrong with her face, but he couldn't tell what at that distance.

"Blame Chad Hilton for the predicament you're in," yelled Swift, raising his voice to be heard over the wind. "If he'd listened to my warning, he'd have backed right off and you lot wouldn't be here. But no, he couldn't do that. Why was that, Chad? Don't you value your girlfriend's life?"

Andrea, Chad thought. Swift had issued a warning that Andrea had chosen not to give him. Christ.

Swift stared at him and then, as if he could read Chad's mind, he let out a long, mirthless laugh. "She didn't tell you, did she? What a fucking bitch she is... Or was." He looked skywards and kicked the grass and sand in front of him. "Ah well, the best laid plans of mice and men, I suppose. And we are where we are." Swift stepped in front of Jas and, in one quick movement, pulled the tape from her mouth. "Wouldn't be the same if they couldn't hear you scream, would it?"

Chad saw Jas licking her lips, trying to get some moisture into her mouth. "Piss off," she said.

Chad could see the cliff top a few yards ahead. He glanced to his right and saw a dust cloud floating into the moonlit air. The seventh cavalry arriving. Shit, this isn't going to end well. Swift had nowhere to run, was out of time and out of luck, and would want to go out with a bang. He was pushing Junior and Jas towards the edge. Chad saw Swift stare towards the dust cloud.

"Hilton," shouted Swift.

Chad looked across. "What?"

"You're to stop them coming any closer. Understand? I want you to get Pop and bring him here to me. The rest of the coppers stay where they are. If you don't return in one minute, one of these two will die. Go."

Chad ran onto the dirt road, pain from his knee screeching up his leg, and saw the lead car speeding up past the first house near the bus stop. He began waving his arms. "Stop, stop," he yelled.

The car pulled up spraying dust and sand into the air, and the other squad cars fanned into a semicircle around it. Pop jumped out.

"No time for talking, Pop. Swift's sent me to bring you to him. If we're not there in about thirty seconds, he'll kill Jas or Junior."

"Let's get going, mate, I've got some business with him as well."

Chad turned and hurried up the track, Pop huffing and puffing behind him.

"Okay, stop there," shouted Swift, when they were about twenty yards away. "Hilton, you go and stand with your mates."

The wind was gusting stronger, and the full beam glare from the squad car headlights illuminated the scene. Chad walked over and stood next to Freddie. He tried to make out what Swift was saying.

"Well done, Pop. You got there in the end."

"We always do. And it's Detective Inspector Murray to you."

"Don't be like that, mate, don't get all formal on me."

Chad felt Freddie's hand on his sleeve.

"I don't like the look of this, bro." he muttered.

"Nor me."

Swift was shouting to make himself heard. "Okay, DI Murray, here's what's going to happen."

"Oh yeah, what's that?" said Pop.

"Well, my plan's gone to shit now, which is your fault and his," Chad saw Swift pointing at him. "So, you're going to pay a price for that and so is he."

"Look," said Pop. "Give it up, Swift. There's a SWAT team down there and you've no way out. Just give yourself up, enough's enough."

"What, for a long stay with a bunch of convicts who hate coppers? No, mate, don't think so. I'm all done. Suicide by cop for me. But the show must go on. Right?"

"I don't know what the fuck you're on about," said Pop.

"There's always a price, yeah? Yours is to take a long jump into oblivion. D'ya get me?" Swift waved his arm towards the ocean. "I count to three and you jump. If you're standing there when I get to three, I start shooting. How many shots can I get off before your lot arrives? We'll see, but I reckon I'll take all of you."

Chad saw Pop trying to comprehend what he'd heard. The big Tasmanian ran his hands through his hair and looked over the cliff edge. Turning, he looked at Chad. Chad held his eye but had nothing to offer, no words to mitigate the horror of the choice. Because there was no choice. Pop knew that, and Chad saw it etched on his face.

"Let them go," said Pop, pointing towards Jas and Junior, "and you have a deal."

"Nah, mate. I can't do that. You see, Hilton's price is Miss Carter here. And Jackson got his thugs to stop me killing Wilcox, so his price is his freak of a son. They're both going to die. You know your scripture, don't you? An eye for an eye."

Pop turned away as if wanting some time to himself…

Then all hell broke loose.

Chad saw a blur of arms and legs intertwining, grappling. The monkeys on Pop's shirt came alive and clambered and climbed over Swift. Chad felt a push on his back and glimpsed Tony crouching, arms outstretched with a gun in his hands, running past him towards the cliff edge where Pop and Swift hovered precariously. Odd Job followed.

Tony's nudge broke the spell and Chad ran hard towards Jas. A loud explosion and the feeling of being hit by a sledgehammer stopped him in his tracks. What the hell was that? Swift was waving his gun, firing wildly as Pop continued to wrestle him. Chad looked down and saw a crimson stain spreading across his shirt. Fuck. Another explosion ripped through the wind.

The world went into slow motion.

Junior was falling like a tree being toppled and Freddie was taking slow, loping strides towards his son. Jas was shouting, then running towards him, terror in her eyes. She was mouthing something at him, but Chad couldn't make out the words.

Then everything speeded up again.

Tony was crouching and firing 'pop, pop, pop, pop'. Swift's head snapped back, and a pink mist rose into the air illuminated by the headlights. His body twisted viciously as one, two, three, four bullets ripped into him. Odd Job dived through the air towards the cluster of limbs and bodies. Swift swayed on the edge, clutching at monkeys and Pop, before they disappeared, leaving the black night sky above.

Chad heard what Jas was screaming. "Chad, you're bleeding."

Pain swept through his torso as he staggered to the cliff edge where Odd Job lay. The wind howled as Chad looked over. Swift lay spreadeagled on the rocks below, the water making his body writhe in grotesque swirling motions. But that wasn't what transfixed his gaze. Floating on the ebbing waves, clear in the moonlight, was a blue Hawaiian shirt.

Chad looked up into the sky. The stars flickered like fireflies, but focussing was difficult. Everything around him seemed fuzzy and his legs were turning to jelly. The stain on his shirt was growing and blood was pouring down his arm over his hand. So, this was the end then? He toppled forward as his legs gave way, but something was stopping him fall. A strong arm around his waist. Then a voice.

"Oh, no you don't, Hoppy. Not tonight."

Epilogue

Chad opened his eyes and tried to focus. He recognised the set up. Hospital, he thought, I'm in hospital. They'd fixed a canula to the back of his hand feeding liquid from a drip and strapped his left arm and shoulder. He wiggled his toes. At least they worked, and he could feel his legs, so he wasn't paralysed. Turning his head to the right he saw Jas asleep in a chair next to the bed. She had an angry bruise across her cheek and she'd be sporting a black eye for a while he reckoned. She stirred, opened her good eye and smiled.

"How are you feeling?" she asked.

"I don't know," said Chad. "But shouldn't you be in a hospital bed?"

"Nah," she said. "I'm from Yorkshire, remember, we're made of stronger stuff than you softie southerners."

"That's very true," said Chad. "What the hell happened?"

"What can you remember?"

Good point, thought Chad. What could he remember?

As it transpired, he remembered little. Chad let his head sink into the pillow after Jas had finished regaling him with the details. There were two bullets that hit him, one in the shoulder and one in the arm. He'd lost a fair bit of blood.

"You've Tony to thank that you're still with us," said Jas.

"Really, why?"

"Because you damn near fell off the cliff edge and I'd grabbed your waist but would have gone over with you if Tony hadn't pulled you back."

Chad hadn't remembered that, but mention of the cliff edge had brought images flooding into his head. "Pop?" he'd asked.

Jas had held his eye then her face had creased into a wide smile.

"He's okay. When he lost his balance and nearly followed Swift over the edge, Odd Job dived and grabbed his leg."

"Jesus," said Chad. "He got lucky."

"And was he grateful?" said Jas. "Not a bit. As Freddie arrived to help Odd Job, Pop shouted something like, 'Don't just stand there, you Pom bastard, help me up.' Went down well with Freddie."

"And what about Junior, is he okay?"

"Swift shot him in the buttock, and he had concussion. He's got a couple of broken ribs as well. The prognosis is that he'll be fine after a couple of days in hospital. Being shot in the bum is probably karma for being a pain in the arse lounging in the apartment all day."

Freddie, she said, had shouted and ranted at anyone who'd stand still long enough until Odd Job and Tony had ushered him away. Pop had wanted to know where Tony had got his gun from, but Tony said he'd found it in Swift's house and it had fallen into the sea when he'd helped Odd Job pull Pop to safety. And if you believed that, you'd believe anything.

Meanwhile, the press were in a frenzy. Leading the tributes to Andrea had been some bloke called Jason Austin who seemed, Jas thought, to have taken over from Andrea as the chief crime correspondent for Channel Nine. They were eagerly awaiting Chad's exit from hospital.

At least the carnage was over.

As he drifted into a deep sleep, he saw Andrea's face when he'd met her at Starbucks. Fringe, nose piercing and an attitude problem. Bless her, he thought, it would piss her off she wasn't there to claim the glory.

One Month Later.

Chad scrolled down the BBC News on his iPad. The sports page had an interview with Freddie focussing as much on his part in Swift's demise as on the winning goal he'd scored for the Rest of the World. He skim read a couple of headlines until one drew his eye in the International News section. '*Former Australian Government Minister dies in a car crash.*' Chad clicked on the article.

'*Michael Wilcox, 59, until recently the Minister for Health and Aged Care, died today when the vehicle he was travelling in left the M31 Hume highway north of Canberra and overturned. First on the scene was a salesman from Newcastle, David Speedy, who said he'd been following the Minister's car when it suddenly veered sharply, left the road, toppled over and burst into flames. The intensity of the fire prevented him from assisting...*'

Chad picked up his phone, scrolled, found the name he wanted and typed.

100 bucks says that Jonathon Swift + David Speedy = Jonathon and David Rasch.

His phone pinged. Pop. *Yep, got to be. And guess what? David Speedy has disappeared*

Chad replied. *They got him in the end.*

Seconds elapsed then another ping.

Btw, I'm being persuaded to take a well-earned leave of absence, so I'm coming to the UK. Jas said you're in a massive house in Harrogate and that you'd be glad of the company. How are you fixed?

Chad paused, then typed.

The second word is... off.

The End

Acknowledgements

To my mentor and editor, the brilliant and indefatigable McIlvanney nominated Mark Leggatt. Thank you!

To Abi Rennison and Victoria McCaskill who's understanding of the world of social media and marketing is greater than I could ever hope to know. Thank you.

To Australia which provided a second home.

To Carrie Benny and Luke, my fantastic children for keeping me grounded…

And most of all to Debi my wife, soulmate and constant inspiration.

Printed in Great Britain
by Amazon

39332749R00189